# THE
# CITY OF THE GODS
# GOLD
## BOOK ONE
### ZACH ERWIN

Maps by Kevin Sheehan

First edition 2024

979-8-9907738-1-3

www.TCOTG.com

EMPIRE CITY
BROOKFIELD
NORTHWELL
TOMPKINS ISLAND
FAYETTE BRIDGE
BUNCHE BRIDGE
EMPIRE CITY
COASTAL HIGHWAY
BROADSHALL ISLAND
SOUTH BRIDGE

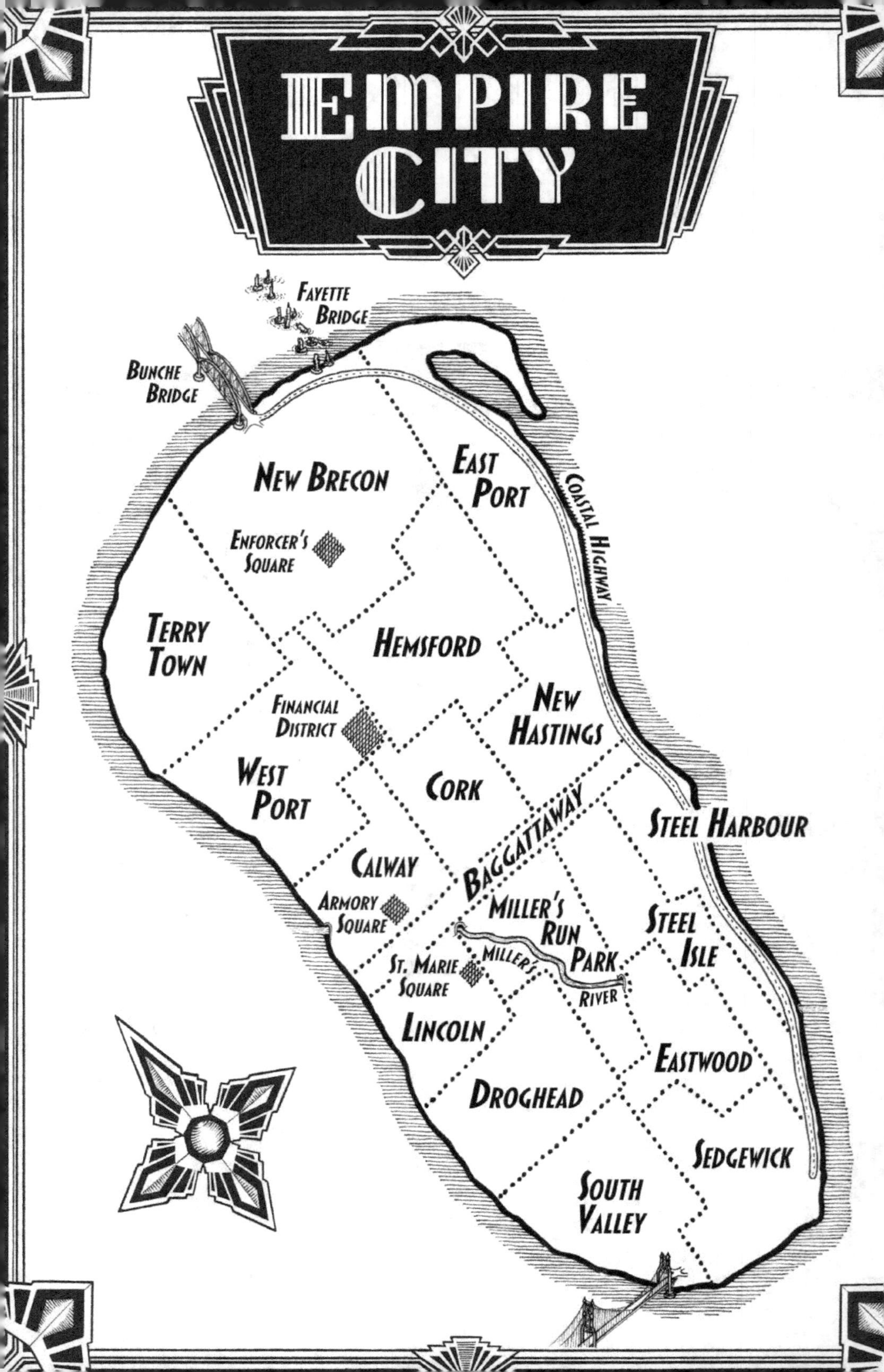

EMPIRE CITY
Fayette Bridge
Bunche Bridge
New Brecon
East Port
Enforcer's Square
Coastal Highway
Terry Town
Hemsford
New Hastings
Financial District
West Port
Cork
Baggattaway
Steel Harbour
Calway
Armory Square
Miller's Run Park
Steel Isle
Miller's River
St. Marie Square
Lincoln
Eastwood
Droghead
Sedgewick
South Valley

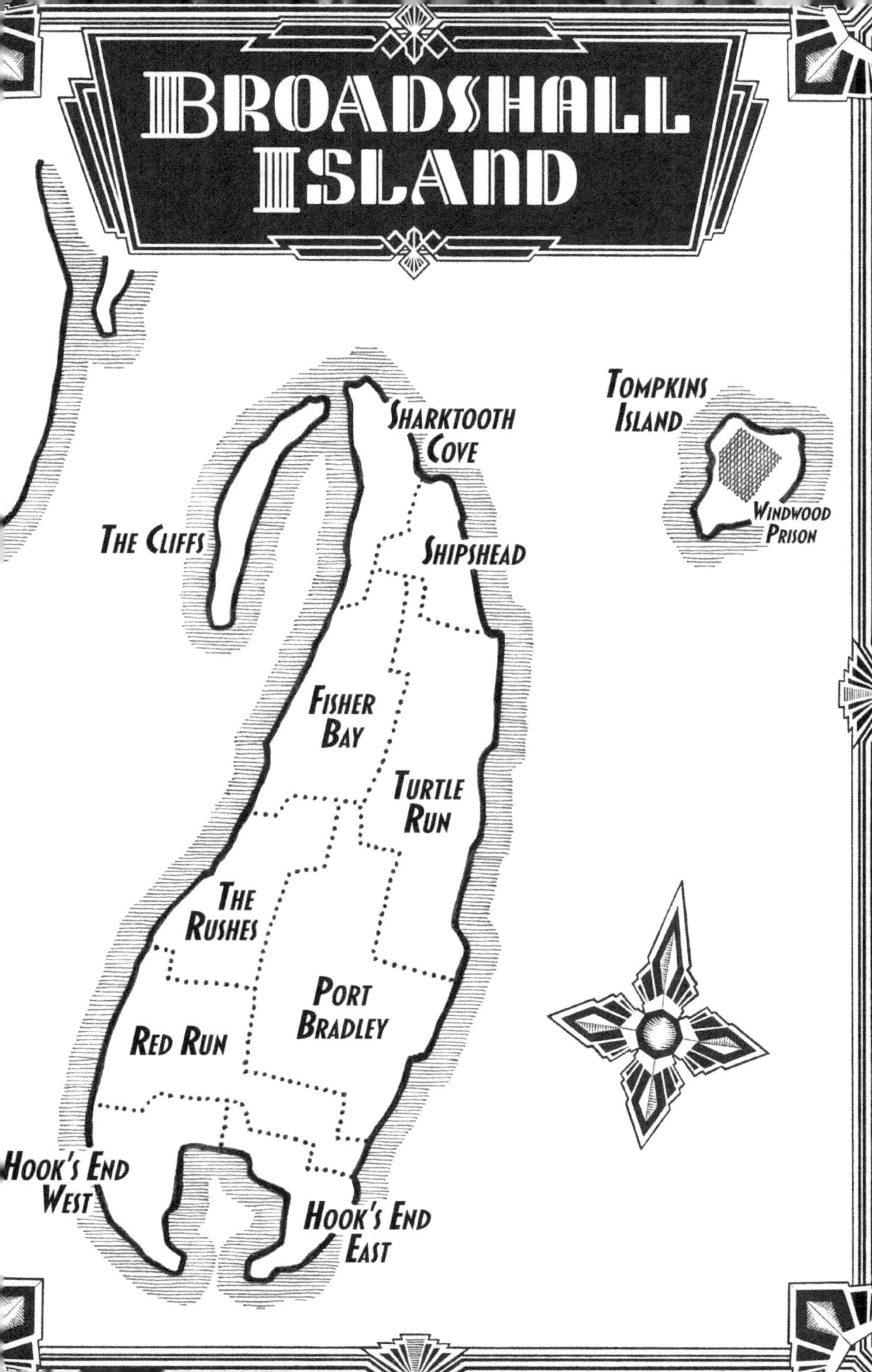

BROADSHALL ISLAND
SHARKTOOTH COVE
TOMPKINS ISLAND
THE CLIFFS
WINDWOOD PRISON
SHIPSHEAD
FISHER BAY
TURTLE RUN
THE RUSHES
PORT BRADLEY
RED RUN
HOOK'S END WEST
HOOK'S END EAST

How do you tell a story with no beginning or end? A story echoing infinitely in two opposite directions.

"This could be the last thing people ever hear. So go, tell them what happened. Make it a good one, one worth hearing."

Those final words were all that remained. This would have been a good story if there had been anyone left to hear it.

INTO
THE
ABYSS

**1**

On the last week of her life, all the repressed personalities that had followed Theodora Connor back from the brink of madness resurfaced, and she recalled having seen the moon in this state before. A blood moon, much larger than usual, glaring like a judgmental eye. On the surface, it was beautiful. However, when it had appeared before, in a dream or past life, lynched over a burning city, it was a bad omen.

She ignored it, instead, looking over her dying yard through the *thump, thump, thump* of her swollen eye. The swing James had hung from a branch over the summer swayed as the wind pushed leaves onto the stone patio. Theo brought a glass to her lips. The whiskey sour stung just right, and the clinking ice cubes played like a symphony. She pressed the cool glass against her cheek, hoping James wouldn't come back this time. It was easier to tell him no one wanted him around when he wasn't around in the first place.

Bonnie was down the hall doing whatever five-year-olds do when left to their own devices, and Theodora was avoiding the inevitable question: where's Daddy? She set her glass down and twisted her bulbous diamond ring, slipping it over her knuckle, the lock holding her captive to this monotonous suburban life.

*This life doesn't belong to you,* she thought, staring at her reflection in the window. *All those accolades and not a shred of self-respect. What would Mother say?*

She scrunched her face and spoke in a high-pitched, nasally voice. "*You never should have married that James Connor. You should have turned my vaudeville act into a motion picture career and run millions of miles away from this rotten Empire City! You sold your soul, kiddo, and for what? A punch in the face?*" Mother was right, and even in death, Theo couldn't outrun her scrutiny.

Theo admired her freckled tan leftover from summer trips to Broadshall with Bonnie. *I could still leave,* she thought. She was only twenty-eight and still pretty enough to contend in Hollywood. 1953 was almost over, but '54 could be her year.

# The City of the Gods: Gold

Theodora frowned. *No, that's just Mother talking again.* She saw the truth in her reflection, a broken woman masquerading as a clown, burying resentment under a grinning, comedic mask. She looked past herself to the Bunche Bridge, glinting in the moonlight and Empire City peering over the horizon. *You're too famous to be an actor, kid. You're the Scarlet Sparrow, and that's all you'll ever—*

A figure slunk along the fence, bleeding into the shadows of the tree branches. Theodora squinted. It was human-sized, too big not to have tripped the perimeter sensors and set off alarms.

"James?"

No, it was more elegant, like a deer, but most definitely a person. Maybe a woman.

*Bang! Bang! Bang!*

Theodora yelped, her drink splashing against the rim of the glass.

*Bang! Bang! Bang!* The knocking came again. She set her glass on the console table and shot herself a forced smile in the mirror, adjusting the bodice of her dress and fingering the charm on her necklace.

"Who is it?" Theodora abandoned her reflection and crept toward the door. Part of her hoped it would be James, but most of her didn't.

"It's Mrs. Braddock," a muffled voice answered.

"Shit," Theodora muttered. "Coming!" She peeled the drapes aside, glanced out the window at a short, frail woman staring angrily through outdated Oxford glasses, and pushed the door open.

Mrs. Braddock's face transformed into something that could almost pass for pleasant as the overwhelming smell of mothballs introduced her. "Hello, dear. I hope I didn't wake you."

Theodora eyed the open iron gate on the edge of the property, a forced smile still in place. "Not at all, Mrs. Braddock. What can I do for you?"

"I'm just checking in. I heard a commotion earlier." Mrs. Braddock's neck stretched and craned back and forth as she tried to peer into the house. "Is everything alright? Where's your daughter?"

Theodora shifted her body to cover the gap. "Everything is fine, thank you. Goodnight, Mrs. Braddock." She pushed the door closed, but the old woman wedged her foot inside.

"I've also been meaning to speak to you about the state of this... *house*."

Theodora sighed and pulled the door back open. "What about it?"

"Well, the neighbors—not me, mind you, but *other* neighbors—have been complaining again." She scanned the horizon. "Fitzsimmons!" she whispered, pointing to the cookie-cutter, three-story mansion towering over the row of shrubs. "*She* says it's an eyesore. All these glass domes and metal walls look like a fortress from a science fiction serial, not a home for you to raise a young girl in, dear." She hid a smile. "I heard her call it something out of a Frank Lloyd Wright fever dream."

"Well, that's almost clever for someone as advanced in age as *she* is. Goodnight, Mrs. Braddock."

Mrs. Braddock shouldered the door. "Hold on, dear. Is your husband home? Perhaps he can—"

"That's none of your concern, Mrs. Braddock."

"Well, as your neighbor, I believe—"

"It's a little late for a social call, don't you agree? Goodnight!" She shut the door forcefully enough to put her neighbor in her place. No amount of phony pleasantries seemed to matter since Theo and James revealed their secret identities after T-Day. Everyone in Empire had an opinion, and not many were positive.

Theodora lifted her glass and pressed it to her lips. She slid the drapes aside, watching Mrs. Braddock scoff at the unraked leaves, and grinned at the idea of turning on the house defenses to scare the old bat. *Maybe a couple of warning shots from the automated M18s would teach her a lesson.*

Her smile faded when the open gate caught her eye again. She turned, glancing across the foyer, through the rear window, to the now still backyard. Her eyes studied the lattice-like shadows from the swaying branches cast against the fence. When all was deemed quiet, she finished her drink, inhaled what courage she could, and went to find her daughter.

<u>2</u>

Bonnie peeked into her parents' bedroom and scanned for movement amongst the shadows, remembering what her daddy had told her. *There's no such thing as monsters anymore.* He'd made sure of it.

"This is typical," her father yelled from the foyer, "starting a fight because you're bored again, Theo."

"Bored? Every time our neighbors forget the Enforcers exist, you decide to suit up with that hussy Lily Larkin and do something boneheaded, James! Maybe a little boredom is what this family needs," her mother shouted. "Can't you spend one night away from *her*?"

"Should we talk about Jerry Smith?" her father responded.

"Fuck you!"

"Theo, I'm not going to rot in Brookfield for the rest of my life. I'm Captain Wonderful, goddamn it!"

Bonnie skipped across the bedroom, humming a song from *The Wizard of Oz* as motion sensors illuminated the recessed lighting.

"That part of our life is over. When will you get that through your thick skull?" her mother yelled.

Bonnie ran her finger across the inlay of the antique vanity. *When I was a little girl, this vanity belonged to Grandma,* she remembered her mother saying.

The funeral was still vivid—an old woman with a face painted like a china doll lying in a casket amongst a bed of flowers. The image stuck when she closed her eyes, but Bonnie didn't recall much else about her. Vague memories of crying, hospital rooms, and shouting, but nothing substantial. She pulled herself onto the stool and scanned the vanity, locating the golden cylinder of lipstick tucked in the back. Sensors illuminated the mirror in a soft glow and a soothing hum, inviting her to try it on.

"You're the one who quit the Enforcers," her father yelled, "not me."

"I quit because I almost lost—I just don't trust Lily, James," her mother said.

"Fine, I'll sell our apartment in the city, close the Hall of Enforcers, and tell the people in Empire: sorry folks, my wife doesn't trust Lily Larkin."

Bonnie squealed with excitement and uncapped the lipstick. "A stiff drink is all that will fix this face!" She echoed something she had heard her mother say once, followed by an imitative giggle.

"We did our part for Empire. Bonnie needs her father!"

Twisted branches on the far end of the dome scraped against the glass, like Bonnie's grandmother's gnarled fingers, echoing an eerie sound and throwing unfamiliar shadows across the floor.

# The City of the Gods: Gold

Bonnie shuddered and closed her eyes. "The monsters are gone." She inhaled and gobbed lipstick across her lips, looping it onto her cheeks and circling it around her mouth until it was a thick, waxy red. In the mirror, Bonnie watched shadows race across the lawn. She dropped the lipstick onto the vanity and slapped her hands over her eyes.

She parted her fingers and scanned the backyard in the mirror. When all was still, she lifted a compact from the vanity and rubbed the sunken gold horseshoes on the lid.

"I'm running late. Let's talk about this tomorrow," her father said.

Bonnie popped open the compact and mashed the applicator into it, discharging white powder. She slammed the applicator into her face and laughed as clouds of sweet-smelling dust floated about.

"No, we're talking about this now. You were a goddamn war hero, James. Now all you do is drink and fuck Lily."

Bonnie froze as a slap rang through the halls, followed by a deep, panting cry.

"Jesus… I'm sorry, Theo, I just—"

"Don't touch me. Leave. Go see your whore."

"Theo, please…"

"Go!"

The front door slammed, and Bonnie flinched. Her mother wailed alone. Bonnie saw her powder-caked face in the mirror and dropped the compact. Down the hall, the cocktail shaker rattled and sloshed.

Bonnie frantically smeared powder across the floor, but the mess grew just as it had on the vanity. She glanced between red, waxy lipstick clumps and the filthy bedroom floor. Footsteps grew louder.

"Bonnie? Where are you, Munchkin?"

The sweet powder smell hung in a thick cloud as a reminder of what she'd done. A door clicked shut down the hall. Footsteps echoed on the hardwood floor again.

"Bonnie?" The door creaked open, and something jumped in Bonnie's stomach.

The light from the hallway backlit her mom. "Bonnie, are you"—she froze—"oh my… Bonnie, how could you? I just"—she sighed and closed her eyes.

"Is Daddy gone again?" Bonnie asked.

Her mother wrestled her face into a smile. "How would you like some ice cream?"

Bonnie dropped her eyes to the floor and twisted her foot. "With a cookie?"

"Sure. You drive a hard bargain, kiddo. You're lucky you're so cute"—she crept toward Bonnie—"but first, the bath police are here to get you!"

Bonnie yelped as her mother scooped her up, and the scent of Moon Mist perfume lifted the rotten feeling from her stomach. Thoughts of monsters, darkness, and strange shapes in the backyard vanished, and the big, dark building was home again.

Her mother laughed and opened the door. "You're a mess. You need to ask me if you want to use my make-up, okay?"

Bonnie's head dropped. Her mother lifted her chin with a finger, met her gaze, and smiled. "Weeeee're off to see the wizard!"

"The Wonderful Wizard of Oz!" Bonnie joined in.

**3**

The water rushed up the side of the bathtub until Bonnie's mom turned off the faucet and kicked her shoes into the corner. "I'll be right back, Munchkin."

# The City of the Gods: Gold

The faucet dripped methodically into the still water. Bonnie hummed another song from *The Wizard of Oz* to kill the silence and eyed the frosted glass window warily. A blurry shape danced across the moonlit backdrop and vanished. Bonnie jumped back, splashing water over the bathtub's edge. The water in the tub sloshed back and forth as she covered her eyes with her hands. The surface stilled, and the faucet dripped slowly again.

"No more monsters." She opened two fingers and peeked out. She swallowed hard and glanced down the hallway. "Mommy?"

Theodora released the weight of the day in a sigh as she walked past framed newspaper clippings plastered to the hallway wall, articles celebrating the League of Enforcers' murders. She remembered how each kill felt and loathed herself for it.

The story featuring The Ivory Icicle caught her eye. When the Enforcers invaded Japan in '45, demanding their surrender, it spawned the Japanese sniper, who somehow made his way to Empire City a few years later, out for revenge.

*Pull the trigger!*

She remembered sitting for hours on that rooftop in Lincoln on that frigid December day with the wind and snow whipping around her, fastened to the railing by fear. The weight of the rifle was unbearable.

Theo could still feel the bone-chilling cold as she trembled against the icy concrete. The snowflakes seemed infinite as they melted on her exposed flesh. James liked her various Scarlet Sparrow uniforms to show a lot of skin, even in the dead of winter.

She stared down the barrel through the telescopic sight of her modified Springfield '03, her heartbeat and the frozen tremble shaking the barrel ever so slightly, but not enough to lose her target.

*Pull the fucking trigger before he does!*

The Scarlet Sparrow was too good at killing to be affected by things as benign as fear or cold.

*Squeeze. Don't pull.*

She remembered the kick of the stock against her shoulder. The sound of the rifle screaming through Sainte Marie Square, and Oroku Kawamata or, as the *Bulletin* called him, The Ivory Icicle slumping forward with a hole the size of a melon in his head.

*Hit.*

Taking lives was taxing, but the moment before the bullet left the gun, pulling the trigger came all too easily.

Theodora shrugged out of her dress and scanned the constellations through the dome over her bedroom. They were prominent, even with the bright city lights on the horizon. She couldn't shake the unease of exposure and familiarity. More déjà vu from a past life, perhaps. The woman with the deer antlers wasn't far.

----

*Tap, tap, tap.* Something rapped faintly on the bathroom window. Lights flickered, and the drip of the faucet sounded like a hammer. Or had any of that happened? Bonnie's father had warned her about letting her imagination run wild. Besides, even if there were monsters, the house armor would protect them. Her mom told her it was like a giant turtle, and they could disappear inside the steel shell if needed. But what if the monsters were magical or got into the house before the armor was on? She couldn't bring herself to look out the window.

"There, much better." Her mother shuffled into the bathroom in her pretty blue nightgown. She ran her hand through her auburn hair and eyed the vent above the tub.

Bonnie followed her gaze. "What's up there?"

# The City of the Gods: Gold

"Nothing, Munchkin. I just can't imagine why the air conditioner isn't working." She smiled and fanned herself with a large book.

Bonnie looked at the window again. "Mommy, are all the monsters still gone?"

Her mom perched on the edge of the tub, clutching the book to her chest. "Yes, baby doll, Daddy and I sent them all away."

"Is Daddy a monster?"

Her mother chuckled. "No, Munchkin, Daddy's just confused by this new world. He misses the old days." She turned her attention to the book.

"What do you mean?"

Her mom shook the curls from her face. "Well, remember I told you Daddy and I were in the war? After we won in Japan, we fought monsters across the bridge in Empire City until one day, a bad man—a monster—destroyed part of the city. We call that day T-Day. And after Daddy banished the monster, you came into our lives, and I rebuilt Empire City.

"Now, your daddy doesn't know what to do with himself. With the monsters dea— gone." She smiled, tucking a rogue wisp of hair behind her ear, and opened the old book. "I found this in my room. It was your grandmother's. Shall we read it together?"

"Yes, please, Mommy!"

She shuffled the pages. "Ah. This is a poem she read to me when I was a little girl, just like you. I thought tonight would be a perfect night to share it."

*Just a little white cottage over the hill*

*All shining and fresh and new*

*With a gray stone chimney and gray-green roof,*

*Shimmering glistening wet with dew:*

*And the chimney seems as a knight of old.*

*Guarding his lady fair.*

*So that worry and doubt and bitter words.*

*May find no refuge there.*

*What a blessed haven for weary hearts.*

*Searching in vain for peace:*

*Leave worry and doubt at the top of the hill.*

*Let all your troubles cease.*

Bonnie smiled. "Can we go to that place, Mommy?"

Her mother stroked her cheek. "It's only in our imaginations. It's a beautiful notion, though, don't you agree?"

"Mmmmhmmm!"

Bonnie eyed the window. "Mommy, can I sleep with you tonight?"

"Of course, Munchkin." She, too, looked out the window. "Maybe that's enough monster talk for tonight." Her mother smiled and sang: "If I only had a brain."

"A-a heart!" Bonnie stammered.

"A home." Her mom tickled her.

"Da noive!" Bonnie squealed.

**<u>4</u>**

Theo woke to a chill, grateful the heat had subsided. Her eyes fluttered, and the blood moon gawked down through the glass dome.

*Where is Bonnie?*

She sprung into a sitting position and gasped, groping the charm of her necklace. She slid out of bed and padded to the door, but the recessed lighting remained off. She waved at the sensor to no avail and scoffed.

"Bonnie?" Theodora sprinted past the blur of gray newspaper articles and gripped the cold, brass doorknob to her daughter's room. She thought of The Ivory Icicle, Doctor Torment, The Dark Plunderer, and The Anti-Angel. All souls the Enforcers had snuffed out.

Theodora ripped open the door and flipped the lights. Tears welled in her eyes. She stumbled forward toward the perfectly flat comforter on Bonnie's bed.

"Bonnie?" Her voice trembled. The room spun.

Bonnie's china doll collection stared down in judgment from their shelves. The empty, soulless eyes brought more memories of a past life.

*Crash!*

Something fell in the kitchen.

"Bonnie?"

*Thunk!*

It came from the study at the opposite end of the house.

"Who's there?" Theo walked back through the darkness to her bedroom, where she kept her hardware. She had pulled out all the stops when designing this fortress. If it had been hard for the intruder to get in, it would be impossible to get out.

She pushed through the bedroom door. A soft clatter sounded behind her, and Theodora spun, staring into the dark abyss. She didn't want this, but it wanted her. The thing from all those years ago was back, pulling her toward her guns like a marionette. She could feel the woman with the deer antlers watching as she slid her hand into the censor slot next to the vanity.

*A turtle,* she remembered she had told Bonnie. *It's like we're inside a giant turtle.* The house shook on its foundation, and the center of the bedroom floor slid apart. Scalloped metal surrounded the glass domes on the outside as other sections folded in.

*Clang! Clang! Clang!*

Metal shutters dropped to the ground with a satisfying thud. It sounded like doom, like death. Theodora smiled as her mind surrendered to the thing she'd been outrunning for too long—the numb, warm feeling like she'd had just the right amount to drink.

She leaped into the chasm on the floor, and her bare feet thudded on the cold metal. She was a panther, silent and hyperaware. It was part of the gift she despised, but it was hers.

Theodora bit her lip to quell the bliss as she scanned the wall of guns. She pulled down a modified M50 Reising submachine gun and clenched the taped stock.

She remembered the rush when blood exploded from the back of those chicken-shit creeps' skulls and painted the wall. A soft giggle escaped her as she slammed a custom four-hundred-round plasma magazine in place. A red light flashed and slowly built into a glowing green bar along its length.

Her thoughts drifted to the intruder, desperately pounding on the six-inch bulletproof glass and pulling on locked door handles. Bloodlust took her. She was a lioness defending her cub. Bonnie needed her now, and she needed her like this, violent and unforgiving.

Theodora pulled herself out of the chasm and bound silently down the hall, stopping at door frames and tables to take cover and aim. Even in her silk pajamas, she felt like she was back in Honshu, gunning down the Imperial Japanese Army. She rounded the corner and scanned the kitchen. Bonnie's glass ice cream dish lay in pieces on the floor. She stepped around the glass shards, steadied the heavy Reising on the counter, and ran her arm over her brow.

Silence. Theo's eyes shot open. The grandfather clock had stopped. She exploded off the counter and doubled back toward the foyer, slamming into the wall beside the study entrance.

She took a few more heavy breaths and spun into the doorway, expecting to draw fire from the intruder.

No. Someone had pulled the grandfather clock away from the wall on its hinge. The hands were frozen.

Theodora stared vacantly into the darkness of the secret tunnel not even James knew existed. A tear ran down her face, then another. She dropped the Reising idly to her side and stared into the passage.

After all her preparation, all her fretting, and building fortress walls to keep the world out, Bonnie was gone, and Theodora Connor, the most powerful woman in Empire City, was powerless.

The Empire Bulletin
Empire City, Friday, October 16, 1953
CONNOR GIRL MISSING

Bonnie Connor, the 5-year-old daughter of retired heroes Captain James Connor and Mrs. Theodora Connor, Captain Wonderful and the Scarlet Sparrow, respectively, was reported missing from the family's Brookfield estate last night.

Mrs. Connor claims she put Bonnie to bed around 8:30 PM. When she returned to her daughter's room at 11:00, she found the bed empty and immediately phoned the police.

Authorities searched the neighborhood before pushing a widespread hunt through Brookfield's surrounding woods and coastal areas using bloodhounds. The Connor's neighbors reported hearing the couple bickering hours before.

Authorities are working on two theories:

Captain Connor took the child without informing her mother, Mrs. Connor.

An enemy of the League of Enforcers took the child; however, there is no ransom note or signs of forced entry.

Mrs. Connor has offered a $2000 reward to anyone with information as to the whereabouts of the missing Bonnie Connor.

From: Commanding Officer, Special Services Division.

To: Chief of Detectives

Subject: Vessel found on South Avenue

Date: 10-15-53

Location: Brookfield

1. Detective Joe Miller, shield #983, assigned to this matter under the supervision of the undersigned reports as follows.

2. On October 15th, 1953, at 11:04 PM, a vessel of unknown origin was discovered on South Street in Brookfield after a Morse code message from the Scarlet Sparrow alerted authorities to the location. The FBI and Allied Science were contacted after an initial search of the surrounding area revealed no suspicious behavior.

3. The FBI searched the immediate premises and surrendered custody of the vessel to Allied Science. Please see the accompanying paperwork signed by Frank Rivoli on behalf of Allied Science.

4. The vessel will remain under the care of Allied Science unless the FBI or ECPD finds cause to remove it.

5. There were 0 incidents in connection with this discovery.

6. This matter will receive continued attention only if and when new developments should occur.

Thomas Edden

Captain

NO PROMISE OF TOMORROW
The Empire Bulletin
Empire City, Saturday, March
DIE DEVIL!

**<u>5</u>**

A neat little blonde crossed Firestone Avenue at the light, and Skip Gibson followed her with his eyes, ashing his cigarette out the window of his 51' Plymouth Concord.

*She looks like Ann.*

The name swam through his mind, twisting his stomach in a knot until a honk from a passing car drew his attention, and she vanished into her routine. He knew he'd see her again in the face of the next beautiful stranger. It was his penance.

"Lucky Tiger Hair Tonic gets the gals!" the radio said. Gibson killed the engine and leaned back. The taste of booze clung to the back of his dry throat, and his head throbbed as the feelings he'd drowned last night resurfaced. He launched his cigarette stub into the empty parking lot and forced another aspirin down, watching Wilbur's Diner.

It was apparent, even in the daylight, that most of the letters on the neon sign had burned out. "bur's Din," it said, and part of the underscore had fallen into the overgrown weeds masquerading as a garden. Gibson stared at the festive cardboard skeletons and pumpkins taped to the front window, caught halfway between a daydream and a thought.

At the ninety-third precinct, Chief Murphy had told him, an eccentric old detective named "Slim" had asked to partner with him specifically. Gibson wasn't one to question authority, but questions still lingered. *Why me? And why insist on meeting at a colored diner in Lincoln?*

Across the parking lot, the Mosley Drive bus bench teemed with folks impatiently checking their watches and fanning themselves with newspapers. Interchangeable crowds splintered off the bus while others boarded, but no one approached his car. Gibson peeled himself off the seat, stretching his cramped muscles, and checked his watch.

*Quarter past nine. What time does this Slim character start work, anyhow?*

# The City of the Gods: Gold

He slouched on the hood of the two-door sedan, pulled out his mashed pack of Lucky Strikes, and tucked a cigarette between his lips. Another bus pulled through the blurry curtain of heat rising from the asphalt. Gibson scanned the crowd for a tall, thin man, but the people in the clumping mass were indistinguishable. The sun bore a hole through his throbbing head, and his gun holster felt like his old M1 Garand was tucked inside instead of a Colt snub nose. He pulled a flask out of his pocket and unscrewed the lid. The scent hit him like a gut punch. "Hair of the dog, I guess."

"Hair o' the dog, my ass!" A tall, obese man jerked the flask from Gibson's hand. "Yer on th' job, sunny boy." His mouth curled into a dumb, playful smile, pushing jowls aside like curtains. Burst blood vessels spiderwebbed over his bulbous nose, a roadmap of bad decisions. Suspenders clung to his pants for dear life, running over his half-tucked-in shirt. A gun holster and a tie partially covered a smattering of sweat stains, old and new. He emptied Gibson's flask into a paper coffee cup.

Gibson pushed himself off the hood of the Plymouth. "Who the hell—"

"Probably shit whiskey anyway." The stranger tossed the empty flask into the car through the open window and ran his hand over the black frame.

Gibson tried again. "Who—"

A sharp whistle from the fat man cut him off. "Sweet chariot." He pulled the door open. "Maybe a little too much car for you from the look of things, but a cherry ride nonetheless." He lowered himself into the Concord with a grunt, and the passenger side dipped.

Gibson ducked his head into the driver's side window. "Now, wait a minute; who the hell do you think you are?"

"Well, I think I'm Slim Shanahan, Len t' my friends, but you can call me Slim." The man lifted the coffee cup to his lips, paused, and lowered it. "And I think that would make you Skipper—you don't mind if I call you Skipper? 'Course ya don't—and that would mean

I'm your partner. If I'm wrong about any o' that, I apologize for getting in your car, friend." Slim slurped at the cup like a mongoloid who had just discovered his lips. "Yep, shit whiskey, just like I thought. What is this, Corby's?"

Gibson flicked his cigarette stub to the ground and yanked the door open, perching on the bench seat. "Now, wait just—"

"Whatever the occasion," Slim said, "it's better with Corby's." He guffawed and slapped his shaking belly. "Whaddaya think, Skipper? Is this occasion better now, with Corby's?"

Gibson jabbed a finger in Slim's direction. "Let's get something straight. My name is Gibson. Detective Gibson, not Skipper."

Slim studied him through beady eyes while silence ate away at Gibson's confidence until the fat man slurped the paper cup again.

"Suppose I tell Murphy you're drinking on the job—"

"Skipper, stop wasting my time. We been put on a high-profile case. I'm talkin' hero-making stuff. You wanna get to it, or don'tcha?"

Gibson cocked an eyebrow. "Case? I thought you were just showing me the ropes today."

"What better training could you ask for? C'mon, get this jalopy in gear an' stop gettin' so hysterical over names. Jesus, you sound like a broad."

Gibson acquiesced and turned over the engine. "Fine. Let me just check in with HQ." He reached for the radio.

Slim slapped a chubby paw over the handpiece. "What are you, a little girl? Ya need t' ask yer daddy if it's okay to come out with the big boys? I'll call it in, t' th' local cops if it makes you feel better. Murphy already knows about this." Slim clenched the paper cup between his teeth and flipped on the radio.

*EeeeEEEEEEeeee!* the speaker whined. Slim twisted the knob off and reeled back.

"What the hell?"

Gibson frowned. "It was working this morning."

Slim took a sip from his cup and grimaced. "Figures, ever since they cut our budget after the big rebuild of Empire, nothing seems t' work right. Even though those crooks in the mayor's office had nothin' t' do with it. Well, that's politics for ya. You see that story th' *Bulletin* put out on Mayor Hall when he retired? You'd think he rebuilt the goddamned city himself. Makes me sick. Stanz is no better neither."

Gibson had no stomach for political talk. "I think there's a callbox on Hunter Avenue, but if Murphy's okay with it, I can handle myself."

Slim grinned, forcing his eyes to squint shut. "Can ya now? Good to know th' rookie's on th' job."

The sun fried the black car on the pavement, and Gibson was sweating gasoline. "Where to?" he grumbled.

Slim took a swallow from the paper cup and broke into a coughing fit, drooling down his shirt. His face turned three shades of red. "Jesus! Shit!" The wet hack turned into a dry wheeze he caught in a trembling fist. "S'cuse me, must be comin' down with somethin'— take th' Coastal Highway north, jus' over the Bunche Bridge." Slim looked to the horizon, blinked his watery eyes, and fell silent.

Gibson pulled the gearshift down and inched onto Ames Avenue. "Is that even our jurisdiction?"

"What, are you writin' a book? Don't worry about it, Skipper." The old man finished a few stray coughs and glanced out the passenger window.

<u>6</u>

The Plymouth rolled through Droghead, another colored section of the city where folks seemed determined not to let their hard lives show on their hard faces. When Gibson was a boy, it felt like enemy territory. Still, he'd always find himself sneaking across Miller's Run Park from his home in Eastwood for penny candy and a Coke at Harvey's, where he'd shared his first kiss with a sweet girl named Claudette.

Next, the Concord dipped into South Valley, aptly nicknamed "Hell's Gate." Blackened remains of old structures creaked and whined, rickety survivors of fires set and extinguished long ago. Buildings that remained livable had busted windows and doors, barely clinging to their hinges, but it didn't stop the dopers, hipsters, and beatniks from squatting.

A naked, dirty toddler followed Gibson's car with runny eyes from a building's stoop. He sat next to a dope peddler with a shifty gaze and a malicious smile, holding court amongst the reanimated dead skulking through the neighborhood around him. The Concord must have stunk like a police cruiser, but the addicts didn't care. Most of them weren't even on this planet anymore, and the ones who saw Gibson offered only matching vacant looks.

"This used to be my beat when I was a uniformed cop, still looks the same," Slim said, yawning. "There was a great coffee shop just down that block."

Gibson eyed him suspiciously.

Slim studied the scenery and chuckled. "I had this partner, McIntire, Stan McIntire. He'd always be scared stupid when we'd have t' be out here past dark.

"One night, we heard strange noises comin' from one o' these buildings just before our shift ended. That one there." He pointed at a nearly collapsed structure and stopped to think. "Musta been back in… thirty er thirty-one, way before th' League of Enforcers.

"At any rate, McIntire an' I hear a noise comin' from that building. He won't go in, too busy pissin' his pants, so I go alone. It's pitch-black, no electricity, but someone's moanin'. Sounds like a girl, ya know? So, I grab my flashlight an' snoop around a bit. I even call out. No response, but the moanin's gettin' louder."

Slim cleared his throat. "Then I see a pregnant lady sprawled out on the floor, all gowed-up on somethin'. So, I yell out to McIntire t' call an ambulance. But what's he do? He comes in t' check it out. McIntire wasn't the brightest, ya see.

"Long story short, this pregnant lady's fakin' th' whole thing, and her boyfriend is waitin' in the shadows t' rob us. Didn't count on us bein' cops didn't matter to him one way or th' other, just wanted money for th' next score.

"So, the boyfriend jumps on McIntire an' somehow gets ahold of his gun. He shoots me right in the arm *and then* tells me to empty my wallet. Luckily, he was about as smart as McIntire. The shot was a through-and-through, didn't hit anything important, so I beat the ever-livin' piss outta that skinny little addict. Left him on the floor t' think about what he'd done while I called an ambulance fer th' girl.

"An' McIntire"—Slim wheezed out a laugh—"McIntire quit then and there. He became a priest! A man o' God still t' this day!" He slapped his shaking belly. "Last I heard, he was over at Saint Paul's in Terrytown."

Gibson weaved around the remains of a scorched black car in the middle of Twin Elms Lane. "Why didn't you take the doper in? Hell, that's attempted murder."

"Nah, can't put a guy like that in jail, not here. He'd just learn how t' get better at robbin' people. Maybe he'd kill the next poor sap he caught in the dark.

"My point is, ya can't trust an addict, an' ya can't trust a McIntire. You don't look like an addict; you ain't a McIntire, are ya?"

"I don't think so." Gibson made a hard left on Lock Alley and headed east.

"Yeah, we'll see," Slim muttered.

They hit two green lights in a row, and decrepit brick buildings transformed into the brownstones of Sedgewick. The Plymouth stopped at a red light, and Gibson scanned the tranquil streets for his old partner, Creed, milling around Temple's Coffee Shop. He made a right onto Loma Avenue. Huller's Restaurant blew by, but still no Creed.

A few more blocks and the city streets gave way to the Coastal Highway's northbound onramp. A flock of angry motorists remained at a standstill, blaring their horns at the gridlock on the southbound side. Gibson hit the gas, and the Concord growled in appreciation as it raced up the open road.

The revitalizing smell of salt air drifted off the ocean, and a gull's scream carried memories of better times. Gibson sighed as the cool breeze kissed his skin and glanced past Slim to Broadshall Island.

*Can we go to Schooners?* Ann would ask with a beaming smile as they window-shopped on Belden Street. If Gibson had an extra dime, he'd oblige, and she'd get a chocolate malt with whipped cream and *two* cherries. Her skin smelled like the ocean, and her long blonde curls were always pulled back with a blue ribbon, matching her sparkling eyes. They were two city kids forced to grow up when the Korean War brought their three-year romance to an agonizing halt. *We'll always have Broadshall,* she'd told him in her final letter.

"So, what's your tale, nightingale?" Slim boomed.

Gibson felt the vice tighten around his skull again and sighed. "Don't worry about me. How'd we end up paired together? Didn't an old timer like you already have a partner?"

"I don't much care to talk about it." Slim stared wistfully out the window.

A passing commuter train thundered by, killing the silence. Gibson pressed the issue. "Chief Murphy said you requested me specifically. Why? You don't know me from Adam."

"That's exactly why. I know the other boys all too well, and I know what they do in their leisure time. I guess you could say I want t' see what you're made of, Skipper."

Gibson shook his head. "Slim, that *Skipper* business again. I told you—"

"Skipper, let me tell you somethin' my old partner used t' tell me. Not McIntire, mind you, a wiser fella. He'd always say: 'live each day as if it was your last…' I can't remember the rest o' the saying 'cause you made me drink this shit whiskey, but at any rate, th' message is the same."

"Which is?"

Slim watched him with a creeping sadness in his features. "Take it one day at a time and keep your nose clean. The rest'll work itself out." His eyes danced between Gibson's. "You seem like a bright guy. You'll figure it out one day, Skipper."

*Figure what out?* He wanted to ask the question but resolved to let the words hang in the air as the Bunche Bridge's arches and trusses rose.

Slim chuckled, scanning the glinting iron. "It always amazes me how the Scarlet Sparrow built this whole bridge an' half the city in only five years. Downright inspiring."

Across the bridge, towering mansions littered the shoreline. Gibson had only ventured to Brookfield and Northwell a handful of times, but there was no getting used to the extravagance. To the right, the old Fayette Bridge stood in shambles as a testament to those lost on T-Day. Part of the road still teetered on the abutments and ramped down into the water. Unnatural striations left behind by Torment's hordes covered the rest of the cement and metal.

Gibson imagined what it must have been like to be on that bridge five years ago. Screaming, terrified people abandoning their cars just as they'd abandoned their lives in the city, destined to become collateral damage in a war they were not part of, with only a broken bridge marking their final resting place.

"You got a wife? Kids?" Slim grumbled.

Gibson drummed his fingers on the wheel. "I was going with a girl, Ann." He paused. Her name still tasted sweet on his tongue. "Uncle Sam had me over in Korea and—"

"Lady troubles, huh?" A smile crossed Slim's lips. "I know all about that. You're young yet, Skipper. There's plenty o' time to be doll dizzy."

With a soft thunk, the bridge ended. The car slowed as it ran into the greenery of suburbia. Large mansions loomed like sentries, and the smell of fall shouldered away the salty air.

Slim pointed casually toward the front windshield. "House is up here on your right, 7674 North Avenue."

Gibson squinted. "That's a house? It looks like something out of a Flash Gordon strip."

Massive glass domes arched into the sky, reflecting a radiant glow through rows of leafless trees. The only thing that insisted it was a house was the little wrap-around porch. Gibson wheeled the Plymouth through the iron gate, around the horseshoe driveway, and killed the engine. His hangover bit at the base of his skull as he scanned the orange and brown leaves peppering the unkempt property. Two jack-o-lanterns gawked from the porch.

Slim wadded his paper cup and threw it on the car's floor. "Alright, Skipper, showtime. This is Mister and Missus James Connor's house. Gen-u-ine heroes. Retired now, well, publicly anyhow. The retired life never seems to stick for their kind."

Gibson's jaw went slack. "You mean—"

"They have a daughter, Bonnie, who's missin'. ECPD already searched the property, took statements, and found nothin'. Not even a ransom note, or so the story goes.

"We're here to check in, see that everyone's feelin' ducky about the process we use to find missing people. Alls you gotta do is shut yer yap an' try not to wear your heart on your sleeve." He popped open the door and heaved himself out of the car.

Gibson ejected, raced around the hood, and pressed his hand on Slim's chest. "Wait a minute!" He scanned the towering glass domes. "Captain Wonderful a-and the Scarlet Sparrow?"

Slim brushed past, trailing a sour, boozy odor. "That's right."

Gibson followed Slim onto the porch, and his stomach lurched. He exhaled and straightened his tie, feeling the weight of the Colt snub nose in the holster and the badge clipped to his belt. Slim pounded on the door.

Gibson tightened his lips and dabbed his sweaty brow with a handkerchief. "I heard most of their enemies are dead, so at least the suspect list will be short."

Slim cleared his throat and furrowed his brow at Gibson.

The door creaked open, and Theodora Connor, *The Theodora Connor*, poked her heart-shaped face out. "Yes, can I help you?" She studied the detectives from under a straw bucket hat, and Gibson tried to place her eye color somewhere between red and brown with flecks of gold. They almost matched the abundance of freckles on her face, chest, and exposed shoulders and arms. Dirt smeared her shirt, and her dainty hand, gripping the doorframe, was missing a wedding ring.

Slim removed his hat, choking it nervously. "Mornin', Missus Connor, I presume? I'm Detective Shanahan, and this is Detective Gibson from the ECPD. I understand our colleagues already searched the premises, but may we have a moment of your time, my dear?" Slim smiled wide, creating large creases under his cheeks and forcing his eyes to squint.

Mrs. Connor ran an open palm over her clavicle. "Of course, detectives." She pulled the door open and presented the house. "Come in, won't you?"

7

*Lucky Tiger Hair Tonic gets the gals.* Gibson recited the ad to keep his mind from slipping into madness as he traversed the Connor estate.

"This way, detectives, we can chat in the parlor." Mrs. Connor's eyes seemed fixated on Gibson as she led the way down a tall, narrow hallway. "Please forgive my hat. You caught me in the middle of gardening, and I'm afraid my hair is a fright."

Slim paused, examining one of the few family photos posted amongst the framed newspaper clippings documenting the Enforcers' accolades. "Beautiful family, Missus Connor."

She feigned a smile and guided the detectives through an ornate door into a large parlor. A rainbow of books covered the walls, contrasting the rich mahogany shelves and a matching desk. The decadent, old-fashioned room didn't look at all like it belonged to the spaceship-looking house.

The tick of a grandfather clock kept Gibson grounded. He eyed his watch. "Your clock is off by ten minutes. It's three after."

Mrs. Connor nodded. "So, it is." She motioned to a red velvet sofa with the same brown frame as the rest of the furniture. "Please, have a seat."

Slim plopped deep into the couch. "Real nice place you got here, Missus Connor, real nice! Ain't it, Skipper?"

Gibson perched on the edge. "Sure is."

Mrs. Connor smiled, sauntering to the matching wooden chair opposite an oak coffee table, and the earthy scent of summer jumped from her skin. Salt and flowers, just how Ann used to smell.

An old tobacco pipe on the desk behind her caught Gibson's eye. "Is the man of the house around?"

Mrs. Connor's lips tightened. "I'm afraid James stepped out."

Gibson furrowed his brow. "Stepped out? Wh—"

"Lovely weather we're having, Missus Connor. I must say it's peculiar for mid-October, but you can't beat these Indian summers," Slim bellowed.

"Yes, it is." She smiled and sucked air between her teeth. "Where are my manners? Can I offer you gentlemen something to drink? Coffee, perhaps, or iced tea?"

"I'm fine, Missus Connor, but I know Skipper here is partial to whiskey. Got any Corby's?" Slim nudged Gibson, wheezing out a laugh. "Just givin' the rookie a hard time. Inside joke, I suppose."

"I'm not thirsty, thanks." Gibson shot daggers at Slim, then regarded Mrs. Connor.

She forced a weak, tired smile. "If you change your mind, you'll let me know."

"Sure." Gibson patted his breast pocket, removing a pad and pencil. He slid forward on the couch and cleared his throat. "Mrs. Connor, I know this may be difficult, but we have a few questions we'd like to ask you."

Her funny-colored eyes found his again, flecks of gold floating amongst the irises that now reflected the brown room. "No need for formalities. Please, call me Theodora."

"Fine," Gibson replied. "Theodora. After Bonnie—"

Slim's hand dropped onto Gibson's shoulder like a vice. "Skipper, this poor woman has been through enough. It would be immoral to hound the poor dear with questions right now. We're strictly checking in on her today."

Gibson eyed the fat man and tightened his lips. Slim draped a cheesy smile across his face. "On second thought," he said, "I'd love a cup of coffee if you don't mind, Theodora." He looked like a teacher's pet who had just asked for extra homework.

Theodora nodded and stood. "Of course. How do you take it?" She glided gracefully across the room, stopping halfway between the couch and the door.

Slim folded his hands neatly in his lap and strained his smile even tighter. "Just black is fine."

*With all my whiskey in it!* Gibson thought. Slim looked like he was waiting for a pat on the head and affirmation that he was a good boy.

"Detective Gibson?"

"No, thank you."

Theodora turned when she reached the door frame, flashing an impish smile. "I'll see if I can rustle up some Corby's." She winked and vanished through the doorway.

"Good one, Theodora!" Slim wheezed.

"What the hell are you doing?" Gibson whispered.

# The City of the Gods: Gold

Slim's face grew solemn. "Detective work. She's too busy bein' cute t' act out the role o' the suffering mother. It'll be easier to get some answers with her out of the room. From here on out, shut yer yap and let me do the talkin', Skipper." Slim shot across the parlor, pouring over photos and rummaging through drawers in the mahogany desk. "Why don'tcha put yer pad t' use an' take notes on how I handle the task at hand?"

Gibson tucked his pad away and eyed the door. Slim was right. Theodora was much too calm, given the situation. "Maybe we can interview some of the help. A house this big must have a staff, right?"

Slim hustled across the room, pulling drawers from a chest next to the large bay window. "Someone who loves their privacy this much doesn't have any use for house boys and the like. Besides, I'm sure she has gizmos that do things you couldn't imagine. She's the Scarlet Sparrow, remember?"

"I prefer to think of myself as multiple people." Theodora's voice carried from the doorway. "Sure, the Scarlet Sparrow has machines that do her bidding, but Theodora Connor—well, she's not afraid to get her hands dirty. And my other personality thinks they're both crazy." She mimicked Groucho Marx, ashing his cigar and laughed. Slim took the hint and smirked. Gibson didn't.

Theodora slid daintily across the floor with the cup and saucer, eyeing Slim. "Is anything the matter, detective?"

"Just admiring the view," Slim responded seamlessly. "Don't get much of this in th' city, 'specially in Calway."

"Do you hail from Empire originally, Detective Shanahan?" Theodora handed him the coffee with a casual smile.

Slim took the cup and saucer delicately in two hands. "Thank you. No, ma'am, farm boy born and raised. More at home in a place like this than Empire City proper. Coffee smells great, by the way, really top-notch!"

Theodora smiled and clasped her hands. Gibson watched her breasts press between her arms and glanced up to find her gaze squarely on him. "Well, you're both welcome to stop by anytime," she said. Gibson cleared his throat, scanning the oriental rug on the floor.

Slim wore his overabundant, cheesy smile again. "Mighty sweet of you, Theodora. I might take you up on that one of these days. I hear Brookfield's lovely in the summertime."

Theodora sunk back into her chair and eyed Gibson. "And you, Detective Gibson, where are you from?"

The lump in his throat made it hard to breathe. "Ahem, excuse me. I am from Empire. Eastwood—"

Slim hacked into a red handkerchief as he dropped slowly onto the sofa. "Excuse me"—he managed between coughs—"funny time of year to come down with something, don't you agree?" He exhaled the red from his cheeks. "Anyway, I'm sorry to have bothered you today, Theodora. Just routine, you understand? An old man like me, well, the ECPD's gotta keep me busy somehow. Plus, I'm showin' the rookie Skipper here the ropes today. First day on the job, sort of a changing of the guard, I guess."

Theodora nodded politely and shot Gibson a smile. "Congratulations."

Slim slapped his belly. "Well, we'll get out of your hair. Might I use your men's room before I leave? I'm an old man, after all." He stared at her through squinted, smiling eyes.

"Of course," Theodora said, "it's the second door on your left. Shall I show you?"

"I can manage," Slim replied curtly. He eyed Gibson, and his smile dissolved. "No more questions, Skipper."

Gibson grumbled as he watched the old man waddle out. He turned to find Theodora's eyes locked on him. The ticking grandfather clock was deafening. He removed the slightly crushed pack of Lucky Strikes from his pocket and extended one to Theodora. "Cigarette?"

She regarded the pack hesitantly and took one. "Sure, why not? I don't usually smoke, but given the circumstances—"

Gibson placed one in his mouth and flipped his lighter open, offering the flame to her.

"Thank you." She puffed until the cherry grew, and Gibson lit his own. Theodora shot a dart of smoke into the air. "I really do appreciate you driving all the way out here from Calway, Detective Gibson."

Her gaze lingered. Gibson glanced out the window uncomfortably. "It's my pleasure." He took a drag. "How are you holding up?"

Theodora's lips curled almost mockingly. "I suppose I'm as okay as one can be." She glanced past him to the door and spoke just above a whisper. "I try to come across as strong, but believe me, underneath this facade, I'm a ball of nerves. Lucky for me, my mother was an actress. She taught me all the tricks."

Gibson nodded. "We're going to find your daughter, Mrs. Conn—Theodora. But I must know"—he took a drag and eyed her sedately—"where is your husband?"

She ashed her cigarette onto the floor and took a long, comprehensive draw. Her gaze locked on Gibson across the table as smoke slowly poured from her mouth. "Can I ask you a question, detective?"

"Sure," he replied.

"What if the laws of man don't apply anymore? What if there's so much more of the universe you don't understand? I mean, it's not your fault; you couldn't possibly understand, not yet anyway. You see, I've seen things, detective." She glanced away and looked to be fighting something deep within herself.

"How do you, as a man of the law, a man who I can only assume has a moral compass, behave when the world you know and love crashes down around you, and there is no right or wrong anymore, just survival? Just preservation of life?"

Her gaze held him in stasis. "I have faith in you, detective, but I'm afraid you don't quite understand what faith is. Not yet, anyhow." Her tone was earnest and foreboding. The ramblings of a lunatic if she wasn't so deliberately sincere and stone sober. It shook Gibson to his marrow.

The silence drove them each into their thoughts. The ticking of the grandfather clock was now soothing, lulling Gibson into a sense of security and order. Theodora was no longer a drop-dead gorgeous bombshell. There was a distinct kind of beauty about her, though, a vulnerability. Her eyes met his, but he didn't look away this time, and Gibson felt, for a moment, that Bonnie wasn't the reason he was here.

Then, the analytical detective took over, and everything fell by the wayside. "I'm afraid I don't follow." It was a half-truth. Some of the things Theodora had said hit him hard in all the right places.

Sadness crept across her face. "And I'm afraid, detective, you'll find out what I mean before you're ready. It scares me."

"Well, Theodora, we'll let you get back to gardening," Slim interrupted. "Thanks again for your time and hospitality."

A forced smile crossed Theodora's lips as she pushed herself to her feet. No tears spilled, but her eyes seemed troubled for the first time. "It's my pleasure. If there's anything else you need, detectives, please feel free to telephone me, or better yet, stop by. I'll be here." Her eyes lingered on Gibson until he turned toward the door.

<u>8</u>

# The City of the Gods: Gold

They said their goodbyes in the foyer, and Gibson and Slim ambled down the porch steps. Gibson glanced over his shoulder at a somber Theodora standing alone in the doorway. Her words drifted in his head. *How do you behave when the world you know and love crashes down around you, and there is no right and wrong anymore, just survival? Just preservation of life?* Theodora clutched the frame, offered a final, weak smile, and shut the door.

Slim marched toward the car. "You were supposed to keep yer yap shut."

Gibson matched his pace. "How can you say that when a little girl is missing? Boy, you sure are a—"

"She's a hero with a reputation whose daughter went missing under her watch. You think she wants us to find her, Skipper? It would be a media frenzy. Afraid we're on our own here, an' as far as I'm concerned, she's the enemy." He tipped his hat back to gaze at the sun like it annoyed him.

Gibson raised an eyebrow. "You think she's involved in this?"

"I don't know, but she ain't playin' ball, neither. As I said, we're on our own."

"What about her husband?"

Slim sighed. "James Connor was never reported missing. Maybe he skipped town. Maybe he's dead. That ain't our problem right now."

"Slim, she said—"

"I heard." Slim flashed Gibson a smile over the Concord's roof. "But I bet I learned more snoopin' around her house than you did from her bullshit tirade. Trust me, Skipper. She ain't your friend."

Gibson regarded the towering domed house and eased into the car. "So, what'd you find, Slim?"

"Ain't you an eager beaver?" Slim's nervous, accommodating facade had ended at the threshold of the Connor estate. He was a raucous old man again.

Gibson sighed. "Playing it awfully close to the chest, aren't you?"

"Always," Slim said.

"Aren't we supposed to be partners?"

Slim looked him over. "I don't know yet."

Gibson turned the key, and the engine roared. "I don't need this. I'm going back to the station. You want me to drop you at Wilbur's?"

Slim pulled a surprisingly pristine pack of Pall Mall cigarettes from his pocket. "Now hold on, Skipper. I said I don't know *yet*. Give it time. One more stop while we're in Brookfield." He lit a cigarette with an old silver Ronson lighter.

"Fine." Gibson shifted the Plymouth into drive and pulled slowly around the driveway, watching the house through troubled eyes.

"110 Pleasant Street." Slim looked Gibson up and down. "You okay, Skipper? You look like you've seen the holy ghost." Smoke floated from Slim's mouth and out the cracked window.

"Not sure what I saw, Slim." The car jostled as they dropped off the driveway onto North Avenue, and Gibson could still feel Theodora's eyes watching him from the window.

"Probably first-case jitters," Slim said. "I still get 'em to this day, you know? The problem is when they stop comin', that means ya stopped carin', and ain't nothin' more dangerous than a cop who don't give a shit."

OLD
GHOSTS

Grease spat, eggs convulsed, and bacon crackled. Cal pushed his stupid paper hat back and wiped his brow, trying to make sense of the final slips of paper scribbled over illegibly with food orders.

It was another hot day on the grill. Another day above ground, but that was the extent of Cal's optimism. He stretched his achy back and bit into an Archway Oatmeal cookie to stave off the gnawing call of the bottle. "Order up."

*Ding!* He tapped the little bronze bell and arranged the plate on the counter in the window.

"I'm comin', I'm comin' keep your shirt on, Cal." Wilbur shuffled across the diner, looking older than his sixty-plus years. Short gray hair faded to patchy stubble on his wrinkled face, which tightened as he shot Cal a smile. The eyes of a young man shone through, eager and passionate. Cal always envied that.

"Hurry up, old-timer, or it'll be cold by the time they dig in," Cal said with a wink.

Wilbur snatched the plate and smirked. "Maybe they'll get tired of waiting and leave. I'd be doing them a favor. Can't imagine this slop is any better than usual, Calvin."

"Better n' you could make, old man." Cal chuckled and watched him hobble across the linoleum.

The already confining kitchen walls closed in as the final minutes of the day drained. Cal leaned into the prep station and thumbed through the box of cookies, longing for his soft, velvet recliner.

Wilbur pushed the kitchen door open and looked Cal over with a bothered smile. "Calvin, you have a visitor," he said in an uncharacteristically somber tone.

# The City of the Gods: Gold

"A visitor?" Cal furrowed his brow.

"That's what I said, Calvin. I'll take care of these last orders, but make it quick; with Darlene off today, we're short-handed." Wilbur donned an apron.

Cal sighed and pushed through the swinging door, eyeing the men slouched along the red laminate countertop, each scanning the *Bulletin*.

"In the corner," Wilbur said through the service window.

A white woman in the far booth gazed out the window, clad in a baby blue dress with a white silk scarf tied under her chin. Cal moved around the counter toward the table and regarded Wilbur, who only shrugged.

The woman watched him approach through ivory cat-eye sunglasses. "Heya Cal, whatta ya say? It's been too long." She smiled.

"Theo," Cal snarled. He slunk into the booth and glared across the table at his reflection in her dark lenses. Theo offered a lady-like grin, but he knew better.

"What are you doing here? It's not like the Scarlet Sparrow to patrol this far downtown. Isn't Wilbur's Diner a little beneath you?" Cal wanted to scream at her. If it had been five years ago, he would have, but time had exhausted his emotions.

Theo removed her sunglasses, and sadness welled in her eyes. One was smaller, maybe swollen, and slathered over with makeup. "It's a little beneath you, Cal. You and Jerry were the best cooks I ever hired. How long are you going to stay in this dump? You should at least go back to catering, if not for your own sake, then for the good of Empire! Everyone in the city needs to taste your food, Bucko. I could help you get back on your feet." She smiled and reached across the table to touch his hand.

Cal reeled away. "Don't say my brother's name. Last time we catered a Connor affair, it didn't turn out too good for either of us."

"Aw. It wasn't all bad, Cal." Theodora flashed a deplorable smile that bound him to the slick vinyl seat and simultaneously shot him into the past. "After what happened—well, at least we got to see the world."

Cal pounded a clenched fist on the table. "The world?" he yelled. "We saw Japan. I saw my brother die!"

Theo looked away. Cal relented with a sharp exhale and scanned the diner over his shoulder. The men at the counter returned to their papers. Wilbur shook his head slowly through the kitchen window, and Cal adjusted the salt shaker flush with the pepper.

He met Theodora's gaze and spoke in a quieter tone. "Uncle Sam didn't even know me an' Jerry were there. We didn't get no golden statue in Armory Square. No fanfare for the colored folks." The heat rose on the back of his neck again.

Theodora scanned the table like a scolded child. "I'm sorry that's how you remember it, Cal, and I'm sorry about Jerry. Not a day goes by that I don't think about him." She sighed, and a slow smile built across her lips. "Why, I remember a time—"

"Why are you here, and what's with the Audrey Hepburn look?" Cal leaned back and crossed his arms over his chest.

"I'm trying it out. Does it suit me, or should I have gone with the Peter Lorre ensemble?" She twisted her face and spoke in an odd voice. "You know Rick, I have many a friend in Casablanca, but somehow, just because you despise me, you're the only one I trust."

Cal sighed, removed his paper hat, and ran a hand through his short, thinning hair.

Theodora smiled weakly. "Not a fan of Peter Lorre? My mother used to take me to see 'Casablanca' every time it pl—"

"Why are you here, Theo? I know it's not to discuss old films."

Theo shuddered. "Calvin, I have no one else to turn to." A well-timed tear rolled down her freckled cheek.

Cal sighed. "The last time I heard that, we ended up in Japan, so Truman wouldn't have to unleash his superweapon—or whatever lie you told us to get us there."

"This is different." Theodora spun the charm of her necklace between her fingers. "I'm sure you've seen the papers—Bonnie's missing. Oh, you mustn't think of me as a bad mother! James is gone too. He—"

"Save it, Theo. I'm not like you, or James, or Lily. I'm sorry, I can't help you." Cal dragged himself out of the booth.

Theo touched his arm. "Cal, this isn't Doctor Torment or The Ivory Icicle. It's Bonnie; it's my little baby. I have no one else to turn to." She buried her face in her hands, sobbing quietly.

"Seems I'm only your friend when you need something. Go talk to the police, Theo. That's their job, and right now, I've got to get back to mine."

Theo leaned out of the booth and grasped his hand. "Please, Cal," she said, "I feel like I'm going crazy. I can't tell if I'm awake or dreaming anymore. Nothing seems real. I know it sounds nuts, but—I keep having visions. I don't know if it's a side effect of what we are or something else. Please, I'm begging you. Help me. The woman with the deer antlers—"

"I'm sorry, Theo." Cal slid his hand from her grip. He'd never seen her so shaken. Even in Kyushu, under a hail of gunfire. He paused and opened his mouth to speak, but no words came—just a slight noise in the back of his throat, then silence.

Theo wiped running mascara from her cheeks, stood slowly, and slipped a white lace glove over her ridiculous wedding ring. "In any case, Calvin, it's always a pleasure to see you." She replaced her sunglasses. "It warms my heart to know you're cooking again. Catering or not, the chef's life always suited you. I'm staying at our penthouse in the

Ironleaf building if you change your mind." The click of her heels echoed through the diner. "I hope you do," she whispered as she passed. "I'll leave your name at the front desk, just in case." The bell rang softly, and the door swung closed.

The mention of the Ironleaf building forced patchy memories to resurface. *C'mon Cal,* Jerry's voice echoed. *One payday from these rich folks, and we can open the restaurant—just one more catering job, and we're on Easy Street.*

He remembered that biting December wind as he and Jerry waited outside for the service elevator. The way Theodora looked poured into that black, off-the-shoulder ball gown. Ron Baxter's malicious glare. The food Cal had prepared: deviled eggs made with his secret ingredients, butter and pickle juice, Belgian endive spears with curried crab salad, Wilbur's special crab Rangoon recipe, complete with the hot mustard dipping sauce and the main event, beef Wellington seasoned with allspice and ginger.

He remembered the smell of rotten meat as he carved into the beef Wellington. The putrid stench as pus ran onto the serving platter, and maggots covered in a thick mucus poured from the food, spilling onto the floor.

Cal gripped the vinyl seat to resist the tainted memories, but still, he recalled splotchy events pieced together with booze-soaked half-visions bordering on insanity. A little girl, a Mexican woman, Ron Baxter's eyes rolled deep into his head, leading a chant in another language. The smell of blood, a rancid iron stench staining the air, and masks. People clad in black robes, peering out of the dark soulless eyes, chanting: *God is dead!*

**<u>10</u>**

Cal locked the diner's front door and watched Theodora through the glass, sitting alone on the Ames Avenue bus stop bench. She was wounded and vulnerable, almost human but an actress, he reminded himself, above all else.

*I wouldn't be much help anyway,* Cal thought. *White folks don't look too kindly on a guy like me asking questions about a young, missing white girl, especially on the Northside.*

Still, there was something Cal couldn't shake. *I can't tell if I'm awake or dreaming anymore. The woman with the deer antlers—*

Theo's eyes met his. She looked like a raw, open wound, festering in the blood-red light of sunset. The bus pulled between them, stopped, and vanished in a puff of black exhaust, and with it, Theodora.

*Good riddance.*

Jerry's reflection watched him from the glass door. Cal closed his eyes. *I'm sorry, Jerry, I'm not like you. I can't forget that easy.* Old ghosts haunted him more often these days. The guilt of his wasted life manifested in the sorrowful eyes of those he'd lost.

*Where is James Connor?* Cal thought. It was well known he stepped out often, but his daughter was missing. *Maybe he took her and ran off with some floozy. If she crossed him, maybe she's already dead.*

*Maybe Ron Baxter took her. Who knows what sick, depraved things he gets into with that cult of his?* Cal thought of the other little girl from the Connors' party, the one who watched him with wide, dark eyes from behind her mother on that cold December night. Rosalita.

*She knows things.*

*She talks to it.*

The masked people muttered as malodorous corruption poured from the girl's dead eyes and gaping mouth.

*God is dead!* The phrase shivered down his spine. Cal winced at what must have been a fabricated memory and turned back to the diner. The comfortable, dutiful course he'd tethered himself to since he'd quit drinking. He approached Wilbur, who stood behind the counter, futzing with the old radio by the cash register.

Wilbur twisted a screwdriver and stuck his tongue out as if it would help move the screw. He spoke without looking up, and a scowl replaced his typical smile. "This damn thing is still busted. How am I going to keep my customers happy if we can't even play music, Calvin?"

Cal smirked. "I could sing."

Wilbur chuckled. "I'd like to keep my customers, not send 'em runnin'."

"You could sing, Wilbur."

"I don't get paid enough for that, young man."

Cal laughed. "Hell, I don't get paid enough to listen to it. When are you going to get rid of this radio and buy one of those fancy jukeboxes? You'd do well to make this place a little more modern." Cal scanned the rusted metal and shoddy vinyl upholstery.

"Right after I make enough cabbage to buy a place on Broadshall Island and right before I marry Miss Marilyn Monroe. Then I'll put in for a nice new Seeburg. Until that happens, this hunk o' junk will have to do." Wilbur pushed back his little paper hat. "I don't understand. This thing was workin' this morning." He glanced up at Cal as if he'd just remembered he was there and clapped him on the back. "You go on home, Cal. This might take a while."

"You sure, Wilbur?"

"Actually." Wilbur cleared his throat. "Can I speak with you a minute?"

Cal slumped onto one of the vinyl stools. "Wilbur, I know what you're going to say, and I—"

Wilbur placed a hand on Cal's shoulder. He motioned to a photo amongst the old menus and ads smattered across the wall behind the counter. "When you look at that photo, what do you see?"

# The City of the Gods: Gold

Jerry, Cal, and their mother, Rose, sat on Wilbur's Diner's front steps some thirty years ago. Rose held Jerry close as young Cal, preoccupied with a toy soldier, stood alone to her left.

Cal eyed Wilbur. "Wilbur, is this one of your riddles? Jerry always loved those, not me."

"Just answer the question, young man. Where do your eyes go?"

Cal shook his head. "Well, I guess I see my mother. She looked happy. Those were easier times for us all, I guess, better times."

Wilbur sighed. "Those days did seem easier, didn't they? That's a nice photo. I remember snapping that shot." He smiled as his voice trailed off.

Cal eyed Wilbur. "But why?"

"How about that one?" Wilbur pointed to a newspaper clipping of James Connor shaking President Truman's hand. Jerry and Theodora stood behind him in olive-drab caps and matching cotton uniforms. As usual, they looked to be sharing an inside joke. Cal stood off to the side.

Cal shrugged. "I guess I see Jerry and Theo acting like fools. Wilbur, what are you getting at with these questions?"

Wilbur smiled. "Well, most folks would look at a photo like that and notice themselves first. They make sure they're represented well, look nice, or what have you. Then, they regard the rest of the people in the photo. It's human nature. But you ain't most folks, are ya, Cal? No, you were always different."

Cal tried to stand, but Wilbur pressed his firm hand on his shoulder, and he sunk back onto the stool. "I haven't made my point yet, young man. Now, I know it's none of my business, Calvin, but I overheard your conversation with... that woman. I knew who she was when she walked in, and I damn sure know you knew her. It's plain to see you don't owe her anything. Hell, I'm sure she's the last person you'd want to see on accounta what happened to Jerry, but"—he scanned the counter—"your mom and I, we came up servin' rich folks like her. I'm talkin' *rich* people who lived over the Fayette Bridge. Real ritzy areas in Northwell an' Brookfield, back when even Armory Square was a rough place. I know how they can get."

Cal pinched the bridge of his nose. "I know, Wilbur. Mom told me that. Heck, you told me that a thousand times yourself."

"I know, I know—as much as I hate t' say it—an' I know it doesn't seem like it t' you—but Jerry's been dead a long time, an' there's no bringin' him back. That Connor child could still be alive. Maybe it's time to let bygones be bygones."

Cal's cheeks flushed. "Wilbur, I can't—"

"I just never known you to back down from helping anyone, is all." Wilbur set his bony, old hand back on Cal's shoulder. "Reason you're here flippin' burgers and fryin' eggs is because I needed your help. You're above this gig, I know that, but you help out. You're a good guy, Calvin Smith." The old man looked Cal over with watery, prideful eyes.

Cal interjected, "Wilbur, I—"

Wilbur calmly raised a finger. "Let me finish." He paused to collect his thoughts. "My point is, I cut my teeth servin' rich folks like that woman. I know the type. She could have thrown around some money. Got herself on television or the radio—not my radio, mind you—but any workin' radios out there." He grinned. "At any rate, she came to you as a friend. She needs you, son. Her little girl needs you. I'm sure if your mom was here, she'd agree with me. An' Jerry"—he chuckled—"that hot head would be halfway to Cork by now."

Cal glanced up at the photo of his family and swallowed. "What can I do? I'm just a—"

# The City of the Gods: Gold

"You're just a what? A diner cook? A grill jockey? You're so much more than this, Calvin. I know I said I needed your help, but please don't waste your life here because of me. You could work anywhere in Empire with the skills you got in the kitchen.

"You and Jerry were practically raised between these four walls when your mom was working here, and I know this is where you feel close to them. Nostalgia is a hell of a thing, but they ain't comin' back. At some point, you need to worry about yourself. Not me, and certainly not those old ghosts haunting you."

"I'm happy here, Wilbur, maybe not with the work exactly but with you and—"

"D'you understand what old ghosts are?" Wilbur stared into Cal's eyes, and the smile dropped from his face. "They're—"

"Unresolved issues," Cal said, rolling his eyes. "I know, I know."

Wilbur smirked. "They'll drive a man mad. They live in our memories, sure, but they ain't nothin' but poison, and they'll consume you if you let 'em." His smile faded. "It kills me inside to see that rage and the pain eat away at you, Calvin. Now, I'm real proud of you for gettin' away from the bottle, real proud! An' I'm not saying you have to run off and help Theodora Connor, but now that you kicked that nasty habit, just get yourself back on track, son, and the rest will fall into place. You got a good heart and a good head on your shoulders. Get out there and use 'em." His smile returned, and his gaze made Cal feel like a child again.

"Wilbur, even if I wanted to—you're so under-staffed."

"Oh, stop making excuses, son!" A smile washed across Wilbur's face. "I'm insisting this time. Darlene'll be back tomorrow. The two of us made it work after the other waitress, ol' what's her name, up an' run off with her husband's brother after T-Day, and we'll make it work again. I'll hop on the grill. Hell, maybe folks will finally get some decent food for once."

Cal laughed. "Watch it, old man; you'll never cook like me!" He ran his hand over the laminate countertop and remembered a simpler time when Jerry would stand on this spot and flirt with the ladies. *Mr. Big Shot,* Wilbur called him.

"I don't know. Are you sure about this, Wilbur?"

Wilbur nodded and looked him over through glossy eyes. "I appreciate what you've done for me, really, I do, but we'll be fine, Calvin." He tightened his lips and exhaled. "Go live your life, young man. The diner will always be here." Wilbur extended an open, withered hand, but Cal embraced the father he never had.

"Okay, okay." Wilbur chuckled and patted Cal's back. "That's enough of that. I ain't goin' anywhere. Like I said, you need me. I'll be right here."

11

Cal pushed the front door open. The bell dinged, and a warm breeze wicked the sweat from his skin as he stomped down the rickety, metal stairs into the parking lot. As the swollen red sun dropped behind the buildings in the west, a frigid wind ate the heat and bulldozed the pleasant evening, rolling over him like death. The sense of leering eyes burned into his flesh, but when he glanced across Mosley and Ames, he was alone.

He shuddered, and each passing moment induced unwanted clarity. The haunting memories of the night he became numb seeped into his subconscious, and the cutting chill spread until his breath rose like a ghost into the bitter cold. Wilbur's Diner faded, and nagging memories warped reality around him as Theodora's words resounded. *I don't know if I'm awake or dreaming anymore.*

The parking lot was replaced by a large, dimly lit room, spreading into obscurity. Cal pressed his hand against a cold marble pillar as chanting echoed down the corridor, the origin impossible to determine. A crowd of faceless men and women in their most attractive formalwear huddled around something in the center. Cal pushed through the masses with a grievous curiosity he couldn't explain. The people disregarded him in favor of a young girl with a white doll face.

A muffled voice called out inaudible commands, and she stepped into the light, staring at Cal through the soulless black eyes of her mask until the sound of a gong ripped through the silence, and she walked toward him.

The chic onlookers watched with emotionless, masked faces, chanting louder, encompassing the room in condemnation.

*Gong!* The girl gripped her mask and slowly pulled it down. *Gong!* Cal fought to look away from her exposed face, but the onlookers drove him to his knees, and cold hands held his head in place. She was horrible, the face of madness.

*Gong!* The girl leaned forward. He could feel her cold breath in his ear. "Find the brothers, Ross."

Behind the girl, the mammoth head of a wolf emerged from the shadows twelve feet in the air. It bared its teeth, and molten fire dripped from its maw, illuminating giant feathered wings. They fluttered and settled back into the shadows.

The stench of blood hung thickly, curdling the air. Incessant chanting thundered through the room. A single phrase uttered over and over, so flat and void of passion that Cal's vision blurred when he tried to understand it, and something tightened like a vice around his skull.

"You are Marchosias," the girl whispered. "Marchosias is you. Until I deem, you are not."

*Gong!* The chanting ceased. The child and the wolf creature were gone. Cal peered up at the vague outline of a woman. Antlers jutted from her head and the shimmer of a blade reflected in the dim light.

The chanting resumed, but the words were sharp and precise. *God is dead!*

Cal broke from the crowds' grasp and staggered to his feet. The world shifted, and he almost doubled over as bile choked him. The hot parking lot brushed his palm as he stumbled, and darkness dissipated.

Cal stood alone in front of Wilbur's Diner again. The cold, achy illness dripped off him like water, and the fall scent rode a warm summer breeze. *I must be exhausted.*

**12**

Cal stumbled into his apartment, flipped on the lights, and tossed his keys into a bowl by the door. He regarded the fat gray cat watching him from the windowsill. "Just where I left you this morning, eh, Stanley?" He sauntered across the apartment and scratched the cat under his chin. "How was your day, pal?" Stanley purred and rubbed his head on the back of Cal's hand.

Cal popped open the freezer and shuffled frozen vegetables around until he came across a Swanson TV Dinner. He scanned the instructions on the back, preheated the oven, and pulled the aluminum tray from the package.

"You know, you got it pretty good here, Stanley." Cal opened a can of cat food and set it on the floor. A yawn caught him off guard. "You just lay around all day without a care in the world." He shuffled across the uneven wooden floor, kicked his shoes off, and sat on the windowsill, scanning the skyline until he found the Ironleaf building. "I don't suppose anyone you didn't want to see came by to ask you for help today?" He sneered and stared vacantly down at Brookhaven Road. "I have to say, Stanley, James Connor is a son-of-a-bitch. No one deserves to suffer through something like a missing child alone. Not even Th—her." He dismissed the thought and placed the dinner into the oven.

With a smile, he slumped into his velvet recliner as the comforting smell of supper drifted across the studio apartment. He opened *Moby Dick* to the dog-eared page, but the words blurred together as one black mass, dripping from the book like wet ink.

# The City of the Gods: Gold

Cal pulled the page away from his face and squinted. "What the hell?" Snowflakes drifted through the open window, and his breath trailed from his mouth, sticking in the frigid air. Goosebumps rolled over Cal's flesh, and the book slid from his shivering hands, dropping to the floor. He pulled a wool blanket from the back of the chair, wrapping it around his shoulders to stave off the biting cold before the numbness took him again.

The lamp flickered and died, then the overhead. Streetlights outside popped and blew in a series of sparks. Darkness engulfed the apartment, and only the sound of his breathing remained.

"Hello?" Cal asked into the inky black nothingness. A bleating sound drifted faintly through the apartment.

"Who's there?"

The lamp flickered on, and Theodora towered over him. Her naked, freckled skin was flecked with blood. She stood perfectly still, except for her chest, which heaved as she admitted short, unnatural breaths.

Cal stared up at her, frozen to the chair. Her eyes met his, and her head twisted slowly to the side, forcing a sharp snapping sound in her neck. Her mouth dropped, and a deep, inhuman voice emerged. "Non sumus Deus!" The end of the word climbed in pitch and volume until it became a deafening scream.

Theodora's eyes dripped from their sockets, and flesh melted away to muscle, then bone, then ash, but the shrill scream remained.

Cal's throat squeezed shut until an unruly cough splattered blood across the floor. He gripped the arms of his beloved recliner, desperately sucking at the air, unable to swallow. He exhaled in sparser, hacking coughs.

*Bang! Bang! Bang!* Cal's eyes shot open, and he sucked in frantically, inhaling smoke. His hands were closed around the crushed arms of the recliner.

*Bang! Bang! Bang!*

"Calvin?" a muffled voice called from behind the door.

Smoke poured from the oven. "Shit!" Cal pushed himself to his feet, shut the oven off, and peered inside. The aluminum tray was intact, but the contents had smoldered down to black ash.

"Calvin, what's going on in there?"

"I'm fine, Miss Johnson, just burned my dinner. Sorry for the trouble," Cal responded, throat sore.

"Oh, okay, Calvin. Be careful now," Miss Johnson replied and audibly mumbled something about an old drunk burning the whole damn building down.

Cal waited for her footsteps to vanish, took the hot aluminum tray out of the oven with a towel, and glanced at the clock. Stanley meowed.

A nervous, thankful laugh escaped and grew until Cal thought his sides would split. He ran a palm over Stanley's back. "It was a dream, pal, that's it."

Across the street, the light in one of the windows of a long-condemned apartment building flickered on. An animal bleated, and Cal's smile faded. The silhouette of a woman stood profile under a dim overhead lamp. Her head turned to meet Cal's gaze, revealing a rack of antlers jutting from the sides of her head. She strode to the blown-out window, watching Cal through the dead, black holes of a china doll mask, and hovered her throat over an exposed shard of glass.

*Death will be my wedding, children, and glory.*

"Don't!" Cal screamed. A soft, scraping noise drew his attention to the tray in his hand, teaming with maggots squirming over moldy food. He dropped the tray to the floor and stepped away. His eyes darted to the window again, but the woman was gone, and the building was dark. His gaze returned to the smoldering, burnt mess spilled across the wooden planks.

*Find the brothers, Ross.*

The horrifying world his dreams inhabited was bleeding into his reality. His arms were growing numb again, just as they had all those years ago, in the coldest December he could recall. He needed answers.

Stanley meowed softly and rubbed against Cal's leg. "Keep the place safe, Stanley," he said and picked up his keys from the bowl by the door.

The Empire Bulletin
Empire City, Saturday, March 14, 1948
T-DAY IN EMPIRE CITY

Doctor Henry Thompson assaulted every significant neighborhood in Empire City's Northside yesterday, leaving behind what eyewitnesses described as "a hellscape of fire and ash."

The attack began at 8:03 AM when (robots) crawled from the Basalt River onto the northeast shore of the city, attacking Eastport and Hemsford. Simultaneously, similar (robots) dropped from a German military transport aircraft (Messerschmitt Me 323 Gigant) on the west coast of Terrytown. Fifteen minutes after they touched down, the machines had spread to Westport and New Brecon. Finally, at 10:40 AM, the Fayette Bridge collapsed into the Basalt River, stranding most of the city.

"Since Japan bombed Pearl Harbor, we have not seen an attack on American soil of this magnitude," Mayor Hall said in an initial statement. "Words fail to describe the devastation that our city has endured."

There were initial indications that Allied Science's Unmanned Vehicle Department had developed these creations. However, Attorney General Herbert Brownell Jr. quickly debunked these allegations when the Empire City Police Department received a call from Thompson's employee, Jacob Landry. (Landry) claimed, "This has gone too far. I didn't think he would go this far." Landry then agreed to assist the League of Enforcers in ending the attack.

The mastermind, Henry Thompson, a.k.a. Doctor Torment, was a former scientist, a respected member of the Manhattan Project, and a one-time colleague of J. Robert Oppenheimer and the Scarlet Sparrow. Although peers held him in high esteem, colleagues often described Thompson as "a ticking time bomb with a Ph.D."

Within hours of these attacks, the League of Enforcers, headed by Captain Wonderful, recently revealed to be James Connor of Empire City, were able to infiltrate Doctor Torment's base of operations on Broadshall Island's Hooks End. The League reportedly made, in their own words, "easy work" of the robotic forces, thanks to the "quick thinking of Captain Wonderful and the even quicker actions of Miss Mercury." They brought "swift and final justice," taking the scientist's life.

Authorities believe Thompson collaborated with exiled Nazis and Communists based on the identity of bodies recovered from his lab on the southeasternmost point of Hooks End.

Hours after Thompson's demise, responders, including police, firemen, emergency medical personnel, and volunteers, are still working around the clock to pull survivors from the wreckage of the decimated city. Much of Hemsford remains unstable, restricting responders from entering and leaving people stranded under broken skyscrapers as extraction efforts continue.

"Although we've lost many and would love nothing more than to lay them to rest properly," Mayor Hall said, "right now, what is important is finding the survivors. We will get to Hemsford and those trapped there as soon as we can, but I won't send more citizens to their deaths."

When James Connor revealed the Scarlet Sparrow to be Theodora Connor, daughter of Nellie Byrne of The Uptown Clowns fame, Hall insisted on conducting an investigation that would "link her to Torment's attacks." Allegations based on her absence during the Enforcer's campaign against Doctor Torment.

# The City of the Gods: Gold

"(Mrs. Connor) was not part of any rescue effort, and even now, when the city is in its hour of need, she is nowhere to be seen. (Thompson) and Theodora Connor worked together on the Manhattan Project. They were close then, and who's to say they aren't still close now?" Hall speculated.

Captain Wonderful came to his wife's defense, stating, "She'd be here if she could. Getting her to sit this one out was more difficult than anything Thompson had in his arsenal. She's pregnant with our child, and after all this madness, the children are what's important."

At a later press conference, a noticeably pregnant, teary-eyed Theodora Connor said, "Henry Thompson has challenged the safety and liberties that citizens of the United States claim as a birthright. The city mourns its fallen citizens, but we must look to the future. We must rebuild the city and our lives with it, or else the Henry Thompsons of the world will always win."

Mayor Hall is still looking for viable options for those who lost their homes. "So far, Zephyr's stadium in Droghead and Bullet's stadium in Northwell appear to be the most spacious, comfortable locations," Hall said. "We have also been looking for help from the Rescue Mission, Salvation Army, and schools or colleges who would open their doors as shelters."

President Truman estimated the body count is in the tens of thousands. He asks, "All of America prays for the citizens of Empire and that God be with Empire City in its hour of need.

THE CALL
TO DUTY
JOIN
THE
ARMY

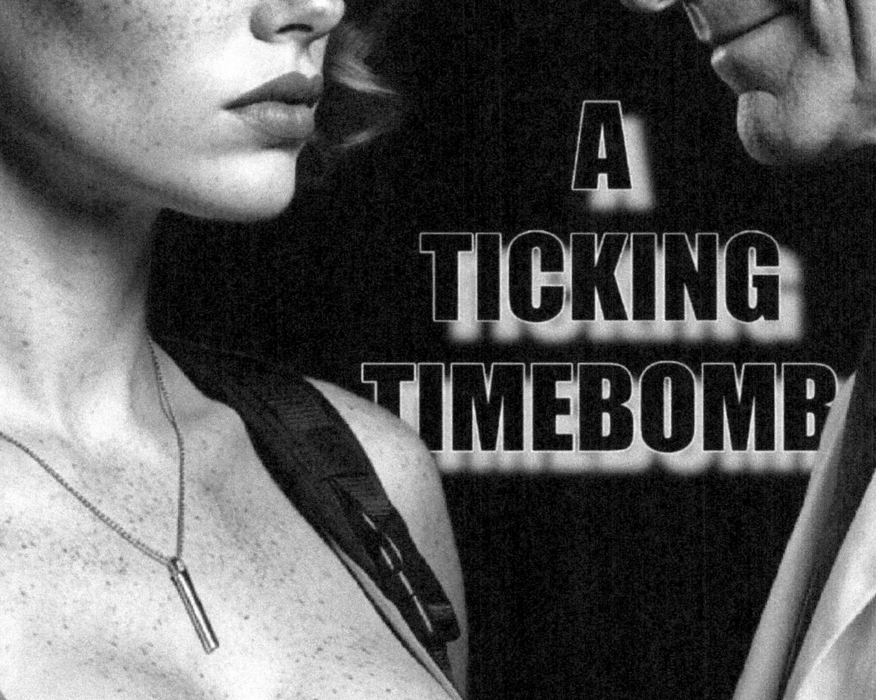

A
TICKING
TIMEBOMB

**<u>13</u>**

Nadir gripped the cool porcelain sink and screwed his face back and forth in the mirror. With each passing day, mortality became more evident as his glory days faded into obscurity. The Tizard Mission, The Manhattan Project, and even the early years at Allied Science were fleeting apparitions of a distant life. He ran a hand over his mustache and chin, catching his palm on the salt and pepper stubble, and sighed.

Steam rose from behind the shower curtain, beckoning with promises of soothing heat for his achy back, but Nadir couldn't leave his reflection's empty gaze.

*Legacy.* The word haunted him. Any interesting work at Allied Science had been covered stem to stern in red tape since Henry Thompson destroyed half the city. "A ticking time bomb with a Ph.D." That was what the *Bulletin* had called him after T-Day.

Nadir remembered the day Thompson was pulled out of V-Site in Los Alamos, kicking and screaming. Away from the atomic technology he'd helped develop, away from the devices, "Fatman" and "Little Boy," his and Oppenheimer's babies. Nadir could still see Henry Thompson's wispy white combover reaching like fingers as he flailed against the military police, his gaunt, reddened face, his wide eyes piercing the Connors, General Groves, Oppenheimer, and the team of scientists. He cursed everyone, threatened them, and told them what a mistake they were making. His voice echoed around the empty bunker but fell on deaf ears. He vowed revenge, scorched earth, the end of everything.

"To be the harbinger of death is my legacy." His bulging, bloodshot eyes locked on Nadir. "The world will burn!" he said. Three years later, half of Empire fell to his automatons and drones.

**<u>14</u>**

"Is the coffee still hot?" Nadir tightened his uneven tie and kissed his wife on the cheek.

Anila let out a surprised yelp. "Probably not." She tried to hide a smile behind her stern voice. "You take so long to get ready. What are you doing in that bathroom each morning?"

Nadir winked. "Unspeakable acts, my dear."

"Well, your breakfast is cold now, and you're going to be late again."

"Nonsense, Anila." Nadir pulled his tie loose. "These Yankees couldn't start the workday without me. They'd have no idea what they're doing. Besides, what's more important than enjoying cold dosas and coffee with my family?" He tousled Ukrit's hair, planted a soft kiss on Pratima's head, and took his seat.

Pratima giggled. "Good morning, Papa." She flashed him her big doe eyes. There was a lot of Anila in her delicate features. The same small nose, round lips, and dark almond eyes—a perfect carbon copy, only smaller.

"Good morning, Duckling." Nadir smiled.

"Father, I'm nearly twelve! You can't call me 'Duckling' anymore!" Pratima responded with the same vigor her mother possessed.

Nadir bowed his head solemnly. "Please forgive me, Lady Pratima. I didn't realize 'Duckling' had an age limit."

Pratima giggled.

Ukrit stared straight ahead with his arms folded, undoubtedly amid a good pout. Although he was only seven, he was clearly his father's son: the same pronounced Roman nose, dark eyes, and a thick mop of black hair sitting in a messy nest on top of his head.

"Good morning, Ukrit," Nadir said carefully.

Anila regarded their son and allowed him a chance to answer before she spoke up. "Ukrit, say good morning to your father."

Nadir forced a weak smile.

"Good morning, Father," Ukrit grumbled without making eye contact.

"Ukrit, is something troubling you?" Nadir walked the minefield that was his son's personality.

Anila broke the silence. "I'm afraid Ukrit had a little kerfuffle with a boy on the playground."

Nadir frowned. "Oh? I hope you didn't resort to—"

"Ukrit knocked his block off!" Pratima exclaimed.

Anila stifled a laugh and tried to hide any amusement behind her disciplinary tone. "Pratima, ladies should not speak like that!"

Nadir took note of Anila's conduct and decided the scuffle wasn't anything with which to concern himself. "Well, boys will be boys, I suppose." He shook out the newspaper and casually glanced around the page. "Ukrit, it's important you don't sink to this boy's level. Use your mind and outthink your adversary. Try not to resort to violence."

Ukrit broke from his trance and glared at his father. "Captain Wonderful would have resorted to violence. He would have shot him dead!"

Nadir flipped the corner of the paper down and shot Ukrit a stern look. "This nonsense again, Ukrit? I thought we agreed you were finished listening to that ghastly radio show."

"You told me to stop. I never agreed!" Ukrit yelled.

# The City of the Gods: Gold

"Well, Captain Wonderful isn't as wonderful as his name suggests. He may be a hero, but he's a very troubled man indeed." Nadir flipped the paper back up to hide his face behind the black-and-white print. "I met him, you know?"

Thompson's howling face flashed through his head at the mere thought of the Connors. *The world will burn.*

Ukrit's eyes turned to saucers. "You did? What was he like?"

"Hm?" Nadir flipped the paper down again. "Well, not one to be admired by a nice British boy such as yourself." Nadir flipped the corner of the paper back up and turned the page over. "Speaking of Captain Wonderful, it seems the Connor girl is missing."

"Missing? Whaddaya mean, where is she?" Ukrit looked back and forth between his parents.

"I bet Doctor Torment took her. He came back from the dead and grabbed her!" Pratima exclaimed.

Anila scowled. "Pratima—"

"If he did, Captain Wonderful would shoot him dead again. Bang!" Ukrit made his hand into a gun and shot at his sister across the table.

"Ukrit!" Anila put her hand across Ukrit's makeshift gun and brought it softly to the table with a grimace. "Perhaps the breakfast table isn't the best place to discuss such things, my love."

Nadir folded the paper, half-listening, and his attention shifted to an advert for men's shoes. "You're right, my dear. I'm sorry." He turned the paper over. "Ah, it seems the Annual Empire City Science Fair is this weekend. Ukrit, how would you like to go with me? The weather is supposed to be positively wonderful for October."

"I want to go!" Pratima said.

Nadir flashed his daughter a smile. "Okay, Duckli—sorry, Madame Pratima—we can all go. What do you say, Ukrit, old boy?"

Ukrit crossed his arms and stared vacantly at the maple hutch, "I don't want to go to the bloody Science Fair!"

Anila glared at him. "Ukrit!"

Nadir sighed. "No, Anila, it's fine. I'm not going to force the boy, Pratima, and I will go." He smiled and placed his hand on Pratima's. She smiled back.

Nadir folded the paper and shot up from his chair, leaving his food and coffee untouched, as usual. "Anyway, I must be off! Science waits for no man! Except for me when I'm running late." He leaned in and kissed Anila's head.

Pratima giggled." Goodbye, Papa."

"My love, when you return home, can you fix the radio?" Anila asked. "It's been making a dreadful hissing sound lately."

Nadir plopped his homburg hat on his head. "I'll take a look when I get home, dear." *Hopefully, that will keep Ukrit from listening to that appalling League of Enforcers show.* "Goodbye all, have a good day at school." He lifted his leather briefcase from where Anila had stashed it by the door and watched his family go about their lives without him.

"Pratima, you make sure to look after your brother if you go back to that playground today after school. I simply can't have him getting into any more scuffles!" Anila said sternly through the clattering of dishes.

"Yes, mother."

Nadir gripped the doorknob, trying in vain to slow time to a halt. His children were growing up while he toiled the hours away, buried alive in an underground lab. He stared at the knob thoughtfully. If he didn't twist it, he could hang his hat back on the metal hook by the door and play hooky. However, time was a currency of which he had none, and responsibility tugged at his sleeve. Powerless, he smiled sadly and pushed the door open.

**<u>15</u>**

The Allied Science building was separated from Sunrise Drive by thirty feet of cobblestone courtyard lined with saplings. Sleek marble layered upon itself, forming a nearly two-story grand archway bent over an ornamentally framed glass face hidden behind ribbed pillars. A carved statue of Athena stood above the arch, watching over the city through blank marble eyes.

Atop the five-story building sat Theodora Connor's crowning achievement: The Powersphere. Curved metal bars whirled around the blinding core in a fury of reflective beauty as it powered the city.

Nadir trotted up the steps with newfound vitality. Even outside, he could almost feel the ideas being born. Knowledge ran through the sleek, blue-veined marble, and each time he entered, he remembered why he could never quit. He pushed open the gold-trimmed door, and his wingtips echoed through the lobby.

Guards clad in standard blue-gray Allied Science jumpers, with matching hats and combat boots, armed with military-issued service rifles, stood at various checkpoints. As usual, where there were brilliant ideas and groundbreaking inventions, the government stood in front of all of it with guns and uninformed men to operate them.

Each wall to the left and right had an Art Deco carving of the Greek gods Zeus and Hera, respectively. Scrawled on the left was the word "Onward," and the right side said "Upward." The official motto of Empire City: "Onward and Upward."

As hackneyed as the display was, Nadir couldn't deny that the energy inside this building was truly inspirational. The more he tried to belittle the art as a cheap attempt at morale-boosting, the more it felt like hope.

He eyed two gruff chaps behind the usually empty reception desk, dressed in black suits with black ties and a black aura about them. Whenever men who looked like that appeared, it usually meant something significant was occurring. The identical, middle-aged men with white hair, stone jaws, and an attitude that screamed, *'I used to be someone important,'* watched him from under matching furrowed brows. They whispered amongst themselves as Nadir passed, sending a twinge of fear down his spine.

Nadir offered a friendly smile. *Why did I refuse to return Frank's phone call last night? Your stubbornness will be the death of you, old boy,* he thought.

He presented himself at the northern bank of elevators with confidence he'd earned through years of paying dues and nodded to scientists from other teams, most of whom he'd never met. Sometimes, Nadir caught himself daydreaming of having these men and their families over to his house for supper. They'd sip wine and pick each other's brains. Perhaps they'd even find some common ground. Alas, it was just a fantasy. The ever-present governmental eye was always watching, and Nadir feared the consequences just enough to not step out of line in a post-T-Day world.

Nadir presented his ID to the guard next to his elevator bank. "Good morning, Nicholas. Subbasement-three, please, as per usual."

"Morning, Doctor Singh." Nicholas smiled and turned the key to call the elevator in the same dull manner he did each day. He was a young man with a thin frame, barely in his twenties, judging by his acne and how the excitement of life still exploded out from behind his eyes. On the uniform, "Berkoski" was printed in big block letters on the left side of his chest. He clutched his M1 Garand service rifle awkwardly, making it appear more cumbersome than it probably was. Nadir smiled, wondering if Nicholas was bright enough to know which end the bullets came out of.

"You didn't catch the game last night, did ya, Doctor Singh? My radio's still on the fritz, and during the playoffs, too. Do you believe it?"

"I'm afraid not; terribly sorry, Nicholas." The doors slid open, and Nadir maneuvered around the boy into the service elevator, unsure what sport he was even referring to.

"Well, the series isn't over yet. Don't count out the ol' Empire City Zephyrs, I always say. They'll surprise you every year!" Nicholas watched Nadir with big, bright eyes like he'd just woken up as a child on Christmas morning.

"Quite." Nadir flashed a hollow smile, and the doors closed.

**<u>16</u>**

The elevator slammed to a stop at subbasement-three, and lights flickered as a reminder Nadir was almost a mile beneath the earth. The doors slid open. He adjusted his tie and stepped into the large staging area.

Empty, dust-covered desks stood like tombstones in a room once full of busy scientists. There had been massive layoffs in '48 and '49, a witch hunt to eliminate those the government felt were at risk of becoming the next Henry Thompson. Now, only four remained.

Nadir approached the large glass cube in the center of the room, referred to unimaginatively as the "Idea Square," probably coined by some corporate fuddy-duddy to build morale. He tossed his hat on an empty desk and inched forward in disbelief.

Suspended from thick metal cables in the Idea Square were two nearly identical ovular objects with scaffolding erected around them. Nadir shot through the ghostly bullpen and punched a code into a keypad. The glass door slid open with a loud, sucking sound. He grabbed a utility jacket from the rack without taking his eyes off the crafts and bypassed the hardhat, silently joining the others. "Good morning, gentlemen. What do we have here?"

Doctor Brown met Nadir's gaze through his outdated, black-framed glasses, making his glossy, tired eyes look cartoonishly oversized. "Good morning, Doctor Singh."

On the other side of the Square, Doctor Wendell scanned one of the ships, oblivious to Nadir's arrival. He moved around the vessel with careful and calculated steps, muttering to himself. Wendell was a young man with long, curly blonde hair and the posture of a vulture. It seemed he could barely tie his shoes, yet he was one of the most brilliant minds Nadir had ever come across from an academic standpoint.

"Who permitted scaffolding in my lab?" Nadir asked.

"Your lab?" Frank chuckled. "Allied Science belongs to Uncle Sam, as do you." Frank's piercing blue eyes followed Wendell, untrusting and attentive. "Nice of you to finally join us, Singh." He turned his upper body to regard Nadir. Frank's neck didn't move quite right because of a grenade injury sustained during the First World War, a story Nadir had heard too often. He was dressed casually today, in a white, short-sleeved bush shirt—Nadir was positive had been popular when Frank had been a young man—tucked into high-waisted trousers. The only thing that set him apart from an ordinary man with a lousy fashion sense was the Colt double-action .38 revolver hanging off his hip.

"Frank." Nadir crossed his arms and watched Brown and Wendell move curiously around the vessels. "I suppose this is what you phoned me about last night?" Neither man took their eyes off the metallic objects.

Frank nodded. "We've been here since, waiting for you. Your wife assured me she'd give you the message, and I was inclined to believe her. Real sweetheart, that one, not sure why she's wasting her time with you."

"She did, but you cried wolf so many times I never thought I'd walk into this." Nadir joined his team. "So, what have we discovered thus far, gentlemen? I want a full report."

"They seem to be metallic vessels, Doctor Singh," Brown answered, "a little larger than a car—"

"I can see that, old boy," Nadir answered flatly. "What else have you found?"

# The City of the Gods: Gold

Brown adjusted his glasses. "We ran a Geiger counter over each of them. There doesn't seem to be any alpha, beta, or gamma radiation."

Nadir nodded, approaching the objects. Each vessel looked like someone had stuck two aluminum bowls together and welded them with uncanny skill and accuracy.

The more pristine-looking ship had a small, unassuming ramp leading into a dark, rectangular hole in the undercarriage. The other was stained and rusted on the bottom, with no hint of a porthole. There wasn't even a crease to match the other ship's door.

"May I touch them?" Nadir asked.

Brown looked to Wendell, who nodded.

"The gas chromatography revealed anything expelled by the vessels is inert," Wendell said.

Nadir ran his hand along the beat-up metallic surface of the closed object. The pale green rust bit at his fingertips and chipped off as heat bled through the impregnable-looking body. The scientists utilized floodlights to illuminate the surface from the ground. However, he could feel heat mounting inside the vessel, even on the edges. "What else?"

"Well, Doctor Singh," Brown said. "It appears the bottom of the closed one is copper, but the top is—"

"Something close to the same composition as gadolinium, but it's like nothing we've ever encountered," Wendell bellowed without taking his eyes off the objects.

"Yes, I see." Nadir eyed the smooth top. "Brown, you're our metal man. What tests have we run?"

"That's where it gets tricky, Doctor Singh. We couldn't run spark tests, Rockwell tests, or Brinell hardness tests because, well, Allied Science doesn't want us accidentally damaging anything inside. However, we found traces of Al2O3"—he eyed Frank—"or aluminum oxide to the layman—inside the open vessel after running an air test. And, as Doctor Wendell mentioned, we utilized optical emission spectroscopy to determine that the outside is possibly an alloy. The top of the unopened one is consistent with the same material."

"So why bother to fuse two different metals? Why not use copper exclusively?" Nadir scanned the edge for a seam.

Brown rubbed the back of his neck. "We think it could be Russian in origin—"

"Soviets often mix materials without much thought. It's a cost-saving strategy," Wendell interjected. "If they have it lying around, they use it. Perhaps they created a new alloy, and it was expensive to reproduce."

Nadir piqued an eyebrow. "But why would they use such a rare metal?"

Frank trudged forward. "Whether it's Russians, Nazis, Japs, Martians, or Jesus himself returned from on high, our job here is to eliminate dangerous possibilities and keep the suits on the board of Allied Science from pissing their pants. We don't care what it's made of. We wanna know what was inside and if it's dangerous."

Nadir peered curiously into the small crevice where the ramp had opened. "You certainly do have a poetic vocabulary, Frank. Perhaps you should have been a writer."

"And miss being here with you, Sunshine?"

Nadir picked up a flashlight and scanned the inside of the open vessel. Metallic mesh covered each side like a tiny chain-link fence. "Am I to assume there were no passengers found?"

"That's classified." Frank crossed his arms.

Nadir peered back into the hole. "Right, well, whatever came in this vessel must have been very small."

"Groundbreaking theory, Singh," Frank said.

Nadir squinted into the hole. "There's nothing resembling flight gear or anything that would generate thrust that I can see. This suggests these were launched from an outside source, presumably close by, or perhaps airdropped?"

"Classified."

Nadir hated the snide grin draped across Frank's face. He circled the other object, scanning the green surface. "Could this one just be rusted shut? Could it be that simple? Was it submerged in water?"

"Classified," Frank grunted.

Nadir sighed and climbed a ladder propped against the scaffolding. "I can't believe I've never asked you this before, but what top brass did you piss off to get this job anyway, Frank? Babysitting us lowly scientists is surely beneath a man such as yourself."

Frank watched Nadir with an amused look unbecoming of such a naturally stern face. "I ask myself that every day, Singh. My boss tells me the only reason I'm here is to make sure you eggheads don't make like Doctor Torment and blow up the city. I should be fishing on the government's dime or whatever it is normal retirees do. I wouldn't know, you see, because I'm stuck underground with you fellas."

Nadir tapped his chin. "Hm. Perhaps it's some sort of new development in space travel? Have Project Mercury or NACA advanced to the point where they have a vessel that could launch across continents?"

Frank eyed Nadir. "Nah, Project Mercury is still drawings on a chalkboard down in sub—" He paused abruptly and tightened his lips. If Frank had leaked a bit of classified information, he hid it well behind a masterful poker face.

"Ha!" Nadir said. "I got you, Frank."

Frank placed his hands on his hips. "As I said, our objective is to get this second… thing open to see if something potentially harmful escaped the other one and is runnin' around Empire."

Nadir peered around the top of the pristine, opened ship. "Doctor Brown, tell me, where and when was this open vessel discovered?"

Andrew Brown looked shocked at being called out. He frivolously peeled back page after page on his clipboard and jabbed at it with his index finger. "Brookfield, near South Avenue. Last night." He flipped a few more pages and looked at Nadir with a nervous twitch in his eye. "All the other information is cla—"

"Classified, right," Nadir groaned. "That usually means it's League-related, or no one knows the answer." He slid his hand across the vessel's surface, where the top piece should have met the bottom. There were no rivets or bolts. He descended the ladder. "And the unopened one? Where, pray tell, was that discovered?" He moved under the vessel and looked up under the green, rust-covered belly.

"That's been here since May eighth, '47," Wendell said. "No official record of it coming into Allied Science, what it is, or even who it originally belonged to." He flipped back a few pages in his notes. "It looks like other objects came in that night, The Ivory icicle's Type 97 bolt action sniper rifle, a canister of The Anti-Angel's sarin toxin, the list goes on. Paperwork was probably lost in the shuffle."

"Lost in the shuffle indeed!" Nadir scoffed. "It seems the League was trying to hide this ship's existence."

"Careful," Frank said.

"Really, Frank, can't you find something else to do?" Nadir put his hands on his hips and stared up at the chassis. "That still doesn't explain what this is exactly. It's obvious why you brought it out of storage for comparison. They're nearly the same vessel, but—"

"Precisely!" Doctor Brown jerked forward with excitement so out of character it was almost jarring. "I came to the same conclusion. So, last night, in sub-five, I looked through all communications received on May seventeenth and eighteenth, 1947. I found a handwritten note from one Marylyn Silver, a secretary here, before David or I started. The odd thing is, all the note said was: 'Do not, under any circumstances, allow Captain Wonderful near the sphere.'"

"You shouldn't be privy to that information, Brown," Frank grumbled.

Nadir smirked. "Curiouser and curiouser."

Doctor Brown shuffled through his notes. "But why would the Scarlet Sparrow hide it from—well—her husband?"

Frank eyed the elevator door. "Is this a necessary conversation? We just want to know what's inside."

Nadir clapped Doctor Brown on the shoulder. "Good question, old boy! Good question, indeed." He maneuvered between the scientists and Frank so he didn't have to watch his scowl. "I have a hypothesis. Have you ever seen the war footage? You know, when they used to run the newsreel at the cinema before the picture started?"

Wendell nodded. Brown shot Frank a nervous look.

"Well, it was never said outright, but James Connor was an absolute brute in Japan," Nadir said. "More often than not, if you look at poor Theodora's expression in the footage, you can tell she was positively terrified of him. Not to mention, if the rumors of him hitting his wife are true—"

"Now, you just hold on!" Frank walked around Nadir.

"Not to say she wasn't a lunatic herself. Still, if she felt the need to keep whatever was inside this vessel from the ever-violent Captain Wonderful, it must be quite dangerous."

"Singh!" Frank eyed the elevator door.

"This is probably not the first or last thing she kept from her husband. That, I can guarantee, but—"

"Singh, let's step outside!" Frank clamped Nadir's shoulder.

Nadir brushed his hand off and eyed Wendell. "Who informed Allied Science of the open ship last night?"

"I wasn't on-site when it arrived," Wendell replied.

Brown looked back and forth between Frank and Nadir and wiped his brow.

"Brown?" Nadir pushed past Frank and gripped Brown's frail shoulders. "Who told us about the open ship, man?"

Andrew Brown swallowed hard. "It was well—Allied Science communications received a Morse code SoS, a location on a map, latitude, and longitude. But when they arrived, there was nothing but the empty ship. Whoever contacted us used the Scarlet Sparrow's Morse Code call sign."

Nadir released the trembling boy. "Wasn't it last night that the Connor girl went missing?" He smirked. "Well, I suppose one can't expect a woman as deplorable as Theodora Connor to win Mother of the Year. She was probably off gallivanting while her daughter was abducted. Still, she couldn't tell the press she was home with the girl and be seen dropping this off at Allied Science at the same time. Calling it in must have been a desperate move at the eleventh hour to keep it hidden. This isn't Russian, Wendell. No, it was built right here in Empire under our noses, but not dangerous enough to be transported out of the city limits."

"Watch yourself, Singh," Frank grumbled, "you're on thin ice! And you!"—he pointed to Brown—"classified means classified. You shouldn't be privy to that information, and the loudmouth who told you has already been dealt with!"

"I'll bet," Nadir scoffed.

"I'm warning you, don't say another word about it, Singh." Frank's ice-blue eyes met Nadir's. "Captain Connor and Missus Connor are national treasures. You wouldn't even be standing here flappin' your gums if it weren't for them!"

Nadir forced a snide smirk. "Noted, and Allied Science and I are just cogs in the wheel, eh Frank? All those men you fired had nothing to do with the good fight? We must bow to the all-mighty League of Enforcers." His face grew warmer with each word.

Frank sighed. "That's not what I—"

"And I suppose violently gunning down Henry Thompson, the most brilliant nuclear physicist of our time, would make one a '*national treasure*.' From here on out, I'll keep my social beliefs to myself and ask that you do the same, Frank!"

Frank's face purpled. "Brilliant? Thompson was a maniac! You can't possibly compare that lunatic to the League of Enforcers! He destroyed half the city, Singh! The Enforcers rebuilt it. End of story!"

"Lunatic? Like someone who acts as judge, jury, and executioner? Folks like Captain Wonderful, Miss Mercury, and the Scarlet Sparrow?" Nadir's words were not the most relevant and soured with piss and vinegar, but they were a long time coming. "You realize it was Doctor Thompson, or *Doctor Torment* as people like you have taken to calling him, who advanced nuclear fission to the point where it could be developed into the Powersphere, the *nuclear* reactor that powers this city? Not Theodora Connor, like Allied Science insists upon."

Frank shut his eyes and inhaled. "It was Theodora Connor who developed that tech—"

"No."

Frank clenched his fist. "Torment just—"

"No, Frank—"

"*Torment just* stole her tech to power his killer robots! You seem to be getting pretty goddamn excitable over Doctor Torment, Singh! Suppose you're a crazy scientist just like he was. Believe me, I won't hesitate to do what's necessary—"

"Agree to disagree, Frank, my dear boy." He turned back to Brown and Wendell. "Anyhow, what if these ships are connected? By more than just their look and mysterious composition, I mean."

Brown tapped a pencil against his lip as he eyed the ships thoughtfully. Wendell stared blankly at Nadir. No doubt, he had already reached this conclusion.

"What are you getting at Singh?" Frank grumbled.

Nadir spun on his heels and strode to the unopened vessel. "If the goal is to open them, we must look past the science to the obvious." He touched the cold chassis of the opened vessel. "This looks like a newer model of the same ship or at least a different brand. Like a Ford Model T compared to a Ford Country Squire. The same manufacturer from different automotive eras.

"I propose these were constructed at different times for the same purpose and, therefore, are from the same point of origin. You could bet your sweet bippy on it.

"There also looks to be no control panel in the open one, which suggests they're controlled remotely, not with the purpose of flying, but the purpose of landing. Like a bomb or something of the sort." Nadir ran his finger over the rusty exterior and rolled particles between his fingers. "However, luckily or unluckily, neither one emits radiation. Finally, we can link them both to Theodora Connor, and whatever is inside is dangerous enough for her to keep hidden but not dangerous enough to dispose of."

"But Doctor Singh," Brown said, "what's it matter if they're from the same place? I mean, that's all well and good, but it doesn't tell us what they are."

"That means they have a similar design," Wendell said, "and there's a door in the older one, but it could be in another location."

"Quite right, Wendell, old boy. Quite right."

"Doctor Singh," Wendell said, "I'm still not convinced it isn't Russian. Perhaps they're closer to space travel than we surmised."

"I suppose we'll find out, Doctor," Nadir said, knocking on the side of the craft.

Michael,

This is not how I imagined we'd rekindle our relationship, but Allied Science has stumbled upon something that requires your attention.

Last night, my superiors asked me to identify a craft, and I immediately noticed the similarities between this discovery and another uncatalogued item in the facility. Both resemble the vessels you may have had a hand in designing.

I do not know what you and Jacob created the item for, nor do I want to, but I cannot and will not risk my career for you. I will deny any knowledge of the craft's origin for now, but something like this appearing twice within Empire City is a mathematical impossibility. The standard curvature of the chassis and the lack of any propulsion mechanism suggest the vessel's origin is nearby. It is only a matter of time before the authorities find anything else you're hiding.

I implore you to come forward. If this item links the Scarlet Sparrow to Doctor Henry Thompson, perhaps you can strike a deal. Your freedom and your life are worth any information you have.

Your brother,

David T. Wendell

Empire City

October 16, 1953

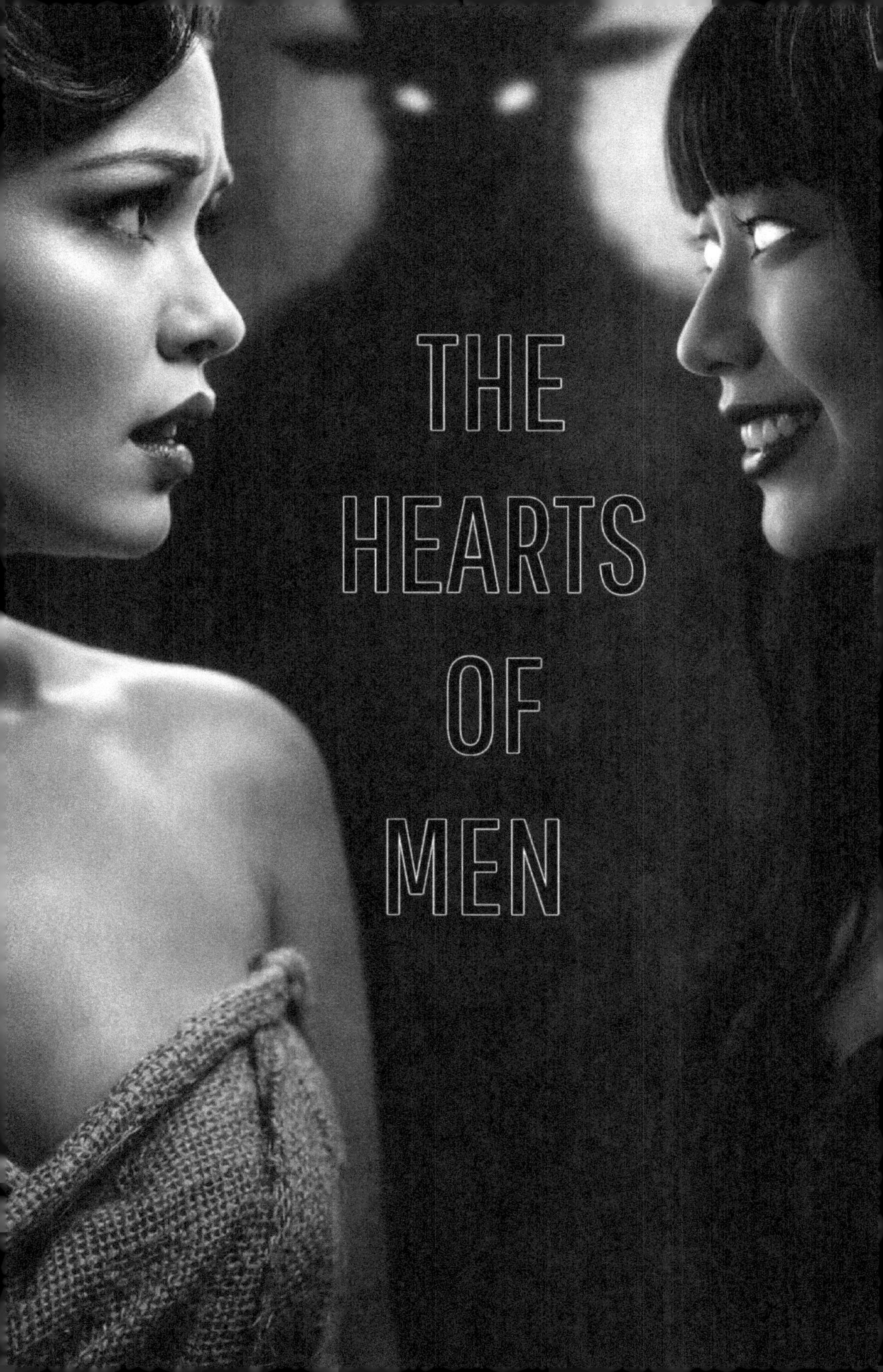

THE
HEARTS
OF
MEN

**17**

*Boom! Boom! Boom!*

The pounding echoed through the foyer and up the eastern staircase, freezing Cassandra and silencing the calming swish of her scrub brush. She hesitantly eyed the front door and scanned the floor for her sisters. "Is anyone—"

*Boom! Boom! Boom!*

Cassandra flinched and dropped the brush onto the marble step. She climbed to her feet slowly, and pins and needles danced across her legs. The pale stone eyes of Athena and Zeus watched the door from their pedestals, standing almost two stories high in front of the white marble balcony.

*Boom! Boom! Boom!*

Cassandra stripped off her yellow latex gloves and dropped them to the floor. *Ron would not approve of all this noise interrupting my chores!* She peered down the long hallway at the top of the stairs nervously. Her sister, Patricia's, faint moans of pleasure carried a shudder through Cassandra's body. The thought of her and Ron—doing that—made her feel like spiders were crawling under her burlap toga.

Her bare feet padded down the cold stairs as her sister Akia emerged from the study. The lanky Japanese woman floated across the foyer to the heavy oak door, pulling it open. Cassandra froze in place and studied Akia wistfully. Her breath stuck in her chest, and the butterflies gathered, beating a gale-force wind against her stomach.

Akia presented the foyer to two strange men with an open hand. The young, thin man with black hair and a whisker-covered jaw removed his hat and glanced around the room through wide, bloodshot eyes. The fat, sweaty, reddish one looked Akia over with a big dumb grin that reminded Cassandra of an excited puppy dog.

"Hello, Miss, I'm Detective Shanahan. This is Detective Gibson. May we have a moment?" The fat one's abrasive voice stained the air with the stench of alcohol and cigarettes. Akia nodded.

The thin man clutched his hat nervously as he looked past Akia, fixating on the towering statues. "And your name, Miss?"

Akia nodded.

Cassandra slunk down the stairs. "Hello, detectives; you'll have to excuse my sister, Aika. She doesn't speak much English. Welcome to The Sibylline Temple. I am Cassandra. Can I help you with something?" She smiled nervously, hoping they couldn't hear her voice tremble. These didn't look like the usual men who came to trade offerings for blessings from her sisters. They were new, and new meant dangerous.

The fat one stepped forward, clutching his hat in his thick, sweaty hands. "Cassandra, is it? A pleasure to meet you." He looked through her to the top of the stairs. "Is the man of the house in?"

Akia slipped back against the white wall next to the pale vase full of white lilies and blended in as if part of the room. Cassandra flashed a cheesy smile. "No, I'm afraid—"

"Detectives Shanahan and… Gibson, was it?" Ron's voice boomed from the top of the stairs. He clapped his hands twice, and Cassandra's sisters seemed to appear from nowhere. "Akia, show the detectives to the study. Barbara, take their hats. Cassandra, don't be rude; offer the gentlemen some refreshments. Mary and Nancy, see if there's anything to nibble on in the kitchen." He descended the stairs slowly.

Despite his loud voice, Ron was an average-sized man who walked with a confidence he hadn't earned. He had a small moon face with beady, sharp, gray eyes, a little pug nose, and thick, pouty lips. His golden toga hung off his left shoulder, covering very little of his pink skin, which was still slick with sweat. The usual smell of fornication and scotch, slathered over with Vaseline cream, trailed him, infecting the room.

"Mr. Baxter, I presume?" Detective Gibson asked. The awe in his eyes was replaced with perplexity as he looked Ron over.

Barbara reached for the young detective's hat, but the fat one placed a hand on hers. "We won't be staying long." The words oozed out as if the sentence had been one long word. Barbara glanced nervously at Ron, shuttered, and disappeared into the kitchen.

"C-can I offer you, gentlemen, some w-water? O-or p-perhaps—"

"Water would be just fine for the both of us," the young detective said.

Cassandra followed the blue veins on the marble floor with her eyes. "R-Ron, can I get you—"

"Shall we, detectives?" Ron interrupted. He clapped twice, and Akia motioned for the detectives to follow her.

Cassandra's chest tightened. *Is Ron angry with me? Was it wrong to allow these men into the temple?*

She leaned on the banister to steady her panicked, heaving breath and glanced at the black broadcloth draped across the doorway under the western staircase. The curtain shifted enough to hold her attention, and a name crashed against her consciousness.

*Master Leonard.*

Cassandra collected herself and pushed through the swinging kitchen door. Barbara sat in the corner, resting her chin on her knees and shuddering in deep breaths. She was a small, mousey girl with frazzled blonde hair and big buck teeth. The youngest of Cassandra's sisters, fifteen or sixteen, no one knew for sure.

Across the room, Nancy peered out of the servant's pantry and smiled wickedly. She was seventeen or eighteen, with long brown hair, blue eyes, and a slightly gaunt but pretty face. Her ribs ran like a ladder along her sternum above small breasts that pushed against her organdy toga. She placed her hands on her hips and shifted her weight. "Look, Mary, it's Fatsandra. She'll know where the food is."

"Yeah," Mary responded, "she can smell it with her pig snout. Go on, find the food, Fatsandra. Ew, look how much she's sweating, like a big fat pig!" Mary was shorter, with an average build, average features, and an average name. She had dull brown eyes and the same mousey hair as Nancy but cut just above her shoulders and turned up in curls. Both girls oinked like pigs and leered across the island. The awful sound grew louder until they stopped to laugh.

Cassandra sneered and inched around the island toward the cupboard. Nancy nudged her with her shoulder as she passed. Mary pushed her and emphasized her horrid nickname. "Watch it, *Fatsandra*!"

Cassandra stumbled and slapped both hands on the red laminate island to catch herself. She closed her eyes and exhaled her anger, focusing on the time Ron had locked her in the basement with a can of dog food and a bowl full of water for slapping Nancy. *You've attacked your sisters like an animal, so you'll be treated as such. Perhaps this punishment will help you lose weight.* Still, her fists clenched as the girls continued oinking.

*Foribus Oraculi.* The words rippled across her skin, leaving a trail of goosebumps even in the sweltering heat. Cassandra ignored it and pushed past her sisters, busying herself in the cupboard.

Mary stuck her tongue out. "Whatever, Fatsandra, go suck an egg."

Nancy giggled. "Yeah, go take a long walk off a short pier."

**<u>18</u>**

The parlor was a two-story room with walls painted like a cloudy blue sky, tapering into a galaxy across the domed ceiling. Ron sat in his decadent white armchair, across from the detectives, on the simplistic blue sofa. The open window carried the scent of fall on a warm summer breeze, and the sheer curtains danced.

Cassandra placed glasses onto the wooden coasters spread across the white oak coffee table and carefully poured water as Ron's gaze bore into her flesh. She backed up to the fireplace beside Akia, whose porcelain skin blended into the painted clouds on the wall. She flashed a smile. Cassandra blushed and dropped her eyes.

The young detective took a long drink. "Thanks." He wiped his mouth with the back of his arm and watched Mary and Nancy enter through the servant's entrance with trays of hor d 'oeuvres. "The girls don't need to be here on our account."

Ron took a cracker with a dollop of Cheez-Whiz from Mary's tray and popped it into his mouth. "Nonsense, it's important my concubines earn their keep. No one lives for free, detective." The girls placed the crackers and cucumber sandwiches on the coffee table.

The fat detective scoffed. "Nice to see feudalism is alive and well."

Ron pulled Nancy into his lap and kissed her neck. She giggled and eyed the detectives wickedly.

"Knock it off, Baxter. Save it for the peepshow," Shanahan said.

Ron peeked over Nancy's shoulder. "Relax, Detective Shanahan, sexuality is very much a part of The Sibylline Religion. In my temple, such behavior is not only accepted but encouraged. These girls may look young, but I assure you they have old souls."

Gibson adjusted himself uncomfortably and took a long drink. The fat detective shook his head.

Ron smirked. "I assume you aren't here to discuss joining us then?" He took Nancy's hair between his fingers and smelled it like an exotic flower. "And indulging in the spoils?"

"Well, Mister Baxter," Shanahan's voice boomed. "I'm pleased to announce it's nothing as provocative as that. Just a few questions, and you're free to get back to molesting children." He inched forward on the couch.

Ron pushed Nancy off his lap and gently slapped her behind. He snatched another cracker from the tray. "Please, detective, call me Ron. Mister Baxter was my father." He licked Cheez-Whiz from his index finger and offered an unsavory smile.

Detective Gibson swallowed the last of his water and eyed Cassandra. She smiled and shot forward to refill the glass.

Detective Shanahan squinted. "Well, Ron, we'll get right down to brass tacks then. You're aware Bonnie Connor is missing, correct?"

Cassandra winced and jostled the pitcher, splashing water onto the table. "Sorry"—she shuddered—"I'm so sorry!"

Ron let out a deep, angry sigh that sounded like the growl of a rabid dog. The sting of tears surfaced as Cassandra desperately searched the room for a towel. Mary and Nancy giggled.

The young detective pulled a handkerchief from his pocket. "It's no trouble, Cassandra. Nothing to get so worked up over anyhow." He wiped the small spill up in one smooth motion. "There, see? All better."

Ron sneered. "Bonnie Connor—hm—I only know what I read in the paper. It's a tragedy, but I'm afraid I haven't spoken to James in years." He leaned back in his chair and clapped twice, but his eyes remained fixed on the table. Akia floated silently across the room to the bar.

Ron regarded the fat detective. "James was a fraternity brother of mine. Legacy pledges to Chi Phi, you see. We were close, but when I founded The Sibylline Religion"—Ron scrunched his pug nose—"that wife of his, Theodora, became jealous. Unfortunately, she wears the pants in the family and drove a wedge between us." He smiled. "But Bonnie. Oh, I love her dearly, and even though we had our disagreements, James saw fit to make me her godfather. It breaks my heart to think any ill could have befallen her." Akia placed a glass of Macallan scotch in Ron's open hand.

Detective Shanahan chuckled and shook his head. "Can't imagine why Missus Connor would disapprove of all this, Ron, ol' boy. Looks like you got a real nice slave labor camp here."

Ron smiled wolfishly. "It's so easy for you to pooh-pooh that which scares you, detective. I understand this is a lot to take in, but let me ask you: what do you believe in? No, let me guess, you're Catholic, correct?"

The fat man crossed his arms and leaned back. "Once upon a time, not that it's any business o' yours."

Ron smirked. "Either way—such a courageous stance you have on religion. You try to burn mine to the ground with words so your beliefs can remain unopposed and keep you feeling comfortable. It's so easy, even a child could do it. But to embrace something seen as different, to embrace something still in its infancy, that takes fearlessness.

"My girls and I went against the grain, a true testament to our courage. You see, the God you know is dead."

"God is dead," Cassandra and her sisters responded in unison.

"Now, in its place, a new way of life rises from the ashes in which we are each reborn as our own god." Ron sipped his scotch.

"We are god," Cassandra and her sisters replied.

The fat detective's saggy jowls hinted at a slight smirk. "Right, well, as George Gershwin says: *tomato tomahto.*' As I was sayin', you an' the Connors also served in the

# The City of the Gods: Gold

Second World War together, correct? Invaded Japan after they refused to call it quits if memory serves. Must have been some scene over there. What with Captain Wonderful, the Scarlet Sparrow, an' all the rest of the heroes runnin' around."

Ron mirrored Shanahan and leaned back in his chair, swirling the scotch around the glass. "It was." The words slithered out of his mouth as he regarded the table. "I don't much like to talk about it. We all know the real heroes were James and Theodora. Well, James, anyway. I was there more for moral support.

"When it was over, the world celebrated the Connors as heroes, and I left Japan with my beautiful Akia, a flower plucked from a garden of weeds." He smiled at Akia, who broke her blank stare with an emotionless smile.

"What about the Smith boys, Calvin and Jerry?" Shanahan asked.

Cassandra eyed Ron, who stared silently at the table. The scotch stopped swirling, and he erupted from the chair, flinging his drink against the far wall. "Cassandra! Clean up that water before it leaves a ring!"

The young detective lurched forward. "Take it easy, Baxter!"

Shanahan placed a hand on his gun.

"I-I-I'm sorry!" Cassandra stammered. She set the pitcher on the floor and scampered to Ron's side.

Ron dumped the young detective's water onto the table and jerked Cassandra by her hair. "Does that look clean to you?"

*Thunk!* The table smacked against Cassandra's face with blinding speed. When the shock wore off, pain radiated through her mouth. She fought to turn her head, sucking at the air through the taste of damp wood. Ron's elbow dug into her back. Both detectives shot up.

"No, don't!" Cassandra screamed. "It was my fault. I'll clean it!" Her cheek was flat against the table, forcing her left eye closed.

Detective Gibson grabbed Ron's arm. "Let her up, you son-of-a-bitch!"

"We all must do our jobs!" Ron pressed on Cassandra's skull until her teeth ground against the inside of her cheek, and the taste of iron rode down her throat. When he finally released her, she rose slowly, fighting involuntary sobs. The young detective placed a hand on her back and offered her the red handkerchief.

"Don't touch her!" Ron screamed.

"I was just—"

"Don't you ever touch my oracle!" Ron spat.

"You alright, darlin'?" the fat man asked, ignoring Ron.

Cassandra nodded.

"You're a son-of-a-bitch. You know that Baxter?" Shanahan took his seat, and the young detective followed suit hesitantly.

Cassandra wiped the spilled water from the table and handed the handkerchief back to Detective Gibson with a shaky hand. She scampered next to the fireplace and tried to force her refractory sobbing to stop. Akia watched her with worry in her dark eyes.

Ron sat. "I apologize, but we all must do our jobs, or else there will be chaos." He closed his eyes, took little breaths in and out of his nose, and ground his teeth into a smile. "I appreciate you are only trying to do yours, detectives, but why bring up those Negros? I knew them, sure. Hardly war heroes, if I'm honest. I don't even know why Truman deployed them at all. James was—"

"But you know they had strange… abilities? Same as Mister and Missus Connor," the fat one interrupted.

A shadow shifted across the room, and a towering form lurked behind Nancy, who didn't seem to notice. Cassandra blinked a few stray tears away, and the wall was blue again.

"I don't know what that has to do with Bonnie," Ron said.

The world spun and shifted, and Cassandra's wet hair froze to the side of her face. She struggled to find breath.

Maggots overwhelmed the Cheez-Whiz on the table and dropped to the floor, rolling around on the oriental rug. Ron popped a rotten cracker into his mouth with a smile.

"Aperi mihi mens onus." The voice rode a frigid breeze as more of a feeling than a sound, shaking the house on its foundation. Searing frost spread over Cassandra's skin like a rash, crawling into her lungs and filling them with a dull ache of ozone. The room grew dark, and cold fingers rested on the nape of her neck. Akia took the pitcher gently to silence the shaking ice cubes. She pursed her lips to call out, but Cassandra shook her head. Everyone was too entranced with the conversation to notice anything was amiss, and no one seemed to see the creature groping Cassandra.

The fat man inched to the edge of the sofa. "You and I both know it has plenty to do with Bonnie."

Detective Gibson placed a hand on his partner's shoulder. "Slim, can I talk to you? Privately?"

"Not now, Skipper."

The chill lifted, and the pain subsided. Cassandra greedily filled her lungs with warm fall air.

Ron tightened his lips. "Well, the Sibylline Religion had nothing to do with their abilities, if that's what you're implying."

Detective Shanahan tossed his arm over the back of the sofa. "I'm not implying anythin'. I'm just a bit of a war buff. Served myself back when I was a pup, liberated France in the Great War, an' th' situation in Japan just fascinates me. So, if you don't mind me asking, or even if you do, I don't really give a warm shit. How'd you kill Jerry Smith in Japan? Seems impossible seein' as he was th' fastest man in th' world."

Gibson grabbed his shoulder. "Slim, stop!"

A slow, thunderous stomping cut through the air like uprooted trees. Footsteps moved across the floor until cracks spread in the marble under an invisible weight. A cold sigh crawled across Cassandra's skin, rattling her bones to the point they threatened to shatter.

Ron sneered. "We are peaceful in this temple. We're not warmongers and butchers like the Connors. You should ask Theodora how he died."

The fat man smirked. "Oh, I will. Just curious t' see what you know. As I said, Ron, I'm a war buff, an' that includes war crimes. Maybe you don't remember due to the other murders you committed. I'm assumin' at a certain point they all run together in yer head."

Cassandra inhaled, gathering the courage to glance over her shoulder. A shadow void of color climbed the wall. Hundreds of thin, gray-skinned arms erupted from the inky blackness, holding her in place and violently forcing her gaze to the window.

*You did this.*

Fingers interlocked and pulled her hair.

*You killed us.*

*You made us.*

# The City of the Gods: Gold

The silhouette of a woman stood against the window, slowly turning her head, revealing a rack of deer antlers jutting from her exposed skull. She watched Cassandra through gaping cavities darker than any black should be.

*Your fault.*

*Unforgivable.*

*Death will be my wedding, children, and glory.*

*Thunk! Thunk! Thunk!* Birds hit the window behind the woman, spraying blood and cracking the glass until a crow shattered the pane and rolled across the floor, flailing wildly and staining the carpet. Gibson smiled at Cassandra and lifted his glass. Akia stepped forward and refilled it.

Ron slid back into his chair, exhaling. "Gentlemen, forgive me, but I was under the impression we'd be talking about the missing Connor girl, not the Smith brothers. I can't have you upsetting my girls. If you want information about Negros, I suggest you go downtown to Lincoln. You'll find plenty of them there."

"No, you know what, Baxter? I'm sorry," the fat detective said behind a cocky smirk. "My old partner used to say you can tell a lot about a man from his past. Jus' tryin' t' get t' know ya, Ron."

"Yes," Ron responded. "I think I may have known your old partner. Harper, was it? Tragic what happened."

Shanahan's smile faded. "That's enough!"

Gibson's eyes moved between Ron and Shanahan. "What's he talking about, Slim?"

"Nothing."

Ron leaned back and crossed his arms. "Oh, doesn't the new partner know? Harper used to talk about you often, Slim, or should I call you Len? It's a shame he never brought you along on any of those private details I hired him for. You could have made a lot of money."

Shanahan's mouth tightened. "Stop it, Baxter. I'm warning you."

"Slim Shanahan... you've gotten so fat, how ironic."

"Et intrabit in vobis," a voice thundered. A crack shot up the wall like a bullet, sending plaster careening across the floor. Any remaining light dulled as red liquid enveloped the sun. Icy fingers clenched Cassandra's heart, and her body convulsed. Something was trying to enter her, thrashing like a wild animal as it worked its way into her soul.

*No!* Cassandra's pulse slowed, and the phantom fingers released her heart. When she refused it, whatever had been reaching for her turned its attention elsewhere.

"That's enough, Baxter!" Shanahan yelled.

A sinister smirk crossed Ron's lips. "Harper, ha! I haven't thought about him in years. I seem to remember reading that the old drunk took his own life a while back."

Shanahan erupted from his seat. "You son-of-a-bitch! I know what you did! I know what you did, Baxter!"

Nancy and Mary cowered behind Ron's bone-white chair. Gibson shot to his feet and pressed his hands against Shanahan's shoulders. "Hold on a minute, Slim, everyone, just calm down!"

Ron remained seated, watching the chaos unfold. "No need to become so hostile, detective"—he clapped twice—"Cassandra, perhaps our guests would like something a little stronger than water?"

"Don't bother. We were just leaving!" the young detective replied.

The ice in the pitcher rattled. Akia's breath staggered, and her eyes rolled back. White froth shot from her throat, across her face, and onto the floor.

Ron popped a cracker into his mouth. "Are you sure, detective? I have a nice—"

*Crash!* The pitcher dropped from Akia's hand, scattering water, ice, and glass across the floor. "Homo sacer!" the Japanese girl screamed between convulsions. Each word spat white bubbling foam from her lips. She fell into Cassandra's arms.

Cassandra guided Akia to the floor as her thin body shook, slapping against the smooth marble like a dying fish. Her eyes turned to black pools, and red tears streamed down her face. The pungent scent of urine engulfed the room, staining Akia's toga and spreading across the floor toward Ron and the detectives.

Akia stared wide-eyed at the ceiling and screamed in a deep, inhuman voice. "Damnatio memoriae! Homo sacer!"

"Cassandra, please take Akia to her room," Ron said.

Detective Gibson crouched beside Cassandra. "Take her to her room? This girl needs an ambulance. She's bleeding, for God's sake!"

"Do not touch them!" Ron yelled.

Detective Gibson hesitated but backed away. Akia's body rippled with terror-induced tremors as Cassandra helped her up. Her wide eyes returned to their normal, dark brown color, and she sobbed, covering her stained toga with her hands.

Cassandra hurried her through the room of gawking eyes. Past the cautious Shanahan and Gibson, past Ron's furious glare, and finally past Mary and Nancy, weeping in each other's arms.

Akia jerked from Cassandra's grip and turned to face the others. Cassandra grabbed her shoulders. Akia pushed her into the door frame.

"Statim finis!" the voice inside of Akia boomed.

"Cassandra!" Ron whined with a hint of terror in his voice.

Cassandra shook the pain from her head. "Akia, stop!"

"Luna est finis mundi!" Akia roared. Her breathing came in short, rapid bursts.

Cassandra grabbed her arm; it was as cold as death, and she was anchored to the room.

"Et mercatores mortem non reddere. Donum deorum non sit capta in modum. Fratres duos. Quaerite ille qui est conservator fui. Alterum malum. Fratres—Ross!"

Cassandra slapped her. "Akia!"

Akia blinked twice, and the glazed look in her eyes faded. Her face twisted, and she threw her warm body against Cassandra, bursting into tears.

Cassandra quickly shuffled her toward the kitchen, and Akia turned to face the others. "Deus est mortuus!" she spat in a low rumble. "Rejoice… God is dead."

**19**

"What in the dickens was that? I thought that girl was Japanese, not Greek!" Detective Shanahan's booming voice sounded through the swinging door adjoining the kitchen and the study.

When the girls were safely out of sight, Cassandra took Akia's face in her hands. "Are you okay?"

"I'm sorry, gentlemen; you see, I brought Akia here from war-torn Japan. I'm afraid she's lost everything, the sweet dear," Ron said from the study. "She can be a bit dramatic and—"

"A bit dramatic? My ex-wife was a bit dramatic. That was downright terrifying," Detective Shanahan replied.

"I-I-we—" Akia stammered through tears. Cassandra hugged her.

"Was that Latin?" Detective Gibson asked.

The girls' bare feet padded through the foyer and up the marble staircase. Cassandra walked Akia into the red room and softly shut the door. Akia threw herself on one of the bottom bunks. The mattress sagged as she collapsed beneath the weight of her pain, crying into the pillow.

Cassandra sat daintily on the edge of the bed and ran her fingers through Akia's silky black hair. "Akia, what was that? Are you—"

Akia's face shot off the pillow. She locked on Cassandra with eyes full of desperate fear. "W-w-w-we go! Now!"

Cassandra tightened her lips. "Maybe you should sleep? Some rest might do you good."

Akia twisted onto her back and shot up into a sitting position. She pulled Cassandra close. "No, we go! Leave!"

Cassandra traced the patterns on the wooden floor planks with her eyes. "Where would we go, Akia? We have no money, no family."

"Please. Please, we go?"

Cassandra rubbed Akia's knuckles with her thumbs. "When I was a child, my mother always said 'debemos conformarnos con lo que tenemos.' We must make do with what we have. In the temple, we have food and a roof over our heads. That's good enough. I don't think we'd survive if we left." Tears welled in Cassandra's eyes.

Akia leaned in slowly and kissed her. Cassandra's heart fluttered, and she closed her eyes, inhaling deeply through her nose. Akia tasted sweet, like honey, just as Cassandra had always imagined. After the shock ran its course, kissing Akia felt as natural as breathing. Still, Cassandra pulled away and eyed the unlocked door.

Akia smiled. "Please, we go?"

Cassandra's heart pounded through her chest, and a smile crept across her flushed face. "We can't, Akia! That's what I'm trying to tell you."

Akia kissed her again and slipped her tongue into her mouth. Cassandra shot off the bed to retreat from the flood of strange emotions. Akia rose slowly, kissed her again, and slid a hand up her toga, forcing Cassandra against the brick wall. Cassandra tried to push her away, but Akia was stronger than her thin frame suggested.

"Akia, stop!"

"This is what you want," Akia grunted. "This perversion is your deepest desire."

"No! No, it's not—I don't—not like this!" Cassandra inched down the rough brick away from her.

"You do not reject me." Akia stood frighteningly still. Her animalistic eyes reflected through the shadows draped across her face. "You do not reject Master Leonard. The one who spawned you gave you to me. Now, I dance with her whenever I choose."

Akia shot across the room, gripped Cassandra's throat in her ice-cold hand, and lifted her. "I should bring death to you, bring you back to the one who created you. She can tell you to whom you belong. Then I'll make this one feast on your corpse!"

Cassandra's neck stretched painfully from the weight of her body. She kicked her feet and gasped for air as she clutched desperately at Akia's outstretched arm.

"This one called Akia is too weak. Being inside it makes me sick. I require a strong host."

Cassandra's mouth gaped open, and the room dimmed into oblivion. A woman with no face emerged from radiant light pouring like a waterfall and brushed Cassandra's fingers. The cosmos spread over her exposed skin. The end and the beginning were clear, the Alpha and the Omega.

*To see too much is to go mad. To remember is to tempt death*, a voice whispered.

Tears ran down Cassandra's face. Dea, the faceless woman. Cassandra knew her from her dreams.

The floor rushed up and smacked against Cassandra's body. Akia hissed and backed into the shadows. The Japanese girl's dead eyes gleamed in the room's low light as she watched Cassandra writhe in agony on the uneven wooden planks. Cassandra inhaled and coughed, gripping her throat as tears poured down her face.

"Consider this your only warning. Reject me again, and I'll drag you to your creator and force you to watch as I defile her. Then I'll rip out your heart." Akia stared through Cassandra with her wild eyes. Her chest heaved in short, rapid breaths. The sound of the cloven hooves beat across the room as the woman with the antlers watched from the shadows.

*Your fault.*

*You did this.*

**20**

Cassandra sat on the top step of the marble staircase, letting out silent sobs like Patricia had taught her so as not to disturb Ron.

"Thank you for stopping by, detectives. It's always a pleasure." Ron's voice echoed.

Mary led the detectives through the foyer. Cassandra lifted the bucket of dirty water she'd left out and watched silently. It was almost time for nightly prayer, but first, she'd need to clean up her mess.

"Don't leave town, Baxter. We'll be in touch," the young detective commanded.

"Why would I leave? I live in paradise."

The door slammed, and Cassandra was alone in hell again. She padded softly across the foyer, scurrying past the black room to dump the dirty water from the bucket in the kitchen sink.

*Master Leonard.* The name stuck in the back of her mind. Vague memories from her childhood slowly revealed themselves but faded just as quickly, like a car engine that wouldn't turn over.

*To see too much is to go mad. To remember is to tempt death.*

The bright white tile in the kitchen was a welcome relief from the gnawing fear the day brought. The bucket of dirty water sloshed back and forth as Cassandra set it on the island. She folded her arms, rested her head on the counter, and sighed. Then she giggled, surprised she could still do that. *I must be tired,* she thought. *Or going insane.*

"Do you think that was pleasant for me?"

Cassandra shot up straight and gasped. Ron sat at the small table in the corner with one arm resting on the surface, ending in an angry, clenched fist.

Sweat trickled down Cassandra's cheek. "I-I'm sorry, I put her to bed."

Ron shot from the chair, sending it careening into the wall with a screech.

"I-I'm sorry!" Cassandra looked away, shutting her eyes as the tears returned.

Ron's steps echoed off the marble floor. "Do you think that was pleasant for me?" he repeated. "I heard you laughing a moment ago, Cassandra. Do you find this amusing?"

*Bang!* Ron slammed the bucket to the ground and slapped her. The sting on her cheek leveled her. She gripped the counter to stop from slipping into the puddle at her feet.

"I won't have that kind of behavior in my house! I won't!" He slapped her, dropping her to her knees. "You go drag that miserable *bitch* out of bed and bring her to me!" he slurred through clenched teeth as he lifted her by her limp arms.

Cassandra's feet tried to find purchase, but she slipped on the slick, wet floor and fell hard on her side.

Ron sighed and kicked her in the ribs. She hacked a wheeze of blood, dribbling it onto the white tile. She sucked air into her burning lungs, coughed, and repeated the process.

"Get up! I want Akia down here now!"

Pain radiated across Cassandra's ribs as she rose to her knees and fell back onto her haunches. She stared up at her assailant through red, swollen eyes and yelled through uncontrollable sobs. "I can't! Don't you understand? She needs rest! It isn't Akia—" She drooled bloody saliva and gripped her bruised ribs with her elbows.

Ron crouched and smiled. "We're so close, Cassandra. Don't you see? It has returned. We just need the missing piece."

Cassandra finished a few stray sobs and sucked air in short audible bursts. "What piece?" She knew, but she needed to hear it.

Ron's smile faded. "Don't you ever listen to a fucking word I say, Cassandra? Why do I even bother? Maybe a few weeks in the basement will bring back my oracle."

"No, please, Ron!" She suddenly remembered the pitch-black from when she was a little girl, the feel of the cold, uneven wall and the smooth, fridged, gritty floor. She remembered the terrible echo from the high ceiling, reminding her she was alone.

*Your fault.*

*You did this.*

She remembered the prayer. She had reached out to something, and it reached back. She remembered now. Master Leonard. She brought it here. It wanted to be part of her, to ride her body onto this plane.

Ron shoved Cassandra back to the floor and placed his bare foot on her face, forcing it into the cold puddle. "Bring Akia to me. She'll explain herself. Then I'll cut out her tongue so this never happens again. You are the chosen one, not her."

"Ron, no, please!" Cassandra cried. She spotted a butcher's knife in the block behind him.

"Well?" Ron pressed his foot down hard one last time and released her.

Cassandra stared at the knife and remembered the rotting bodies Master Leonard left in its wake. The ceremony that summoned it, and the gifts and premonitions it brought. The creatures who fastened themselves to people. "Ron, I-I can't."

Ron lifted Cassandra by the toga and slammed her against the wall. "Go—"

*THUMP!*

Something hit the ground outside.

Cassandra stared into the dimly lit, bone-white trees and the beautiful sunset backdrop. A murder of crows took flight, and her heart sank.

Ron Baxter's Journal

December 17, 1939

I arrived in Yerba Buena, Mexico. A little backwater farming town where my brother Robert has been hiding from American authorities. I hope whatever reason he's called me here is worth the trouble. In his letters, he told me my knowledge of ancient religions would be paramount in his new project.

The deeper I delve into this town, the more I imagine this must seem like a prison to Robert. In Empire, duping marks out of money was his forte. As plentiful as the marks are here, the money appears minimal. Perhaps that's why he reached out to me.


Ron Baxter's Journal

December 18, 1939

I've met the woman Robert refers to as his wife, Carmela. She speaks not a word of English, and Robert not a word of Spanish. However, I can tell she doesn't care much for me. I don't believe their marriage to be legal anyway.

Carmela has a two-year-old daughter, Rosalita. Robert never struck me as the fatherly type, but he's very protective of her.

Ron Baxter's Journal

December 20, 1939

I awoke early to find Rosalita standing at the foot of my bed, watching me sleep. When I called her name, she ran.

Today Robert revealed why he brought me here. It seems my brother and his wife stumbled upon some ancient artifacts in a cave on the outskirts of town. Jade facemasks and small quartz statues, as Robert has vaguely described them. When I asked if they were Aztec or Incan, he had no idea, and Carmela seemed hesitant to involve me.

They appear to be face masks used as a mark of rank by the Olmecs, and I believe the statues are Kunz axes.

After much-unwarranted anger and confusion, Carmela confirmed what I believed; that these statues do indeed symbolize gods. One of these figures appears panther-like, while the other looks serpentine. If I were to venture a guess, I would surmise one represents the demon Bael.

Depending on the year of their origin, finding these pieces could prove my college thesis. Although God and Satan, as the civilized world knows them, began in the Abrahamic Religions, I stand to argue that demons existed in polytheistic belief systems as gods by different names. Proving this would solidify my theory: these entities are real or based on some form of reality.

Ron Baxter's Journal

December 21, 1939

I've convinced Robert and Carmella to conduct a ceremony in the cave where they found the artifacts and suggested we involve locals to show them our awesome power. I fear it is something far more sinister, though. If I understand what these masks represent, there may need to be a sacrifice of blood.

Ron Baxter's Journal

# The City of the Gods: Gold

December 23, 1939

The ceremony was a success. Although Carmela now believes the Incan goddess Supay possesses her, I know better. My studies in ancient religions have led me to the conclusion that Carmela was, in fact, in contact with something otherworldly. Whether it is Bael or some other entity remains to be seen.

My brother insists his wife is acting. He thinks she is creating this ruse to get the local farmers and other uneducated townsfolk to worship her and bring her money and gifts, but I know the truth. Last night's blood rituals and orgies indicate something is reaching out. Something older than the earth itself. Unfortunately, my short stay has ended, but I will be back soon.

SACRIFICE

## 21

"You're a fucking asshole," Gibson said.

Slim marched across Baxter's front lawn full tilt toward the Plymouth and gave him nothing but ice.

"What the hell was that, Slim? What the hell is your obsession with Jerry Smith?"

"Drop it. You sound like an old woman. I let Baxter get under my skin, is all. Won't happen again."

Gibson moved briskly to keep up. "You're damn right it won't. We'll never be allowed back in there." He glanced over his shoulder at the towering mansion and sneered. "Not that I'd want to, but Baxter knows something about Bonnie, and you blew our shot at finding out what."

Slim stopped short and eyed Gibson from beneath a furrowed brow. "Let it go."

Gibson grumbled, watching the sun dip below the horizon. "How do we stop, Slim? How do we punch out and forget about this little girl?"

Slim's stern gaze broke. "You don't. You don't sleep. You don't eat. You don't consume anything but cigarettes, coffee, an' booze to numb yerself. You take years off your life an' hopefully give 'em back to Bonnie Connor."

"Then we need to work together," Gibson said. "What'd you find at the Connor place? And why were you berating Baxter about Jerry Smith?"

Slim sighed. "I'll explain everything in time. You're right about that miserable son-of-a-bitch Baxter. Might be he didn't take Bonnie hisself, but he's involved."

"Well, you were too busy attacking him to get any information. All this personal bullshit needs to end here, Slim. I'm your partner. I need to know everything you do."

He scoffed. "Partner? Ha! You need t' calm down is what you need t' do. You don't know what the fuck you're talking about, an' the way you're carrying on makes you sound like a rookie."

Gibson jabbed a finger inches from Slim's bulbous nose. "I am a rookie. I'm also the only—"

"Well, you sound like one." Slim forced a smirk. "Matter-o'-fact, you sound like a damn yappy dog, an' I'm growin' tired of it." He sighed heavily. "Listen, there's no need to get all worked up. You ain't helping anything by doin' that. We're in agreement; Baxter's crazy as a loon. Sounds like the guy read a little too much Nietzsche if ya ask me. Now, can we please focus on the task at hand?"

"I'm trying to focus. I'm doing the best I can with a partner who can't get out of his own way: an old drunk who's too afraid to set foot in the police station on accounta they'd laugh him out the front door."

Slim's face twisted slowly into a smile. He chuckled, which grew into a belly laugh, and doubled over, wheezing with his hands on his knees.

"Something funny?" Gibson muttered.

Slim rose with a beet-red face, and a few more titters escaped as he wiped a tear away. "Woo-boy, Skipper, that's a real knee slapper. Who told ya that? Briggs? It sounds like something he'd say."

"No, I—"

"Don't matter, I guess now I know what I assumed to be true."

"And that is?"

Slim smirked, and a soft chuckle left his nose. "Well, two things; first, you don't know jack shit about that station o' yours. Place is dirtier 'n mud. That's why I steer clear. I don't want to wet my beak, an' cops on the take don't look too kindly on that." Slim trudged toward the car. "Th' second, and probably most important thing, is you ain't in Baxter's pocket like every other cop in Empire. Not yet anyway, which is a good start."

Gibson froze and clutched the iron gate. "You're way out of line."

Slim let out a defeated sigh and leaned on the Plymouth. "Goddamn, your naivety is impressive, kid. Where was your beat when you were a uniform cop? Sedgwick or Steel Isle, right?"

Gibson stared at Slim across the roof of the car. "Sedgwick, what about it?"

"Because, Skipper, that's where they put all the soft, goody-two-shoe little boys to keep 'em sedated. You go t' work every day, do your job, an' if Internal Affairs comes a-knockin', you're the one Commissioner Harry Evans points 'em toward. The dumb, deaf an' blind boys down in Sedgwick.

"Now, if you're a boat rocker like me, they stick you in places like Hell's Gate, with morons like McIntire, hopin' you get shot, or worse. Why d' you think it took me so long to make detective? They don't want a guy like me movin' up in rank. They want me dead.

"Every time a new detective comes through th' ninety-third precinct, I try an' get 'em before Baxter's wallet does. Sometimes, there are a few good eggs, sure, but that usually doesn't last long when they see a pile o' cash."

Gibson cocked an eyebrow and forced a smile. "Boy, you must be drunker than you smell, old man." When Slim didn't respond, a gut-churning pain replaced Gibson's conviction. "Well, what about the Enforcers?"

"What about 'em?"

"If the cops in Empire were dirty, wouldn't the Enforcers have something to say about it? Next, you're going to tell me they're dirty too." Gibson smiled nervously.

"That's a whole 'nother can o' worms, kid. They have a history with Baxter, but they ain't dirty like the cops are dirty. They're killers, make no mistake, but th' League an' the cops are like oil an' water. They don't get mixed up in each other's affairs. Scarlet Sparrow cleans up after herself, an' cops look th' other way when they happen upon a body or somethin'. That's the extent of their relationship. Hoover's boys in the FBI are more interested in the Enforcers. Got a real hard-on for 'em. You shoulda seen 'em after T-Day, crawlin' around the station like roaches."

Gibson shook his head. "I just—I can't believe this. I won't!"

Slim popped the car door open and rested his arms on the roof. "Boy Skipper, sometimes I wish my head were as far up my own ass as yours is. Sure would make things easier. How else do you think Baxter gets away with his… lifestyle?" Slim smiled. "Ah, don't feel bad about bein' in th' dark. I've been looking into this for years. The DiLilo family owned the town 'till the Enforcers killed big Sal, then Baxter swooped in and picked up the tab when Sal's son, Francisco, jumped ship after T-Day. It ain't just the cops neither, lawyers, politicians, the whole lot belongs to Baxter's daffy cult." Slim shrugged.

"Then why the hell were you given such an important case?" Gibson asked.

"Don't worry about that jus' yet, an' don't go askin' Murphy neither!" Slim's fingers drummed across the top of the car door, and he gazed longingly at the sunset. "Baxter wants that Connor girl if he doesn't already have her; I seen it in his eyes. An' those dirty cops will deliver her like Chinese food if they find her, but why?" He shook his head. "I just hope th' Enforcers ain't involved."

"Why would the League kidnap a little girl?" Gibson swallowed a lump in his throat as he stared wide-eyed across the car at the fat man.

"You really don't know much about the Enforcers, do ya, kid? Never heard rumors about how they got their abilities? Them bein' devils or Martians or gods, or what have you?"

Gibson scanned the driveway. "I guess I assumed the Scarlet Sparrow made them—or Allied Science. Ya know? Like the radio program said."

"Radio program?" Slim wheezed out a laugh. "How old are you, eight? That theory holds about as much water as a sieve. You never heard any o' the other stories? You sure you grew up in Empire?"

"No. I mean, yes, I did," Gibson stammered. "But, you heard Baxter. He said he hadn't seen James Connor in years. Why would he—why would Theodora—" Gibson pinched the bridge of his nose. "Maybe someone is holding Bonnie ransom, and that's why Theodora was acting so odd?"

Slim eyed Baxter's menacing estate. "Doubt it. Who'd be dumb enough to threaten Captain Wonderful an' the Scarlet Sparrow? No, th' League has a history with Baxter. Whole thing could be staged to look like a kidnapping. You know Theodora Connor an' her mommy used t' be actors, right? Maybe it's not a coincidence that James Connor hasn't surfaced yet. Maybe he got in th' way."

Gibson felt the relentless heat pushing down on him. He sighed and ran a palm over his tired eyes. "Maybe you're just growing senile?"

"Heh, maybe." He dropped onto the Concord's seat with a grunt.

Gibson scanned the porch's shingled roof, eyeing the stacks of dark windows. The mansion felt too empty, like the curtain had been drawn after Baxter's performance, and all the players had retreated backstage. A light breeze carried the dying scent of summer across the lawn, the same essence Theodora had exuded, salt and earth, and he could hear her voice in his mind. *My mother was an actress. She taught me all the tricks.*

Something shifted through the fading light on the widow's walk. Gibson squinted. The silhouette of a woman inched along the railing. Her long, black hair snapped in the wind as she lifted her hands to her face and put one foot forward.

*No!* Gibson exploded through the gate and sprinted across the lawn.

The woman dropped off the edge. Her hair floated upward like a winding river. A faint thump cut through the still evening, and a murder of crows screamed as they took to the sky.

**22**

A sour stench rode the wind as Gibson high-stepped through the overgrown brush on the side of the house. The trickle of a brook merged with angry crows' screaming from the birch trees. Ron and Cassandra stood eerily still over the Japanese girl's twisted body, matting the tall grass. Her leg bent unnaturally away from her below the knee joint, and a bloody, splintered bone jutted from her forearm, but her chest still rose and fell. Gibson shut his eyes to keep the hot bile down.

"Is she breathin'?" Slim wheezed from across the lawn.

Baxter crouched. "Yes, barely. Oh, my beautiful Akia, what have you done?"

"Yagi," the Japanese girl whispered faintly through the rattle in her chest. Baxter slowly brushed the hair out of her face, yanking at her snarled bangs. He gasped.

"Fuck," Gibson muttered to keep the dry heaves at bay. Blood pulsed from Akia's empty eye sockets, and her gore-stained fingers were red up to the second knuckle.

"Skipper!"

He heard his name but couldn't look away from the girl's mutilated face.

A hand clamped Gibson's shoulder; he turned slowly. Slim nodded toward the front door. "Go call for an ambulance."

Gibson blinked twice, following a firefly across the lawn with his eyes. The brook's earthy aroma returned with the crickets' shrill song. "What-what about the radio?"

"It's busted, remember?"

Gibson tried to glance over his shoulder again, but Slim grabbed him squarely and shook him.

"When you call it in, tell 'em you're Briggs."

Gibson shook his head. "Why? Wh—"

"Just do it! Now, Skipper, go!"

Gibson scampered across gnarled roots and jutting stones toward the white wood paneling on the side of the mansion.

"Badge number one-fourteen!" Slim yelled.

The gravel pathway crunched under Gibson's Oxfords as he rounded the house and took the front steps two at a time onto the wrap-around porch. He pushed through the heavy oak door and found himself alone in the foyer.

Gibson frantically scanned the labyrinth of hallways and staircases, eventually making a hard left down a long white corridor, skidding to a stop in front of a black door and bursting through it. A black rotary phone sat on an oak desk across from the entrance. He bobbled the receiver, dialed the operator, and poured himself a glass of scotch from a crystal decanter on the corner of the desk, downing it with a shaky hand.

"Operator," a friendly-sounding woman answered.

"Get me Empire City PD dispatch!" Gibson pulled a chain on the green banker's lamp, illuminating the room. He lifted the phone base and dragged the cord, squinting through the dim light at the hanging photos behind the desk. "Hurry it up, will ya?"

"Hold the line," the operator responded.

Ron's old memories watched Gibson from the black-and-white photos. Mostly a smattering of Ron and the Enforcers in Japan, with Jerry and Cal Smith resigned to the background.

Gibson glanced at a photo of a young Ron Baxter standing in front of a barn next to another young man who didn't appear in any other pictures. The man was slightly taller than Ron but had similar features, including a matching underbite. He was holding a voluptuous woman with long black hair close to his chest. Hispanic, maybe Mexican.

Gibson set the phone's base back on the desk amongst the messy collection of books, magazines, and newspapers and brushed aside a copy of *Playboy* magazine with Miss Mercury staring seductively from the cover. His eyes lingered curiously until a thick book open to *Agamemnon's sacrifice of Iphigenia* caught his attention.

"Sorry for the delay, sir. Connecting you now," the operator said.

"Dispatch," a woman's tired voice came through the receiver. Gibson's eyes ran across the open book, trying to make sense of the underlined sentences.

"Hello?"

"Yes, this is Detective… Briggs"—Gibson's mouth soured with the lie—"badge number one-fourteen, we need an ambulance at one-ten Pleasant Road, in Brookfield. There's been a 10-56A."

"Right away," she said.

# The City of the Gods: Gold

Gibson dropped the phone onto the base and jerked the book from the desk, scanning each underlined section hungrily. "Agamemnon's sacrifice of Iphigenia. Sacrifice the daughter for fair winds. Sacrifice the daughter for the gods' favor." He turned the book over. *Iphigenia at Aulis,* translated by Jane Lumley.

*It's nonsense; what was I expecting?* He settled into the soft leather chair and set the book down cautiously. Then he eyed the long dark hallway leading back to the foyer as he opened a leather-bound book with gold letters: *The Key of Solomon.* A printed drawing of a circled star covered most of the first page, with Latin phrases scrawled across it in ink. They ran upside down, right, left, and backward. He thumbed through the rest of the book and found more of the same.

Gibson sighed and opened an older-looking text: *Pseudomonarchia Daemonum.* Inside was more Latin, which might as well have been a Martian language. Something shifted in his periphery. He spun toward it, nearly falling out of the chair, but he was alone.

"Goddamnit." Gibson desperately searched the desk, shifting a few old copies of the *Empire Bulletin* to reveal a horrid-looking ink sketch of a twisted man holding a cane. His V-shaped smile was unnerving, and his bulging eyes seemed to follow Gibson. Underneath the word "Ronove," Jerry Smith's name was burned into the page, and under that, "Lillian Larkin."

Gibson curiously ran the supple leather-like material the image was printed on between his thumb and index finger curiously. It felt like flesh. He turned the page and the smell of rot lifted from the book. He glanced over his shoulder again, but all he found was his own shadow.

"*Charles,*" a voice whispered.

"Hello?" Gibson's eyes darted to the open door. After a few moments of silence, he examined the next page. A drawing of a man with a lion's head adorned in medieval armor riding a pale horse. "Sabnock," it said. Underneath, "Theodora Connor" was burned onto the page, and under that, the faded name "Gordon Ross."

The next page featured a wolf with large, feathered wings and the tail of a snake.

"Marchosias," Gibson read. Burned into the page were the names "Calvin Smith" and, underneath that, "Walter Ross."

James Connor's name was burned into the next page with a single line through it under an image of a knight riding a horse made of bones and the name "Eligos."

Gibson's gut tumbled with nervous agitation. Slowly, he turned over the heavy flap to find a vile creature atop a throne of onyx glaring from the page. "Master Leonard, the Baphomet." It had a human body with large breasts, an erect male member, the head of a goat, and cloven hooves.

"*Charles, come home.*" The whisper rode a crisp breeze. He jerked his head toward the sound, but the room was empty, and when he regarded the page again, the drawing was gone.

Something slithered within Gibson's bowels, bulging through his skin from the inside. He pushed himself away from the desk, opened his mouth to cry out, and sprayed the walls and ceiling with hot, visceral bile. Tears poured from his squinted eyes down his gaping face as crippling pain shot through his insides. His stomach sank and withered away until his gray skin was stretched tight over his bones.

Gibson's heart beat like it might explode, and his emaciated reflection stared pitifully at him from the window. He pushed helplessly against the desk, trying to rise without the strength to do so.

The door slammed shut. A bitter gust of wind blew the light out and trailed across Gibson's flesh, freezing him to the leather chair. The house shook as something spoke in an ancient, forgotten language. A frozen, dead maw slid over his body, swallowing him into a pit of decomposing, putrid remains that cried out in agony. Pale arms pulled at Gibson's loose skin until it tore.

He screamed, and the desk lamp flickered, bathing the unaltered room in a soft glow. Frantically, Gibson eyed his reflection in the window and found his features had returned to normal, and the desk was clean of bile. He slammed the book shut and pushed it off the desk onto the floor.

Gibson ripped his handkerchief out of his breast pocket and wiped the sweat from his brow with a shaky hand. His eyes jumped around the room but found no one. He exhaled and slowly opened the cover to a small black journal with a black ribbon marking one of the pages, waiting to fall into another fit of madness. When nothing happened, it only fed his apprehension. He scanned the pages hesitantly.

The handwritten passages were the writings of a madman. Phrases had been scrawled across the page in as many different handwriting styles as there were sentences. Most of the words were Latin, but Gibson read whatever English he could decipher from the chicken scratch.

"Heroic families of Attica, endowed with immortality." He ran the back of his forearm over his brow and flipped back a few more pages where the goat-headed creature was waiting again, crudely drawn in crayon.

"Deus est mortuus" was scribbled over the drawing in red. The only other words on the page were in English: "Spawn of the gods for the chosen."

The opposite page had been torn off in a hurry, judging by the frayed edges still sewn into the spine. He ran his index finger along the edge, collecting ancient fibers on the pad of his finger.

"You shouldn't be in here."

Gibson's head shot up, and he regarded the doorway. A tall, thin woman in a robe leered at him.

"Who are you?" Her tangle of messy blonde curls bounced as she pushed off the frame and stomped across the wooden floor, spreading the scent of stale booze around the office.

Gibson smiled sheepishly and lifted the copy of *Playboy* to show her the cover. "Ya caught me. I was taking a peek at Miss Mercury in her birthday suit." He opened the magazine, scanned the copy of a Schiaparelli cologne ad, and whistled. "What a doll!"

"What is your name?" Panic built in her voice as she called out to her master. "Ron!"

"Hey, no need for hysterics." Gibson slid the black journal into his waistband and inched toward the door. "I'm a police officer." He slapped the magazine onto the desk and offered the woman a sympathetic expression. "I'm afraid there's been an accident."

**<u>23</u>**

Gibson wandered across the front lawn toward the gate through the muggy humidity to the soothing melody of the crickets, trying to convince himself what he'd seen was in his head. He followed the blonde girl with his eyes as she approached her people on the side of the house. She whispered something to Ron, who nodded solemnly and glanced in Gibson's direction.

"So, did ya find anything inside?" Slim's eager face floated in the darkness under a towering maple, illuminated by the glowing cherry of his cigarette.

Gibson brushed the book hidden in his waistband and elected to pull the pack of Lucky Strikes from his pocket instead. "Not really, just a bunch of books with titles I can't pronounce."

Slim nodded. "Figures. Well, it was worth a shot, I guess." He regarded Ron and his girls. "That poor Cassandra looks like a frightened rabbit over there. She don't belong in that house."

Gibson lit a cigarette and turned away, but Akia's blood-soaked face wouldn't leave his thoughts. "None of them belong there."

Sirens wailed, and the circus pulled up the driveway: an ambulance, a Ford police cruiser, a Pontiac that said "Brookfield County Coroner" on the side, and an unmarked black Cadillac Eldorado. The sound died, but red lights continued to spin shadows around the yard, and the slam of car doors announced Briggs and Goroski. Briggs nodded to Slim with a mocking smile, and the harder, more serious Goroski brushed past without so much as a glance.

"Blow it out your ear, Briggs," Slim croaked as he watched the men approach Baxter and his harem. Words were exchanged, and the homicide detectives vanished into the house with two of Ron's girls, the skinny one and the plain one.

"Call it." A paramedic shook his head and motioned for the coroner from the weeds. Time stood still as a camera flash illuminated the darkness, freezing poor Akia's mangled face for all eternity.

"Let's get outta here," Slim grumbled, walking toward the Concord. The zipper from the black bag echoed across the yard, the red lights cut off, and the ambulance pulled away behind the meat wagon. There was no need to rush now.

"Shame, she was so young," Slim said.

Gibson slammed the black iron gate behind him and tossed his cigarette stub into the gravel driveway. "She's in a better place now, Slim."

Slim snorted a laugh. "Ain't that the truth? She's away from Baxter."

Gibson watched Ron lead a terrified Cassandra back inside, then turned back to Slim and leaned on the roof of the car. "Something doesn't add up."

"Yeah, I'd say about a million things," Slim sneered. "Baxter, Briggs, and Goroski in that big ol' house with a bunch o' young girls, for starters."

"That's not what I mean, Slim. I mean Akia, her death, something doesn't add up."

"Looked like suicide t' me. She was a troubled girl; you saw it yerself. As morbid as it sounds, I can't say I blame her, an' if th' coroner needs a statement, that's what I'm tellin' him." He pointed a stubby finger across the Plymouth's roof at Gibson. "Matter-o'-fact, yer doin' the paperwork, 'cause we know Briggs sure as shit won't. Just say we showed up after 'em. Happened t' be in the neighborhood or something."

Gibson watched the lights cut out in the house. "I don't know, the way that girl was carrying on inside before she died —call it a hunch, but I think it had something to do with Baxter. Something he did to her. What else would make a young kid like her jump off the roof?"

Slim followed Gibson's gaze. "Baxter seemed pretty shook up, an' jus' as surprised as the rest of us. I mean, I trust th' guy as far as I can throw him, but what could he have possibly done t' her to make her do that? 'Sides, ya can't arrest a man on a hunch, Skipper, even if he is a lousy man."

Gibson fired up the engine and backed out of the driveway. He cracked the window. The crickets still sang, moonlight still dripped off the branches in the rearview, and life went on without that poor girl. Hope for Bonnie Connor still clung to a threadbare rope.

Slim rolled his window down and launched his cigarette stub onto a lush, green lawn. "Well?"

"Well, what?"

"Whatcha find, Skipper, in Baxter's house? I know you're holdin' out on me. You're white as a ghost."

# The City of the Gods: Gold

Gibson could feel the stiff journal tucked in his waistline. He could see those creatures watching him from the pages of that book containing the list of names. He eyed the house in the rearview, and sweat snaked down his face. "I told you, not much—a lot of Latin books with some creepy photos of people with animal heads. You know, things the average creep has in their house." He ran his arm over his brow.

Silence hung like a guillotine between them, and Gibson exhaled. "I don't know, Slim. It seems they actually believe in that nonsense, and somehow, all this religious stuff connects with that Japanese girl's suicide. How'd she suddenly speak fluent Latin with no hint of a Japanese accent?" He sighed. "It connects somehow, but it doesn't make sense."

"Well, keep thinkin' about it. Something you saw is bound to come back up. This is what being a detective's all about, comin' across nonsense and makin' it into something solid. The hardest part is having the patience to wait for it all to fall into place. Jus' be careful. As I said, Baxter has powerful friends, an' he ain't as stupid as he looks."

Bright lights on the horizon grew more vivid as the Bunche Bridge rose like a giant glowing beast guarding Empire City. The salt air drifted in through the windows again, and Gibson finally found serenity amid the chaos.

"Say, you want to get a drink?" Slim asked.

"Sure, there's no way I could sleep after that."

"Great, head to Eddie's Place. You know it?"

"Yeah, I practically lived there when I was a beat cop."

Slim flipped his hat down over his eyes. "Good. Rookie buys on the first day, Skipper. Sorry, I don't make the rules."

Gibson eyed a young Dominican woman in a nurse's uniform, waiting on the curb for the light to change. "Slim, there was one more thing I saw at Baxter's."

"Oh?" Slim responded from under his tipped hat. "Do tell."

"Well, it's probably nothing, but there was a framed photo on Baxter's wall. Ron Baxter, younger, with another man, and the man he was with was holding a woman with long black hair, maybe Hispanic?"

"Hm, guy coulda been his brother."

Gibson slid his elbow out the window. "He has a brother?"

"*Had*," Slim responded. "He died back in '44. Ol' Bobby Baxter, good riddance, I say. He was even worse than Ron, constantly in and out of jail for running scams all over Empire. Whenever he'd get caught, his daddy would bail him out just as fast. Then he'd be right back in for the same shit th' next day. We used to call him 'Bad Luck' Bobby Baxter before he became a serious offender."

Gibson eyed the old man. "Serious offender?"

"Well, it was never proven, but I'll go to my grave believing he murdered his parents to get that inheritance money. When the ECPD was looking for him for questioning, he left the country. Word is he got involved with the DiLilo Family or some such thing. I assume it had somethin' t' do with him hiring DiLilo muscle to off his parents an' being too cheap to pay them, but that's just my theory. Anyway, I heard he died in whatever hole he'd been hidin' in not long after."

"So, who's the girl?"

"Probably some local in whatever dump he lived out the rest of his days." Slim tipped his hat back and glanced at Gibson. "Don't think it pertains to the case anyhow, seein' as he's dead as a doornail."

"How'd he die?"

"Don't know, don't care. Enough questions, Skipper. Anyone ever tell you you're exhausting?"

**24**

Slim yanked open the door to Eddie's with the excitement of a kid on Christmas morning and held it for his partner. The bar was haunted by the same drunks, leaning on the same carved-up wooden tables as the last time Gibson had come here with Creed. A unifying sadness held the spirit of the long, narrow dive together, encompassed in Eddie himself, standing behind the old oak bar drying glasses, as usual.

The jukebox belted "I'm Looking Over a Four-leaf Clover," as Slim strolled through the room like Dwight Eisenhower, shaking folks' hands or greeting them with a friendly smile. He'd have probably kissed a baby if one had been available. He turned to Gibson and yelled, "It's too bad the Connor girl ain't here at Eddie's, eh Skipper? Woulda found her ages ago."

"If only."

Slim mounted a stool like a horse and slapped the bar. "Hey, Eddie! Get me a scotch, I'm starvin'. An' set the rookie Skipper up, too!"

Eddie whipped his rag over his shoulder. "Sure thing, Slim. You still owe me from last week; don't forget now."

"I'm good for it, you know me. I'll settle up as soon as payday comes 'round. Tonight, Skipper's treatin'."

"Skipper? You mean Gibson here? This bum still owes me from over a year ago," Eddie said with a chuckle. "I'm just joshing you; what'll it be... *Skipper?*"

"Whiskey, neat, Eddie," Gibson said with a friendly smirk. "And don't get too used to this Skipper business. It isn't liable to stick." He took the stool next to Slim, removed his hat, and set it on the bar.

"Make it Corby's!" Slim exploded with laughter and squinted through tears at Gibson.

Gibson dusted a bit of lint off the top of his hat. "Laugh it up, Slim."

Eddie nodded, oblivious to the joke, and went to work on the drinks.

Gibson eyed his watch. "Is this the best use of our time?"

"Can't think of anything I'd rather be doin'." Slim pulled a Pall Mall from his breast pocket and stuck it in his craw.

"But Bonnie is still—"

"Hey, Eddie, you haven't seen a young girl around here, have ya? About yay big." Slim raised his hand a few feet off the bar.

"I see a lot of young ladies around here, Slim. None that want to be found by an old-timer like you, though," Eddie replied with charmless wit, and set the drinks on the bar.

"Aw, Eddie, you're breakin' my heart!" Slim leaned back and extended his arms like he needed a hug.

Gibson fished around in his pocket and dumped a wadded-up dollar and a quarter onto the bar. "Don't encourage him, Eddie." He swirled the brown liquid, watching it swish dangerously close to the rim. "What are we missing, Slim? I feel like we overlooked something."

Slim dumped the contents of his glass down his gullet. "Aw, Skipper, do we have to talk shop? I was just starting t' enjoy myself." He lifted his smoldering cigarette from an ashtray, glanced at Eddie, and lightly tapped the rim of his glass. Eddie lifted the glass from the bar and replaced it with a full one.

Gibson left his drink untouched. "God is dead. We are god."

"Skipper, lemme tell you something my old partner used t' tell me." Slim lifted a dollar off the bar and waved it like a flag. "Money is the only god these people worship. It's the root of their power, the Connors and the Baxters.

"They were gods long before Ron started his bullshit religion, an' James got his little magic abilities. It's all about clams for their breed, always has been. Makes their little world go 'round. Hell, makes everyone's little world go round." He slapped the dollar back down on the bar and sipped his drink.

"So where does the money come from?"

"Connor Steel, obviously." Slim downed the rest of his scotch and looked at Eddie, who was busy. He glanced back at Gibson. "Over in Steel Harbor, that big building on Columbus Avenue? That's where James Connor's granddaddy made his fortune. Pretty sure the Baxter family had a hand in it, too." He glanced across the bar, growing visibly irritated. Finally, he got Eddie's attention and tapped his glass again.

Gibson smacked his palm on the bar and looked at his partner with newfound vigor. "Of course, Connor Steel, why didn't I make that connection? I mean, if Baxter's involved and maybe the League, as you said—" A vision of Bonnie Connor's bloated little body drained of color and floating in Steel Harbor shot through his mind. "We gotta get down there, Slim, right now!"

Another drink miraculously appeared in front of the old man. "Easy Skipper, you think I didn't already think of that? James Connor owns Connor Steel like I own my coin collection. It sits in my closet, gathering dust, and I forget I have it 'till someone brings it up. Other people run th' business for him. I bet he hasn't been there in years." Slim tightened his lips and placed a giant mitt on Gibson's shoulder. "Believe me, no one's hiding little Bonnie Connor there without people seeing something. It's a working steel mill, for Christ's sake."

Gibson met his gaze. "But—"

"That's enough for tonight, Skipper," Slim said forcefully. "I appreciate the vigor, but you're going to wear yourself out."

Gibson slapped Slim's back. "I gotta run, old man. I'll see you tomorrow. Get some rest, huh?" He maneuvered behind Slim and into a growing crowd of people.

"Where ya goin', Skipper?" Slim asked in a dejected tone.

"I have something I need to do." Gibson pushed through the front door of Eddie's and fingered the journal tucked in his waistband.

Ron Baxter's Journal

October 14th, 1940

I have returned to Yerba Buena, and the heat is unbearable. This will be a short visit. For now, I must get settled and end this entry. There is much to do and little time to do it.


Ron Baxter's Journal

October 15th, 1940

I fear the ceremony I introduced to these people during my last visit has spiraled out of control. It seems the locals now worship Carmella as a goddess. It proves my college thesis correct but with no evidence save the claims of small-minded townsfolk. Tonight, I have agreed to bear witness to one of her ceremonies that, according to Robert, she insists on performing each week.


Ron Baxter's Journal

October 16th, 1940

The insatiable lust-fueled power Carmella holds over these people is unlike anything I have seen in my years pursuing Theology. People willingly gave their lives to Carmella, while Rosalita received premonitions from a deity she referred to as Master Leonard. She spoke perfectly, not the broken language of a toddler. With my limited understanding of Spanish and Latin, all I could discern from the phrases were "moonchild, doom, and brothers." No one else seemed to take heed of these warnings. Instead, they focused all their unwavering attention on Carmella.

This morning, when I asked Carmella what Rosalita was saying, she had no recollection of her daughter being there.

Ron Baxter's Journal

October 19th, 1940

Robert is dead, stabbed multiple times. Carmella told me it was a robbery. I write this passage with a heavy heart, but it is necessary to mark this significant moment.

I have paid a local pilot to fly Robert's remains to California along with Carmella, Rosalita, and me. Once there, I will make other travel arrangements to get us all safely to Empire City. I cannot, in good faith, leave them here.

ALLIES
AMONGST
ENEMIES

**25**

Leering eyes burned into the back of Gordon Ross's head as he pumped the pedals on his Roadmaster Luxury Liner, gaining traction up Sunrise Drive, past Armory Street, and down Spring, keeping a wary eye on the road behind him. A few old people glared from stoops, and high school kids lingered outside corner stores, smoking cigarettes and catcalling girls, but the steely gaze of something else bothered him.

He made a right on Albert Street. The city gave way to suburban homes with maintained lawns and families enjoying the beautiful fall afternoon from their weather-stripped porches. The salty sea air burst through the humidity. Gordon put a few more cookie-cutter houses behind him and made a right across Mister Johnson's yard.

The old man yelled an inaudible threat from the window as Gordon blew past and leaped the ridge at the edge of the property. He skidded sideways and scanned the ghost-white birch trees as the smell of the rotting wet leaves wrestled away the stench of the sea air.

"Hello?" Gordon called into the pale woods. A loon wailed in the distance, and the trees swayed with a gust of wind, but something else was there, too, watching. He tore down the narrow path, and his bike clattered over rotten wooden railroad ties, overgrown with crabgrass, and beaten into the ground.

Gordon dumped the Roadmaster at the end of the clearing and peered down the old railroad track as he covered the bike in leaves for safekeeping. "Who's there? Walt? Billy?" When no one answered, he crawled quickly through the brush to the next clearing.

The sun dipped into the western sky; it would be dark in a few hours, and if the streetlights went on before he was home, his father would give him another knuckle sandwich. Gordon knew his old man's schedule all too well. He knew it was Friday,

# The City of the Gods: Gold

October Sixteenth, and Pop didn't have a shift at the fire station or poker tonight. So, he'd be home, probably angry, definitely drunk.

He'd been completely blotto since Gordon's mom ran off with his uncle Tommy after T-Day. All she'd left behind were a few wire hangers, the dwindling scent of perfume, and a note scribbled over a receipt from the A&P: *Don't look for me.*

For a few months, Gordon's father had remained hopeful. Maybe she'd come crawling back. Maybe things could return to the way they'd been. Maybe she was afraid of the city after T-Day. The maybes piled up optimistically until the old man received a letter from his brother. Hope faded like his health as he drowned himself in drink after drink, night after night, flooding any chance of moving on with cheap bourbon and Schlitz beer. Now, he existed as a walking corpse with his only purpose to make his boys' lives a living hell.

"Where the fuck have you been?" A small, pudgy boy with a swollen black eye and a head full of thick ginger hair waddled through the clearing toward Gordon.

"H-hi Billy—"

"H-h-h-hi Billy, what are you, some sort of retard?" Billy mocked. "I was waitin' here forever. I cut Buchman's class so we could finish today."

"Sorry, I took the long way. I—"

"Bullshit, did that old hag Miss Sullivan keep you after class again? I told you, next time she tries that shit, tell her a woman's place is in the kitchen, not the classroom. That'll shut her up."

Gordon looked past Billy at his fortress and smiled. Four nearly even plywood walls fastened together with second-hand nails and covered with a rusty tin roof. "Look at her, Billy. The Scarlet Sparrow will be proud."

The shadows stirred with the wind, and Gordon scanned the brush at the edge of the clearing. "You weren't following me through the woods before, were ya?"

"Following you? Didn't ya hear me? I've been waiting here forever. I thought I was going to die from boredom," Billy said. "I brought my old man's hammer to finish up, and he said we could keep his hunting chairs until deer season starts in November."

Gordon nodded. "Good. The Junior Enforcers will need 'em when we're on duty." He high-stepped through some bushes and dragged out a long piece of waterlogged plywood. "Last one, pal. We just need to reinforce the door, and our fortress will be complete."

Billy gripped the board. "I'll knock it in. Last time, you almost bashed my fingers. You don't even know how to use a hammer. You're like half a fag or something."

Gordon tightened his grip. "Nuh-uh, I'm hammering."

"It's my old man's hammer!" Billy whined.

Gordon tossed the wood to the ground and ripped Billy forward by his shirt. "It's my fortress!"

"Okay! Jesus Christ, Gordon. Uncle!" Billy pleaded.

"Can I play?" a small voice asked.

Gordon sighed. "We're not playing, Walter. This is serious Junior Enforcer business."

Walter scampered from behind the fort, peering out from under his old man's herringbone flatcap. Gordon's hand-me-down striped collared shirt and slacks hung off his slight frame, dragging in the dirt. "Well, can I be in the Junior Enforcers then? C'mon, I'm your brother, Gordie!"

Billy flashed his bulbous decoder ring. "No fuckin' way, Walter! You ain't Junior Enforcer material."

"I am so, Billy!"

"Then where's your decoder ring?"

Gordon sighed. "You're only seven, Walter. You're not old enough to join the Junior Enforcers yet."

Walter crossed his arms over his chest. "Stupid Billy got to join, and he's only ten!"

"Hey, watch it, you little shit," Billy sneered. "I'm eleven going on twelve. I flunked the second grade, duh!"

"Well, you're only ten, Gordie!"

Gordon slapped Walter's cap down. "When you're old enough, you can join. Heck, I'll initiate you myself. By that time, I should be a full-fledged member of the real Enforcers."

Walter knocked the brim back. "Well, when will that be? I never get to do anything!" He shrugged his shoulders and forced a dry whimper.

Billy sighed. "Are we going to hammer this board in or—who's that?"

Gordon turned slowly and followed Billy's gaze, but the anxiety that followed him through the woods was gone. This was something else. Dark eyes peered out sideways from behind a tree until a look of surprise shot across them, and they vanished behind it, leaving a mop of black hair exposed.

"Hello?" Gordon slowly approached.

"Wait a minute! That's the little ass hole who sucker-punched me. He's spyin' on us!" Billy said.

Gordon forced his voice into a deeper register. "Hey! Are you spyin' on us? This is Gordon Ross, leader of the Junior Enforcers, speaking."

"He's bad news, Gordon," Billy said. "I think he's one of the Dark Plunderer's Voodoo Zombie Assassins. He already socked me. Maybe he's back to finish the job with a ray gun or something."

Gordon set his hands on his hips. "Hey, you behind the tree, do you swear allegiance to the Dark Plunderer?"

"No," a timid voice answered through a thick British accent.

Billy shook his head. "Oh boy, it's worse than I thought. Listen to the way he talks. I bet he's one of the Ivory Icicle's men."

Gordon nodded and regarded the tree. "Who is your master? The Dark Plunderer or the Ivory Icicle? Are you a Voodoo Zombie Assassin or a Frozen Fiend?"

"Neither," the small voice behind the tree responded, "I go to Baggata Elementary."

"Oh shit, Gordon!" Billy's good eye grew wide. "The Changeling himself! Must be! There's no way he goes to our school, not with that Limey accent. He's only pretending to be a kid. I remember when the League tangled with him on the radio show. He was pretending to be Captain Wonderful's long-lost brother."

Gordon shushed him. If this was the Changeling, talking about him within earshot wasn't doing any good.

"Show yourself, kid!" Walter yelled.

Gordon regarded his brother with wide eyes. "What the hell are you thinking?"

"Great," Billy exclaimed. "Now we're as good as dead!"

A scrawny, feeble boy stepped out from behind the tree, scanning the forest floor.

Gordon laughed. "That's the kid who gave you the shiner, Billy? He's half your size."

"No, he must be some sort of villain or at least have powers. He's stronger than he looks—or—he snuck up on me, yeah, that's it. He snuck up on me and popped me one!" Billy whined.

"He's even smaller than me, Gordie," Walter exclaimed. The new kid snickered.

Billy stomped toward the small boy. "I'm gonna cream you!"

Gordon placed a hand on Billy's chest and stepped between the two, but the kid didn't even flinch.

"Yeah, cream him!" Walter yelled.

"Now, wait a minute!" Gordon struggled to hold back the ball of rage that was his friend. "This isn't the Junior Enforcer way! Remember what Captain Wonderful said in episode fourteen: "It Came from Beyond the Stars?" When they found those Martians who they thought were dangerous, but then the spacemen ended up helping them against the Nazis? 'We have to assess the situation first, then act.'"

Billy stopped and glared at the kid.

"How 'bout it, kid? Are you a foe or a friend?" Gordon asked.

"You bet he's a foe. He attacked me!" Billy pushed against Gordon.

"No, I'm not. You called me a name, so I hit you," the kid said.

Billy stood up straight and slapped Gordon's hand away from his chest. "This is bullshit, Gordon. This kid sucker-punched me! I demand satisfaction. Lemme at him!"

"Kill him!" Walter growled.

Gordon stifled a laugh and shot Walter an angry look. "Walter, pipe down! Billy, if you touch him, you're out of the Junior Enforcers. It's not our way. You know that."

Billy muttered, retreating into the fort and slamming the makeshift wooden door.

Gordon regarded the new kid. "What's your name?"

"Ukrit."

"Funny name."

Ukrit shrugged.

Gordon crossed his arms. "What are you doing here, Ukrit? If you're not here to attack us?"

Ukrit pointed at Walter. "He told me to come. He said you were playing Enforcers, and I wanted to play."

Walter's jaw dropped. "No!" He looked at Gordon. "Nu-uh! He musta followed me, Gordie. I didn't tell him to come, honest Injun."

Gordon crossed his arms and glanced from Walter to Ukrit and back again. The kid was brave, and if he could take on Billy without so much as a scratch to show for it, he may have been Junior Enforcer material. Gordon smirked and placed a hand on Ukrit's bony shoulder. "You want to join the Junior Enforcers, kid?"

Billy exploded through the door. "What?" The shock on his face almost opened his swollen eye to its normal size. "Didn't ya hear what I said? He socked me, Gordon!"

Ukrit eyed Billy. "That's because you called me a—"

"I don't care who did what," Gordon interjected. "On the radio show the Scarlet Sparrow always says, 'We're stronger as one unit,' remember? She also says, 'Make your enemies into your friends.' Now, can you fellas do that?"

Billy glowered. "I guess."

"I just want to play!" Ukrit said.

Gordon stepped back hesitantly. "Shake on it."

Billy leered at Ukrit as he spat in his hand and extended it. Ukrit tried to do the same but drooled onto his open palm. Billy shot Gordon a look of disgust and shook Ukrit's hand.

Gordon crossed his arms. "We don't play in the Junior Enforcers, kid, remember that. This is serious business."

**<u>26</u>**

Long shadows stretched eastward across the forest floor as Gordon smacked the final nail into his fortress. "I declare the Junior Enforcers open for business! 'We help those who can't help themselves,'" he quoted Captain Wonderful.

The animosity hanging over the group snubbed the sense of accomplishment. Walter approached his brother. "Can I be on the team too, Gordie? If Ukrit can, why can't I?"

Gordon sighed. "Fine, you can be in on a trial basis for now, but if things get dangerous, I want you to stay in the fort, deal? We already lost mom and—just promise me?"

"Deal!" Walter drooled into his palm and offered a handshake. Gordon chuckled and slapped his brother's cap down over his eyes.

Walter shrugged and clapped Ukrit's back. "Doesn't this fella have a funny voice? All the kids in my class say so." Walter's blue eyes twinkled under the shadow of his hat. "It's okay; we'll teach you how to talk regular, won't we, Gordie?"

Gordon eyed Ukrit. "Hm, how can we test your allegiance to the Junior Enforcers?"

"You have to eat dog doo-doo!" Walter yelled excitedly.

Gordon sighed. "No, Walter."

The bushes rustled, and Gordon's heart leaped.

A fed-up-looking girl stumbled through the thicket, looked up to speak, and tripped over a branch, catching herself on an elm tree. "Bloody hell!" She smoothed her dress, scanning the boys with a sharp glare and singling out Ukrit. "Ukrit! You can't run off like that! Mother said I'm to watch you, and I'll not spend all day traipsing through this sorry excuse for a forest!" She tossed her long black braid over her shoulder and fanned her flush face.

Billy snickered, and Ukrit's face grew three shades redder to match the girl's. "Not now, Pratima!

Gordon crossed his arms. "Is that your babysitter, kid?" He looked her over with a cocky smirk to hide his nerves, excitement, or whatever was gnawing at the pit of his stomach.

"He has a babysitter? What a sissy! I told you, Gordon, I bet they have to go home to comb each other's hair and get ready for their tea party!" Billy raised his stubby pinky and guffawed.

"No, this is my sister, Pratima." Ukrit kicked a rock.

Gordon swallowed a lump in his throat and watched the late afternoon sun glistening off her smooth, black hair. Her beautiful eyes and soft lips reminded him of candy. "She seems irritating," he blurted out.

Pratima scowled and snatched Ukrit's hand. "Come, Ukrit. You must get away from this South Empire trash before you catch something!"

Gordon frowned. The storm in his stomach whipped into a frenzy as he fought words through whatever slight breath he could still draw. "South Empire trash? Better than being a snobby broad. Come back tomorrow without your dumb sister, Ukrit. We'll have a place for you in the Junior Enforcers."

Ukrit pulled from Pratima's grasp. "I'm sorry, fellows." He kicked a stick and glared at his sister. "You always ruin everything, Pratima!"

"She always turns up like a bad penny, huh? I know the type." Gordon didn't know where this malice was coming from. He didn't even know which way was up when Pratima's beautiful eyes met his. The scent of her shampoo rode the breeze, and he leaned on the wall of the fortress to catch himself from falling into it.

Pratima gasped. "My mother insisted I look after Ukrit! If it were up to me, I'd be as far from this disgusting place as possible. Do you realize you're basically playing under the Coastal Highway? Look at the lot of you. Junior Enforcers? Ha! More like—like Baby Enforcers!"

Billy watched her with an ear-to-ear smile, interrupted by occasional laughter.

Walter stepped up to meet Pratima's fury. "You're just jealous of us because you can't be in the Junior Enforcers, you dumb girl! Boys only, right, Gordon? No girls allowed, right, Gordon?" He crossed his arms and nodded hard, forcing his hat to fall over his face.

Pratima rolled her eyes and placed her hands on her hips. "I don't want to be in your dumb Baby Enforcers anyhow! Besides, aren't the *real* League of Enforcers predominantly female?"

Walter tilted his hat back, clenched his tiny fists, and leaned into his words. "I don't know what you're saying, you smelly ol' girl!"

A shrewd smile crossed Pratima's lips. "You're the smelly one!"

"Everyone, relax." Gordon pulled Walter back. "She can be the Junior Enforcer's secretary." The need for her presence overcame common sense. Girls were disgusting creatures.

"Ha!" Pratima exclaimed. "I am *not* a secretary! If I were to stay, which I probably won't, I'd be a science officer! *The* science officer!"

Billy erupted with laughter, holding his jiggling belly. "Girls can't be science officers!"

Pratima's face reddened as she stomped toward Billy and grabbed him by the lapels. "I believe the Scarlet Sparrow is the science officer of the real League, and last I checked, she's a girl!" She locked eyes with Billy and craned her neck forward, moving her chin close to his.

Billy lifted his hands. "Okay! Okay!"

Gordon stepped in to separate the two, but his eyes never left Pratima. "Alright, that's enough. We'll let you in on a trial basis," he said, trying to cover his desperation with confidence.

"This is stupid!" both Pratima and Billy said. Billy grimaced. Pratima stuck her tongue out at him and made a soft "mmm!" Sound.

Billy threw his hands up and stomped toward the thicket. "This is bullshit, Gordon. I'm out of here! The day some broad joins the League is the day I quit!" He climbed halfway through and peered back at the group. "There will never be a girl science officer! They belong in the kitchen!"

Pratima screwed her face. "Bloody ape." She stomped toward the other side of the clearing. "Come along, Ukrit."

"But—"

"Now!"

Ukrit sighed and followed. Gordon watched them vanish through the brush. He gripped his belly and sighed blissfully.

*She smells like flowers and bubble gum,* he thought. *She looks like a rainbow after a summer storm.*

"Gordon," Walter said.

"What?"

Walter pointed west. "The sun's going down!"

<u>27</u>

"Follow me and stay close, Walt!" Gordon turned the pedals as fast as they'd go, charging past the A&P, the unofficial border of Steel Harbor. In the distance, whitecaps crashed onto Eastview Beach, leaving a trail of wet sand as the water retreated.

Gordon flew down the long, steep Signal Ridge hill into Steel Isle, and the ocean vanished behind a blur of rundown houses. The sun was a sliver of gold, surrounded by red fire spewing through the light cloud cover. It looked like Hell, but the streetlights were still off.

The boys dropped their bikes on the unkempt lawn and sprinted through the tall grass to the broken concrete path. Gordon froze. His shadow flickered onto the dilapidated porch as the fluorescent bulb of the streetlight hummed behind him. The giant Victorian mansion spread infinitely into the dusk. There was nowhere left to run.

Half of the first floor was theirs, converted a few years ago into a split level full of bad memories. Walter didn't know any other home, but Gordon missed the old apartment across town in Lincoln. The last place his family had been happy.

Gordon slowly reached for the chipped, green door as cold sweat trickled down his back. *Maybe Pop is out, or maybe he's passed out on the couch again.* The driveway was empty, but that didn't mean his father hadn't abandoned his maroon Chevrolet Stylemaster at some bar. He took a deep breath to steady his hand and pulled the handle on the screen door, yanking it open in one fluid movement, creating a soft, yawning sound.

The boys inched across the threshold, stepping around empty Schlitz beer cans and old newspapers toward the kitchen. Bent nails marked the wall where long discarded photos of his mom, baby Walter, and Uncle Tommy posing with his prize buck once hung. Pop had said they were too painful a reminder of this perfect life stolen from him as he took a baseball bat to the wall last year. Gordon could still hear the shattering glass as his father destroyed the final images of his family.

*We ain't rich, but we have each other*, Gordon's mom would often say over a dinner of leftovers she'd bring home from her job at Wilbur's Diner. He'd hear his father climbing those old, creaky stairs in the Lincoln apartment. Pop would open the door smelling like Lifebuoy soap from the fire station, say something fresh, and wink at Gordon. His mother would giggle, and he'd dip her for a kiss. Now, the memory seemed like he was watching another person's life, fading each day until it became twisted with nostalgia like the photos once hanging proudly in their home. His mother called memories like those *old ghosts*, and they weren't to be trusted.

The only remaining picture was his Uncle Robert standing proudly beside Engine 23 in the Lincoln fire station. He died on the Fayette Bridge during T-Day. Pop called him a hero as if he hadn't been fleeing for his life—another old ghost.

Gordon motioned for Walter to stop as he inched along the skirting board between the small foyer and the living room. There was no snoring, so he peered over the ledge through the broken spindles at an empty couch and sighed. "It's alright, Walt. He isn't home."

Walter emerged from the doorway slowly. "Phew!" He kicked a beer can against the wall. "Hey, Gordie, do you think Ukrit will—"

The toilet flushed up the four stairs of the split-level house. The toilet flushed! It wasn't supposed to do that; they were supposed to be safe. Gordon met Walt's wide gaze; his muscles tensed, and his breath left him until a word shuddered out. "H-h-h-hide."

"But, Gordie!"

"Go!" Gordon craned his neck to watch the stairs. Trees danced against the backdrop of the streetlight, casting sinister shadows across the room. He clenched his fists. Walter slunk into the coat closet next to the front door and disappeared into the musty darkness.

"Walter? Is that you?" His father's voice dripped with malice for the boys who—as he said—reminded him so much of his bitch wife. It was lethargic and slurred. Hatred reinforced with booze. "Where you been?"

The floor creaked as he edged down the stairs and buttoned his trousers. His dark, bloodshot eyes bore a hole through Gordon, and the smoldering cigarette pressed into his salt-and-pepper beard bounced as he spoke. "Oh, it's Gordie. You're late." His voice was gravel pouring into Gordon's shoes and fixing him to the floor. Smoke shot from his nose like some sort of horrific dragon. "Where's your brother? If you left him behind, I swear to Christ—did you leave him somewhere?" The scent of Lifebuoy soap struggled beneath the stench of booze and cigarettes as his father pressed his face close to Gordon's. He smelled like an ashtray someone had spilled whiskey into. "I asked you a fucking question, boy!" He bounced Gordon's head off the wall and stepped back to let him fall.

Gordon's body slapped the floor, and pain radiated through his arm. He wanted to get up, to stand up to this man who had replaced his loving father. This wasn't the sweet man he had known in Lincoln, or was it? Old ghosts.

Gordon threw his arms up over his head and rolled into a ball. "Please, Pop!" He wanted Captain Wonderful to kick the door in and shoot this man, or Miss Mercury, to carry him to the Hall of Enforcers with her superspeed and put him behind bars. Warm tears ran down his face, or so he thought, until droplets of blood collected on the floor. Then the tears came, angry and hotter than the blood gathering in his eyebrows.

He retreated into a memory where he was a little boy, playing with his mother's raven-black hair as she rocked him to sleep. She would hum a song, sweet and wordless. It existed only as music with no name, something that pure couldn't be named.

"You sissy, crying on the floor like a girl over a little scrape." Pop flicked his cigarette stub, and the spark smacked Gordon's arm. He scrambled away, leaving the ember to fade on the linoleum.

Walter pushed the closet door open. "Stop it!"

"Ah, there ya are." His father flung the thin wooden door into the wall and threw Walter to the ground. Gordon hummed his mother's lullaby.

"You little shits think you can pull one over on your old man, huh? Sneak in here after dark, and I wouldn't notice? I'm the king of this castle! I'm—" Pop's face reddened, and veins bulged in his neck. "Shut up with that fucking song, Gordie!"

Gordon hummed louder, and his father snatched a half-full beer bottle off the table by the door. "I said shut the fuck up, boy!" His eyes widened as he cocked the bottle back like a baseball pitcher. "Do not test me!"

## The City of the Gods: Gold

The song faded into Gordon's mind, and his father casually tossed the bottle to the floor. "You're both like your mother, stupid, just like she is." He glanced out the window with his hands on his hips. "Get my belt, Walter," he growled.

Walter jumped to his feet, kicking a few beer cans as he scurried up the stairs like a shot. Gordon remained in a fetal position, staring at the deep black of a crack in the wall.

*The cellar door*, a voice called out from the darkness, and a hundred eyes watched from the window. Gordon could feel them, the same voyeurs who had followed him through the woods. Somehow, he didn't want to disappoint them.

Walter crept down the stairs, clutching the black leather belt in his tiny hand.

"It looks like I'm raising a couple of blubbering girls," Pop exclaimed with a twisted smile. It was forced. His eyes didn't smile; they never did anymore. "Looks like you're first, Walt. Bring it here." He extended a large, rough hand.

"No." Gordon lifted himself up. "Walt didn't do anything. I'm the one who made us late."

*Bang! Bang! Bang!* Something beat on the window in appreciation, but only for Gordon to hear.

The old man's eyes flashed in the darkness. "Well, shit, look at Gordie, the hero." He snatched the belt from Walter, stumbled, and caught himself on the wall. "Ya know your Uncle Robbie was a hero—now he's dead. Go watch the television, Walter. Your brother saved you an ass-whoopin'." He regarded Gordon. "Grab me a beer and meet me in the dining room, Gordie. You're just like your mother, stupid."

Gordon moved into the dining room, possessed by duty to his brother, and set a cold can of Schlitz on the table. His father towered over him, and the light from the television accentuated his sunken, cadaverous eyes.

"It's the Uptown Clown Show, live from Empire City!" the TV said. Walter peered back from where he sat cross-legged in front of the glowing set. Clowns paraded around on a stage behind him in scrambled black and white.

"Turn around, Walt, or you'll get the leftovers. You ain't safe yet." Pop coiled the belt around his arm, and Gordon closed his eyes.

*Standing up for the little guy, that's what we do because no one else will!* Captain Wonderful's voice rang through his head as the clowns hit each other with pies, and laughed, sprayed the audience with seltzer and laughed, fell over, and laughed, laughed, laughed, laughed.

Gordon pulled his pants down and braced himself with a deep, shuddering breath. His father screamed incessantly, but the laughter engulfed it, crawling from the television and into Gordon's mind.

*Cellar door,* something whispered.

His father worked the leather against Gordon's exposed behind with a recurring *whap!* Pain flared until numbness crawled over his bare skin, and the *whap, whap, whap* of the belt vanished into the laughter.

A figure stared out of the shadows behind the television, humming a song, sweet and wordless. Gordon could feel her smile as she tilted her head, allowing her dark hair to tumble across her shoulders. *Come find me, Gordon. Become the hero I know you to be.*

Pop spun Gordon around and backhanded him across the face. "And one to grow on! Get to your room, you little son-of-a-bitch! You too, Walter! And think about that next time you decide to sneak in here after dark, you dumb son-of-a-bitch!"

Gordon pulled his pants up and wiped the blood from his split lip. Expected tears never came, just excitement beyond anything he'd known.

*Come find me.*

# The City of the Gods: Gold

Walter hurried up the stairs and down the hall until his little footsteps faded into silence, and Gordon eyed his father.

*Cellar door.*

The broken old man stared out the window toward the ocean, and a single tear cascaded down his weathered face. "I said, go!"

Gordon limped through the living room as feeling returned and throbbing pain with it. One clown gazed dead-eyed from the television, tittering nervously. "Come find me, Gordon," its voice warped into a goofy low pitch. Gordon shut off the set, and the clown faded into a small circle of light, lingering in the center of the screen. "CeLlAr DoOr."

Gordon flung the bedroom door open. Walter jumped and discarded the piece of paper he was scribbling on. "Gordie, are you okay?"

"I'll show Pop, wait 'till I join the Enforcers!" He ran a hand under his sheetless mattress and pulled out a copy of a "Playboy" magazine with Miss Mercury smiling seductively from the cover.

"Thanks for takin' my whoopin' Gordie. I was sure I was finished," Walter hugged his legs to his chest and glanced at Gordon with wide eyes. "Woah! Is that Pop's dirty magazine? He is going to be maaaad if he sees you with it."

Gordon flipped through the pages of seductive, leering eyes and supple nude bodies. He traced the outline of Miss Mercury's jet-black hair with his finger. "You gonna tell him?"

Walter pushed himself to the edge of the splintered bed frame. "Nuh-uh, I ain't a rat, Gordon!"

Gordon regarded the magazine and smiled. "None of this will matter when I marry Miss Mercury and become a hero, anyway."

Walter scrunched his nose. "Ew, why would you marry a girl?"

"You don't see the bigger picture yet, Walt." Gordon hummed an old, familiar, wordless song and stared out the window at the figure cast in shadow. "You will."

*Come find me, Gordon.*

Ron Baxter's Journal

November 20, 1940

Since returning to Empire, I've had the most vivid dreams of that ceremony in Mexico. Carmella's followers' commitment was boundless. That kind of power can not be bought or earned but must be bestowed by something we, as a society, don't quite understand— the power of a god.

I believe Rosalita is the key to unlocking this higher power. I often recall waking on my first day in Mexico to find her glazed stare studying me. Something was behind those eyes.


Ron Baxter's Journal

November 21, 1940

Another night, the same dream. Throughout my Theology studies, that ceremony remains the most spectacular proof of higher power I have ever experienced. After much research and deliberation, I have decided to form a religion built on what I witnessed in that cave in Mexico. It will be called The Sibylline Religion, based on the Greek myth of the great Oracle Sibyl. Carmella will be necessary. However, the most crucial piece will be whatever lives within Rosalita.


Ron Baxter's Journal

November 25, 1940

I awoke to Rosalita standing over my bed. She spoke in Latin, but I understood each word: Master Leonard does not travel alone and will require vessels to carry its army. She told me the God I know is dead, and through Master Leonard, the chosen of the Sibylline congregation, will become gods.


Ron Baxter's Journal

November 26, 1940

Dea. The name haunts me as a faceless woman with luminous skin and hair. Dea, Dea, Dea. It has invaded my dreams, insisting I am on the wrong path. Through Rosalita, Master Leonard had warned me not to trust it.

HUMANITY
EXCEEDED

*Ding!* The elevator jerked to a stop, and the golden door slid open. "Penthouse suite, Mack. All ashore that's goin' ashore!"

Cal sighed, tossed the operator a nickel, and stepped into the darkness. The smell of mothballs wafted from a dingy room opposite the elevator, where dusty sheets clung to the silhouettes of furniture. The moon's pale glow gleamed through large, floor-to-ceiling windows, tucking itself into the gloomy shadows.

The building had been rebuilt and changed drastically since he was last here, but the extravagance was still evident, as was the evil. He remembered what the girl had told him almost nine years ago: *You are Marchosias. Marchosias is you. Until I deem, you are not.*

"Hello?" Cal glanced past the dark room down the narrow hallway toward a hint of fluorescent light. He inched along the length of the marble corridor and froze mid-step when he saw two people's silhouettes.

"Theo?" The forms remained frozen, and hints of the woman with deer antlers lingered in the shadows, too solid to be a dream and too fantastic to be real.

Cal ignored the creeping vision and tried again. "Hello?" A tinge of fear stole into his tone. "Theo?" The silhouettes remained fixed in place. "Lily? James?" He inched closer. "Hello? It's Calvin Smith. Theodora asked me here."

No answer.

Cal approached and let out a relieved sigh, placing a hand on one of the figures' bare marble arms. *Statues. They're statues, you ol' scaredy-cat.* He barked out laughter and met their blank marble stare as he crossed into the light.

# The City of the Gods: Gold

The hallway opened into a three-story palace with a sunken living room. A giant television screen stood across from a long orange sofa and a lime green easy chair with an odd triangular coffee table between them. Behind an elaborate chandelier, white tapestries hung from the ceiling, each showcasing stylized illustrations of the Scarlet Sparrow and Captain Wonderful.

"Theo? Are you home?" Cal scanned the railing of the grand balcony behind the narcissistic decor and glanced down another extravagant marble hallway on his level to a shiny, golden door marked: "private elevator." He walked past the bar along the floor-to-ceiling windows and peered over the outdoor terrace. The garden and the pool butting up to the railing felt out of place this high up.

Beyond that, Empire City stretched for miles, dwarfed by the colossal Ironleaf Building. Cal stood at the top of the world, watching the tiny lights of vehicles as they scurried around the streets like comets amongst stars.

"Theo? Hello? It's Cal. Calvin Smith." Heavy, unnerving silence shrouded the penthouse, too high even to be bothered by street noise. The scent of cigarette smoke drew his attention to a chair resembling a hollowed-out ball across the sunken living room under the balcony. A burning cigarette rested in a crystal ashtray on an end table next to a sweating glass containing brown liquid and one large, melting ice cube.

"Theo? Are you here?" He watched the long finger of ash grow on the smoldering cigarette. "Th—"

*Boom!* It came from upstairs. Cal scrambled around the island in the kitchen to try for a better look at the sound's origin.

*Boom!* Something crashed against a wall on the second floor, rocking the chandler. Plaster from the ceiling dropped into the hallway under the balcony. Footsteps scrambled, and a woman screamed.

*Boom!* The balcony exploded.

Cal covered his face. Rubble peppered his skin, and a loud tearing sound left something tangled in the Captain Wonderful tapestry.

*Brap! Brap! Brap! Brap!* A semi-automatic rifle chattered, and the tapestry landed, cracking the marble floor. Smoke curled from the huddled mass.

"Cal?" Theo peeked over the edge of the balcony, backlit and draped in a purple silk robe with her hands wrapped around a rifle stock. A three-ringed tip smoldered at the end of the gun, trailing smoke into the air. Light from the rocking chandelier strobed across her skin and lit up her smile. "I'm so glad you—*watch out!*"

Cal turned into a punch, launching him across the room and into the Frigidaire. The black metal folded like paper around his body, and cold air licked his back as the refrigerator bulb clutched at flickering life and faded.

Cal gulped at the air as an unfamiliar feeling of helplessness hit him harder than his assailant. The stench of loose food and milk rode the cold into his lungs. He pushed a messy assortment of metal and slop aside, fighting his way to his feet.

Theodora cut the lights and dropped off the balcony into the darkness. She plunged a knife into the hulking mass under the tapestry, and moonlight glistened off the slick blade. Something snatched at her, but she reeled away and drove the knife into the material again. The bloody iron scent stirred something within Cal. He smiled, ran into the fray, and connected a hard right hook, sending a soothing numbness down his arm.

The thing under the tapestry staggered into the drywall, exposing the brick and knocking a framed photo of Bonnie onto the floor. A whimper climbed from under the bloody textile, but Theo was too far gone for sympathy. She slung the rifle around on the strap, answering the whines with a few rounds of plasma.

*Brap! Brap! Brap!* The semi-automatic lit the room with a yellow, alien-looking beam, tearing the draped cloth to smithereens as the target slumped on its side. The charred form filled the room with the stench of boiled garbage.

"Your turn." Theo shot Cal an ominous glance and offered the gun. He snatched the M-1 Carbine, eagerly steading it on his shoulder, and smiled. He gave himself over to the urge as pale, eyeless faces watched from the shifting shadows. Numbness infected his body, and cold breath rode the still night.

*Brap! Brap!* He let off two quick shots into the mass at his feet, lighting the room and scattering the ghostly apparitions. The creature groaned and swiped a long, bulky metallic arm at Cal. He stumbled backward, catching only the putrid wind.

The creature rose slowly, eight feet, ten feet, twelve feet, and a single glowing red orb emanated from the top of the form. Cal tossed the gun to Theo. She braced it against her shoulder and fired a yellow burst of light into its face, illuminating human-like features. The Carbine kicked, rocking her back and sending the creature to its knees.

"What the hell is this thing?" Cal yelled.

Theo's eyes shone in the moonlight like a cat's. "Does it matter? I haven't felt this good in a long time." She smiled and peeled off her torn robe, revealing a small harness with blinking green lights over a leotard. Cal had seen her, Jerry, and James wear something similar in Japan.

A hand shot through the darkness. Thick metallic fingers wrapped around Theo's torso. The metal seemed to be shifting like a river. Like it was alive. The thing rose and launched her at the window. A cocoon of orange light flashed around her body as she crashed through the glass, skipped violently across the pool, and burst through the railing on the far end of the balcony, draining the water slowly over the edge.

"Theo!" Call cried. When he turned, the creature was gone. He spun, scanning the room for movement. Finding none, he sprinted toward the cracked granite deck. A red glow slowly built in the hallway between the statues.

*Boom!* The sound came with a red flash and then darkness.

<u>**29**</u>

Cal's eyes fluttered open to a rush of cold air and the howl of the wind. Buildings rose, and bright yellow windows flashed past. Before he could scream, the roof of a building reached up and met him with the force of a train.

He bounced twice, cracking concrete and tar. The numbness spread through his body in place of pain, returning his strength and bringing forth unquenchable bloodlust.

*Boom!* The creature landed on him, a flurry of hulking metal and flesh. The remaining human eye stared dumbly at nothing while the glowing red circle jammed into its other eye socket gawked from its small, hairless head. A dry tongue drooped from its dead, mangled mouth. It stunk, even in the open air, like rotten cheese.

Blow after blow, piston-like fists rained down upon Cal. Blood filled his mouth as the comfortable, numb feeling faded. He tried to move his arms to block the onslaught, but his body refused. Something was terribly wrong. Or finally, right.

Cal's nose burst like a tomato. His eyes swelled shut as punches bounced off his battered face, and old ghosts met him from within his consciousness. The end was near.

He turned his head to take one last look at the city he loved and spotted Theo hanging from the penthouse balcony, fighting against the slowing waterfall that had once been her pool. A final punch split his bottom jaw, and everything went black.

A dream spirited Cal away from the madness, or perhaps he was dead. Pinpricks shot across his body, but he didn't mind the sensation of little insect legs massaging his battered flesh. When they reached his face, he instinctively opened his mouth, and the tickle ran down his throat in large droves, becoming part of him. A sharp pain shot through his neck.

*I'm sorry if that was jarring, but it's necessary, Calvin.*

Numbness crawled over his body, and he smiled.

"Cal? Cal, are you with me?" Theo's voice woke him with a jolting snort. He tried to move, but pain fastened him to the roof. The Ironleaf Building towered over him. He was still in Hemsford.

Theo crushed a vial with her foot, and the meter on her armor-harness screamed a red sliver of warning. "Stay with me!" Her voice was distant and muffled. "I need you, Cal!"

*I need you, Cal,* Jerry's voice echoed in his mind. *I need you to go get Theo. Tell her to tell Baxter I'm ready—it's time for plan B.* Cal shook the memory from his mangled head.

A red beam emanated from the creature's eye, sweeping across the roof toward Theo. She leaped aside. The beam reset and fired again. She bent backward over the second attack and sprung onto her arms like a circus tumbler.

Cal could feel the crumbled roof on his back, the debris sticking to his forearms. He lifted one finger and let it twitch, then another.

Theo leaped away from another blast and bound to a neighboring deco balcony. The Carbine trailed her on a black strap as she jumped from building to building.

Cal pushed himself up. His black, singed shirt dangled off his massive frame. He grunted through his broken jaw, but the creature's attention remained fixated on Theo. It was backlit and shadowed. Cal limped forward, ignoring the pain climbing his legs. The numbness was clawing to get out and the strength that came with it. His body was knitting itself back together. That was new, but so was taking damage in the first place.

*Bang!* Cal shielded his eyes from the red flash of the creature's eye. The blast caught Theo in mid-air. She careened, head over heels, into a plate glass window. *Crash!*

Cal roared and shuffled toward the monster, landing blows on its fleshy face and chest. It was no longer a grotesque creature. It was James. It was Ron. It was Theo. All those who'd had a hand in ending Jerry's life.

The creature caught Cal with a hard right hook, twisting his head. He staggered but refused to fall until it dropped him with another right. His vision blurred as his face slapped the gravel. The creature lifted him by the throat and threw him across the roof. As his limp body rolled, he called out desperately to the numbness, hiding amongst the old ghosts, the white grinning masks, the bleating woman with deer antlers smattered through his mind, and the girl who made it all happen. He needed to be invincible again.

*Crash!* Theo exploded through a neighboring building's window, emptying a magazine into the creature.

*Rat-tat-tat-tat-tat.* She landed on the roof, rolled to absorb the impact, and dove to the side to avoid a punch.

"Hey!" Cal stammered through his healing jaw. He spat a gob of blood, and Empire City dimmed. He put his fists up anyway. The creature spun and thundered toward him.

He recognized the grotesque horror of metal and seared, bubbling flesh in the moonlight but couldn't place it. One glowing red eye lit its human mouth, moving wordlessly. A patchwork of metal arms and legs, flesh, and exposed shoulder bone protected a glass tube, standing in for its abdomen, fused to mangled pectoral muscles, and housing a floating mass in green liquid.

Theo fidgeted with the box on her chest, tossed the gun aside, and bound away across rooftops until she disappeared.

The creature caught Cal on the jaw with a jab. Cal returned the favor. He knocked a few punches away and ducked under some but took the majority on the chin and ribs. Then, he pushed it off balance and slammed his fist into the glass tube. There was a *thunk* where Cal had expected a *smash*, and it swatted him with a backhand.

Cal skidded across the roof. He hated fighting. It was fear that drove him and fear that stopped him. Fear of letting go entirely and becoming the numbness inside him, the part of him that enjoyed this.

Theo sprinted back across the roof with a cable in tow. Where she pulled it from was anybody's guess. Cal rolled between her and the creature, pushing himself to his knees with a painful grunt. Her hard, calloused feet scrambled up his back, and she flipped over, lassoing the monster's throat. The roof whined. Cal leaped from a crouching position and punched down on the creature. Theo pulled the cable tight. Glee shot across her eyes as the roof gave way. She giggled, and the building collapsed around them.

Each floor attempted to stop them with bone-shaking thuds as they exchanged blows with the creature, falling as one mass through eighteen painful stories to the ground floor. Plaster, brick, and steel rained, and everything went black.

**<u>30</u>**

Cal woke to the distant fire of a Type 96 machine gun, echoing through the stone formation of a Japanese pillbox. Dust kicked up overhead, peppering the foxhole.

Jerry slumped against the wall, smiling his bloody smile. "I didn't realize the armor-harness was empty." He chuckled. "Pretty stupid, huh? Wilbur'd call me a knucklehead for sure if he could see me now." The moonlight glinted off his dark eyes as he gazed at the stars. "What a ride, though. Huh, brother?"

Cal slid to Jerry's side. "Don't talk like that, Jerry. You're gonna be fine. I'll get Nurse Larkin; she'll fix you up—"

"It's over, Bucko. Look at me." Jerry scanned his bullet-riddled legs, pumping blood into the soil.

"Aw, Jerry…" The sting of tears welled in Cal's eyes. "Naw, c'mon, man! We're going to get you—"

"Cal, go get Theo. Tell her to tell Baxter I'm ready—it's time for plan B." He laughed softly. "Whatever it takes, eh, Calvin?"

Cal watched his little brother fade behind a blur of tears. "What's plan—no! Jerry, c'mon! You're the fastest thing on two feet. How did this—"

The Type 96 thundered until Jerry's labored breathing eclipsed it. "Just go get—tell Baxter it's time—" his head dumped to one side, and his eyes fluttered shut. "Love you, Cal—"

In the distance, there was a deafening growl, ending in a horrifying sputter.

Cal gasped, and his eyes shot open. Pain radiated through his cramped body in shifts. The world was upside down, and red lights flashed through cracks in the shroud of darkness in front of him. He bent the rebar, pinning his leg, and slid down a brick wall onto his head.

When the throbbing pain faded, he rose, pushing aside piles of rubble as easily as cardboard. The humid air coated his exposed skin, and he coughed a painful, bloody phlegm wad. That was new. He hadn't taken damage like this in years.

"Don't move!" a nervous voice stammered. Cal's weary gaze met a .38 Special shaking in his face. The uniformed officer attached to it had a proud-looking rat face that Cal wouldn't have minded caving in under different circumstances.

"Get away from him!" Theo climbed the pile of rubble behind the cop. Moonlight glinted off her shiny black uniform, containing a failing armor-harness.

"But Missus Connor. He's a—well—he's a—"

"A what? A hero?" She snatched the officer's gun, emptied the shells into the rubble, and tossed it into the street. "Go fetch!"

The cop scampered off. Theo smiled and brushed a stray lock of hair behind her ear. "Sorry, Cal. They can be—Well, not much has changed around here but the scenery, unfortunately." She offered a hand to pull him up. Cal ignored her and climbed out himself.

Theo fingered the charm of her necklace and regarded a parade of police cars and ambulances. "The thing I miss least about being an Enforcer is dealing with these creeps after a big event like this."

Cal nodded and wiped his mouth with the back of his hand. A thin layer of white dust covered his bruised and blood-caked body, and his clothes hung off him in ribbons. "Mind if we go someplace else, Theo?"

She smiled again. "Yeah. Sure, let's get you inside. I already gave my statement. I think we're done here."

The private elevator shot to the penthouse, but inside, time ground to a halt. Theo ran a hand through her wet hair. "God, I must look a fright." She frowned at her reflection in the golden door. "I'm sorry about all that, Cal, truly." She laughed. "But, I like this new look you're trying. It could be—"

"I thought all your enemies were dead." Cal crossed his arms, trying to come off as dignified as possible in his ragged clothes. Making eye contact was unbearable, so he opted not to.

"So did I." Theo exhaled overdramatically.

"Then what do you call that?" Cal asked.

*Ding!* The elevator doors slid open. Theo sniffled and pushed out ahead of him. "Beats me, but it's kinda like old times, eh Bucko? Like we were back in Japan. You haven't lost a step, Calvin." She marched a bit quicker and ejected a smoldering black mass from her chest harness, letting it fall to the ground. "Maybe later we can try the Charleston." Her dismal tone did nothing for the jokes.

Cal winced in pain as he increased his stride to catch her. He grabbed her by the arm and spun her against the wall. "Theo, what the hell was that?"

She gazed down the long hall, avoiding his eyes. Her chin quivered, and she fell into his arms, sobbing. Cal sighed, and something broke inside of him. He wrapped his arms around her and stroked her damp hair.

Theo pushed away. "I'm sorry, I'm a mess." She walked quickly ahead of him again. "Where are my manners? You must be famished. Can I fix you something to eat? I'm not much of a cook, but I can probably whip something up."

Cal's jaw dropped. The apartment looked like nothing had happened. The Frigidaire stood like new, and the window was repaired and cleaned.

"Theo, how—the glass—the refrigerator—"

Theo regarded him somberly. "Oh, my nano-mites fixed the place up."

"Your what?"

"They're little machines I created, untraceable to the naked eye. They... build things, I guess. How else do you think I rebuilt Empire in only five years?" She let out a sigh, and composure seemed to return. "That building we knocked down was commercial, by the way, I doubt anyone was in there at one o'clock on a Saturday morning. It should be standing again by the time the sun comes up." She smiled. "I'm always telling Bonnie to clean up her toys, and what kind of terrible hypocrite would I be if I didn't do the same?"

"Theo, if you have these little things that can fix everything, why not use them all the time?"

"Where's the fun in that?" she asked with a sad smile. "I'm not afraid to get my hands dirty, Cal. In fact, I enjoy it. I wouldn't want to lose all my humanity, hiding behind machines and little gadgets. I clean my own house and water my own plants. Doing mundane chores keeps me sane. Sure, the Scarlet Sparrow can erect cities, but no one can tend to a garden nearly as well as Theodora Connor." She winked.

Cal crossed his arms. "But with these—nano—whatever—we wouldn't need to fight anymore. They would have taken that creature apart piece by piece."

Theodora cleared her throat. "I don't—they aren't for that. They also burn out far too quickly and interfere with radio frequencies. I haven't been able to perfect them yet, but this is the last defective batch. Hopefully, I can get the kinks out next time. Besides, you can't tell me you didn't enjoy that." She opened the fridge and closed it thoughtfully. "I could use a drink first, whaddya say, Calvin?"

Cal eyed the towering wall of bottles behind the bar. "Maybe later."

"Suit yourself." Theo dipped under a service door and looked over the collection of booze.

Cal took a seat on one of the stools. "Why are you in the city anyway? I read in the *Bulletin* Bonnie was taken from your place in Brookfield."

"Are you sure I can't fix you a drink?" Ice clattered in the silver shaker as she pounded it up and down.

Cal climbed the wall of alcohol with his eyes. "I'm fine."

Theo set the cocktail shaker down and took her necklace between her index and middle finger, twisting it as she glanced out the window. "Truth is, that house in Brookfield feels too empty. I haven't been back there since the night Bonnie disappeared. Besides, I keep a lot of my tech here, and I had a feeling I needed to check up on it. Good thing too, or else I wouldn't have run into our ugly friend." She half smiled and didn't even try to make it look happy. Tears welled in her eyes again, and she scanned the ceiling to fight them back. "Cal, I think that thing took Bonnie. It could have easily broken into my Brookfield home. It was very quiet until I caught it sneaking around in my office." She sighed again and strained the drink into a rocks glass. "Luckily, I was able to slip into my armor-harness before it attacked me."

"How do you know James doesn't have Bonnie?" Cal asked coolly.

"James and I got into a little quarrel the other night, the same night Bonnie went missing. Things have been on the rocks for a while, and"—she trailed off—"he doesn't have Bonnie. If I know James, he's probably with Lily Larkin."

Cal nodded slowly. "Miss Mercury? The one who inherited my brother's speed after he—"

"Right," Theo said. "James loves Bonnie, but he's only her father when it's convenient. Being a dad was never his strong suit, neither was being a husband, I guess."

"So, what do you think that thing was that just beat us senseless?" Cal asked.

Theo smiled. "Between you and me, it looks like one of Doctor Torment's. I mean, it isn't the same tech we saw on T-Day, just the kind of crazy contraption he would make. That thing looked like it was human at one point, and Torment and the people he associated with loved to play God."

Cal shook his head. "I thought James killed him. Hell, didn't James kill everybody?"

Theo took a drink. "You seem to know a lot about the Enforcers for a guy who refused to join." She paused to smile and waited for a response. Cal ignored her.

She shrugged. "I don't know, Cal, honest Injun. I was pregnant with Bonnie when James went after Torment. He said he put him down, but who knows? I begged him not to. He was crazy, sure, but he was such a brilliant mind. As sick as it sounds, part of me hopes he isn't dead." She shook her head. "I never got a straight answer out of James. We weren't talking much then, either. I guess our marriage has been falling apart for longer than I care to admit."

"But why would Thompson take Bonnie?"

"To get my attention? I don't know. I keep asking myself the same question. The thing is, I have jewelry and money, all sorts of expensive junk all over this apartment. That creature went right by all that stuff and got into my safe."

"What's in your safe?"

Theo leaned across the bar and dropped her voice to a whisper. "Weapons, blueprints."

Cal scowled. "Did it get in?"

Theo nodded.

Cal sighed. "What did it take?"

Theo stood slowly, rested her hand on her hip, and scanned the bar. "It knew right where the safe was."

Cal leaned forward. "What did it take?"

Theo took a drink. "Blueprints… for a recon vehicle I designed years ago. It's harmless on its own. An orb with four legs designed to be launched into hostile territory, but it could be weaponized."

"Great," Cal said.

"I have a feeling that creature is connected to Bonnie's disappearance. I've been retired for a few years, and everything was quiet. Suddenly, Bonnie goes missing, and that thing shows up. Torment or not, there hasn't been a substantial villain in Empire for years. Heck, there hasn't been a small-time one."

Cal nodded. "Everyone's too scared of the big bad League of Enforcers to start any trouble."

Theo dropped her eyebrows. "Everyone's too scared of James, you mean?"

"Sure."

Theo yawned into the back of her hand. "Anyway, I'm bushed. Help yourself to anything in the fridge. You're obviously a better cook than me, anyhow." She lifted the hinged part of the bar and slid out from behind. "There's a guest room upstairs when you're ready, second door on the left from the elevator. The bathroom is across the hall. Oh, and lay your clothes out. My nano-mites will take care of the rest." With a wink, she made her hasty escape to the elevator. "I'll see you in the morning, Calvin. We have our work cut out for us."

The elevator doors closed over her silhouette, and Cal collapsed onto the couch.

Ron Baxter's Journal

August 2, 1942

The Sibylline Religion has accumulated more followers from the civilized world of Empire City than I ever thought possible. Although most are drawn by my concubines' private blessings, I can sense a few who are genuinely moved by our way of life. With such a fragile, budding religion, I found it necessary to hire off-duty policemen as private security for gala events. These parties, thrown each month, have tempted only the most forward-thinking members of our community, but Master Leonard has not yet chosen vessels for its army.

What most would label debaucherous activities exist as a mere prelude to the future, and we will pass no judgment within these walls. Whatever one's deepest desire, one is free to fulfill it here. I must admit that part of me is worried this will become a common whore house rather than a temple, but my lover, Carmella, reassures me free love is paramount at the juncture.

As of this entry, we have been unsuccessful in bringing the presence forth into Carmella as we had in Mexico, but I believe we are close. Each night, Rosalita visits my room with new instructions, and I have not dreamt of Dea for months.

Ron Baxter's Journal

August 5, 1942

I awoke at 1 AM to a scream and found Rosalita in my study, scribbling madly into one of her journals. It was well after 2 PM when she finally stopped. Rosalita's message will take time to decipher, scribbled in unfamiliar languages. My love, Carmella, grows concerned for her daughter. I can't be certain it isn't jealousy.

Ron Baxter's Journal

August 9, 1942

Four days ago, Carmella instructed me to lock Rosalita in the basement. She has been growing more violent, even in the daytime. Last night, I awoke to find her standing over my bed, reciting a poem. Today, I cannot remember the words, but I recall it involved Master Leonard. This morning, I found the child back in the basement where I'd locked her four days ago, and when I asked her to recite the poem, she had no recollection of it.

**Master Leonard comes to my house Monday, bringing with him cheer.**

**He loves to play, but if I'm away, he'll wreak havoc here.**

**Master Leonard comes to my house Tuesday, bringing with him toys.**

**He may jest he likes you best, but he loves all girls and boys.**

**Master Leonard comes to my house Wednesday, with a book to read.**

**If you dare to stop and stare, your eyes will surely bleed.**

**Master Leonard comes to my house Thursday with a goose that's fat.**

**If you kneel to make a deal, he'll match you tit for tat.**

**Master Leonard comes to my house Friday when the moon is new.**

# The City of the Gods: Gold

Stop in the town and look around; many are now few.

Master Leonard comes to my house Saturday, smelling strong of ash.

Stroll through the town and burn it down, or you will earn a lash.

Master Leonard comes to your house Sunday when the moon is red.

If he does not like what he finds then you will end up dead.


I awoke sitting at my desk with the poem above this entry burned into the page.

THE
FAMILY
AND THE
MISTRESS

The clamor from the street carried through the open window, riding the never-ending heat from the restless city. Nadir's eyes shot open, and his mind rushed back to the twin vessels like his brain had been on pause for a few hours of sleep. *Perhaps there's something inside that would condemn Theodora Connor, so she hid it. But why open the second one? And where did whatever was inside go?*

He pushed himself to the edge of the bed, following the sunlight along the tear in the wallpaper with his eyes. *And why hide the original vessel at Allied Science?*

Anila stirred behind him. "You're up early, darling," she squeaked.

Nadir smiled and kissed her forehead. "Yes, busy day."

She giggled and watched him from the pillow, her hair splayed over it. "It's sweet of you to take Pratima to the fair. She was so excited last night. You should have seen her."

He traced the grooves in the floor with his eyes as his thoughts shifted back to the vessel. *What could be so important to make Connor break protocol by not recording the original discovery? She was always the most by-the-book member of the team.*

Anila touched his arm. "My love?"

*The world will burn!* Nadir shook the memory of Thompson from his head.

"Hm?" He regarded his wife. "Sorry, love. I was miles away."

"I asked if you ate the leftover rajma last night."

"Of course, delicious as always."

"Did you heat it up?" A broad, knowing smile spread across her lips when he didn't answer. "Did you at least use a plate?"

"Well, I must be off. Busy day for Pratima and I; as you know, science waits for no man… or girl, as it were." Nadir sprang to his feet and proudly marched to the bathroom, kicking the kinks from his weary legs.

Anila rolled over and shut her eyes. "If you decide to have breakfast, please don't teach the children to eat like animals."

Maurice Avenue glistened in the morning sun as Nadir and Pratima walked hand in hand toward the Chapman Street train station.

Pratima smiled. "Thank you for taking me to the Science Fair, Papa."

"Of course, Duckling." Nadir regarded his daughter and was immediately infected with the whimsical feeling radiating from her eyes. She was still young enough to be his little girl, but that connection was hanging by a threadbare string.

Nadir fished two tokens from his trouser pocket and ran his thumb across Hermes's face, glaring profile from the coin. He slipped it into the slot by the turnstile, guided Pratima through, and followed her closely after pressing one in for himself.

They inched up the concrete steps, but Nadir's mind was still in the Idea Square, swimming amongst theories too impossible to be true. *Could the Scarlet Sparrow be involved with T-Day?*

He saw her in his mind, watching with malice as Thompson was escorted from V-Site in New Mexico, ranting and raving like a lunatic.

*No love was lost between Thompson and Connor, but was it all an act? The Enforcers are known murderers. There isn't much Connor would need to hide from the public at this point, let alone her husband, but what would she have to gain by involving herself with T-Day?*

"Come on, Papa! I don't want to miss a minute of the fair!" Pratima called out from the top of the stairs.

Nadir chuckled. "Settle down, Duckling, the fair isn't going anyplace." When he broke the cusp, Pratima had already merged into the masses of Empire City citizens. Nadir fanned himself with his tweed flatcap and scanned the ocean of people nearly overflowing from the platform.

"Look, Papa! The train's coming!" Pratima hopped up and down and pointed to the sleek tubular vessel rounding the bend.

Nadir forced a smile and pressed his way through the crowd, standing his ground for some semblance of a chance to board. The train sighed as it lowered to the platform, and the door opened. Nadir took Pratima by the hand, wedging into the car between a rather buxom woman and a full-grown man waving a "Miss Mercury" pennant.

"All aboard the northbound red line, this train is making express stops at Beecher, Hornview, Clark, Tallman, Enforcer's Square, and Stinson. Next stop, Beecher Street Station. All aboard!" The conductor cried out. The doors slid shut, sealing Nadir in.

**<u>32</u>**

The train hissed into a slow whining standstill. "Last stop, Stinson Street station, everybody leave the train in an orderly manner."

An outpouring of people rushed onto the platform like a burst dam. Pratima tugged on Nadir's hand, "Let's go, Papa! We're going to be late!"

"Slow down, my dear." Nadir chuckled.

Pratima yanked Nadir through the crowd and under a large archway, opening into what looked like a newly discovered village. Futuristic-looking cars and structures sprinkled the fairgrounds with no rhyme or reason. Everything seemed to have a bubble or a glass dome and odd three-ringed antennas jutting every which way.

Nadir scoffed. *Preposterous science-fiction nonsense.* He tried to conceal his disgust from his young, impressionable daughter with a smile to match hers, but this new display was heartbreaking. In 1952 he missed the event, but it changed so drastically in one year to something almost unrecognizable.

Regardless, Pratima pulled him through crowds of gawking people, stopping at each attraction. Nadir eyed a mirror with a ridiculous-looking space suit drawn on in acrylic paint, reflecting his face in the visor of the helmet, and two green men behind it with ray guns. "See what you would look like living on Mars!" it read across the top.

"Ridiculous!" He caught Pratima watching him with her big doe eyes and smiled as he trudged onward. She stopped at a small glass dome with some sort of translucent blue bean in the middle and pressed her face and hands against the glass.

"Ooooh, this is so pretty! What do you think it is, Papa?"

"The bean of tomorrow, or some such nonsense," Nadir muttered.

"What?" Pratima craned her neck back to look at her father.

"Ahem, let's find out together, shall we?" Nadir pressed the red button next to the speaker.

"The pill of tomorrow is also the food of tomorrow!" a narrator yelled with a nauseatingly phony cadence. "Soon, this little miracle pill will replace food on earth as we know it! That's right! Mom's famous meatloaf dad can't get enough of! Or even little Billy's favorite peach cobbler, all available in this wonder pill!

*"Bark!*

"Ha ha! Yeees, Fido, even your dog food—"

Nadir slid his hands into his pockets and excused himself, allowing the children and some of the simpler adults to engulf the display. Despite the phony, cardboard atmosphere, he couldn't help but smile as he watched his daughter soak up all the information. Pratima had always taken after her old man with an unquenchable thirst for knowledge, fictional or otherwise.

He leaned against a light post and adjusted his cap, trying to force his sour mood by the wayside. This fair was supposed to be a chance to bond with his daughter, not a stuffy affair where people discussed things like anodes and flux density.

"Step right up, folks, meet the League of Enforcers, the gen-u-ine article here in the flesh!" A man with a waxed mustache and shifty eyes yelled through the thoroughfare.

Nadir scanned the crowd, eyeing a woman dressed in the same uniform the Scarlet Sparrow wore at V-Site. It looked like a bright red bathing suit with a tactical leather "E" strapped across the front, standing out like a beacon against the sea of people.

Again, Nadir thought of Thompson's words. *The world will burn!*

He moved through a break in the crowd for a closer look. The woman's face was turned away, but she didn't possess the effortless elegance of the real Theodora Connor either.

*An actress, perhaps?*

Nadir looked past her, locking eyes with a freckle-faced woman wearing sunglasses and a sunhat, holding a small child in a matching hat to her chest. Her lips turned up at the corners. Pratima pulled Nadir's hand, demanding his attention. "Hurry, Father! I want to see it all!"

Nadir turned back, but the woman and the child had vanished into the masses. He regarded his daughter and smiled thinly. "Of course, Duckling."

*I must have Theodora Connor on the brain*, he thought.

Pratima yanked Nadir in front of a towering bronze statue of the Powersphere. "Wowwee! Look at that, Papa!" She pressed a button next to a speaker in front of the replica. Nadir peered over his shoulder through the heat lines climbing off the cement, but all the phony Theodora Connors had vanished.

"Developed by Allied Science and the brave heroine, the Scarlet Sparrow, the Empire City Powersphere contains a state-of-the-art reactor that powers all of Empire City. Utilizing the latest nuclear technology first developed during the Second World War, this device powers all of Empire City. Everything from mom's vacuum cleaner to—"

"Did you help build the Powersphere, Papa? You work for Allied Science, right?" Pratima asked.

Nadir sighed and gave up his hunt. "I'm afraid not, my dear. I had a hand in creating the reactor that powers the core during the war, well before Allied Science existed, but this recording is wrong. It was actually a scientist named J. Robert Oppenheimer and"—he paused—"a few others who developed the sphere." He couldn't bring himself to tell his impressionable daughter this modern marvel was mainly Henry Thompson's, the same madman who turned Empire City into scorched earth.

"Well, I'm going to tell the students at school that my papa helped build it."

Nadir smiled, and Pratima dragged him to the next nauseating exhibit.

### 33

Nadir watched folks on the opposite platform funnel out of the northbound train and battle their way into the fairgrounds.

"Southbound Red Line to New Hastings, next stop, Enforcer's Square," the conductor called out. The doors slid closed, and the train came alive with a jolt and a hiss.

"Did you have a good time, Duckling?" Nadir placed a hand on his daughter's back and smiled.

"Oh yes, Papa, I had a wonderful time," Pratima said.

The deco buildings of New Brecon overtook the desolate landscape of Terrytown, and the smooth rumble of the train forced Nadir's heavy eyes shut.

"Father, do you think I could ever be a scientist?"

"My dear, you understand most of those things you saw today were pretend, right?"

She gazed up at him. "I know, Papa. It's all very silly. I just want to do what you do. Do you think I can? I mean, when I'm older?"

Nadir sighed, watching sleek glass buildings whiz by. "Oh, Duckling… It's extremely hard and—" He felt her big, hopeful eyes on him, and a smile crossed his lips." Of course, you can. You can do anything you set your mind to."

The train jerked to a stop at Tallman Street, and faceless masses left the car while others replaced them. Pratima eyed some old gum on the floor and kicked her little white party sandals back and forth. "A boy on the playground told me I can't. He said only boys can be scientists."

Nadir sighed. "What does he know?"

"It was the same boy that Ukrit socked. He *really* knocked his block off, Papa!" She smiled.

Nadir nodded, and his eyes drifted to the window again. The sun reflected off the Ironleaf building in the distance, creating a glass-like ripple effect. It was a beautiful day, even through the glaring pain in his tired eyes. "You can't let closed-minded people dictate who you are. Look past them, little Duckling. Or, rather, look at the inverse. Reach deep down inside for the strength to prove them wrong. Gender has little to do with what's inside your heart. Although some may not be ready for a female scientist in 1953, if you're ready, start now. *Be* a scientist today, my dear, and society will have no choice but to follow you."

Pratima turned on the bench seat and gazed out the window. "Do you have *any* girl scientists at your job, Father?"

"Well, no, but who can say what the future will bring?" Nadir placed a gentle hand on her back.

"What about the Scarlet Sparrow?" she asked.

"She isn't one to be looked up to, darling."

Pratima ran her eyes along the floor.

Nadir wrapped his arm around her. "Maybe you could be the first woman to work at Allied Science. Wouldn't that be something?"

Pratima turned excitedly. "We could work together, Father!"

Nadir forced an empty smile. "Maybe." He turned away from his window and gazed out the far one overlooking Hemsford. "Maybe."

He wanted to tell her what a long, hard road she had ahead of her if this was indeed the life she desired. Thompson had made people afraid of scientists, while the Scarlet Sparrow had rendered them virtually obsolete. Pratima nuzzled against Nadir, and she smiled up at him.

*The heart wants what it wants,* he thought, *but science is, and will always be, a needy bitch of a mistress.*

"Beecher Street, transfer here to the Green Line," the conductor yelled as the train came to a screeching halt. Nadir leaped to his feet, snatched Pratima by the arm, and rushed off the train as the doors closed.

"Papa, what are you doing? This isn't our stop!"

Nadir smiled. "I have a surprise for you."

Pratima jumped up and down, clapping wildly. "Are we going for ice cream? Oh, Papa, this has been the best day ever!"

Nadir winked and took her hand. "Better than ice cream."

**<u>34</u>**

"Wooooowweeee!" Pratima screeched. She stopped short in the middle of the cobblestone patio, shielded her eyes, and followed the golden arches past the statue of Athena to the Powersphere, spinning endlessly amongst the towering skyscrapers. The heart of Empire City, beating as strong as ever.

"The real-life Powersphere!" Pratima looked at her father wide-eyed and gasped. "That means—"

"Yes, my dear." Nadir held out his hand. "What better place to start your career as a scientist than Allied Science?"

Pratima scampered up the steps, pulling Nadir along, and put all her weight into the heavy door. She scurried into the lobby and ran her hands over the intricate designs carved into the golden inlay of Zeus's wall.

"Now, you mustn't tell your mother," Nadir whispered. "She'd have a fit."

She nodded. "I promise, Papa."

"Good girl."

Nadir sauntered to the security station and cleared his throat. Nicholas turned the corner of the *Empire Bulletin* down, folded the page back on itself, and casually glanced up. Nadir smiled wolfishly.

"Doctor Singh!" he belted out. The chair tipped, but Nicholas steadied himself and stood up. He snatched the M1 Garand, leaning, barrel up on the wall. "What brings you here on a Saturday, sir?"

"Hello Nicholas, pay me no mind, old boy. I seem to have forgotten some paperwork in the lab. May I pop down and fetch it? I'll just be a moment."

"Of course, Doctor Singh. I'll call the elevator."

Nadir eyed the gun and smiled. "Please." He tightened his lips and leaned across the desk. "However"—he sighed—"I have my daughter with me."

Nicholas stretched his neck to peer over Nadir's shoulder. "Cute kid. I'm sorry, sir, but I'm afraid she has to wait up here," Nicholas stammered.

Nadir leaned on the desk, glancing casually at Pratima, who was staring up at the wall of Hera across the room. "Of course," he whispered softly enough to force Nicholas to lean across. "Just please keep an eye on her. She's had a tummy ache all day and may have to use the little girls' room. I just pray she doesn't have an accident."

Nicholas traded glances between Nadir and Pratima. "Accident? Alright, alright. Take her with you, Doctor Singh. Please don't tell anyone, huh? I need this job."

Nadir clasped his hands together. "Well, if you insist, Nicholas, we'll just be a moment. Come along, Pratima." His voice bounced around the empty marble room, and Pratima hurried along, giddy as a child on Christmas morning.

Nicholas turned the key and followed the two with wary eyes as Nadir shuffled Pratima into the waiting elevator.

"Hey, kid, try eating some crackers," Nicholas said.

Pratima stared at her father. "What?"

"Won't be but a moment," Nadir said through a cheesy smile. The elevator closed, enveloping the two in complete darkness. Pratima clutched Nadir's shirt until the lights turned on overhead, and the elevator dropped slowly.

"Did you lie to that man, Papa?"

Nadir chuckled. "No, Duckling, I merely stretched the truth."

"Well, it seemed like you lied, and Mother told us never to lie. Ever!"

Nadir crouched and placed a hand on her shoulder. "It was a small lie, but you're right, it was a lie." He looked away thoughtfully. "You must understand that sometimes, the truth can be used as a tool. Just as I'm always telling Ukrit, you must outsmart your adversary. Violence should be an absolute last resort."

She watched him with uncertainty still lingering in her tiny features. "That man was our adversary? I thought he was your friend."

"Yes, well, he is, but"—Nadir sighed—"look, Pratima, sometimes people will try to come between you and your goals, even friends. In this case, your goal of becoming a scientist and my goal to get us both into this elevator were not mutually exclusive. Nicholas didn't want to let either of us advance, so I had to tell him a little white lie." The elevator lurched to a stop. Nadir placed a hand on Pratima's back. "So, we could experience this together."

The doors slid open, and Nadir guided his daughter into the room. She glanced skeptically around the empty desks, scrunching her nose as Nadir threw a switch. The lights illuminated slowly, humming like stubborn old spirits.

"Do you understand, my dear? If you want to be a scientist, this world will be harder on you than it was on me. You must do everything in your power to help yourself."

She nodded. "Yes, Papa—Woooooowwiiiiiieeeee!" Pratima ran toward the Idea Square and pressed her hands on the glass. She looked over the two suspended crafts with the same awe her father felt.

"'Wowwie' indeed, well put, my dear."

The humming lights were the only sound until the questions spilled from Pratima's mouth. "What do those do? Why's that one so dirty? Can we ride in them? What are they? Where did they come from?"

Nadir leaned on a desk and crossed his arms, beaming at his daughter. "This, Pratima, is science at work, and we're trying to find all the answers. That's an excellent start, however. A capital line of questioning. You are hungry for the truth and thirsting for knowledge as all scientists must be."

Pratima turned back to the ships, and her breath spread across the glass in a thin fog. "But what are they, Papa?"

"Well, that's what we're trying to figure out, my dear. We're going to open the one over there. That one that's closed, you see? We just need to figure out how."

Pratima nodded. "What abouuuuut… a crowbar? I once saw a Charlie Chaplin movie at the cinema, where a robber used a crowbar to open a lock."

"Well, I'm afraid it's much too large and tough for that, isn't it?" Nadir said. "But you're thinking, and there are no bad ideas at this stage in our scientific endeavor."

She studied the ship. "Hm. What abouuuuut... a magnet? We're learning all sorts of things about magnets in science class. Did you know you can make a magnet from barro… barromagnetic metal? It means magnetic metals." She beamed up at her father.

"*Ferromagnetic* metals, Duckling. No, I'm afraid that wouldn't work. You see how the metal has a green hue? That means it's copper and not magnetic, and the other half is— Hm." Nadir inched toward the glass. "Hold on, you could be onto something. If the top half of the ship is indeed gadolinium-like, it could have a Curie temperature of around twenty degrees… if we could cool the Idea Square… Yes! There is a refrigeration element that drops the atmosphere inside down to zero. If we cooled it to twenty degrees Celsius, the metal might become ferromagnetic!" Nadir lifted her up, spinning her around. "Oh, you're well on your way to becoming a scientist, my little duckling! Well, on your way!"

Pratima giggled. He set her back on the floor, and an eerie silence made the room feel too big.

"What if there's something bad in there?" Pratima asked.

"There won't be; if there is, we have Nicholas and the boys upstairs to protect us." Nadir smiled but failed to capture any reassurance.

Pratima stared at her father. "You mean the man you lied to?"

### 35

The family had supper together. However, in Nadir's mind, Theodora Connor and her mystery vessel eclipsed conversations of the science fair and some club or something Ukrit had joined with boys from school. Nadir excused himself with a friendly smile and a promise to return soon. He snuck into the bedroom, lifted the phone receiver, and asked an operator to connect him to a number he'd memorized ages ago but never imagined he'd use. The receiver rang once, twice, and a third time.

"Hello?" a tired voice answered.

"We need to open the ship tomorrow."

There was a pause on the other end. "I had a feeling you'd call, Singh. I don't know how, but I knew. I guess my weekend was a little too peaceful up to this point." When Nadir didn't answer, he cleared his throat. "Why tomorrow? Tomorrow's Sunday."

"I cracked it. I know how to open it. I'll call Brown and Wendell to ensure the material can be cooled to the point where it becomes ferromagnetic. We did it when Richards was still working there, testing the durability of elastic, remember? Can you get the fire brigade to send some men?"

"Singh—"

"And someone who can operate a saw?"

"Singh, c'mon—"

"And a few of the guards, but not too many. And we'll need to ensure no one is occupying subbasements two and four tomorrow. Is it possible?"

"Singh, what the hell?"

"You need to trust me, Frank. Can it be done?"

There was another long pause, then a sigh. "I'll do what I can."

Nadir held the phone to his ear until it clicked, then he hung up on his end and smiled.

----

The old wooden Smith's alarm clock on the nightstand openly mocked him. Nadir closed his burning eyes, but sleep wouldn't come. There was a lingering feeling like he'd forgotten something. He threw the blankets to the side and trudged across the dark room with a grunt and a sigh, stretching the nagging kink from his back.

The blankets rose and fell on the bed as Anila dreamed behind him. He pulled drawers out of the small desk in the corner until he found a sheet of paper and an envelope and moved silently to the kitchen.

Nadir flipped the overhead light on and sat at the table. The words he was unable to find earlier poured effortlessly from his pen.

*To my duckling, on her graduation day.*

To Police Captain Thomas Edden,

I, Dr. David T. Wendell, spent extensive time and effort inspecting the item collected by Allied Science and your officers on October 15th from South Avenue in Brookfield. Under the supervision of Dr. Nadir Singh and Lt. Frank Rivoli, I ran tests and recorded my findings in layman's terms.

A swab under the mesh barrier in the aperture revealed what I initially surmised to be aluminum oxide particles. Upon further inspection, I found the particles do not react like aluminum oxide. For example, aluminum is paramagnetic, whereas this material was unaffected by magnets. It also has a very high thermal conductivity, which is not uncommon for aluminum; however, this material's thermal conductivity was far higher. This leads me to believe this material is unknown; as I can discern, there is no substance like it on earth. However, it seems to be harmless.

Further analysis proved that although this has the crystalline properties of aluminum oxide, it is almost as if it is trying to mimic the chemical compound. Perhaps the subatomic structure was altered to create a new element. We will continue to run tests and keep your department updated.

 Sincerely,

David T. Wendell

Empire City

October 17, 1953

SINS
OF AN
IGNORANT PAST

## 36

Cal cracked an egg, adding it to the dozen already spread across the sizzling grill, and peered through the service window. "Any orders yet, Wilbur?"

Color died at the front door, and darkness flooded the dining room, shifting in the deep crevices where shadows lingered. Wilbur stood frozen behind the counter, gray and lifeless—like stone—with a half-crazed smile.

The kitchen door pushed open and rocked back and forth until it stopped mid-swing and slowly settled closed. A small child with big, happy eyes watched Cal. "I'm seven, you know?"

Cal smiled and cracked another egg. "You're getting big. Do you want some breakfast?"

"I can't eat that," the boy responded, "it's rotten."

Cal regarded the stove. Legions of maggots crawled across the eggs, and the stench of corruption overtook the billowing smoke. Blood ran from the yolks, and half-formed chicken embryos, leaking pus, screeched as they fried alive on the grill. Cal cracked another egg.

"What has to be broken before it can be used?" the boy asked.

Cal smiled. "That's an easy one, an egg." He turned around, and the boy was gone.

*Thunk-thunk, thunk-thunk, thunk-thunk.* The free-swinging door rocked back and forth until it almost tore off its hinges, stopped mid-swing, and closed with a slow, creaky whine.

Cal left the grill and smiled, pushing through the door into the dining room. "Do you want to play?"

Thunder shook the restaurant's foundation, and the sky turned overcast gray through the window, threatening to dump at any second.

Cal scanned the dark dining room. Broken tables and bench seats spread forever in two directions like infinite reflections in a mirror. "Do you have any more riddles for me?" He peered under the booths, one at a time, scanning the inky black for movement.

Laughter echoed, and the boy's voice overlapped itself with riddle after riddle:

"What is always in front of you but can't be seen?"

"I've been around for millions of years, but I'm never more than a month old. What am I?"

"The more that there is of me, the less you see. What am I?"

Cal smirked, peering over the laminate countertop into the darkness. He glanced up into Wilbur's dead, milky-white eyes. "Wilbur, have you seen him?"

The old man stood frozen, staring blankly out of the front window.

"Sorry, Cal. I can't play anymore."

Cal whirled around. A giant pale hand with long bony fingers and knobby knuckles, like exposed roots, rested on the dejected boy's shoulder. The owner of the arm stood around eleven feet tall. Its emaciated face peered out from a curtain of greasy hair. Egg-shaped eyes locked on Cal while its nostrils greedily sucked in air from a fleshy mound above a wide, beak-like smile. Dead, white skin stretched over the skeletal frame.

*Bam! Bam!* Its long staff called the room to order.

Disregarding the creature, Cal crouched to meet the child's eye line. "But you just got here, Jerry."

Outside, hundreds of people gathered in a mass of exposed pink flesh, watching from behind masks of broad, toothy smiles and little china doll faces with puckered black lips.

Cal held the boy's hand. "Stay a little longer, please, Jerry?"

Jerry looked away. "I can't stay, Cal. I'm dead, remember? But you can come see me. Master Leonard can help you. Master Leonard bound me to this one, remember? Now I'm his." He eyed the creature affectionately. "You abandoned yours, but it's not too late for forgiveness. Marchosias will help you again if you let it." He regarded his captor. "Say this one's name, won't you?"

*Bam! Bam!* It bounced its crooked staff on the floor twice.

Cal tightened his lips. "I won't."

"Say its name."

*Bam! Bam!*

"I refuse."

"Ronove!" Wilbur shouted. He slowly pulled the front door open, and grim silence overtook the laughter. The still air froze, and a woman strutted into the diner, her black hair spilling out from behind a puckered doll mask. Lily Larkin. She nodded to the tall, spindly thing holding Cal's brother in its gnarled grip.

Jerry turned from Cal, and his hand slipped away. "Now, Ronove is her gift."

*Bam! Bam!* Ronove bounced its staff and touched the woman's covered face with its massive thumb as it growled. "Meus es."

The diner rumbled, and the ground split. Ronove turned to Cal, and its black pupils dilated over the field of yellow sclera.

Jerry looked up. "Remember how we tied ourselves to them? Remember the deer?"

Lily's icy hand grasped Cal's arm, and antlers erupted from the sides of her head.

Jerry was a man now. He smiled his bloody smile. "He comes to bedsides, icy bridges, battlefronts, and crumbling ridges. When he comes, he comes alone, taps a shoulder, then he's gone."

*Bam! Bam!*

### 37

Cal's eyes fluttered open, but the smell of breakfast followed him from his dream.

"Morning, Bucko. I hope you like your eggs runny."

He shot up to a seated position on the couch and gasped. Theo stood at the edge of the kitchen, holding a blue ceramic plate like a wife in a Norman Rockwell painting, right down to her ruby-red lipstick, soft bob, polka dot summer dress, and golf ball-sized wedding ring.

Cal snatched his newly mended shirt from the coffee table and pulled it over his head. "What time is it?"

"Quarter past six." Theo's eyes met his, and he saw the poorly hidden worry tucked neatly on the edge of her phony housewife persona.

Daybreak poured across the living room, bringing the chandelier to life. Cal watched the sun through the floor-to-ceiling window, kissing the sky beyond the uneven horizon and painting an orange canvas with wisps of bluish-white clouds.

He planted his bare feet on the ground and waited for pain that never arrived. There wasn't a scratch on him; even his trousers had mended on his body as if last night's battle had never happened.

Theo set the plate on the breakfast bar. "You should eat up, Calvin. We have a busy day."

Cal plodded toward her like a dog who didn't entirely trust the hand feeding him. He sat but couldn't help feeling like this was his last good meal before being taken behind the barn to end it all. "Aren't you eating?" He unfurled a silk napkin across his lap.

"Not right now," she said with a perfunctory smile as she rested her hands on her hips.

Cal hunched over the plate. Eggs, bacon, sausage, wheat toast with butter, and strawberry jam. Even freshly squeezed orange juice.

*Why?* That word haunted him. Regardless, Cal dug in.

Theo sat across from him, bouncing her knee and scanning the *Empire Bulletin*. "It doesn't look like our scuffle made the paper."

Cal shoveled a forkful of eggs into his mouth. "That's good, right?"

Theo sighed. "I don't know. We can't wait around for that thing to make a move. If it builds anything from the blueprints it stole from me, it could—" She pinched the bridge of her nose. "This is all I need right now."

Cal sipped his orange juice.

Theo's eyes darted between his plate and the clock above the stove. "We have to go to the Hall of Enforcers. I can't have our friend from last night stealing any more of my designs, and if it took Bonnie, well—" She grabbed Cal's plate as he took his last bite of bacon. "Finished?"

"I guess so," he responded.

Theo floated across the kitchen and dumped the plate into the sink. She leaned on the counter and sighed.

----

The elevator doors slid open, and gasoline-scented darkness rode the cool air into the elevator. Theo stepped daintily into the garage. "Figured we'd ride in style, Bucko," she said. Lights turned on consecutively overhead, revealing cars, motorcycles, and even a disassembled M4 Sherman tank lined up along the wall. An engine turned over at the end of the corridor, and headlights beamed. The sleek body of a Rolls-Royce cut through the darkness and stopped short in front of Cal. Theo popped open the door, motioning for him to enter. He shot her one last discerning look and slid inside.

Cal scanned the front seat, expecting an uncomfortable look from whatever snooty driver the Connors employed, but it was empty. The lush, ornate wood interior looked like it belonged in someone's study, and futuristic metal knobs and switches ran across the dash. A small television set housed in a sleek oak frame sat between the driver and passenger seat.

Theo scooted in next to him and slammed the door. She adjusted her dress and smiled. "That's more like it."

The Rolls jolted forward, weaving through the cavernous underground tunnel, gaining speed toward a sliver of natural light that grew until daylight bled in, engulfing them. The car thumped onto Wexford Street, weaving in and out of traffic.

"Theo, who's driving?" Cal stared at the road ahead wide-eyed.

Theo gazed out the window passively. "The car's driving itself, Cal. When I rebuilt Empire, I relayed the street grid through my global positioning satellite into all my vehicles. It's safe, Bucko, trust me."

Cal grunted and gripped the plush, black leather. "So why did you take the bus to Wilbur's? It doesn't seem like you have any shortage of transportation."

Theo sighed. " I like to be anonymous sometimes. I like to be out amongst the people. Believe it or not, being Theodora Connor can get rather lonely." She eyed a woman pushing a baby carriage down the sidewalk and turned the charm of her necklace over. For a moment, her smile almost made her look human.

"That's a nice necklace, Theo," Cal said.

She turned, lifted her shoulder, and scrunched her nose. "Aw, thanks, Cal. It was my mother's. She passed away, wow, three years ago. Sometimes, it seems like just yesterday, though. I haven't taken it off since."

Cal nodded. "I lost my mother, too, when I was a young man. I suppose that's why Jerry and I were so close."

Theo's eyes sparkled. "Mother always wanted me to be an actress, like she was, but then the war, and T-Day, and"—a sad smile crossed her lips—"well, you know… life.

"Mother was a vaudevillian, one of the greatest Empire City had ever seen." Theo inched across the bench seat toward Cal excitedly. "She started the Uptown Clowns. I was part of the act before they were on television. I was just a girl, but oh, what fun it was!" She looked away, but the nostalgic smile remained. "After we became—you know—I abandoned my dreams, and my mother and I never had another pleasant conversation. I guess saving the world wasn't as important as my acting career." She watched the streets of Empire speed by over Cal's shoulder, and her smile faded. "Heck, I've wanted to act since I was a little girl." She glanced back to Cal. "What's the point of having a world left to live in if you aren't really living?" Her voice grew softer. "I would have been great."

*Old ghosts,* Cal thought.

"Listen to me carrying on, but reminiscing about my mother makes me happy. Even if we ended on bad terms, I still love her. I still look up to her. I still hope I end up being half the mother she was." Theo gazed out the window again. "I would have been great."

The Rolls stopped abruptly halfway down Ives Avenue and backed itself into an open spot on the street. The back door popped open.

"Here we are," Theo said. She sprung out of the car, donning the same pair of white cat-eye sunglasses she'd been wearing at Wilbur's. Although her dreams never came true, she still carried herself like an actress, sent from Hollywood to play a disheartened mother. Cal climbed out behind her and glanced around uneasily.

The Hall of Enforcers was an unimpressive white, three-story structure pushed deep into the back of Enforcer's Square. Buildings shot up on the outskirts, dwarfing the short row of evergreens leading up the walkway toward a reflecting pool.

Cal ran his fingers over the sunken letters of the names of those lost on T-Day carved into the lip of the pool and surrounding benches. Some of these people still lay beneath the city or turned to ash when the bombs went off, and the automatons roamed the streets. He watched the fountain climb from the center in an infinite loop. This wasn't the Enforcer's base, he realized. It was a humble reminder of Empire's strength—a testament to the power of the human spirit in the face of annihilation.

Theo placed a hand on Cal's shoulder. "Jerry's name is carved over there. I made sure—"

Cal brushed her off and walked toward the Hall. "We don't have time for that."

The sound of rushing water faded with his sentiment as he climbed the concrete steps. Statues of Ares and Artemis watched over the square from under the roof gable. "Onward and Upward" was carved amongst the ivy vines behind them. Thick pillars supporting the roof spread as far as the eye could see in each direction.

Theo plodded up the steps behind Cal, pulled him behind one of the columns, and pressed her hand against the marble. She shot him a tired smile as a ray of blue light scanned her palm, and the pillar spun open with a sigh of cool, stale air. She pulled Cal into the pitch-black, and the door slid shut.

## 38

The room exhaled, the floor descended, and the lights flickered to life around the glass cylinder that Cal hadn't even realized they were standing in. It dropped slowly into a cavernous room of platforms adjoined by paths and staircases, stretching for miles into the darkness like a lost city.

The elevator jolted to a stop, and the platform spun toward an opening in the glass. Theo stepped out onto the concrete floor. "Make yourself at home, Bucko, the maid's on vacation." Lights illuminated overhead as she marched down an aisle of glass cases containing mannequins clad in various uniforms and alien-looking weapons. She stopped in front of an empty tube and sighed. "Damnit, James." Her eyes flashed at Cal. "He's always moving things, can't leave well enough alone."

Cal glanced at the plaque. "Who is the Shadow Butcher?"

Theo chuckled. "You mean you don't listen to the radio show, Calvin?" She regarded the glass thoughtfully. "He was pretty scary. When we found him, he was using a flamethrower to burn people alive in the financial district. I have no idea why the *Bulletin* named him that." She shot Cal a humorless glance. "Believe me when I tell you, he didn't have a cute catchphrase and definitely wasn't going to tie us up until next week's thrilling conclusion. He was out for blood. All these people were. That's why we put 'em d—"

"Let's get what you need and get out of here," Cal sneered.

Theo nodded. "Fine by me. I don't like being here anymore than you do."

Cal scanned each display thoughtlessly: The Dark Plunderer, The Anti-Angel... Mostly, the uniforms looked like regular clothes sewn together as a hodgepodge imagined in a fever dream. Some even looked like a child had made them.

The reflection in the empty Shadow Butcher display caught his attention; he didn't want it to, but it did. Cal turned slowly toward an old army uniform hanging proudly in front of a tattered American flag. He didn't have to read the plaque; the bullet holes across the olive-drab cotton said enough. He could still hear the Japanese Type 96 machine gun firing in his head, and he recognized the uniform his brother died in from his nightmares.

Theo timidly placed a hand on his shoulder. "It was Jerry's—"

"I know it was Jerry's!" Cal shrugged her off. "What the hell is it doing here? They never recovered his body after he—How did you get this?"

Theodora's eyes welled. "Cal, I'm sorry I should have told you." She wrapped her arms around herself and looked away. "I'd give anything to trade places—"

"You never should have involved us in the first place!" Cal turned to face her. "There's a special kind of Hell waiting for you!"

"I'm sorry!" Theo lunged forward suddenly, clawing at Cal's chest and sucking in air between bursts of hysterical tears, but he didn't move to catch her. "Cal, I'm so scared. Lately, I've been reliving that night that changed us, but I can't remember—"

"I know," Cal grumbled, wrapping his arms around her. They stood huddled together in the dank basement before the uniform Cal's brother died in.

Theo glanced up, shuddering. Mascara ran down her soft, freckled face. She seemed small, like a little girl herself, certainly not the same woman who once called herself the Scarlet Sparrow. "The visions are back, and those—"

A shrill beeping noise pierced the moment, and Theo pushed off Cal's chest. She sprinted around a metal workbench, past a row of whirring machines and gadgets, and fell into an oversized, throne-like chair in front of a giant screen. Her fingers danced across some sort of flat typewriter. Wheels spun, tape whirled, and twisted inside a blinking wall of lights.

"Someone's tripped the perimeter alarm, but there's no one there." She turned in her chair and smiled up at Cal. "Must be some tourist wandering too close to the entrance, is all." She spun back around. "But now that I'm here, I might as well—" She scanned the green symbols on the black screen. "It doesn't look like any of my blueprints are missing from this database, but someone's stolen one of my ships. The CCTV is missing thirty-one seconds of footage as if someone had magnetized the tape. I'm willing to bet it's the ol' tinman we went ten rounds with last night."

"You don't seem worried," Cal said.

She smiled. "The fact it has my ship will make it easier to track." She clicked away on the keyboard again. "It's still on the move now, but It'll be easier to get the drop on whoever took it once it lands. Unfortunately, that means we have to wait." She kicked her feet up on the console and smiled. "Up for some Gin Rummy?"

"Not much of a card player, I'm afraid." Cal scanned Jerry's uniform pressed behind the glass like a trophy. Theo was all smiles again. It was becoming more difficult to tell which was the real woman and which was the mask.

She stood and looked up at Cal with her big, brown eyes, her fingers twisted and turned the charm of her necklace. "You ever think about leaving Empire, Cal? For good? Just picking up and going someplace where nobody knows your name? It's kind of a romantic thought, don't you agree?"

Cal trudged toward the tube housing all that remained of Jerry Smith. "Nobody knows who I am here." He pressed his hand against the glass. "Why would I need to leave?"

"Cal, I didn't mean—"

"I have to know, why were we chosen?" Cal's eyes followed the polished brass buttons down Jerry's uniform. "There were plenty of people at the ceremony who wanted what those things gave us. Why Jerry an' me? We weren't guests. We were just there to cook."

# The City of the Gods: Gold

Cal leaned his head against the glass. "Why us?" Tears he'd been holding back for ten years burned, threatening to fall, but he wouldn't give Theo the satisfaction.

She dipped her chin away, but her eyes stayed locked on his reflection. "You think I wanted this? I was only nineteen. I adored James. Back then, I would have followed him to the ends of the earth if he'd asked." She smiled ruefully and gazed into the distance. "When he told me about the party, I was expecting the usual beer, games, and songs from his fraternity days. He bought me a little black dress, 'something to make the other fellas jealous,' he said, and I felt like a princess when he told me the party would be in the Ironleaf building. Suddenly, it was larger than life, so I hired you to cater it because—well—I'd heard through my mother's nurse you and Jerry were the best. When Ron returned from Mexico with that woman and that *girl*, I certainly didn't know about his plans. Honestly, I thought the whole affair was a chance to get dressed up with James and see what it was like to be the prettiest girl in the room, like a movie star." She smiled.

"Didn't you find it odd that Ron had private security?" Cal asked. "Or that everyone was wearing masks?"

Theo shook her head. "Cal, how could I have possibly known this would happen? I hate this goddamn life. This thing is eating me from the inside. I can feel it each time I build something. I want it to end so badly. When I rebuilt the city, it was to be the Scarlet Sparrow's tombstone. That didn't work. The urge is too powerful. So, I decided once I find my daughter—well—you'll never hear the name Theodora Connor again."

"No, you don't get off that easy," Cal yelled. "This curse may have stabbed my brother in the back, but you twisted the knife when you took us to Japan."

Theo pressed a finger into Cal's chest. "You obviously didn't know your brother, Cal. Invading Japan was his idea. I told him about the horrors of the atomic bomb, and he understood." She paused. "The reason he's dead—the *real* reason—is because he snuck his last power-magazine into my armor-harness when the Japs had us pinned down in Honshu. Mine was empty. He gave his life for me."

Cal lurched forward. "Bullshit!"

"He did, Cal. And not a day goes by where I don't think about it. Jerry Smith, your brother, sacrificed his life for mine."

"No, he wouldn't—" But Cal knew she was right. Jerry had always been the type to offer the shirt off his back to anyone in need, and they didn't even need to say please.

"Cal, your brother was my—"

"I don't want to hear it." Cal refused to dishonor Jerry's memory by thinking of him as a homewrecker. The beeps and clicks of various machines made the silence more palatable. Still, Cal couldn't stand it. He took a breath and met Theo's gaze. "We need to focus on finding Bonnie. Who would want to hurt you?" He regarded the museum of uniforms. "Who's still alive?"

"I don't know, Cal, honestly." Theo sighed.

"Maybe it's not anyone you suspect," Cal suggested. "Could it be Ron or that Mexican woman? Carmella?"

Theo's eyes widened. "Carmella? Oh god, Cal. I remember now—those girls. I watched... *We* watched them suffer. I never wanted this! I was supposed to be an actor. I-I-I didn't know this would happen!" Theo collapsed onto the floor and stared up at nothing, half-crazed. "That little girl, she killed—dressed them up like animals—antlers."

Cal saw it, shifting in the shadows, watching him. Memories manifested as apparitions, antlers fastened to a human face, burning eyes, refusing to relent. *Death will be my wedding, children, and glory.*

"That girl," Theo stammered. "That child, Rosalita, she's not human! She took my— Oh god, please forgive me." She stood and opened a rusty metal drawer in the workbench, shoving a shaky hand into it.

Cal inched forward. "Theo?"

Her hand rose from the drawer clutching a Smith and Wesson revolver. Her chest rose and fell quickly, and her eyes widened.

Cal froze. "Theo? What are you—"

She jammed the barrel against the side of her head. Her eyelids dropped. She grimaced, squeaking out one final sound.

"No!" Cal reached for the gun.

The pistol clicked. Theo blinked twice and dropped the revolver to her side, dazed and catatonic. She let the gun tumble from her grasp and blinked again.

Cal snatched the gun and popped open the cylinder. It was empty. He tucked it carefully into the back of his trousers.

"Cal, I"—something was missing from Theo's once lively eyes as she watched the far wall—"I almost—"

He lifted her up to her feet, but she pushed him away. "It hurts so much, Cal! Oh, god. It hurts! I wish I were dead!" She sobbed, fighting to pull in a breath against her building panic.

A sharp zip tore the bodice of her dress from her shoulders. She ripped the fabric from her hips in two swift pulls and tossed it to the floor. Her empty, wild eyes watched him through smudged mascara, half-crazed. Her chest heaved in and out until each of her exhaled breaths sounded like a low growl.

Cal gathered her discarded garment from the floor and pressed it to her chest. "Theo? What are you—"

"It's all I'm good for, right?" She pushed him away, reached behind her back, and unsnapped her bra. "Just good for a fuck! First, James, then Ron, then Jerry, now you!" She skulked around Cal in a slow circle, taunting him with a sick smile as she kicked off her undergarments. "Come fuck me, come on, big man!"

Cal followed her with his eyes until the shadows shifted behind her. Something rose fluidly against the wall cloaked in black, so dark, Cal's eyes burned. The outline of a thick shock of hair burst outward, and two shiny reflective eyes watched Cal silently. He'd seen it before.

"C'mon, you sissy, fuck me!" Theo snarled.

Cal pressed the torn garment to Theo's chest again. "Stop this." It seemed like a stupid thing to say, but he was out of ideas. He wrapped his arms around her and pulled her close. She kicked and struggled, but he held on. When he lifted his eyes, the shadow was gone.

"For the good of Empire! That's what they told me! We did this ritual for the good of Empire! Jerry died for the good of Empire! One day, I'll—for the good of—" Theo fell into a sobbing fit and pressed herself against Cal. He released her, and she tumbled to the floor. "My child—she didn't even get to have a life."

Theo pulled her knees to her chest and snorted. "I just wanted to feel something, Cal. Something other than this numbness." She gazed up at him through slitted, ugly, swollen eyes, and a bit of spittle dripped from her mouth.

Cal yanked an old sheet from a nearby table and shook it out with a dusty snap. He wrapped it around her shoulders.

Theo touched his face softly. "Please, Cal. I just want to feel something." She forced a smile.

Cal sighed. "This isn't doing us any good, Theo. Bonnie is still out there. You need to pull yourself together."

She smiled. "Theo's gone, and I don't know if she's coming back this time." She threw her head back and howled: "Oh my god, my baby!"

Cal yanked open an old rusty folding chair, leaning on the workbench, and took a seat.

Theo rested her head on her knees and moaned. "Do you want to know a secret?" she croaked. "I'm not afraid to die, but I'm afraid of whatever is inside me. It's closer than ever. Sabnock."

Cal's eyes grew heavy, and the room turned dark.

"There's one inside you, too, but you're broken. I want to be broken, too. The end is close. That's where we'll be together."

A growl sounded, stuttering at the end.

**<u>39</u>**

The grill sizzled, and the man in the kitchen jabbed his forehead. "You want to do anything right," he said, "you start up here." He had kind eyes and a familiar face. "People say it's women's work, but make no mistake, Calvin, this hot stove doesn't care a lickspittle about what's down between your legs. Boy or girl, it'll break you if you let it, but it can also make you. Work hard, and maybe one day, you'll be the man in the kitchen. For now, eat up." He pushed a plate of writhing crickets across the table.

`"I don't want that!" the boy responded.

A swift jerking motion tore Cal from a sound sleep. He sat up on the old, rusty folding chair and rubbed his stiff neck. The wall of lights whirred and beeped in front of him. He shot to his feet, wide-eyed. "Theo?" He scanned the empty room and reached into his trousers for the gun, but it was gone.

"Cal?" Theo touched his shoulder and smiled. "You nodded off for a bit there. Do you feel better?" She was wearing the same form-fitting black leotard from last night. "The ship finally landed." She pointed at the screen. Analytics trumped her emotions for now, or had her mental breakdown even happened? The horrifying world Cal's dreams inhabited seemed to be bleeding into his consciousness.

"I thought you"—he chuckled—"never mind. Where did it land?"

The overhead lights died, and the screen powered down. Cal froze in the stillness of the pitch-black room. Behind them, a generator came to life. Red emergency lights flooded the room with an unnatural, hellish glow. The computer flickered on, and a solitary green hashmark blinked in the center of the screen.

"This is impossible!" Theo took her seat and anxiously clicked away on the keys. "I'm locked out of the security system." She pressed a combination of buttons and slammed her fist onto the console, but the screen remained frozen. "This is my tech!"

Theo spun out of the chair and ripped a panel off the giant metallic wall, revealing a miniature city of turning wheels and blinking lights. She jerked a few wires loose and looked over the small labels taped to each. "I don't understand. Everything is working."

A bright yellow light cut through the dim, red room behind them. Theo and Cal whirled around, each lifting a hand to block the blinding glare.

"You shouldn't be here, Calvin," a deep, distorted voice called from the shadows.

Cal shifted his hand, but the person's shape was too obscured to determine whether it was a man or a woman. "Who's there?" he asked.

Theo ducked and slunk along the edge of the workbench. Slowly and silently, she slid open the metal drawer and removed the revolver that Cal thought he'd tucked in his pants.

"I'm a friend," the distorted voice said, "to both of you. I'm here to tell you Bonnie is safe. You need to trust me, but Calvin, you can't be a part of this. You need to leave."

# The City of the Gods: Gold

Theo looked over the gun and prowled around the table, disappearing entirely into the darkness.

Cal squinted. "If you are a friend, you'll have no problem showing yourself."

"I can't do that, Cal. I'm sorry. You need to trust me. You aren't safe here."

Cal chuckled. He was tired of mysterious things lurking in the shadows. At least whatever attacked them last night had the common courtesy of throwing punches outright. "Is that a threat?" he asked." I thought you were a friend, or did you change your mind?"

Theo rose and aimed the pistol. "Where's my daughter?"

"She's safe, Theodora. Calvin, go, please." It was a desperate command but not a threat.

"Theo, wait!" Call yelled.

*Bang!* The gun rang out. The bullet froze inches from the intruder, and orange light rippled outward, flashing off the wide circular glass eyes of an old gas mask, hiding the stranger's identity. A familiar crazed look crossed Theo's face, and she emptied the rest of the chambers until the gun clicked.

"You'll see your daughter again soon, Theodora. When this is all over, you'll be together. I'll make sure of it," the voice responded somberly.

"You're not the Shadow Butcher," Theo said. "I saw him die. Who are you?"

Cal leaped over the old metal workbench and sprinted toward the mysterious person. The invisible barrier pushed back, and the orange light burned across his body. His clothes were shredded, and he could smell burning meat. His horrific reflection stared back from the dark eyes of the black mask, bubbling flesh searing over his frame.

A ball of light exploded behind the stranger, illuminating the room. "Go home, Calvin, please. Stay out of this. Theodora cannot be trusted."

The abyss of unconsciousness called out. "Wait," Cal said. "Tell me where Bonnie is, and I'll go!" He shuddered the words through the searing pain. His eyes rolled back in his head, and darkness fell.

"Don't trust Dea. Don't trust the girl. The old man has the answers. Bonnie is not Theo's firstborn."

"What? Who are you?"

"What can be big or small? Anywhere in the world, near or far? It can stay the same or change over time. It's different for everyone, but everyone has one."

"Jerry?"

"Everything you've seen has been real. Get away from her. She *will* kill you. She is poison. Dea is poison." The voice gave way to the yawning void of oblivion.

**<u>40</u>**

"You're not using your noggin, son," the familiar man in the kitchen with kind eyes said. "You need to think, or else you're going to burn the whole block down." He pushed a stack of old books forward. "Here, read these before you kill us all." He chuckled.

The boy scanned the books' spines: *Serve It Forth, Consider the Oyster, How to Cook a Wolf, The Gastronomical Me.*

"All of these, Wilbur?" he whined.

"Every word. If you want to do anything, you have to start at the beginning." Wilbur smiled. "Now eat up, Calvin."

The crickets exploded off the plate in a frenzy of chirps and crawled down his throat.

Cal's eyes fluttered open to the blinding overhead lights and deep, heart-wrenching sobs. Cal sat up, waiting to feel every inch of the blinding pain he'd earned by foolishly running headfirst into that orange shield. It never came. His clothes were pristine, and he didn't have a scratch to show for his foolhardy escapade.

Across the room, Theo's slight shoulders bounced with every sob. Beside her, the empty pistol lay shunned on the floor. "They have my baby, Cal!"

Cal staggered to his feet and waved a hand to test for any remnants of the wall of light. The cement floor was singed and faded where the shield had been.

*What can be big or small? Anywhere in the world, near or far. Can stay the same or change over time? It's different for everyone, but everyone has one.*

Cal closed his eyes. "Home," he whispered. Jerry had told him that one when their mom died. He regarded Theo. "Who do you think that was?"

She squinted up through swollen red eyes. "It was The Shadow Butcher's uniform, the one missing from the display." She inhaled and shuttered. "But it wasn't Leland Thorp, I watched him die."

"And the"—Cal struggled to find words—"wall of light? Who do you know who can do that?"

"Me," Theo said.

"You?"

"That was my tech. Those were my weapons, my shield generator. I'd know it anywhere. That son-of-a-bitch took everything from me." She stood abruptly and stomped to the workstation. "I bet whoever that was is also responsible for that creature attacking us. And if they have that tech, I'm sure they have more." She slumped into the chair.

Cal approached hesitantly. "Whoever it was knew both of our names. Who would know me? I'm nobody in your world." He eyed Theo in the monitor's reflection. Her hands floated across the keyboard.

"It's Thompson. I'm sure of it now," Theo said.

"Even if he was alive, how would Thompson know me, Theo? It doesn't fit."

"He has my ship, and he's in *my* workshop. He must be. This has Doctor Torment written all over it, Cal. Don't you see?"

Cal eyed the blinking green hashmark on the monitor. "Isn't this your workshop?"

"Calvin, do you really think I would leave all my dangerous weapons and blueprints lying around here? My real workshop is on the moon."

Cal's eyes widened. "The mo—"

"—Bonnie—has her." The computer interrupted.

"Shh!" Theo hunched over the console and went to work, adjusting knobs and flipping switches. She pressed a button, and the message reversed, played again, and reversed once more. Cal leaned in to pick the words out of the shoddy reception.

A woman's voice poured through the speakers: "—found Bonnie—DiLilo family has—come quick."

"It's Lily Larkin," Theo said. The rest of the message was a garbled mish-mash of static, but it seemed that was all Theo needed to go to war.

Ron Baxter's Journal

October 13, 1944

Last night, I awoke to Rosalita standing over my bed, reciting the same four phrases in Latin and striking me with a switch:

Eligos, the death merchant

Sabnock, the builder

Roanove, the messenger

Marchosias, the armored

I believe these are the beings Master Leonard plans to call forth. After showing Carmella the wounds Rosalita inflicted, she told me she worries her daughter is lost and has suggested, with a heavy heart, that we end her life before she spirals completely out of control and kills us. I have another plan, however. I will acquire the power of one of Master Leonard's followers and contain the creature within Rosalita. I will hold another ceremony. I will obtain the power of a god.

A
USEFUL
SERVANT
A
DANGEROUS
MASTER

## 41

Ash grew long on the cigarette pressed between Gibson's lips as he hunted and pecked the typewriter keys, filling the empty ninety-third precinct with the clatter of clicks and dings. Each word of the report fed his guilt. A girl had killed herself on his watch, and last night, the haunting image of eyes wrenched from their sockets wouldn't allow him to sleep. Reality seemed to be the only escape, and keeping busy sustained reality.

He'd pored over Ron Baxter's stolen journal into the wee hours of the morning. *Dea and Master Leonard.* Those words had been repeated ad nauseam in the mad writings and now stood firmly in Gibson's thoughts. Their identity, however, was hidden within illegible Latin, containing no clues as to the whereabouts of Bonnie Connor.

Gibson stretched and yawned, settling in for a long morning of paperwork. *The glamorous life of a detective,* he thought. *One day, you're rubbing elbows with the Scarlet Sparrow; the next, you're chained to a desk. Not that there's anyone at home missing me.* He leaned back in his chair, scanning the other desks in the bullpen, littered with photos of cop's families.

Detective Carl Anderson and his son, holding up a prize bass by the gills, smiling from the bow of a brand new Richline boat. Detective Ralph Jasper presented his children with a Lionel train set on Christmas morning, wearing a ridiculous conductor's hat. And, of course, Detective Jack Briggs with his arm around his beautiful wife in front of his brand-new Chrysler Imperial. The influx of money was so apparent Gibson couldn't believe how blind he'd been. They were all dirty, their perfect lives paid for with cash from Baxter's pocket.

Gibson mashed his cigarette in an ashtray that said, "Visit Broadshall," over an illustration of a woman in a striped swimsuit and an oversized sun hat relaxing on a beach. It sat alone in the corner of his army green desk, mirroring his personal life, empty but clean.

"Gibson?" a voice called out.

He jumped and turned.

"What the hell are you doing here on a Saturday? Sucking up to Murphy won't get you anywhere, believe me." Creed smiled from the doorway.

Gibson went limp in his chair and laughed. "Creed? You ol' so-and-so, what the hell are *you* doing here? Scared me half to death."

Creed strolled up the aisle of desks on his short gorilla legs, carrying two steaming paper cups with that familiar smile resigned to his lips. The smell of bad coffee and Old Spice aftershave brought Gibson back to his salad days.

"You look like you could use some coffee, pal," Creed said. "All the way from Temples, your favorite stop on our beat before you left me high and dry." He surrendered one of the steaming cups.

"Thanks, Creed. Boy, you're a sight for sore eyes." Gibson set the coffee down on his desk. "Say, how'd you know I was here anyway?"

Creed laughed. "Man alive, making detective sure has made you paranoid. I'm a cop," he said, "catching up to low lives like you is what I do, or have you forgotten?" Creed's little mouth was always raised at the corners like he knew something no one else did. He turned to grab a chair from a nearby desk, and the metallic hint of a gun gleamed where his trousers and shirt separated.

"You packin' in civvies?" Gibson brought the paper cup to his lips. "Now, who's paranoid?"

Creed pulled the piece and set it on the desk. "Just my .45. You can never be too careful in Empire, now that the heroes are gone." He smiled and took a seat opposite Gibson. "How you holdin' up, pal? Paperwork on Saturday? That Slim Shanahan's a real slave driver, huh? Remember, there's only one 't' in fatass and one 'b' in slob." He slapped his nonexistent belly to mock the old man, but his anxious demeanor ruined the delivery. Creed had always been one of the funniest guys in the ECPD, but today, he was off.

"How do you know Slim?" Gibson asked.

"Just what I heard; I hear a lot of stuff from my new partner." Creed dropped his eyes to the gun on the desk.

Gibson smirked. "Who'd they pair you with, some rookie?"

"Nah." Creed sipped his coffee, and the silence continued where Gibson expected an explanation.

Gibson slapped Creed's shoulder across the desk. "Well, it's good to see you, pal. How's our ol' beat treating you? Did you ever get the number of that waitress from Hullers? I remember she had those pegs you used to go crazy f—"

"Shame what happened to that Jap girl." Creed's ever-present smile faded.

Gibson tried to hide his shock behind a stern gaze. "Where'd you hear about that?"

"Like I told ya, I hear a lot of things from my new partner," Creed said.

Gibson forced a smile. "I'm sorry, Creed, I was just stepping out. We'll have to catch up soon." He snatched his hat and pushed against the desk, but Creed put his hand on Gibson's shoulder, forcing him back into his chair.

"Before you go"—Creed glanced at the ceiling—"I have a little proposition for you, pal. How'd you like to make some extra lettuce?" His mouth curled into a smile.

"And how would I do that?" Gibson asked.

"It's kinda like... private security detail, off the books, of course. A lot of the boys use it to make ends meet. I mean... you may have to look the other way every once in a while, but it's really no big deal. Shit happens, you know?"

"What kind of shit?" Ice pulsed through Gibson's veins.

"Well, you may come across a few... dead cons or working girls—chuckleheads who were in the wrong place at the wrong time. People Empire wouldn't miss. Hell, they'd be dead from opium or something eventually. The Orientals are still running it into Hell's Gate, even with the DiLilos out of the picture. But this way, you don't have to report it." Creed sat up straight like a huge weight had been lifted. "And hey, less paperwork." His smile returned, more devious than jovial.

"Oh yeah, Creed? And how, pray tell, would these hypothetical cons and khaki-wacky working girls meet their demise if not for the opium in Hell's Gate?"

Creed leaned in, meeting Gibson's gaze with his sea-water eyes, and spoke in a coffee-scented hushed tone. "You're not seeing the big picture. Our man, Baxter, is very interested in getting you on his payroll. You must have made some impression yesterday." Creed slapped his hands on the desk, and his eyes went wide. "You should see these parties he throws, Gibson. He says the old ways are dead, God is dead, and now we are each our own god. I'll admit it took a while to get used to—what with growing up Catholic—but, holy shit. I don't know how I ever lived before the Sibylline Religion."

Gibson stood and slammed his chair under the metal desk. "You think you know somebody. I gotta get going, Creed. You tell Ron Baxter I'm not interested."

Creed watched him with that little smile that suddenly made Gibson sick to his stomach. "Think about it, Gibson, it's a big opportunity." He threw his arms over his head and leaned back in the chair.

Gibson ripped the paper from the typewriter and stuffed it into the desk drawer, shaking his head. He turned to leave, but he could feel Creed's eyes on him.

"I know Slim told you to stay away from Baxter, but Shanahan is bad news. I'm telling you, pal. He used to work for the man, himself, until they had a falling out."

"Bullshit!" Gibson spun around, surprised by his enthusiasm to defend a man he didn't entirely trust.

"Ask him if you don't believe me. He and his ol' pal Harper were Baxter's security detail." Creed smirked. "And while you're at it, ask him why you two are pussy-footing all over Brookfield. Murphy wouldn't assign that fatass to the Connor case. That fatso technically isn't even a detective anymore. He's just a geriatric asshole who burned all his bridges, and the only reason he has a job is because he and Murphy have a history. Ask him."

"Fuck you, Creed!" Gibson turned to leave.

"You ever end up reconciling with that bird you were dating before Korea?" Creed asked. "Ann, right?"

Gibson stopped in his tracks and shut his burning eyes.

"Cute name, Ann, Annie, Little Orphan Annie. You and her an item again?"

Gibson peered over his shoulder. "Leave her out of this, Creed. I haven't seen her since I've been back." It was the hard, grueling truth. The last time Gibson heard from Ann Listman had been a postcard from Broadshall he'd received overseas. She had decided to go steady with Bobby Fletcher.

"Well, I saw her the other day—such a lamb, and that keister… man-o-man. Maybe I'll check up on her again, see how she's doing," Creed said. "You can never be too careful in Empire, now that the heroes are gone."

"Drop dead, Creed," Gibson said.

"What, and look like you, Gibson?" Creed made a gun with his fingers and mimed firing a shot. "I don't think so, pal. Think about the offer. It's in everybody's best interest."

**42**

The Concord raced into Wilbur's parking lot, and Gibson cut the engine. He peeled himself off the sweaty leather and looked for a tail. When he was satisfied he hadn't been followed, he padded up the metal stairs. A bell rang above the door, and all eyes were on him.

Gibson scanned the shabby tables and rusty stools along the counter, stuffed wall to wall with patrons. Slim glared at him from a booth in the back. The sweet, stale air stunk as Gibson shuffled through the busy restaurant.

"You're late." Slim's loose skin jiggled when he chewed like an old bloodhound.

"Late? I was doing paper—"

"Baxter get t' you yet?" When he spoke, he spat a bit of egg onto the rickety linoleum table.

"No, but not for lack of trying."

"Then take a seat. I ordered you a cup o' joe." The stench of cigarettes and cheap booze wafted across the table as Slim shoveled another forkful of eggs into his mouth.

Gibson slid into the booth. "Jesus, Slim, you been to bed yet?"

Slim's gray eyes fell to his plate, and he pushed eggs onto the fork with his index finger. "I've been working, Skipper. Ever heard of it?"

A lanky waitress approached the table with a badge pinned to her chest that said *Darlene* and a paper hat on top of a mess of blonde hair. She set a coffee cup on the table and smiled.

"A coffee for the rookie," Darlene said through a nasally Empire City accent with a bit of Brooklyn peppered in.

Slim grinned. "Thanks, Darlene."

She popped her gum and winked. "Slim told me t' say that." She regarded Slim, who was beaming up at her and silently moving his mouth. "Oh, and also—um—oh yeah, do you want some Corby's in it? The coffee, I mean, I'm supposed to say that too, but I already told Slim we don't carry Corby's." She finished with a flat delivery that would make Claudia Barrett blush.

Slim slapped his fat belly and wheezed and coughed in tandem. "That's the—that's the best part!" He wiped a tear away.

Gibson forced a smile. "Thanks, Darlene. It's fine as is."

"Okie-dokie, can I get you some food or somethin', doll? Wilbur makes a great short stack."

"Coffee's fine, thanks." He lifted the small ceramic cup from the saucer and smiled as he tipped it to her.

Slim's grin faded, and his fork froze mid-air. "Hey, Darlene, is Cal Smith working today?"

Darlene pouted. "Nooo. He don't work here no more."

"Hm." Slim shoveled another forkful into his craw.

"You boys need anything else, holler." Darlene said with a wink.

"Cal Smith works here? The war hero?" Gibson asked.

"Worked here. You heard Darlene."

Gibson scanned the diner, watching the waitress vanish into a sea of customers. "You think there's something there?"

"With Darlene and you? Not a chance, Skipper." Slim chased a bit of egg around his plate with his fork.

Gibson narrowed his eyes. "No, Slim, with Cal Smith and the case we've been working... Even though it isn't our case."

Slim froze mid-bite. "You been talkin' t' someone. Briggs? What else did he tell you?" He dropped a wadded napkin on his plate.

"My old partner, Creed, told me enough. He told me you used to work for Baxter."

"Not exactly. Look, we can sit here all day and argue, or we can find Bonnie Connor. Our case or not, don't you think she's a little more important than you judging a pissing contest between me an' one of Baxter's errand boys?"

"I need to know the truth," Gibson said.

"And you will," Slim responded, "in time. Right now, we need to focus on the task at hand."

"What did you find at the Connors' house?"

Slim's mouth became a straight line. "So, Creed came to see you today? Offered you some money, did he?"

"That's right—"

"So, take the money."

"I don't—"

"Or don't take the money and help me find this little girl, Jesus Christ, Skipper. If you aren't with me, you're in my way." Slim crossed his arms. The indistinguishable voices from other tables and the clank of flatware slapping ceramic plates fell to the background as the detectives watched each other across the table.

Gibson sighed. "You think Cal Smith is involved?"

Slim cracked a smile and wiped his greasy face. "No, Cal's a good man. He and Baxter have a history, that's all. I wanted to ask him about... something I found. One thing's for sure, Baxter offering you money is a good sign, means we're gettin' somewhere he don't want us t' be."

Gibson glared across the table and took a sip of coffee.

Slim chuckled. "Anyone ever tell ya yer real cute when yer angry?" He lit a cigarette and stared at Gibson through the curtain of smoke.

"Well?" Gibson said.

Slim clamped the cigarette between his lips and flopped a brown cardstock folder onto the table. "Take a gander."

Gibson opened the envelope. A naked woman's vacant eyes watched him from a three-by-five black-and-white photo. She had been propped against a wall, held up by deer antlers haphazardly attached to the sides of her skull with roofing nails and suspended by a thick rope. Dried blood flowed from her open throat and across her chest like a bib, and behind her, written on the wall in blood, was the phrase: "Deus est mortuus."

Gibson shut the folder. "Jesus, Slim, what the hell is this?" His shaky hand reached into his breast pocket for a Lucky Strike.

There was a hint of sadness in Slim's eyes as he offered a lit match across the table. "Look again, Skipper. I wouldn't show you if there wasn't a reason."

Gibson lit the cigarette off Slim's match and opened the folder. He brushed his fingers across the words, using his other hand to cover the poor dead girl's exposed body. "As depraved as it is, it's familiar."

Slim stretched his arm across the back of the bench seat, shooting a dart of smoke into the air. "It should be. That dead girl over at Baxter's was yellin' it at the top o' her lungs yesterday."

"Yeah, I remember." In Gibson's mind, pus and blood poured from Akia's hollow eye sockets onto the dead leaves like the guts from a pumpkin as Baxter brushed her hair out of her face. He shut his eyes. "What are the rest of these photos? The same type of horror show?"

"Unfortunately." Slim's unwavering gaze made Gibson consider he was in over his head. "Lookin' at this type o' shit is a professional hazard in our line o' work. So, get used to it."

Gibson sighed and took a long, comprehensive draw from his cigarette to steady his hands as he flipped forward through the well-documented nightmare. "These all from the same place?"

Slim nodded.

Gibson shut his irritated eyes and saw Creed's twisted little smile. *You may come across a few dead cons or working girls—chuckleheads who were in the wrong place at the wrong time. People Empire wouldn't miss.*

Gibson dropped the folder onto the table and took a long drag off his cigarette. "That's what you found at the Connor house?"

Slim looked Gibson up and down. "No."

"Then where'd you get them?"

"These don't exist, you hear me?"

Gibson regarded the fat man, recalling something else Creed had said. *Shanahan is bad news. He used to work for Baxter until they had a falling out.*

Slim swatted his palm on the table, and the coffee cups jumped. "Skipper! You hear me?"

"Loud and clear," Gibson obliged sullenly, bouncing his cigarette on the edge of the ashtray.

Slim exhaled a final drag and dropped the spent cigarette into a coffee cup. "My old partner Bill Harper treated this as a… passion project, let's say." Slim patted the envelope. "These here are human sacrifices that happened smack dab in the middle o' Empire. According to Harper, the Connors and Ron Baxter were on the scene. Others too, judges, th' DA, Mayor Hall, you name it."

"Sounds like you have them in the palm of your hand; why don't you squeeze?" Gibson asked.

Slim spoke in a hushed but firm tone, scanning the restaurant. "There are a lot of dangerous people involved. James and Theodora Connor are the least of it." His finger crashed onto the folder. "You squeeze, an' they'll squeeze back. Harder. I jus' wanted you t' see what could potentially happen to little Bonnie Connor, an' maybe these glamor shots could shed some light on somethin' you saw inside Baxter's house? They're yours now. I'm too old and tired t' be lookin' at dead people anymore."

Gibson yanked at his tie. "What do you want me to do with them?"

Slim shrugged. "Compare 'em with your notes. I dunno, be a detective. Good grief, do I have t' keep holdin' your hand?"

Gibson felt the evil seeping through the top of the cardstock folder. "You really think the League is mixed up in this? C'mon, Slim, you really think James Connor would—I mean, Ron Baxter, I get it, he's one sandwich short of a picnic, but Captain Wonderful?"

"James Connor, Theodora Connor, Ron Baxter. All of 'em are a lot of sandwiches short of a lot o' things," Slim responded.

Gibson shook his head. "But these people don't look like criminals. Some of them are women, and Bonnie Connor is a child."

"You watch too many movies, Skipper. The world ain't all bubblegum an' rainbows. Ron Baxter an' the Enforcers crave power, an' they ain't too keen on being told no." Slim cupped his mouth with the back of his hand. "Harper said this is how they got their abilities. Human sacrifices, magic mumbo jumbo, devil worship, yadda-yadda, above my comprehension.

"Harper was there, an' unlike you, he lived in the real world, wasn't one to exaggerate. The Enforcers have killed thousands. What are a few more heroin addicts or working girls if it means becomin' super-powered heroes?"

Gibson remembered the low, earth-shaking register of the Japanese girl's voice as she snarled Latin phrases. "If this is true, how does it connect to Bonnie?"

"Well, Skipper, that's the big question. That's where we have to earn our paycheck. Alls I'm sayin' is don't count out Theodora or James Connor, or Miss Mercury for that matter. Much as I'd like to pin this kidnapping on that lowlife, Baxter."

Gibson's face flushed red hot. "So why wait till now to tell me this? We were at James Connor's house yesterday. You didn't think this would have been important information?"

"I needed to know if I could trust you first," Slim responded. "Still don't know if I do."

Gibson slammed his fist on the folder. "Then why even show me this?"

Slim sighed and looked over his hands with a sad, creeping smile matching his dejected eyes. "Well—truth is—it's out of necessity. I'm dyin', Skipper. Got the cancer a few months back. Wife left me, got no kids, no one I can trust in the ECPD with this." He paused thoughtfully. "She always wanted kids, my wife. I never saw the point of bringing life into the world while I was busy extinguishing my own. I don't blame her for leaving. Just wish the timing was better." Slim gazed out the window and chuckled. "Ya know, I've been comin' here for years. Every day, I sit in this booth an' look at that building over there." He pressed his index finger on the glass. "Right there, to the left o' the Ironleaf. It's not finished. Never was. The Scarlet Sparrow rebuilt the city in five years an' never bothered to finish that one building. I always wondered why."

Gibson sighed. "Look, Slim—"

"Bonnie Connor is missing," Slim interrupted, "an' I think this—whatever this is"—he slapped his hand on the photos —"this is why. Her parents were wrapped up in somethin', and now I think it's got her too. I still don't know if I trust you, but you could be my last shot at retribution." He stared across the table, and Gibson saw him for what he was, not a hero or a martyr, just a broken old man trying to do some good on his way out.

"You could be Bonnie's last shot at life an' maybe the avengers of these dead folks, but so could anyone with a set o' morals." He sighed and stared out the window again. "Oh, to be young an' have your whole life laid out face down in front of you like an unspent deck of playing cards. I'd give anything to be sittin' where you are, Skipper. Don't squander it with greed"—his troubled smile faded—"an' don't go gettin' a big head about it, neither!"

Gibson focused on the wet trail the single tear had left as it ran down Slim's face and dripped onto the table. "We're going to get this little girl back, Slim, if we have to take on the Enforcers ourselves."

"Cocky bastard, ain't ya?"

"Yeah, I learned that from the self-proclaimed 'great' Slim Shanahan."

Slim chuckled. "Don't let these assholes change ya, Skipper. You can have it all in this world. Money, family, friends, but if you aren't okay with the man in the mirror, you aren't going to be ready for life, and you're damn sure not going to be ready for death. Like Bill Harper used t' say, live each day as if it was your last." He pushed the folder toward Gibson.

*Crash!*

The front window exploded inward, ripping across the dining room like bullets. Gibson raised his arms over his face and fell into the booth. Steel girders whined as the earth heaved under the diner.

"Holy cats!" Slim yelled. Patrons screamed and gasped. The shaking ceased, but the ringing in Gibson's ears immobilized him.

Blood pooled under a large woman's baby blue summer dress. An elderly man staggered forward, clutching his glass-riddled arm. Others stared at the window wide-eyed, some with injuries they hadn't even noticed. A few people slumped over the counter. The radio popped and screeched until someone ripped the plug from the wall.

An old black cook exploded from the kitchen through the free-swinging door and crouched by the bleeding woman, applying pressure to her wound with a towel. "You're going to be alright, Missus Mitchell," he said, but the fear dancing across his face told another story. "Darlene, call an ambulance!"

Darlene peered over the counter with black mascara tears pouring down her face, but there was no one home behind those wide eyes.

"Darlene!"

The young woman blinked, moved slowly down the length of the counter, and lifted the phone with a shaky hand.

Gibson stared at the shattered front window as Slim screamed his name.

"Skipper, are ya still with me? Skipper!"

Gibson blinked and regarded the tower of smoke in the distance. People's voices joined into an angry and horrified jumble, filling the room with nonsensical and unnervingly possible theories.

"Skipper, don't get involved! We have too much on our plate already!" Slim grabbed him, but Gibson wrenched his arm away. He looked over the sea of terrified faces. Some stared catatonically, while the smart ones ran for the door.

"I gotta go help, Slim." Guilt Gibson had always carried with him pulled him away from his partner, the case, and Bonnie Connor. He'd been at the police academy in Northwell during T-Day while Empire suffered and people he'd known all his life died. He was locked out of the burning city, helpless and forced to watch the smoke in the distance as hundreds of thousands of lives were extinguished.

"Skipper!"

Gibson stepped through the blown-out window and landed ankle-deep in a putrid collection of dead leaves and trash. The blistering sun beat down as he took off, sprinting across the hot concrete toward the tower of smoke.

**43**

Gibson ran through the pea-soup humidity down Longdon Lane, a narrow one-way street with old brownstones and fenced-in trees growing from the sidewalk. Folks gathered on stoops, watching smoke pour into the sky as radios screamed high-pitched static from open windows.

Trepidation clung to Gibson like his sweaty clothes. The same fear of civic annihilation his friends likely fought, riding Fire Engine 33 into hell on T-Day. Three kids from

Eastwood who had vanished somewhere amongst the falling skyscrapers on the Northside of Empire.

Gibson bolted past wary people scattered in the street, gawking at the tower of smoke like curious deer, ready to bound off at the first hint of trouble.

*Boom!*

They fled, and a black cloud pushed from the south, encompassing everything from the street to the buildings. Gibson turned away, covering his eyes as a wall of dust enveloped him, but pressed on.

The cloud settled, and a terrified mob exploded forward, covered in soot. Screams echoed off the buildings as they trampled each other to get away from the column of smoke. Gibson waited in a doorway until they dissipated, then continued through the dust toward the source.

He stopped short on the edge of Sainte Marie Square, a once lively mecca reduced to a smoking crater. The hole in the center was half the size of a football field. Around the edge, concrete bent inward, crumbling into the black unknown. Rubble from apartment buildings scattered the street amidst furniture and clothes—people's lives strewn amongst the brick and stone that once sheltered them. The buildings around the square gaped open, in danger of falling like they were children's blocks. And the radios still screamed from open windows.

People wandered around the pit's circumference, calling out names. Others stood tall and angry like they were invincible, waiting for whatever had created the giant crater to emerge. Gibson shut his eyes, inhaling to steady his nerves. He yanked his colt snub nose from the holster. "ECPD! Clear the area! Everyone behind me!" he yelled. A few people looked in his direction, but that was the extent of any civil obedience. There were sirens in the distance. At least the cavalry was on its way.

Metal groaned, the ground shifted, and debris tumbled into the dark abyss in front of him. He scampered back. Two people across the way lost their footing as Forman Avenue surrendered to the earth, and screams echoed around the empty square. A thunderous mechanical clamor rose from the hole, eclipsing the screech of the radios. The earth quaked, and Gibson gazed into the pitch-black, yawing like a grave dug for Empire City.

The sirens grew louder, and Gibson gained new confidence. "Clear the area, now!" He tried again. The remaining wide-eyed citizens on each side stared at the pit as another loud whirring noise echoed from the darkness.

A metallic cylinder as big as a building erupted through the sidewalk to Gibson's left, sending most of the walkway, a few trees, and some shrieking people flying. A three-pronged claw popped open at the top, arched, and shot toward the earth, gripping into the cement a few feet away from Gibson. He braced himself but tumbled backward as the ground shook.

Another cylinder shot upward through the original hole in front of him, turned into a three-pronged claw, and gripped the other side of Sainte Marie Square—more whirring. Gibson swallowed and grabbed the churned cement from his seated position. Something giant and metallic crested the concrete, glinting in the sun. He was close enough to see the Buick-sized gears turning along the surface. Nearby apartments and cars with radios screeched.

The form rose between its metal appendages. Bits of concrete, burst sewer pipes, and anything long buried under Sainte Marie Square slid off as gears and pistons spun and pumped. It spanned fifty yards at least.

Gibson scooted backward along the ground, like a crab, and aimed his shaking gun. His commanding officer from Korea cried from the back of his mind: *You're a piece of equipment, a killing machine. When you walked across the 38th parallel, you gave up the freedom of an American man!*

The mechanical noise ceased, pistons sighed, and the metallic body froze. Gibson aimed his gun, but his finger wouldn't squeeze. *If you pull your weapon, you better—*

His commanding officer's voice faded, and all he saw was Ann. *I'll love you forever,* she said. He could smell the sea as her hair tumbled into his face, and she kissed him softly. In her place, Theodora Connor's image stared back at him with fire dancing across her eyes. *How do you behave when the world you know and love comes crashing down around you, and there is no right or wrong anymore, just survival? Just preservation of life? I have faith in you, but I'm afraid you don't quite understand what faith is. You're not ready.*

Sirens wailed. Police cars and ambulances crashed into the shifting stone that had once been Longdon Lane. Two more arms shot from the mechanical body above him, tearing into the street and expelling dust and debris into the polluted air. The thing jolted forward, and Gibson aimed. The street cracked. A Studebaker rolled down the sloping tarvia, and the ground heaved to swallow him. *Heroes die. It's what they do best.* He couldn't remember where he'd heard that, but he knew it would be his last thought.

*Boom!* An explosion ripped through the air with a flash of gold. The soft touch of an angel pulled Gibson through the dust, and his feet were back on Longdon Lane.

"Dropped your hat, doll." A beautiful woman in a strapless navy blue and gold swimsuit and a dark, painted smile across her lips presented Gibson's fedora. She winked through yellow goggles framed by black hair falling to her pale-white shoulders.

Gibson swallowed and met her gaze, unable to speak.

"Excuse me, won't you?" She vanished in a gust of wind that nearly ripped Gibson's tie from his neck and threatened to pull him to the ground.

He stumbled and blinked the dust away. One by one, a crowd of cops and civilians materialized from the gold blur. Shocked, terrified faces turned to applause and cheers when the people got their bearings.

"It's Miss Mercury!" a man yelled. "She saved us!"

"Not yet, I haven't." Miss Mercury appeared in a flash, eyed the square, and sped off.

"The League of Enforcers is back!" a woman cried.

The uniformed officers snapped into action and pressed back against the advancing crowd. Gibson flashed his shield and pushed past the cops, advancing until the churned streets became too precarious.

Flashes of Miss Mercury's figure sporadically froze in time amongst the blur of blinding speed. Somehow, she'd turned the giant mechanical creature away from the crowd and back toward the hole. The thing froze, and steam expelled in a hiss from crevices along its surface. A small egg shape with one flat edge rose from the top of the original sphere, spinning in a circle following the gold blur that was Miss Mercury. Red particles danced in the air across the flat side of the new orb, and a beam erupted.

Gibson lurched forward and held his breath. Miss Mercury skidded to a stop before the light touched her. Concrete folded like a rug under her feet and sent a Buick sedan tumbling end over end as she exploded in the opposite direction. The oval on top faced the crowd, and the crackle of red light particles built again.

"No!" Gibson tasted copper, and a blinding red beam turned the world red, sliding across the onlookers with a deafening, high-pitched scream. The spectators who'd gathered to watch Miss Mercury triumph over evil burst, and the smell of singed meat replaced the electrical scent. Gibson watched ash drift in the breeze, forming a mass grave along Longdon Lane.

Miss Mercury yelled something inaudible. The ear-shattering crack of a whip from one of the creature's arms sent her careening into a nearby brownstone, fracturing the foundation and almost toppling the building. She bounced off the second story and hit the pavement with a thud.

The hair on the back of Gibson's neck rose. Red light crackled along the creature's orb. "Brace yourselves!" He yelled before ducking and covering.

The beam never came. Gibson lifted his head, following the golden blur of Miss Mercury across the robot's surface. The egg-shaped orb on top trailed her adamantly until it detached and slid down the body into the crater. Miss Mercury dove into the hole the missing piece created, and the thing stumbled as gears, pistons, and shrapnel collapsed into a heap.

Gibson could breathe again.

The onlookers refused to leave the scene, and the raucous sound of an unstable crowd grew, even as policemen tried to usher them away. Some displayed disgust for Miss Mercury and the League, while others cheered her.

Gibson returned his hat to his head, fired up a Lucky Strike, and gazed at the ash scattered along Longdon Lane. *Things like this never play out like the pictures,* he thought, watching the growing crowd overtake the ambulances that had come for the injured and dead. He turned, scanning the pile of metal that was once Empire's doom, took a long drag, and pushed into the crowd.

Miss Mercury stopped abruptly with a smile locked on her face, dumping screws from her palm. The crowd silenced. All the naysayers and champions of her cause stood in awe of the goddess.

"That mechanical menace won't be troubling you anymore, citizens!" Miss Mercury called out in a cheerful, sing-songy voice.

The press slithered to the front, yelling Miss Mercury's name until it became droll and meaningless. They asked her empty questions. She grinned ear to ear, posing like a cover girl as flashbulbs popped and twinkled, and when she'd had enough, she vanished into the wind.

The crowd slowly dissipated. Uniformed cops escorted the gawkers behind the perimeter they had established far too late. Gibson flicked his cigarette stub onto the giant smoking crater in the middle of Sainte Marie Square.

"She's amazing, huh?" Slim said.

Gibson hadn't noticed the old man approach. He offered a dented flask to Gibson, who shook his head.

Slim took another swig and returned the flask to his back pocket. "Saw her up close like this back in '51, but it ain't the type of thing you ever get used to."

"Yeah, I guess not," Gibson responded.

Slim clapped Gibson on the back. "Alright, that's enough. Quit drooling on yourself, Skipper. Act like you've seen a lady before."

"That's not it." Gibson's eyes refused to leave the giant crater.

"I know, how many dead this time?"

"I saw six fall in, and a handful vaporized."

"That's also not the type of thing you get used to. I told you not t' get involved. Big thing like that requires a big response, bigger n' we can handle. I knew she'd come. They always come; retirement be damned. The gods of Empire will be watching over us forever, if we want 'em here or not."

Slim was right again. That woman couldn't help herself. The adrenaline-fueled brawl, the fame that came with it, the infamy if she died protecting the city—it was a disease. She played the actress, the beautiful bathing beauty, while the citizens she was sworn to protect slipped through her fingers.

"What's a human life worth to the Enforcers?" Gibson asked. "Is one girl's life worth more than the promise of more power? Even if she's a Connor?"

"That's what I been tellin' ya, Skipper."

Theodora's words came crashing into his thoughts. *How do you, as a man of the law, a man who I can only assume has a moral compass? How do you behave when the world you know and love comes crashing down around you, and there is no right or wrong anymore, just survival? Just preservation of life?*

Gibson scanned the crack in the building Miss Mercury hit. *Will killing Bonnie Connor preserve the Enforcer's power? Will it preserve their lives? Is that why they retired? Are they running out of power?*

"You owe me a nickel for that coffee, by the way. I don't know what kind of arrangement you had over in Sedgwick, but at Wilbur's Diner, cops pay for things," Slim said. "I got your folder o' photos too. Pretty sloppy leaving stuff like that behind, Skipper. Call yourself a detective, ha!"

"Whatever you say, Slim." Gibson shoved his hands into his pockets and looked out over the path of destruction.

Slim followed his gaze. "You got a bee in your bonnet? What's with you?"

"I thought I heard Miss Mercury tell a reporter that thing was made with Connor Steel. You recall them ever making anything like that? Ya know, because the Scarlet Sparrow, a.k.a. Theodora *Connor,* has been known to build big, dangerous things from time to time."

Slim scratched his chin and scanned the broken street. "Ha, you ever seen anyone other than Torment make anything like that?" When Gibson didn't respond, he cleared his throat. "During the war, they made ships an' naval guns. Now that we won, it's all heating ducts an' things o' that nature—no killer robots that I know of. Besides, why would the Scarlet Sparrow want to tear down the city?"

"I don't know, to keep us busy? Maybe she wants to rebuild the Southside like she did the Northside. Maybe there was a rift in the ranks, and she meant to attack Miss Mercury. Could be any number of things."

"Or maybe it's to appease the Martians, or th' Communists, or th' heavy from the sci-fi serial?" Slim chuckled.

"Is it so crazy?" Gibson asked. "The daughter of two of the Enforcers goes missing while some killer robot strikes? And one of her parents has been known to dabble in building things like that?" Gibson found his sudden passion alarming. "All I'm saying is we should check out Connor Steel."

"This again?" Slim clapped Gibson on the back and wheezed out a long laugh. "You think the Scarlet Sparrow took Bonnie and is now hiding in Connor Steel when she owns more property than I got coins in my pocket? Don't get all excited, Skipper. Just 'cause a giant—whatever that thing was—came from Connor Steel doesn't mean that's where Bonnie Connor is, and it certainly doesn't implicate Theodora Connor."

Slim eyed the crater. "Besides, stuff like this used t' happen daily in Empire, don'tcha remember? Probably stolen product or something. It's a cold lead. Can we focus on the task at hand, now that you had yer little... hunger to be a hero satisfied?" Slim shook his head and casually strolled into the crowd behind the police barricade.

Gibson watched him go as two men in identical black suits and black fedoras stepped in front of him.

"You Gibson?" the older one with horn-rimmed glasses asked.

Gibson reeled away. "Who wants to know?"

"Come with us, please. We need to ask you a few questions." The second man in black flashed a gun pressed into a leather holster under his black coat.

Gibson surveyed the people collecting behind the barricade. Slim shook his head, fired up a cigarette, and faded into the crowd.

The Empire Bulletin
Empire City, Sunday, October 18, 1953
MISS MERCURY MINCES
MECHANICAL MENACE

An unidentified object landed in Sainte Marie Square yesterday, killing 79 people while 13 remain missing.

Around 9:30 AM, an entity of unknown origin fell from the sky, creating a nearly 140-square-foot crater in the middle of the thoroughfare. When the initial impact subsided, authorities reported tremors and aftershocks as far north as Westport and dust spreading up to four city blocks away from the initial point of impact. As responders rushed to the scene to treat the injured and assist trapped people in and amongst collapsed buildings, the large object rose from the crater on "long, metallic legs," witnesses say.

Miss Mercury of the League of Enforcers arrived soon after, pulling citizens to safety as the automaton fired a beam, killing an estimated 6 people before Miss Mercury disassembled the creature.

After the battle, when asked about the robot's origin, Miss Mercury said: "That certainly wasn't a Martian. Someone built that mechanical miscreant out of good old-fashioned American-made Connor Steel. Must be why I had such a hard time taking it apart."

She spoke on the League of Enforcers and retirement rumors, stating, "The League never left. Captain Wonderful and I, Miss Mercury, have and always will be watching over the sons and daughters of Empire." No statement was made about the Scarlet Sparrow, leading us to believe she is officially retired.

## The City of the Gods: Gold

Miss Mercury also had no answer when asked what her thoughts were about the disappearance of Bonnie Connor. The 5-year-old daughter of Captain and Mrs. James Connor reported missing days before.

At press time, the death toll has risen to 81.

RAZOR'S
EDGE

## 44

Dust particles drifted through the sunrays, landing on the pile of beer cans in the corner. Gordon's mind wandered as the soothing two-note "see-saw" call of a chickadee carried through the open window on a warm breeze, inviting him to come play.

"So long, kids! See you next Sunday!" Howdy Doody said from the television set. The credits rolled, and Gordon climbed to his feet to shut it off. A little jingle stopped him in his tracks, and his hand reeled away from the knob when a reporter's face appeared. He fell backward onto the edge of the couch with his eyes glued to the screen.

"Good morning, Empire City. This is Jim Essex, reporting," the man said in a gritty but pleasing old man voice. "Recapping yesterday's top story, we take you to Sainte Marie Square." Gordon's eyes widened. He slid down the couch and crept forward on his knees toward the images of a giant, ovular robot flashing across the screen. "Where, as you can see, a large mechanical monster was overcome by the might of Miss Mercury. NBC's own Bert Mitchell was able to get a statement from our speedy savior."

The screen went black, and then, as if she was standing in the living room, Miss Mercury, *the* Miss Mercury, posed in front of a towering pile of rubble. Gordon gawked at the television. Words caught in the lump in his throat and died as small noises.

Miss Mercury pinned her black hair out of her face with her glasses, and her sultry eyes locked on the camera. One wink sent butterflies beating against Gordon's stomach and froze his breath in his chest. Reporters yelled indecipherable questions over each other in the background.

"One at a time, gentlemen, please. I'm only one girl." She giggled.

The man with the microphone said: "Bert Mitchell, with NBC News. Does this mean the League of Enforcers is back?" The microphone jammed into her face.

Miss Mercury smiled, and her eyes met Gordon's through the television screen. "Hello, Gordon," she said through a flicker in the reception.

Gordon inched closer to the set. He ran his fingers over the smooth glass, trying to memorize her seductive eyes, pouty lips, and raven hair.

"The League never left. Captain Wonderful and I, Miss Mercury, have and always will be watching over the sons and daughters of Empire"—static buzzed—"until Gordon Ross joins our ranks."

Gordon gripped the television. Everything around the screen blurred. He followed her body with his eyes, studying each curve of her milk-white skin running in and out of her strapless swimsuit-like uniform.

"I see, so where is Captain Wonderful?" the reporter asked. "Surely, he helped you win the day."

"He helps me from time to time"—she sighed, and the set buzzed with static—"but I've since found a real man with a fortress—well, look at me, telling a newsman old news. Isn't that your business, Bert?" Her voice was honey, poured over each word.

Miss Mercury waved. "I'm afraid that's all I have time for right now. Make sure to tune in to the *Ed Sullivan Show*, where yours truly will be a guest next Sunday." She regarded the camera. "Gordon, I'm waiting for you." She winked again and vanished in a blur.

The camera panned across the metallic wasteland as dust trailed over heaps of steel, and a loud sonic boom echoed in the distance. The reporter crushed his hat into a pile on his head to keep it from slipping into the wind. "Well, there you have it, folks—Gordon Ross, she's waiting for you." The television hissed.

Gordon's beating heart threatened to rip from his chest. All sensation drained from his legs and collected in his groin, pressing it against his pajama pants, which were soaking wet.

# The City of the Gods: Gold

Someone snickered, and Gordon felt a leering gaze through the open window. The porch creaked, and the shadow of a tall, thin figure slunk across the floor. Gordon gasped, but when he looked out the window, he was alone. He eyed the towering buildings in the distance and smiled. She was out there somewhere, amidst the jungle of skyscrapers and parks, concrete and iron. *She's waiting for me.* His smile faded as shame overcame him, and he walked to his room, trying in vain to adjust his sodden pants around his erection.

In the bedroom, Walter sat facing the corner, commanding an army of tin soldiers. Gordon threw open the door and pulled his pajama pants down quickly. He flung them into the closet with his foot before his brother noticed the stain and yanked on yesterday's seersucker shorts. "Walt, we have to go."

Walt eyed him over his shoulder. "Aw jeez, Gordie. I was just gettin' set up for the war!"

Gordon spotted his canvas rucksack on top of the faded antique bench with the broken leg. He turned it upside-down and shook it, scattering school supplies across the floor.

Walter's eyebrows dropped. "Hey! Don't mess up the room, Gordie. You're getting stuff on my side!" His voice turned to a shrill whine as his eyes followed a pencil rolling into his soldiers.

Gordon ignored him and kicked aside a rubber ball, scouring the floor. He spun thoughtfully and shut the door, revealing his trusty Daisy Red Ryder Carbine BB gun leaning against the crayon-covered wall.

Gordon lifted the gun eagerly, checked the stock, and yanked back on the cocking lever. He pointed it at the drawing of a crayon house on the wall and pulled the trigger. It clicked unenthusiastically. He turned it and peered down the barrel with one eye closed like he'd seen the cowboys on *Death Valley Days* do. Satisfied, he shoved the gun into the rucksack along with a box of Revelation BBs and his old wooden Sharpshooter Slingshot.

Walter broke his feigned pout. "What's the Red Ryder for?"

Gordon ripped his pajama shirt off and tossed it onto his messy bed. He kicked around the dirty laundry on the floor, sniffed an old green knit sports shirt with a yellow stripe, and slipped it over his thin frame. "We have to get to the fortress, Walt. Something big happened."

Walter turned back around to face his army of tin soldiers. "I'm sick of playin' Junior Enforcers. I wanna stay here and play army men."

Gordon shoved his hand under his mattress, sliding it across the box spring until his fingers brushed the glossy paper of the forbidden *Playboy* magazine. He scanned the cover, running his hands over Miss Mercury's black hair before sliding it into his rucksack.

"Nuts to that! C'mon, Pop'll be mad if I leave you behind," Gordon said. "Besides, Billy and Ukrit are probably already there."

"And Pratimaaaaa?" Walter added.

"Shut up, Walt." Gordon's face flushed red. "We can stop at Marly's for a malt on the way home. I still got a little money from my paper route."

"Fine!" Walter slapped the collection of soldiers onto their sides, rose to his feet, and flopped his oversized flatcap onto his tiny pinhead.

The boys exploded into the hallway, racing down the stairs. They burst through the broken screen door and let it bang against the frame. The ghost of summer still lingered, perverted with the stench of fall.

Gordon lifted his dew-covered Roadmaster from the front lawn and threw a leg over the seat. Old Missus Storrier and her dumb Pekingese peered out from the neighboring window with a matching scowl on each of their faces.

*She was probably the one laughing at me earlier,* Gordon thought. Heat rose on the back of his neck as he studied her old, wrinkled face through the window.

"Ready?" Walt asked, drawing his attention.

"Ready!" Gordon repeated. "Let's gooooo! Junior Enforcers awayyyyy!" He made a trumpet sound with his mouth, and they were off.

**<u>45</u>**

The sickening sensation of leering eyes stopped for a while, but maniacal giggling still came in spurts. Gordon heard it when he almost spilled his bike on the Signal Ridge hill and again when he tripped in the woods on his way to the fort.

"Stand guard for a minute, Walt," Gordon said, eyeing the tree line and pushing through the fortress's entrance. He slumped into one of the leather tripod chairs, rifling through his rucksack. "One Daisy Red Ryder BB gun, BBs, one slingshot, and branches, we can use as weapons."

Something shifted in the corner, crackling like lousy television reception, and the scent of burnt popcorn filled the room. Gordon shot out of the chair.

Walter burst through the plywood door, puffed his chest out, and saluted. "Ukrit and his dumb sister are here." He pushed his hat back and smiled.

"Good job, Walt." Gordon eyed the now still corner. "Say, do you smell anything funny?"

"Like girl?" Walt asked, flaring his nostrils. "Yeah, Ukrit brought his sister, like I told ya."

Gordon licked his palm and ran it through his hair, scanning the door over his brother's shoulder. "Never mind."

"I don't want to be a guard anymore, Gordie."

"Okay, Walt. Uh, take five. Smoke 'em if ya got 'em," Gordon echoed the quote from the radio and pushed through the plywood door. He strolled around the fort slowly, but his legs felt jerky and unnatural like he was walking on stilts. His pulse raced, and his breathing came hard and fast.

Ukrit bound excitedly toward Walter, who threw an arm around him like a funny little drunk. "Heya, pal!"

Pratima inched into the clearing, feigning a bored look. When Gordon caught her staring, she looked away quickly.

"Well? Did you see the special report?" Gordon asked Ukrit, but his gaze fell on Pratima. Their eyes met, and they both turned away in horror. Gordon's face flushed red, and he scanned the fort, trying to make the same serious face his father made whenever he fixed something around the house.

"I didn't see any reports," Ukrit said, "but I read about the attack on Sainte Marie Square in my father's newspaper. Was the creature *truly* as tall as the Ironleaf building?"

Walter raised his arms, howled, and stomped around on dead leaves. "Bigger! It was a million feet tall!"

"This is so stupid," Pratima muttered, nervously caressing her long, black braid. She was wearing a red plaid shirt and dungarees. It wasn't the most combat-appropriate outfit, but it created a beautiful reddish aura in her dark eyes.

Gordon sneered. "If it's so stupid, I guess we shouldn't take our new science officer to investigate."

Pratima's eyes grew wide. "Wait, you're actually going to Sainte Marie Square? You can't be serious!"

"We're going to need samples for our science officer to make weapons, just like the Scarlet Sparrow does for the League of Enforcers," Gordon said.

"Yeah!" Walter yelled.

Pratima's eyes widened. "But, we can't—"

"C'mon, science officer, we need you." Gordon smiled.

"Yeah, we need—we need her, Gordon?" Walter asked.

Ukrit placed a hand on his sister's shoulder. "C'mon, Pratima, it'll be fun."

Pratima smiled bashfully, and her mocha-colored skin reddened. "Fine, but we aren't to tell Mother."

The bushes rustled. Gordon stepped in front of the others and swallowed hard. "Wh-who's there?"

"Shit!" Billy stumbled through a thicket and fell to his knees. "I don't know about this fort, Gordon. It's kinda a pain"—he scanned the group, and his brow dropped—"what the hell is going on?"

Gordon extended a hand to help Billy to his feet, but he pushed it away and got up himself. "It's bad enough we have this little shit in our group, but now his sister is hanging around? Gordon, c'mon, we talked about this yesterday." He spat a gob of phlegm into the dirt.

Gordon sighed. "She's—"

"Oh, haven't you heard?" Pratima exclaimed. "I'm the newest member of your Junior Enforcers. You'll refer to me as Science Officer Singh from here on out."

Billy glanced back and forth between Gordon and Pratima as little noises of disbelief crawled from his throat. "Gordon, c'mon, is this a gag?"

Gordon smiled at Pratima, who blushed again. "Nope. Meet the newest member of the Junior Enforcers. Science Officer Singh."

Billy exploded in a fury. "This is bullshit! It's bad enough that little sucker-puncher joined! Now you're letting broads on the team? She doesn't even have a decoder ring!" He looked like a gorilla, throwing his arms up and kicking dead leaves and branches around as he circled the forest floor. "Mutiny! If you let these foreigners in the League, I'll mutiny!" He stopped suddenly, and his eyes rose to check if his tantrum had paid off.

Pratima crossed her arms. "We aren't foreigners. We go to the same school as you. Also, the United States and England are allies, you buffoon."

"Yeah, you balloon!" Walter crossed his arms over his chest.

Pratima and Billy stared at each other, and Billy suddenly looked like he might cry. Gordon threw his arm around his friend before he did anything irreversibly embarrassing.

"C'mon, Bill," Gordon whispered, "it's only a trial. If she doesn't work out, we'll send her packing. I promise."

Billy followed a drifting leaf across the ground with his eyes and tightened his mouth into a line. "Fine, but if she doesn't work out, her little-shit brother goes too."

Gordon glanced over his shoulder at the others. Ukrit and Walter chased a butterfly while Pratima scolded them; then Pratima let out a playful scream and scurried away when the butterfly landed on her shoulder. *Some League, we might as well be a bunch of kids playing hero without Billy.*

"Fine." Gordon had already forgotten what the deal had been. Like a good leader, his mind was already on the mission, but Pratima looked so beautiful in the morning sun.

**<u>46</u>**

The heat baked the concrete, rising in thick waves as the Junior Enforcers headed west away from the coast toward Lincoln. Gordon clutched the straps of his rucksack as he walked, and sweat gathered in a soggy puddle under its weight. The swishing of the BBs made the silence more natural as Gordon and Pratima settled for awkward smiles met with red, blushing faces. Ukrit and Walter giggled behind them, and Billy drifted further back, pushing the bicycle he insisted on bringing through knots of people on the sidewalk.

At Grandview Avenue, words erupted from Pratima's mouth. "So, h—"

"When did—" Gordon interrupted her. "Sorry, go ahead." He chuckled.

"No, please," Pratima replied with a bashful smile.

"Well," he said, "I was just gonna ask, why did you decide to come to Empire City?"

Pratima giggled. "It was never my decision. My father was part of the Tizard Mission in the States before I was born and the Manhattan Project after." Her dark eyes met his and darted away nervously. "When the war ended, he got a job, so he moved us all here. I do miss England, though. My grandparents live in a beautiful house in the countryside with a pond and little ducklings." She blushed and smiled, looking at the sidewalk. "There's even a tire swing hanging from a wonderful old oak in the back. Of course, I'm far too old for that kind of thing now, but the view is stunning."

"Well, I'm glad you're here—that is to say—"

"Goooorrrrrddddiiiieeee! Are we almost there?" Walt interrupted.

"Alright, alright!" Gordon reached into his pocket, removing a crude, hand-drawn map of Empire City based on a newspaper article he'd kept from T-Day. "It shouldn't be much further." He unfolded the paper and flipped it right side up, laying it on the roasting hood of a parked Plymouth sedan.

253

Billy approached. "Are you even reading that right?"

Gordon glowered, ignoring him. "We're at the corner of Munson Avenue and Julian Place. It should be close."

Ukrit shrugged. "Maybe someone cleaned it up already."

Gordon sighed. "How could they have"—he scanned the street frantically—"where's Walt?"

"Hey, fellas, over here!" Walter called from across the street.

"Walt! Don't run off like that!" Gordon darted into traffic, forcing a Ford Angelina to stop short. The old man behind the wheel laid on the horn and yelled something inaudible through the windshield as Gordon rounded the corner after his brother.

Walter stood beside a short brick building, craning his neck, trying unsuccessfully to see over a much taller group of men. Voices meshed into an inseparable web of theories and rumors as Gordon pushed through droves of wide-eyed gawkers. Pratima, Ukrit, Billy, and his bike brought up the rear, and the crowd closed in behind them.

Gordon stopped short. A pile of steel and rubble jutted from a crater in a messy five-story heap. It was so dead and motionless that he couldn't imagine it rampaging through the city. Men moved about the debris like ants, some in police uniforms, others in black suits with matching fedoras.

Something soft brushed Gordon's hand, igniting a spark of energy followed by churning in his gut. He looked down to find Pratima's fingers wrapped around his. They each smiled, and the world fell away.

"Well, we're here. So, what's the plan now?" Billy grumbled.

Gordon ripped his hand away from Pratima's, shuffled to an open area next to a run-down building with blown-out windows boarded up with plywood, and dropped the rucksack on the sidewalk. He snatched the BB gun by the barrel and forced an authoritative cadence into his voice. "I'll find out how we can help and report back here. Until then, at ease, Junior Enforcers!" A smile spread over his face, and breathing came in euphoric gulps as he weaved around tangles of people.

A collection of wooden sawhorses stacked side by side blocked the street between a handful of police cruisers pulled along the perimeter haphazardly. Each vehicle came with one or two miserable-looking cops standing sentry.

As Gordon approached, the closest officer tended his sweaty brow with a handkerchief. "You look like a man who needs a break, and I'm happy to oblige." He saluted. "Gordon Ross of the Junior Enforcers, reporting for duty, sir. How can we help?"

The officer tilted his hat back, scratching his head like he was trying to comprehend some great riddle. Then he shoved Gordon aside, making a noise between a sigh and a laugh. "Get lost, kid."

Gordon stumbled, and the cop turned to talk to another officer. "Matthews, how you holdin' up? These goddamn Indian summers, huh? Makes me long for—"

Gordon tugged at the officer's shirt and backed up. "Didn't ya hear me? I'm—"

The officer regarded him with a scowl. Gordon held his hands up. "Wait! You don't understand! I'm here with the Junior Enforcers on official League bu—"

"I said, scram!" The officer stomped forward once, but Gordon stood his ground, ready to fight his way through if necessary. The cop stood upright and knocked his hat back again. "Goddammit, kid, beat it. You're starting to bother me. You want me to call your parents?"

A belt snapped in the back of Gordon's mind. He turned in a huff and pushed into the dense crowd, back toward his friends.

Billy dropped his bike. "Where do they want us positioned?"

Gordon kicked a stone into the gutter. "The dumb cop told me to get lost!"

Billy stepped forward excitedly. "Did you tell him—"

"I *tried* to tell him we were the Junior Enforcers here on official League business, but he didn't care," Gordon said.

Billy threw his arms up in a huff and shook his head. "Shoulda let me go. You aren't even wearing your decoder ring!"

Pratima regarded Gordon with a relieved smile. "So, that's that?"

"That can't be *that*, Gordon!" Billy said. "We came all the way down here, wasted the whole goddamn Sunday!"

Gordon looked over his troops. "Bill's right, it's our duty to help Empire City!"

A look of worry shot across Ukrit's face. "Maybe we should play something else."

"Yeah! Like cowboys and Indians!" Walter pushed his hat back and made little six-shooter guns with his fingers. "Bang! Bang!"

Pratima placed a hand on Gordon's shoulder. "If the police officer said no, maybe we should—"

Billy grimaced. "What a fucking waste of time!" He threw a leg over his bike and rang the pathetic little bell on his handlebars, vanishing into the crowd.

"What? No, c'mon," Gordon pleaded. "What about the Junior Enforcers' duty to Empire City?"

*Everyone is so selfish. What about you? What about Gordon Ross?* a woman's sultry voice answered from the depths of his mind.

Pratima's eyes met his. "We can go back to the fortress and regroup. My father always says there's no shame in finding a less worn path to our goals." She reached timidly for his hand and smiled.

*What does a snobby British girl spoon-fed a perfect life know about your goals?*

Gordon pulled away. "You don't understand! How could you? You have everything: a family, a nice life. I'm just-I'm just South Empire trash, like you said!" Tears streamed down his face, forcing his voice to tremble. "This is all I have! Without the Junior Enforcers, I'm nothing!"

"That's not true, Gordon!" Tears formed in the corners of Pratima's eyes. "I didn't mean what I said. I'm sorry—"

"Just get away from me!" Gordon pushed between two smoking men and sprinted west to throw Pratima off, wiping his nose with his hand. His mother's tune ran through his head.

*It's okay, Gordon,* a woman's voice whispered through his mind like a cool breeze.

Gordon steadied himself and scanned the crowd for Pratima. When he didn't see her, he sprinted toward the colossal heap of metal and slammed into a police cruiser parked diagonally across Union and Longdon by the sawhorse barricade. The scent of Pratima's shampoo caught the light breeze, and his eyes welled again.

*I am a piece of shit, a real fuck-up, like Pop said. Stupid, just like my mother.* Gordon inhaled the dusty city air through his nose and blinked away the tears.

"Can you believe this mess?" said a cop from the other side of the car. "Here we are cleanin' up after Miss Mercury again. It's a crime, I tell ya."

"No, what's a crime is that skimpy costume she wears," another officer responded.

"Ha! Tell me you don't like it, and I'll call you a liar."

"Did you see her in that girly magazine?" He whistled.

"Boy, did I. Hey, I gotta take a whiz. You mind coverin' for me for a minute?"

"Sure."

Gordon clutched the Red Ryder's stock in his sweaty hands, waiting as the man's shadow slid across the pavement and moved around the police car opposite him. The officer whistled "Please, Mr. Sun" as he passed. When the whistling faded, Gordon darted behind a piece of hot metal debris and peered over.

The other officer turned to tilt his hat to a woman in a summer dress, and Gordon bolted for the ocean of steel detritus. His worn-out Poll-Parrot shoes slapped a metal panel, bouncing it like a springboard, but he didn't dare look back. He skidded to a panicked stop as it teetered. A chasm yawned underneath him. "Hey!" the officer cried out. The metal plank whined, shifted, and dropped.

**47**

Gordon gasped. His eyes shot open, and the world was a pitch-black dream. The rotten, chilly smell of sewer and concrete gushed, engulfing him, and the screaming pain in his back assured him he was still alive.

He sat up, squinting through the gloom, and instinctively turning toward Walt's bed when an oddly cheerful whistle began.

"H-hello. Who's there? Walt?" The ground was freezing like Gordon was sitting on an ice block. He shivered, groping for his blanket, but found anything solid was smooth, cold, and relentlessly rigid.

Metal groaned. Hot liquid dripped off Gordon's hair. Sweat? No, thicker, hotter. He winced in pain as his fingers found the deep gash in his forehead and the all-encompassing panic that came with it. The whistling wouldn't stop.

# The City of the Gods: Gold

"Hello?"

All sound ceased abruptly. Gordon's eyes slowly adjusted, and he found his green shirt was now tinted red. The sight made his eyes dip back into his skull, but he fought the urge to pass out. He rose slowly, ignoring the pain radiating from his head and back, flailing his arms desperately as he inched forward. His fingers brushed something as cold and stiff as the ground had been. He pressed his hand flat against the smooth surface. The ground shifted and whined. Gordon steadied himself.

*I'm in Sainte Marie Square. There was a police officer. I was running. If I yell, I'll be caught, and Pop will—*

Gordon placed a hand on his throbbing head, and the world tumbled in front of him. He leaned against the smooth wall. *I can't look weak in front of Miss Mercury. Was she there? Did she tell me to run?* Gordon's hand brushed his soaked shorts, and he scowled. *I pissed myself! Like a baby!*

Something shifted in the shadows. A flicker of white drew Gordon's attention and an electrical burning smell, like when Pop had tried to fix the porch light and nearly electrocuted himself. The white flicker came again, intermixed with glowing black light and all the grays in between. Electric snow danced without touching the ground, stuck in space, like bad reception on a television.

Gordon stared in awe until the metal shifted again. He glanced up, almost losing his footing off the edge as the sliver of natural light faded. His heart jumped, and he dropped to his knees, staring at the wall where the electric snow had been until his eyes grew tired and out of focus. In his periphery, a human-looking figure skulked slowly across the open area repeatedly, caught in a continuous loop. When Gordon regarded it, a touch of red bled into the crackle of electric snow, resembling eyes. They turned to stare at Gordon, looping over and over. His stomach churned when it changed course, approaching him repeatedly, inching closer with each cycle. Fingers snapped shut inches from Gordon's nose.

He pulled his knees to his chest, cradling his head in his arms and shutting his eyes tight. The air crackled, growing louder until it was almost unbearable. Then, all at once, the scent of electricity faded, replaced by the sour stench of the city's underbelly. Gordon gathered his courage and glanced up to complete darkness. He sighed, and a hint of a smile crossed his lips.

A dull, frigid object brushed against the nape of his neck like a finger. He spun quickly but found only darkness.

"Gordon?" a voice whispered. It was distant and reserved, like a lousy connection echoing through a telephone receiver. Unmistakably, his mother's voice, but not her cadence. Gordon's eyes welled up, and panic forced him to his feet. He stepped forward a little too hastily, and the ground whined, a sound that made his blood curdle. He glanced up in time to see a small shard of metal falling through the darkness. Instinctively, he covered his face with his arms and stepped backward. The metal sparked as it bounced off the ground, illuminating a grinning black-and-white face before him.

"Gordon?"

Red eyes burned for another second and vanished. Gordon knew the face; he'd seen it before but didn't want to admit it. That sick, twisted grin and those deep, burning eyes belonged to the clown from Walter's "Uptown Clowns" program. The one who watched with glee as his father beat him.

Gordon stepped away, slowly losing focus. The natural light grew dimmer, and the unnatural glow illuminating the face brightened. Dark shadows accentuated deep smile lines and a gaping jaw.

"Gordon?" it asked in his mother's voice. Although its mouth didn't move, he knew that was the origin of the sound. "Gordon? Gordon? Gordon? Gordon? Gordon?" it repeated in the terrified voice of his mother. Black-and-white static ran over its body like snow, like it had stepped directly out of the television.

Its jaw dropped until it snapped, pulling the flesh around its face unnaturally tight. The bottom jaw stopped at its belt buckle. "Gordon? Gordon? Gordon? Gordon?" His mother's voice grew louder as the creature advanced, forcing him into its gaping maw.

Gordon awoke, standing in front of exposed brick. As the familiar, warm evening swaddled him, he ran his fingers along the rough surface. *Am I dead?*

*You're not dead,* a familiar voice answered.

Gordon slowly turned, allowing his eyes to adjust, and the Longdon Lane street sign came into view. The heaps of broken metal that had buried him moments ago glinted down the block, and his burning chest heaved with labored, phlegmy breaths like he'd been running. People passed on the street, staring. One old lady approached with concern in her eyes, and her mouth moved wordlessly.

*Follow me,* a voice cut through the overwhelming silence. Gordon couldn't find the origin amongst the leering crowd, but he knew her voice. It was all he could hear.

The sun was a whisper of yellow over the horizon, and the sky was blood red, inviting another night forward, inviting another beating. He sprinted away from the people, and the world tossed and turned, trying to throw him to the ground.

*Keep going.*

Color bled from the city as it grew darker, and Miss Mercury stood down the street, watching him with a seductive smile. *I'm here, Gordon. I came for you. You're mine now, and I'm finally yours.*

"Gordie?" The voice was small and quiet, but it rang through his head. Gordon turned and stumbled into Walter's arms, and the world fell into darkness.

Ron Baxter's Journal

October 14, 1944

Today, I met with James Connor, an old college friend and Chi Phi Brother. Although he was skeptical when I brought the Sibylline Religion to his attention, he has since had a change of heart. He has agreed to host my event in the penthouse suite in the Ironleaf building. Although I suspect James's fiancé, Theodora Byrne, had something to do with convincing him, it makes no difference. However, I have a sinking suspicion that once she discovers the party's true intentions, she will be wholeheartedly against it. I've left the event's planning and preparation to her as a distraction.

HELL
IS EMPTY
AND ALL
THE DEVILS
ARE HERE

**<u>48</u>**

Gibson took a cigarette from the crushed pack of Marlboros on the table, lit it, and took a deep, stale drag, pacing along the outskirts of the interrogation room. Smoke danced under the lone sweltering light, creating ghostly images resembling Bonnie Connor's face until Gibson could almost hear the grandfather clock ticking from Brookfield.

"Let me out!" he yelled at the door. The humorless men in black suits who had taken him in were almost as robotic as whatever Miss Mercury had toppled in Sainte Marie Square. They had grilled him about Miss Mercury's whereabouts like he'd been her partner in a robbery. When he couldn't provide the information they wanted, they threatened him: "How would Ann Listman feel about visiting you in Windwood Prison?" That made him chuckle, and they didn't like that. He rubbed the nagging pain in his ribs.

The latch clicked. Gibson backed against the table like a feral animal as the door swung open, revealing a shadowy visage against a far too bright backdrop.

"What are you waitin' for, Skipper? A kiss hello?" Slim's gravelly voice filled the room. Gibson snatched his hat from the table and pushed past the old man into the police station. Slim matched his stride, handing him his gun and a bloated manilla folder of personal effects as they rounded the corner into the bullpen. Phones rang, and typewriters clacked. The ninety-third precinct was bustling with unfamiliar men in black suits and matching grim resolves.

"Who are these fellas, anyway?" Gibson whispered.

Slim ran his thumb over the wheel of his stubborn Ronson lighter, eventually sparking a battered cigarette. "Fuckin' G-men, good for nothin' but givin' me the creeps."

"Why are they here?"

"They're like fuckin' cockroaches. Show up whenever the League so much as sneezes an' crawl up our collective ass. Got a hard-on for this shit. Haven't seen 'em this excited since T-Day." Slim poked Gibson in the chest. "Told ya to stay out of it."

Gibson sighed.

Slim leaned against a desk. Smoke snaked from his mouth as he said: "It ain't all your fault, Skipper. Someone told these slimy bastards you had an in with Miss Mercury. I set 'em straight; told 'em a monkey was more likely to have an in with the League than you." He chuckled, which turned into a coughing fit. "Anyway, if someone's tellin' tales outta school, then we're probably being set up."

"Creed." The name tasted like bile.

"Could be," Slim replied. "Could be any number o' people. I'm gonna see what Murphy knows."

Gibson cocked an eyebrow. "Murphy's here on a Saturday?"

"I called him." Slim looked Gibson over thoughtfully. "You should make yourself scarce. He ain't gonna be happy." A snide smile crossed his chubby face. "Yer welcome, by the way."

Gibson glanced around the bullpen and fingered his tender ribs, suddenly conscious of something interrupting the fraternal order. "Thanks a million, pal."

Slim's smile faded. "I'll talk t' Murphy. Go get some rest."

Gibson shook his head. "There's work to be done. You still have those photos you showed me at Wilbur's?"

Slim smiled and opened his palm like a magician, revealing a cardstock folder on the desk behind him. Gibson reached for the files, but Slim slapped his hand over them.

"There's a library," he said, "across the park. I'm not much of a reader, but my old partner used t' go there often. Said it helped him think. Sometimes quiet is what a case like this requires."

Gibson nodded, collected the files, and walked toward the door. Something Creed said wasn't sitting right. *He's just a geriatric asshole who burned all his bridges, and the only reason he has a job is because he and Murphy have a history.* He met Slim's gaze and leaned into the door, wondering why his partner suddenly wanted him out of the way.

The sunlight almost forced Gibson to his knees. Spots swam in front of his tired eyes, and the world became an oven. He clutched the files to his chest, moving briskly across Currie Park.

The city rose around the sprawling lawn, and folks meandered aimlessly, enjoying the beautiful day. A young couple spread out on a blanket laughed at a private joke, and Ann's blue eyes plagued Gibson's thoughts. In another life, they used to walk through this park hand-in-hand, naming their unborn children. Playing family. Then Gibson was shipped off to Korea, forced to grow up under a hail of Communist China's gunfire as the all-powerful Soviet Union loomed in the distance with their atomic weapons. The same weapons Doctor Torment once had access to if the *Bulletin* was correct.

*You can never be too careful in Empire, now that the heroes are gone.* Creed had been right. Constant annihilation threats still plagued Empire, and if the rest of the Enforcers were truly gone, Miss Mercury couldn't protect them forever.

A woman in a summer dress and a red shell hat pushing a baby pram flashed a smile. Gibson tipped his hat. "Ma'am." These were his people. This was his city. The clamor of honking traffic, the crowds, the smell of exhaust, and the dirty sidewalks ran through his veins. The skyline had changed since T-Day, but the soul was still there. The energy nourished him through the sleepless nights, and the hustle and bustle kept his heart beating. Empire was alive, and so was he. As long as he drew breath, he couldn't give up on his people, including Bonnie Connor.

## **49**

The library's musty smell matched the old decor. Ornate mahogany pillars, bookshelves, and tables sat opposite gothic windows overlooking the park.

A gaunt woman with cat-eye spectacles resting halfway down her pointy nose scanned a book behind the front desk. Gibson removed his hat and cleared his throat. She finished the page and regarded him. "Yes?"

"Hello—I need, um—I guess I need help finding books on religion."

The old lady slid her glasses up her birdish nose. "You guess?"

"Yes, ma'am. No, I mean—I'd like to see the books you offer on religion."

"Please?"

"I'm sorry?" Gibson responded.

"You guess you'd like to see the books I offer on religion, *please.*"

Gibson sighed and nodded. "Please."

"What religion, sir?" she asked lazily.

"Anything you have handy, specifically with the words 'Master Leonard' or 'Dea' included. Also, any nonfiction associated with witchcraft or sacrifice. Oh, and Latin, any English to Latin books available. *Please.*"

The woman stared at him, and her leathery jowls tightened. "What is this pertaining to, exactly? Maybe I can help narrow your search." She eyed the cardstock folder.

"I'm a detective with the ECPD, investigating a missing persons case and—"

"And you think God will help you? Or is it the witches who will be assisting?"

"What? No! Look, I just need any books you have containing the words 'Master Leonard' or 'Dea.' Please."

The woman sighed. "Follow me." She moved like a specter across the library, pushing in chairs and tidying as she went. She pulled a wooden chair from under a matching table. "Wait here."

She vanished amongst the shelves. Gibson slumped into the chair, casually glanced across the sea of mahogany to ensure he was alone, and slowly opened the folder.

The dead woman locked eyes with him from the black-and-white photo. Gibson looked past the gore and deviance and wondered who she had been. She was pretty enough, and her hair looked as if it had been in pin curl waves like she'd come from a gala. Then he regarded the deer antlers fastened to her skull with roofing nails and sighed.

*Why deer antlers?*

The photo reminded Gibson of a hunting trip he'd taken as a child. He remembered that cold winter day like he was still that same boy, watching silently as his uncle stalked a deer. The frigid air gnawing through his gloves and boots, leaching all feeling from his digits. The bitter taste of his first sip of beer after his uncle finally deemed him a man. Gibson enjoyed the attention and comradery until he saw the kill, sprawled in the snow with wide, stark black eyes. The vacancy and fear in the dead creature's face resembled the woman watching him from the photograph as if begging for an end to the suffering. He shut the folder.

*Could someone do this to a child, to Bonnie Connor?*

Gibson couldn't help but think there were clues hidden within the collection of strange and terrible things he'd seen over the past few days.

# The City of the Gods: Gold



Gibson ran a hand over the stubble on his chin and thoughtfully gazed out the park window. A young mother laid her newborn on a plaid blanket as her husband fished inside a picnic basket. An eerie passage from the book he'd found at Baxter's jumped through his mind: "The sacrifice of the daughter for the gods' favor."

Something about the phrase didn't sit right. Sacrifice *the* daughter for *the* gods' favor, *the* gods' favor, not God's favor. *We* are god. Not *I* am God. God is dead. *We* are god.

Gibson sighed and flipped through the photos. Another woman, another lurid death. She had the same hairstyle as the first, naked with the same open throat and blood running down her chest. However, she lay on her back in the center of an elaborate star with candlesticks melted at the apexes.

"Ahem."

Gibson glanced up to find the librarian's stern face. He shut the folder and smiled.

She motioned to a cart behind her. "These are some of the religious titles we offer. Leave anything you don't need on the cart, and I'll return the books when you're through."

"Yes, ma'am," Gibson said.

She scowled. "I've also included a Latin phrasebook. We have no text with a direct translation in this branch of the library. Perhaps in our Cork branch. I can call them if you'd like?"

"No, thank you. This might just be the ticket."

"There's also a microfilm reader over there, should you need it." She pointed across to the opposite wall.

Gibson nodded. "Well, thanks again. You've been a tremendous—"

"There was another detective who came in here looking for books like these," she interrupted. Gibson waited for her to add more to her statement. Instead, she turned and strolled back to her desk.

Gibson watched her go curiously, then regarded the overwhelming stack of books and frowned. *One in a million shot, any of these have anything to do with Bonnie's disappearance. I should be out there, boots on the ground.* He glanced across Armory Square at the glistening, life-sized statue of the three Enforcers.

*t's not enough to know the heroes are watching over the city. Empire needs tangible idols when faith isn't enough.* The gold glinted in the sunlight like a shroud over their violent past. *We citizens ignore the Enforcers' death toll as long as the city feels safe, but is anyone really safe anymore? Any day, the Soviets could attack. Even in Empire, I saw a dozen or more people die in Sainte Marie Square this morning.*

*The Enforcers can't guarantee our safety any more than the government can. Still, we live our lives believing everything's hunky-dory while they hide their violent ways behind that hokey radio show.*

Gibson closed his eyes, and the dead stare of the woman with deer antlers watched him. *The Enforcers gained our trust,* he thought, *and all the while, they were possibly involved in the horrific murder of innocents.* He eyed the folder. *These women and men died years ago, but what are the Enforcers hiding now? Or what am I, as a citizen of Empire, choosing to ignore because of who they are?* Gibson sighed. *Am I just growing cynical, or am I finally seeing the truth?*

He remembered what Theodora had said. *How would I behave when the world I know comes crashing down, and there is no right and wrong anymore?* He stared at the golden heroes. *Was there ever a right or wrong for them?*

Gibson sighed and pulled the first book from the cart. *Dictionary of Phrase and Fable* by E. Cobham Brewer. He thumbed through the pages until the name jumped out at him: Master Leonard.

# The City of the Gods: Gold

The text melted into a blurry jumble of black and white. Gibson rubbed his tired eyes and squinted through the words.

*Grand-master of the nocturnal orgies of the demons, he is represented as a three-horned goat, with a black human face, he marked his novitiates with his horns.*

A drop of blood splashed across the page, then another. Gibson watched them flow into the book's spine and ran his hand under his nose. Blood poured down his fingers.

"Jesus!" Frantically, he pinched his nose with his handkerchief and shoved the book aside. When the bleeding stopped, he grabbed another volume from the cart: *Eliphas Levi's Ritual of Transcendental Magic.* He opened the glossary and found "Master Leonard" listed under "Chapter XV, The Sabbath of the Sorcerers."

"To Sabbaths dreamed in this manner, we must refer the accounts of a goat issuing from pitchers and going back into them after the ceremony; infernal powders obtained from the ordure of this goat, who is called Master Leonard; banquets where abortions are eaten without salt and boiled with serpents and toads; dances, in which monstrous animals or men and women with impossible shapes take part; unbridled debauches where incubi project cold sperm. Nightmare alone could produce or explain such scenes."

The page blurred again, and Gibson's head pounded. Something in the back of his subconscious begged him to stop as a ringing grew louder. He slammed the book shut and slid it across the table with the others, staring at it with wide eyes.

Eventually, he chalked it up to sleep deprivation and opened the Latin phrasebook. "Damnatio memoriae—" He underlined the word with his finger. "Condemnation of memory? 'The goal of damnatio memoriae is to erase any shred of evidence certain people ever existed. The ultimate mortal punishment performed by many cultures through the ages.'"

*It would make sense for Ron to ensure these victims became a bunch of John and Jane Does, but why celebrate it by writing damnatio memoriae above the corpse? It seems redundant.*

He flipped back to the glossary and found the other phrase from the photos. "Homo sacer. 'Roman law stated the homo sacer or the accused man was banned from society, and their life was forfeit"—he raised an eyebrow. *Cons fit that description, transients, working girls, queers, commies. None of which are Bonnie Connor.* He shut the book, added it to the shunned pile with a sigh, and thumbed lazily through what remained on the cart.

"'Iphigenia at Aulis,' translated by Jane Lumley.*"*

*I saw this same book,* he thought, *in Baxter's study.* He flipped a few pages into the lengthy text, finding passages marked with black ink and dark circles encasing phrases:

"He loves power. A terrible love."

"Death will be my wedding, children, and glory."

An image of the goat-headed creature was etched next to the passage:

"Oh, where is the noble face of modesty, or the strength of virtue, now that blasphemy is in power and men have put justice behind them, and there is no law but lawlessness, and none join in fear of the gods?"

Gibson flipped the cover closed but found none of the Armory Square Library's stamps or markings on the book's spine.

"He said, if anyone ever came in here asking about Master Leonard, give him this book," the librarian's voice echoed off the high ceilings. Gibson spun around, startled.

"The detective who used to study here. He told me you'd come one day. Luckily, I was here when you did."

"What detective?" Gibson asked.

"The gentleman never gave me his name. He insisted it was safer that way. An older fellow, I haven't seen him in years."

*Harper,* Gibson thought.

She made a face that almost looked like a longing smile. "I forgot all about this sordid affair until you mentioned Master Leonard. It's funny how the mind works like that." Her scowl returned. "Well, good luck, young man, in whatever it is you hope to accomplish here, and please, take that awful book with you." She turned and strode elegantly back to the front desk.

Gibson flipped to a random page, blotted out with black ink. He tried to make out the words, turning and twisting the book in the dim light. Something shifted a few pages deeper. He fanned them, and a small piece of paper dropped onto the table. He glanced at the front desk, unfolded it, and read the handwritten note silently:

*Lenny,*

*I took the coward's way out. I'm sorry. Add it to the ledger of my regrets. I'd say this whole caper unfolded like a Greek tragedy, but it isn't as dramatic as that—just people playing games that got out of hand. Still, I'm afraid 62 is too old to fight the good fight anymore.*

*Who am I kidding? I quit because I can't live with what I've done. I count it a blessing that I lack the courage to end it myself. Life is too fragile a gift to squander in that manner. Alas, I'm a haunted man with more bad memories than good.*

*Who knows? Maybe I'm already dead. If not, then they'll see to it soon enough. At any rate, I hope it's you who finds this note. I couldn't leave it in the open, as people and their belongings seem to be disappearing more permanently these days. Soon, I'll vanish along with them, but you'll remember me, won't you, Lenny? Don't worry; no one knows what you're keeping for me. I made sure of it. Now it's time to see the rest. Don't let this haunt you, pal. It was never your battle, but I'm afraid I've dragged you into it. Get that little girl out of that house, do what I couldn't.*

*We'll always have Eddie's Bar and Wilbur's Diner. If anything happens to me, Lenny, remember our time at Eddie's and Wilbur's, won't you?*

*-W.H.*

Gibson touched the frayed bottom and left edges and flipped the page over, revealing a drawing, crude and poorly sketched but unmistakably the creature with a goat's head. The intensely etched lines made the image look like a madman drew it. Beneath it, sentences were scrawled backward and forwards up and down in at least three different handwriting styles.

"Eligos, the knight, a master of strategy. The death merchant."

"Sabnock, the creator. The builder."

"End the war before it begins or annihilation."

"Ronove, the quick, lingers with the dying. The messenger."

"Marchosias, the warrior, wishes to be on high. The armored."

"An uncorrupted offering: a pure soul."

"No beasts, only the gods' spawn."

"Dea is death."

Gibson flipped the letter over. One sentence stood out: "Protect that little girl."

His mind raced. *Obviously, W.H. is William Harper. So Lenny must be Len "Slim" Shanahan.* Gibson slid the note into his pocket and mindlessly scanned a few more pages. When he was satisfied there were no more notes, he gathered his effects and the book and moved briskly toward the exit.

"Thank you for your help, ma'am," Gibson called out as he passed the front desk and the stern old woman who sat behind it. She nodded joylessly, eyeing the book under his arm. Gibson slid his hat back onto his head and pushed open the heavy wooden door.

**<u>50</u>**

Gibson turned on the lights and glanced up the stairs to ensure no one followed him into the police station's basement. He set his documents on top of a row of army-green file cabinets and opened the drawer marked "H," flipping through the names. "Hader, Hardy—no Harper."

*Damnatio memoriae. Condemnation of memory.* He slammed the drawer shut. The right people had made sure all traces of Harper were gone. Another dead end in a series defining Gibson's detective career.

He pulled the note from his pocket, meticulously scanning each word. The phrasing at the bottom flowed differently, like a desperate love letter: *We'll always have Eddie's Bar and Wilbur's Diner. If anything happens to me, Lenny, remember our time at Eddie's and Wilbur's, won't you?*

Gibson folded the note. *Why was Harper so adamant about remembering an old diner and a dive like Eddie's? Slim doesn't seem like the sentimental type—and to mention it twice—there's no way he'd be able to hide anything at either of those places without folks noticing.* Gibson's eyes found the file cabinet marked "W." *It's a long shot,* he thought.

He pulled the drawer open and walked his fingers over the folders. "Warner, Watson, Washington." He froze breathlessly. "E. Wilbur," the worn tab said in block letters. It was a file thicker than the rest, standing out like a beacon.

Gibson pulled the folder with shaky hands, dropped it on the table in the center of the room, and gawked like it was a ghost. He glanced up the stairs and slowly pulled the cover down.

On top was a sepia-toned glamor shot of a woman gazing optimistically into the distance taken in the mid-forties, judging by the victory roll updo.

*That sure as shit isn't Edward Wilbur.*

Underneath was an unofficial death certificate. "Betty Burton, April 17, 1926 - December 16, 1944." He flipped past it, and like a recurring nightmare, the photo of the woman with deer antlers met his gaze.

Gibson flipped forward to a similar death certificate clipped to a picture of a woman with shorter cropped black hair and cat-eye spectacles. A slight obligatory smile graced her bookish face.

"Dorothy Mautz, September 6, 1927 - December 16, 1944." He flipped the page down and, as expected, found the photos of the second, dark-haired woman with a slit throat sprawled inside a star.

Gibson passed through a collection of make-shift legal documents and stopped at the picture of a man with a caved-in head. He flipped forward and found a mug shot with a piece of paper clipped to the front.

"Carl Curtis February 2, 1921 - December 16, 1944." The man had oily black hair, a hard, remorseless face, and wild animalistic eyes.

*Well, there's your accursed man.*

He flipped through more men's mugshots, birth certificates, death certificates, driver's licenses, arrest records, and police reports.

# The City of the Gods: Gold

Gibson dropped the file and pinched the bridge of his nose. The mounting stack of dead bodies fit with the League of Enforcers' habit of acting as judge, jury, and executioner, but why hurt these women? They seemed innocent. He shuffled through the photos again. Near the back was a black-and-white picture of a man with a military crew cut. Deep creases ran across his forehead, at the corners of his eyes, and down along his slight jowls. His strong jaw, thick neck, and joyless, hard stare suggested he was not a man to be fucked with.

Gibson flipped the photo over and found William Harper's death certificate: "September 3, 1882 - December 13, 1945."

*How could Harper be in this folder if he created it?* Gibson Thought. *And if Bonnie is five now, Harper wouldn't have known her. So, who was the little girl he was talking about in his note?*

He thumbed forward to a black-and-white image of Harper sprawled, shirtless, in a bathtub. His throat was open, and his feet hung over the edge, one bare and one clad in a black dress sock with the sock suspender still attached. His face looked alive and angry, but the light was gone from his eyes. As expected, above his dead body, written in blood, was "damnatio memoriae." This was the worst kind of dead end, one that begged more questions than it answered.

He flipped past the photo to a small slip of paper and unfolded it with hesitant anticipation. The dark, scratchy pen marks scrawled messily over the page were familiar, but the words were meaningless. It was unmistakably the bottom of the page where Harper had written his note. He turned it over.

*Lenny,*

*If you're reading this, I failed, but the mission must continue. Get Rosalita away from Baxter. Now that her mother is dead, she's too dangerous. Do what I couldn't.*

*-W.H.*

The note was wrapped around a small, cropped photo of a woman with long dark hair dumped into a bathtub, just as Harper had been. She looked like she'd suffered multiple stab wounds. Gibson had seen a picture of the same woman in Ron's study—the Hispanic woman posing with Ron and his brother.

Gibson shoved the new note into his pocket and stacked the folder with the rest of his documents. No one at the ninety-third precinct would miss ol' Eddie Wilbur, and these people needed validation. He climbed the stairs.

----

"We're off the case," Slim said as Gibson entered the bullpen.

Gibson eyed the few remaining G-men meandering by the water fountain and tightened his grip on the folder. "Slim, this is bigger than—"

"It's over, Skipper." Slim listlessly pulled a Pall Mall from his shirt pocket and set it between his lips. "Murphy made it clear that I'm only on the force as a—how did he put it?—in an advisory capacity. Or I was, at least."

Gibson glanced across the bullpen into Murphy's office, where he hunched over his desk. "Let me buy you a drink, Lenny. I know a place. It ain't Eddie's, but it'll do."

Slim froze with the flame of his lighter inches away from his cigarette. "What did you call me?"

"C'mon. A drink'll do you good."

## 51

Lost Lake was a little revolting, but it served booze and wasn't a cop bar like Eddie's. Gibson used to come here after his beat when he wanted to escape the cop life. Today, the bar was so empty that Gibson could hear rats in the walls and the labored breathing of the fat bartender as he thumbed through the *Bulletin*.

Slim sat across from him at the small, wobbly table in the back of the room, lighting match after match, watching them burn down to his stubby fingers. "Look, Skipper, I appreciate what yer tryin' t' do, but it's the end of the road. Murphy took my badge an' my gun. You'll be reassigned—"

Gibson shook his head. "Slim, there's something bigger at play here. We're so close. You can't throw in the towel, Harper wouldn't do that."

"Ha! You don't know Bill Harper." Slim leaned back in his creaky chair. "He killed hisself, or so people say." He took a swig of whiskey.

"Bill Harper was murdered," Gibson said.

Slim let out a long wheeze, which turned into a boisterous laugh. "Murdered? How do you know that? I know that 'cause I know Bill Harper, and I know he wouldn't even think o' suicide, but all his mortal items were destroyed. He don't even have a grave." Slim's tone grew more sullen, and his smile faded as he lit another match.

Gibson slid the pile of documents in front of Slim. "Ever heard of Eddie Wilbur?" He took a swig of his Schlitz beer.

Slim eyed Gibson and opened the file cautiously. He moved his mouth as he read, flipping each page over, giving the files the time they deserved.

Gibson couldn't have said how long they sat there, but there was a calming silence between them. The rats scurrying through the walls and the bartender's labored breathing meant Slim was learning what he needed to know. His eyes glazed, and his expression traded fear with anger and anger with grief. "Do you know what this is? How'd you come across this, Skipper?"

"Harper." Gibson spun the empty beer can in his hands.

Slim watched Gibson cockeyed. "Harper's dead, fella. You seen one too many episodes of *Tales of Tomorrow*."

Gibson dug into his pocket and slid the first note from Harper across the table. Slim eyed him and unfolded it hesitantly. His mouth tightened as he read, and he nodded solemnly half a dozen times. "Where'd you find this?"

"The library, across from Armory, he meant for you to find it."

Slim dropped his head to look over the note again. "Harper was a drunk, a sentimental drunk from the look of it, but this don't mean a thing."

"Look closer," Gibson said. "On the other side."

Slim flipped the page over, and the insanity of the passages registered on his face. "It's nonsense."

"No, Slim, I saw this same thing at Baxter's. A whole book of it, and I'm pretty sure Baxter wrote it. Harper tore this page out on purpose. He's leading us somewhere." He tapped *Iphigenia at Aulis*. "I found another copy of this book in Baxter's study with a passage circled about sacrificing children for the gods' favor.'"

"No, this is wrong." Slim flipped the note over and over and stared at the carpet. "Harper wouldn't know about Bonnie Connor."

Gibson slid the second note to Slim.

"How about Rosalita? Any idea who that is?"

Slim scanned the letter and looked up. "No. You seen how Baxter is. He always has girls hanging around."

Gibson tightened his lips. "Did Harper have a relationship with—"

"No. Harper wouldn't play ball with Baxter aside from that one time in December '44, but he wasn't stupid, neither. He stayed out of his way but still took his cut, I guess. We never talked about it. He gave me th' photos of th' dead girls when shit started t' go south, but not all of 'em. He said he wanted to keep me away from it as much as possible." Slim patted the folder. "I guess this is the rest of 'em."

"Any idea who put Harper's files under Eddie Wilbur?" Gibson asked. "He obviously didn't do it himself."

"Probably Denton. He worked th' Connors' party with Harper."

Gibson's eyes widened. "Can we ask him——"

"He's dead, had a heart attack in '50." Slim shuffled through the file again. "Who's the Mexican broad?" Slim lifted the small photo out of the file.

"No idea. No documents involving her, aside from the picture. I saw her in a photo in Baxter's study, though."

"Hm. Harper did have a pet project, something about Mexican immigrants. He wouldn't tell me much because he thought it was too dangerous. She could be Rosalita." He chuckled. "An' if she is, there's not much I can do for her now from the look o' things."

Slim shuffled back a few pages. "Why the deer antlers? I never been able to figure that one out. It's barbaric. Somethin' out o' a Greek tragedy, like Harper was saying in his note."

"That's it! 'This whole caper unfolded like a Greek tragedy, but it isn't as dramatic as that. Just people playing games that got out of hand.' Like it says in the note. Slim, Harper wasn't being melodramatic. He was warning us." Gibson remembered the cold, dead eyes of the Greek gods watching him from Baxter's foyer. He opened *Iphigenia at Aulis* and scanned the pages until something spoke to him.

"Let me see that note," Gibson said.

Slim handed it over.

Gibson flipped it. "No beasts, only the gods' spawn. Baxter wanted this to unfold like one of his beloved Greek stories. There's a reason Harper took this specific book and left it in the library for you to find."

Gibson dropped the note and tore through the book, trying to remember where he'd seen the passage. "In this book, a deer was sacrificed at the altar instead of Iphigenia, the daughter! For the gods' favor!" He pressed his finger down on the photo of poor Betty Burton with deer antlers fastened to her head.

"It says so right here: 'And the miracle happened. Everyone distinctly heard the sound of a knife striking, but no one could see the girl. She had vanished, the priest cried out, and the whole army echoed him, seeing what some god had sent, a thing nobody could have prophesied. There it was, we could see it, but we could scarcely believe it: a deer lay there gasping, a large, beautiful animal, and its blood ran streaming over the altar of the goddess.'"

Slim sipped his drink. "So?"

"So, that was the first time. The first sacrifice—the one Harper and Denton were at. The woman with the antlers was a sacrificial deer." He pointed back to the note. "It also says no beasts, only the gods' spawn. There are no more Greek gods, no more Artemis, to sacrifice deer to, to gain her favor. They were offering this to that, Master Leonard, thing. Now it craves the gods' spawn. The League of Enforcers is the closest thing to gods the world has now. That would make Bonnie the spawn or the child of the gods. That's why Baxter wants her."

"This is so far-fetched, Skipper. I don't know."

"You saw that Japanese girl, same as I did, Slim. That thing is back—Master Leonard—or at least Baxter thinks it is, and if Baxter thinks it wants Bonnie Connor, she's as good as dead."

Ron Baxter's Journal

December 19, 1944

All the arrangements have been made, and favors called in. I will send Carmella to the Ironleaf building early to ensure all is well. As much as it pains me, I must stay behind to deliver Rosalita. I cannot trust her to be left alone with anyone but myself.

James informed me this morning over a short telephone call that, using his father's connections, he was able to convince Mayor Hall, the DA, and many of the prominent men of the ECPD to attend this evening. I pleaded with him not to involve them, but he was insistent.

Rosalita said whosoever offers Master Leonard an acceptable sacrifice shall inherit the power of the gods. After studying Greek myths, I believe I can appeal to that which gave the goddess Artemis her power. Just as Agamemnon sacrificed Iphigenia only to have her replaced by a deer at the last moment, I will offer a sacred deer and a daughter as one.

BRIDGE
TO
OBLIVION

## 52

"Hold it steady, goddammit!" the man screamed over the roar of the circular saw, echoing through the Idea Square. He approached the vessel, suspended upside down from the ceiling by thick cables. Two equally sweaty men yanked at chains attached to either side to steady it.

"Go ahead, Leo, that's as good as she's going to get," one man yelled.

Nadir paced along the outskirts of the Idea Square to stave off the anxiety creeping through his subconscious like a predator. "Do be careful."

The man with the saw eyed him belligerently and slowly forced the whirling blade against the hull. Nadir cringed, and red-hot debris shot like tears onto the flame-retardant blanket draped over the electromagnet bolted to the floor beneath it.

The contractors looked like circus clowns, fighting the tethers to a million balloons as their associate ran the dreadfully deafening machine around the vessel's circumference. Nadir felt Frank's resentful stare boring a hole through him from behind the glass, where he stood with Brown, Wendell, a group of firemen, and a handful of armed guards.

Extensive dye penetrant, radiography, and ultrasonic tests concluded the vessel's rust-covered side was intact and, indeed, copper. However, the cleaner half was an unknown metal, close to (or possibly) gadolinium. All that mattered was that it could be ferromagnetic when cooled. Still, questions continued to pile up, but the most haunting enigma remained at the forefront: Why did Theodora Connor feel the need to keep this vessel's identity from her husband?

The scent of burning metal forced Nadir forward. "Careful, old boy. Careful!" Every precaution had been taken, but his insatiable worry forced him through the checklist again:

*We've returned the other vessel to storage on sub-five. The smoke detectors and sprinkler systems were disabled. The Idea Square's cooling system is able to reach ten degrees Celsius. Men from the fire brigade are waiting in the staging area, forced to sip coffee with Frank, poor chaps. And guards are standing by, armed with M1 Carbines—or rather, they will be armed once we're through with the magnet.*

Nadir peered at the soldiers through the glass and sighed. They were only on-site on the off chance something hostile was inhabiting the ship. However, their presence brought a lot of unwanted attention from Frank's faceless bosses and the men in black who seemed to be infesting the building as of late.

The man holding the saw circled slowly with the same anxious face one might make when trying to push a grand piano up a set of stairs alone. "Hold her steady, boys. We're almost there!" He traded glances between the ship and his footing as he rounded the edge and disappeared to the other side.

*CA-CHUNK!* The saw's hum came to a sputtering halt, and smoke billowed.

"Goddammit! This fucking thing broke my blade!"

"Did you happen to finish scoring the hull?" Nadir yelled.

The contractor moved into view. "Yeah, but—"

"Good, good." Nadir marched eagerly across the concrete floor, throwing an echo around the mostly empty room.

The other men removed the chains. "I need a cup o' joe," one said to the other.

"Hell, I need a beer," the second man responded to the first man's amusement.

Nadir pressed a button under the speaker by the door. "We're ready for phase two. Doctor Wendell, if you would be so kind as to fetch the generator from sub-five? Doctor Brown, would you prep the cooling mechanism?" There was a wave of movement behind the glass, and Nadir hastened across the floor toward the ship.

# The City of the Gods: Gold

Two of the contractors smiled at a private joke, most likely at Nadir's expense. He recognized the superiority complex in their dim, thoughtless eyes and stupid grins.

"Gentlemen, if you'll excuse me," Nadir said.

"Not so fast, pal," the man holding the saw replied. "What about my saw? This thing cost me a mint."

"Yes, yes, of course. Go out that door there and ask for Frank. I'm sure he'll compensate you." Nadir smirked. "He's my secretary, not a very good one, mind you, but it's so hard to find good help these days, don't you agree?" Nadir eyed the grinning buffoons and waved dismissively toward the exit. "Do stick around, however. We may require your services again later." He began the tedious job of inspecting the room.

----

The sucking noise of the opening door announced Frank. He stomped across the Idea Square as theatrically as possible to accentuate his anger. Nadir glanced over his shoulder with an appropriately audible sigh.

"What's the big idea tellin' those contractors I'm your secretary, huh?" Frank prodded his chest. "Jesus, I'm a goddamn laughingstock out there!"

Nadir smirked. "I have to keep you honest, old boy. We can't have you getting a big head, can we?" He ran an index finger across the fresh score in the ship, eyeing Frank, who was purple with rage. "Cat got your tongue? Good, I'll do the talking. I'm not sure I like the guards milling about. Their presence is rather unsettling." He pulled the tarp from the electromagnet.

"You're *rather unsettling*, Singh; they're necessary," Frank huffed.

"Yes, good one, Frank. I thought you might say that." Nadir stepped over two insulated wires taped along the floor and removed a pair of wire cutters from his pocket.

He crouched and stripped the insulation from one. "Be a dear and hand me that duct tape, won't you?"

Frank slapped the roll into his outstretched palm. "You know you're unbelievable, Singh. I'm here on my day off. The least you could do is treat me with a little respect!"

"And why would I do a crazy thing like that?" Nadir peeled a piece of tape from the roll and smoothed it over the wire. "Here, Frank. Make yourself useful and strip this other wire, like I've done with the first."

Frank shuffled around him and snatched the wire cutters. "The lack of respect is unbelievable. The only reason I'm doing this is so we can get out of here at a reasonable time, not because you told me to!" He crouched and stripped the insulation.

"Don't worry, Frank, it's a soundproof room. The men in the office, whom you are so desperate to impress, can't hear me ordering you around."

Nadir scanned the magnet. It was roughly four feet in diameter, with an eight-inch hole bored through the center containing coils. He flipped through Brown's notes. "Fifteen kilowatts would essentially rip the magnet apart or, at least, bend the copper coils inside enough to render it unusable. That's why Theodora Connor reinforced it with silver. Smart girl, despicable, but smart. Will it be enough to separate the ship, however?" He scanned the vessel thoughtfully. "When you've finished there, Frank, the ship's chassis could use a good buffing." Nadir tried to hide his plaguing doubts behind a veil of nastiness, but they became more substantial as the moment of truth approached, and hints of Doctor Thompson's insanity invaded the flavor of the day.

*The world will burn.*

"You know I could be fishing with my cousin right now? Instead, I'm here, listening to a pompous windbag disrespecting me." Frank grunted.

"Yes, well, it looks like your cousin is the lucky one." Nadir strode past Frank and slapped a red button, opening the door to the office. "Take five gents," he said to the crowd of onlookers, sliding between them and nodding to Nicholas, whom he had only just now recognized under his cap.

Nicholas smiled. "Hey, Doctor Singh, congratulations."

Nadir clapped him on the back. "Congratulations aren't warranted yet, my dear boy."

Nadir sauntered to the desk on the other side of the room and slumped down, eyeing the people gathered to watch his folly around the partition. He lifted the phone handset off the cradle and dialed his house.

The phone rang twice, and Nadir's anxious fingers tapped the desk.

"Singh residence," Anila finally answered.

Nadir smiled. "Hello, darling."

"Hello yourself, how is work, my dear? Have you met any Martians yet?" she teased.

"Not yet, but we haven't even had lunch, so there's still plenty of time." Nadir tilted his chair back on two legs. The room dissolved, and it was just the two of them.

"Well, you positively must discover what they eat for lunch. We wouldn't want Martians to think Earthlings are rude."

Nadir chuckled. "With my luck, we'll find out they eat Earthlings."

The silence on the other end of the phone lingered. Nadir returned the chair to its four legs and leaned forward on the desk. "I'm just calling to check-in. Are the children home?"

"No, they've gone out to play with a few of their classmates."

Nadir glanced around the partition and through the glass at the hanging ship.

"Ukrit's friends, *not* Pratima's! Can you believe it?"

Nadir tapped his fingers. "Well, that's—"

"Doctor Singh!" Brown motioned for him. "The Idea Square has reached ten degrees. We're ready."

"I'm afraid I must go, Anila. As you know, science waits for no man," he exclaimed. The other end of the phone fell silent, and that unsettling feeling came crashing back between Nadir and his wife.

He closed his eyes. "I love you, Anila." He pictured her as she was when they were first married, young and sweet—and unable to foresee what a mistake she'd made. "Give the children my love as well. I'll be home in a few hours."

"I love you," she responded. The phone clicked. Nadir held it to his ear for another moment and gently set it on the cradle.

He forced a smile as he walked across the room and clapped Frank's shoulder. "Well, shall we make history?"

**<u>53</u>**

Frank's reflection glared at Nadir from the window. "Are you sure about this, Singh?" he whispered. His breath smelled like someone had opened a septic tank, but aside from that offense, he was now a docile creature.

Nadir sighed. "*This* is why we're here, old boy."

Nadir edged his finger up to a button trapped under a protective glass shield. "Well, gentlemen, we've done the math, and here we are. Hopefully, we've remembered to move the decimal points to the correct number of places and carried whatever numbers felt the need to be carried. Care to place wagers on what we find inside?"

Silence blanketed the room.

"Very well, then." Nadir clicked his tongue against the roof of his dry mouth, flipped the casing, and pressed the button. Red lights circled the bullpen, and an alarm screamed as metal shutters lowered on each side of the Idea Square.

Nadir focused on the ship as it vanished. When the clamor ceased, he eyed his team. "Doctor Brown, on my mark."

Brown wiped his brow.

"Three, two, one, now!" Nadir said. There was an anticlimactic click as Brown threw the switch, and the generator sputtered alive.

"We're running at four kilowatts," Brown squeaked.

Nadir nodded, watching the shutters. "Bring it up to eleven!" he yelled over the motor.

Brown turned a knob on the side of the generator as Wendell flipped through a notebook, no doubt triple-checking the math.

"Eleven kilowatts, sir," Brown stammered.

The fillings in Nadir's teeth tingled. He stepped back. "Keep it there for a moment, Doctor Brown."

"Doctor Singh," Wendell interjected, "the coils on the magnet will crack if we keep it here. I'd advise we go full power right away, sir."

Frank placed a hand on Nadir's shoulder. "Is that a good idea?"

Nadir brushed him off. "Anyone with dental fillings or plates in their head might want to stand back. Twenty-one kilowatts, Doctor Brown."

Brown made the Christian sign of the cross against his chest and cranked the knob. There was a sharp fracturing sound as the windows blew between the shutters, followed by the groan of twisting metal.

"Singh, that's enough!" Frank yelled.

The room's temperature dropped, and Nadir pressed his hand on Frank's shoulder. "Just a few more seconds, Frank." The shutters buckled inward.

Frank pointed at Brown. "Shut it off! Now!"

"Do not touch that switch!" Nadir yelled.

Brown followed their voices with wide eyes.

"This is over, Singh!" Frank screamed.

The ceiling whined, and Brown white-knuckled the knob. The rest of the group had their backs pressed against the far wall.

The ceiling groaned again, followed by a crash, then another.

"Singh!" Frank gripped his arm.

Nadir slapped Brown's shoulder. "Shut it off!"

**<u>54</u>**

The motley group stood stagnant, waiting for the construction crew to return with a blowtorch. Nadir paced, eyeing the damaged steel doors. The men had managed to lift one of the outside shutters halfway up and prop it open using a desk turned on end. Broken glass from what had once been a window spilled across the floor.

The contractors had also attempted to lift the inside shutter, but it was "bent to hell," as Frank had so eloquently put it. A blowtorch seemed like the best bet and, more importantly, the fastest way to get back into the Idea Square.

Nadir stopped, scanning the crowd. "Does anyone have the time?"

The fireman with a thick salt and pepper beard checked his watch. "Ten-forty."

Nadir nodded and continued pacing.

Frank followed him with his eyes. "Singh, calm down. Whatever's in there ain't—"

The freight elevator doors slid open, and the entire crew regarded the contractors.

"—Just don't tell my wife!" one of the men exclaimed boisterously, followed by his companions' uproarious, wheezing laughter. They strolled into the office, quelling their amusement.

Nadir plodded toward them, trying his best to hide the desperation from his words. "Alright, gentlemen, what do you need me to do to help move this process along?" He placed a hand on the headman's shoulder.

"Stand back." The man set the torch on the floor and lit the drip pan. "Get that glass outta there," he yelled to his cohorts.

When he passed, one of the men muttered something ending with, "fuckin' janitor," as he lifted a shovel and moved spade after spade of glass into a pile.

The headman flipped a heavy-looking metal visor over his face and turned a knob on the back of the torch. "Spread out!" he cried from under the welding helmet.

The blowtorch hissed, and white-hot sparks scattered over the floor as the flame tore through the metal, leaving behind a molten trail. The shutter wiggled and fell forward with an unsatisfying, wobbly woosh, expelling dust and debris.

The lieutenant barked out the containment plan again. Nadir slid behind the contractor as he killed the torch, grabbed a flashlight, and slipped into the darkness.

"Wait, Singh!" Frank yelled. "Let the boys check it out first!"

Nadir inched through the pitch-black, running his hand over something at a sloping angle. The room was no longer cold. He flipped the switch on the flashlight. Frank and some others continued to call his name from the office.

"I'm alright!" Nadir answered.

"Get outta there, Singh!" Frank yelled.

"Do you see anything?" Wendell asked.

"Not yet," he answered both men in the same breath.

"At least put on a hazmat suit!" Frank yelled.

"This isn't the Great War, Frank. The Geneva Protocol prohibits chemical weapons, and Connor would never risk associating herself with something that heinous," Nadir called back. "Or, at the very least, she has more sense than to store a chemical weapon at Allied Science."

The yellow circle trailed across the shambles of the Idea Square as other lights joined behind him, scanning the rubble.

"Jesus Christ," someone uttered.

Half the ceiling had come down. Nadir ran his flashlight over the hole above him. The heating ductwork was exposed and bent, but the girders remained intact.

# The City of the Gods: Gold

Most of the cables suspending the ship were severed, and the vessel drooped at a forty-five-degree angle, throwing unfamiliar shadows across the wall behind it. The bottom gadolinium-like portion was connected, albeit bent, contorted, and almost unrecognizable.

"I don't suppose telling you the room could be structurally unstable will get you to leave?" one of the firemen asked.

"Not a chance," Nadir said.

"Your funeral, pal."

Nadir moved around the ship carefully, stepping over rubble but keeping his light locked on what remained of the top half. He hadn't noticed Brown and Wendell behind him until Brown's nervous voice sounded. "Boy, oh, boy, this is the end of our department for sure."

Nadir ran his light along the interior of the copper half of the ship, locating a small opening in the center, like the other one. However, the door underneath seemed to be rusted shut or nonexistent. He didn't dare get too close without the proper equipment, but on the first inspection, it appeared empty, and if something had been in there, it was no longer.

He scanned the little mesh walls lining the side. The other ship had the same design, but here, the area behind this mesh seemed to be a solid silvery substance, with some sort of transparent shield containing it.

Aside from the small cavity in the bottom, there wasn't much more to the vessel. Nadir moved his light down, lingering on the bottom half, a solid mass of now-contorted metal. As he had suspected, there was no engine.

The contractor previously holding the blowtorch whistled a long, impressed whistle. His flashlight danced across the ceiling. "A lot of damage here; this'll be a big job. You got major structural damage; a couple of bent I-beams, a warped ceiling and wall, and ceiling cracks. I'd have to get the lights back on before we can give you a full estimate, but it won't be cheap."

"Alright, alright," Frank said. "For now, try to clear the rubble off this ship. These scientists have work to do."

Nadir rewarded Frank's respectful display with a smile and a nod, then regarded his team. "What are your first thoughts?"

Frank placed a hand on Nadir's shoulder. "Maybe you should take this outside."

"Not a chance, Frank." Nadir eyed his team. "Thoughts?"

Brown cleared his throat. "The top half seems denser, the gadolinium side, which is odd seeing how it was most likely resting in the water on the lighter metal."

Nadir nodded. "Yes, I noticed that too. Unless it was completely submerged, and the alloy is rustproof." He trained his light on the ship.

"That would mean we also had it upside down," Wendell said. "And that means it wasn't a ramp. It was something else entirely."

One of the firemen tripped, and the ship spun, flopped, and angled to one side. Nadir jumped back.

"Jesus, Ross! Watch it!" one of the firemen yelled. "What are ya, drunk again?"

"Hey fuck you, Miller."

"Eh, go crawl up your thumb, pal. No wonder your wife left you."

"Enough!" Frank yelled. "One more outburst, and you can kiss your money goodbye!"

Nadir raised his arms. "Quiet!"

Everyone froze as a hush fell over the room. There was a slow-spreading crack, like ice breaking, followed by a leaking hiss.

"What the hell is that?" someone said.

Flashlights danced around the room.

Nadir whipped his light toward the ship. The metal behind the mesh and glass ran like a river; a pop echoed through the Idea Square and the transparent material behind the mesh burst. The hissing grew louder. The soldiers raised their guns nervously, scanning the room as thick smoke enveloped everyone.

"C'mon! We gotta get out of here!" Frank motioned to the door.

The men stumbled through the open shutter into the office, coughing and gagging. The lieutenant was the last to emerge. He slipped through the hole amid a coughing fit and vomited green bile onto the floor. "Drop"—he said amongst violent coughs—"Drop that shutter!"

Nicholas burst through a group of squabbling men and helped Frank and one of the contractors move the desk. The shutter fell, but tendrils of smoke seeped under, crawling up the wall and across the ceiling. Nadir tasted the sour hint of metal.

"It feels like bugs are crawling across my skin!" Brown yelled.

Frank moved toward the elevator. "C'mon, it's not safe—"

"Everybody, stay where you are!" The lieutenant said, wiping his mouth with the back of his hand. The guards blocked the freight elevator, training their weapons on the group.

"What the hell?" said the bearded fireman. "You can't do this."

"What's the big idea?" a contractor added.

"This is now a contaminated scene!" the lieutenant yelled. "No one leaves. You all signed contracts and knew the risks associated with this particular job. We will shoot you if we have to."

Nicholas watched his lieutenant through frightened eyes but lifted his gun to shoulder level. Nadir eyed Frank.

"Not a chemical weapon, huh?" Frank growled.

## 55

Fourteen men sat in the dimly lit room, keeping to themselves, aside from the odd rhetorical question. The remaining hazy smoke danced amongst the neon lights mockingly.

Nadir stretched his achy back and walked across the room where Wendell sat alone against a desk divider. "May I?" He motioned to the floor beside him.

Wendell glanced up with a deeply haunted look on his usually emotionless face. He slid over. "Did you notice it too?"

"Notice what?" Nadir made a face like he'd smelled something disgusting as he sat.

*Don't say it.*

"Before the room filled with smoke, something moved inside the ship. Not a biological form. I saw—well, the walls moved." He hugged his legs and stared at the floor.

"Honestly, Doctor Wendell, I thought I did see something, but it could have been shadows. Everyone had flashlights, and—" He shot a passing glance at one of the guards. "Let's keep this between the two of us, shall we?"

"Yes, of course, but I also noticed after the smoke entered the room, well—"

Nadir inched closer. "Well? Well, what? Out with it."

Wendell's eyes dropped. "Well, whatever the mass was behind the mesh—it was gone, Doctor Singh."

"Are you certain?"

"Yes," he said with cold, unchallenged certainty.

----

Each man had a five-minute telephone call to offer their family peace of mind under the watchful eye of an armed guard. Frank and the lieutenant brainstormed quite the yarn involving a small elevator fire. When Nadir explained the situation to Anila, she didn't press the matter if she had any reservations. The only man who didn't make a call was the fireman with the beard.

After his call, one of the contractors decided he didn't work for the United States Government and could leave whenever he "damn well pleased." The man was beaten and confined with an M1 pointed at his head.

Finally, after what seemed like hours, the freight elevator opened. Men with service rifles and hazmat suits shuffled into the office, resembling giant bees.

"Everybody up against the far wall," one of them ordered, motioning with his rifle to the fallen shutters.

As the crowd obliged, the lieutenant saluted, barely containing a snide smile. "I'm Lieutenant Falso. Who's your commanding officer? I'll see you are well—"

"Sir! I need you against the wall! Guards, drop your weapons!" the man barked in the same authoritative voice he'd used to herd the others to the back of the room.

The lieutenant cycled through each emotion, settling on anger, and tossed his Colt Government pistol to the floor.

"All clear!" the second soldier in a matching hazmat suit yelled when everyone had settled. Two men emerged from the shadows of the elevator, clad in identical hazmat suits but with clear visors over their faces.

Nadir shut his eyes, fending off the bout of terror. *If we were infected, someone would be showing symptoms by now. This is just a precaution,* he told himself.

A final man emerged from the elevator and looked on with subtle interest through the clear visor of his suit as he advanced slowly through the room.

"Great, whenever the fuckin' G-men show up, it's a problem," one of the guards whispered to another.

As soldiers collected the scattered rifles from the floor, one of the hazmat-suited men pulled an instrument from his sash. Another leaned in and spoke to the aforementioned "G-man," who nodded in confirmation.

"Alright, everyone, back to the center of the room," the man said. "This will go quickly if everyone cooperates."

Each of the now captive men shot each other a look. Nadir's gaze fell on Wendell, who seemed to be muttering.

One of the firemen stood, eyeing the others as he slowly walked around an old metal desk and stopped a few feet from the scientists.

A hazmat soldier lifted his service rifle. "That's close enough!"

A second fireman stood and joined him timidly, then the third, then the two well-behaved contractors, the scientists and Frank, then Nadir, and finally, the man who had complained, followed by Nicholas and the unarmed guards.

One of the hazmat scientists moved down the line with his small, handheld whining machine. It looked like a ping-pong paddle with two antennas at the top. The tone it emitted remained a slow, electronic hum until the antennas rose when brushed against one of the firefighters, and an unsettling clicking noise followed.

The scientist paused but ultimately moved on when the antenna reverted to its original state. After a second pass and more of the same, now familiar hum, he nodded to the other scientist, who whispered something to the man in charge.

"Alright, everyone, strip down," the hard-boiled man said through his respirator. There was a clamor amongst the group, primarily light defiance and nervous titters, but also some outright refusal.

"If you want to get out of here"—the man's voice rose over the complaints—"you'll comply."

The silence returned, broken by exasperated sighs and the sucking of teeth. Eventually, the firefighters stripped, followed by the contractors, each holding their hands over their genitals. The soldiers' stone faces remained an even keel, and Brown looked as if he might cry.

"Bloody hell!" Nadir unbuttoned his shirt, shut his eyes, and pulled his trousers and undergarments down. When he opened his eyes, they remained forward, scanning the elevator door as he imagined himself to be anywhere but here.

*Tomorrow, we'll all share a laugh about this whole sordid affair.*

All the men stood naked, displaying signs of discomfort mixed with anger or feigned amusement as the schoolboy in each of them rose to the surface.

One of the hazmat soldiers shouted over the clamor: "Everyone up against the western wall!"

Silence washed over the room. Once again, the firemen took the lead, followed more quickly by the others.

"Place your hands flat on the wall!"

Everyone complied.

Nadir glanced over his shoulder and noticed Frank staring daggers up at him. "What the hell did you do, Singh?" he bellowed in a half-whisper.

Nadir scowled. "Yes, Frank, it was always my intention for this to happen. You, me, and the other chaps, all nude, missing dinner with our families. Perhaps next time, I'll ask instead of proceeding with all the theatrics of destroying sub-three."

"It seems whatever leaked was unharmful," the hazmat scientist said. "Most likely some sort of carbon-based fuel." The machine clicked off with a fading hum. "As a precaution, we'll be dousing you with Rinzo soap and rinsing each of you with a fire hose. After that, you're free to go, but we'll need to keep your clothes."

The men formed a line over a grate on the southeast corner by the chemical shower that had been, ironically, shut off with the sprinklers.

"I hate you, Singh," Frank said adamantly.

"The feeling's mutual, I assure you," Nadir responded.

Past the grated area, soaked men were trying on clothes brought in from the Salvation Army for such an occasion. In front of Nadir, the final naked construction worker gritted his teeth as the turbulent stream of water forced him against the wall. Then, Nadir begrudgingly took his place. The sharp edges of the grate bit into his bare feet as he inched forward. Nadir covered his genitals with his hands. "Let's get this over with, then!"

A puff of powdered soap floated down softly, and the fire hose forced him against the cold, metal wall. He shut his eyes, and as quickly as it had begun, it was over.

----

Nadir pulled on a pair of knickerbocker pants and held up a blue, striped shirt with a missing collar and a hideous Hawaiian button-down. Frank approached, naked and dripping wet.

"Which do you prefer, Frank? The Hawaiian shirt or this collarless, striped number?" Nadir asked.

Frank snatched clothes without much deliberation and dressed quickly. Water spotted through the far-too-small button-down and oversized pants as he shot Nadir one final piercing look and shuffled angrily to the elevator.

"Alright, well, I'll see you tomorrow, Frank. I suppose we'll find a temporary workspace?" Nadir asked casually, eyeing both shirts, waiting for one to jump out as better than the other.

"Like hell, you will!" Frank spun on his heels and stomped back toward the group huddled around the clothing pile. He poked Nadir in the chest. "You're done, Singh. This was the last straw. The men upstairs have been trying to shut this department down since T-Day. I was the only person keeping us afloat! Me! But now, after this—" He shook his head. "You rubbed my nose in shit, Nadir. I'm done with you. Expect a call from Robert Cutler. My boss."

Nadir blinked away the surprise as he watched Frank shuffle toward the elevator. He slipped into the Hawaiian shirt and bound after his one-time workplace adversary. "You can't be serious! Frank I—"

"You're fucking dangerous, Singh!" Frank's stare was sharp. "Allied Science doesn't need you. They'll reassign Doctors Brown and Wendell, but you—you're finished!" He turned as the elevator arrived and stomped inside. Other men who had been waiting shuffled in silently after him.

Frank stood amongst a group of mismatched, poorly dressed people in the dimly lit box, glaring like a rabid dog. His last words came like a bullet. "You're just like Thompson, Nadir. The only difference is he was certifiably insane. What's your excuse?"

*The world will burn.*

The doors closed with a heart-wrenching swish. Nadir slumped into a chair and stared vacantly at the wall.

Sometime later, the elevator returned, and people filtered in. Brown and Wendell tried to speak, but Nadir met them with deflective smiles, handshakes, and attaboys. They'd learn the truth soon enough. He peered into what was left of the dark Idea Square housing the ship as the hazmat-clad scientists maneuvered inside. He'd found something in the vessel, after all. The end of his career.

Nicholas was the last to dress from the dwindling pile. He moved toward the elevator in his chocolate-brown short pants and oversized button-down combo but stopped when he saw Nadir. "You okay, Doctor Singh?"

Nadir chuckled. "Not really, Nicholas. I can't seem to get out of my own way today."

"I'm going to go get a drink, Doctor Singh. C'mon, you look like you could use one, too," Nicholas said with a friendly smile.

On any other day, Nadir would have dismissed the boy with some offensive thought that insulted his intelligence. However, today, the idea of facing his family with this news made him ill.

"You know what, Nicholas?" Nadir stood and slipped his feet into mismatched shoes. "That sounds like a fine idea."

**<u>56</u>**

# The City of the Gods: Gold

The hole-in-the-wall pub had a tiki theme, a perfect match for Nadir's offensive shirt. Sunday drunks lingered at the bar, around the jukebox, and hunched over tables that looked like they had floated ashore on some polluted beach. The floor, presumably wood, was covered in peanut shells and discarded cigarettes. The barstools were metal, something the designer had no doubt overlooked when trying to keep with the theme. Still, the bar had a bamboo inlay, which Nadir found charming.

They took seats between a fat woman sucking something blue through a straw from a faux human skull and a tall, lanky man drinking a pint of beer. Nicholas eyed the bartender. "Hey, Midge, how goes it?"

Her surly face lit up. "Nicky! Great to see you!" she said in a sing-songy voice that sounded like it came directly from an ashtray. "It's been too long." She eyed Nadir.

Nicholas smiled. "This here is Doctor Singh. He's a big deal over at Allied Science. Doctor Singh, Midge."

Nadir nodded. "Nadir is fine."

"Pardon?" Midge asked, extending her neck and bulging her eyes.

"Feel free to call me Nadir—it's my first name," he reiterated.

Midge laughed politely. "What'll it be, fellas?"

"A couple of Old Viennas and maybe two Jack Daniels, neat. It's been that kind of day," Nicholas said.

Midge nodded, snatched two dripping cans from the well, and poured two fingers of whiskey into rocks glasses. The scent brought Nadir back to his formative years in Liverpool.

Nicholas raised a glass. "Cheers, Doctor Singh. Big day for you," he said obliviously or politely.

"Cheers," Nadir repeated. They clinked glasses, and the whiskey started a fire in his empty stomach, a feeling he quite enjoyed.

"So"—Nicholas sipped the beer—"how's your family, Doctor Singh?"

Nadir took a swig of Old Vienna. "Oh, just fine, and how is—" He realized he knew nothing about this man he'd spoken to every morning for the past two years. "My apologies, but I can't seem to remember if you have a wife, my boy."

Nicholas opened his wallet and produced a worn photo of a beautiful woman with long, chestnut hair holding a small child in a little pink dress. The image looked like he'd clipped it from a *Good Housekeeping* magazine.

"Wife and a little girl, Doctor Singh." He smirked. "That's why I let you bring your daughter into the lab yesterday. I know how important it is for kids to see who their father is."

Nadir smiled. "How did you—" He sighed, eyeing the drinks lined up on the bar. "You have a beautiful family, Nicholas. I really should be getting back to mine." He extended his hand. "Thank you, my dear boy, for everything. I wish you the best."

Nicholas eyed his hand curiously. "You're not coming in tomorrow?"

"I'm afraid not," Nadir said, and a strange, relieved smile crossed his lips.

Nicholas smiled and shook his hand. "Good luck, Doctor Singh."

Jacob,

Allied Science has opened the vessel you designed for Thompson. I need to know if the contents are dangerous.

I initially believed we experienced metal vapor deposition or physical vapor transport. I discovered an aluminum alloy-like substance in a similar open vessel a few days ago that was perhaps the remnant of this same phenomenon. However, MVD would entail extreme heat or some other conversion tactic, but in all the literature I have come across on the subject, the metal always forms a solid mass when cooled. This has not.

Jacob, where did the contents go when settled, and what happens if it is inhaled?

If I do not receive correspondence by midweek, I will have no choice but to bring this information to the authorities.

Sincerely,

David T. Wendell

Empire City

October 18, 1953

THE MANY
DEATHS OF
COWARDS

<u>**57**</u>

*Saturday, October 17, 1953*

*I had the dream again. The same one that has plagued me for as long as I can remember, but last night was different. I wasn't frightened when the tides raged, and the moon burst into a billion pieces. It was almost beautiful. Still, I can't be sure whether it was because I'm used to the devastation by now or because she was there.*

*She doesn't always come, Dea, the Faceless Woman, but when she does, there is a feeling of transcendence I can't explain. It might be what some people call God or love.*

*Each time I dreamt this dream, I awoke before the end. This time, I stayed. I saw what came after. The grandeur, the disorder, and the faceless woman spoke:*

*"Isn't it divine?"*

Cassandra shut her diary and ran a finger over the gilt inlay on the cover. "Memories," it said aptly. She clutched it to her chest, revisiting her dream. A glimpse at the end of the world. *Isn't it divine?* She ran the phrase through her head until it lost meaning and tucked the diary under her mattress with a smile.

The secret journals hidden throughout her bedroom acted as a window to her soul, a life outside Ron's mansion, and sometimes, a tether to the faceless woman. Each entry celebrated the part of Cassandra that no one could control, and when she died, she would not be forgotten like her mother.

The morning bloomed, and an azure aura flooded Cassandra's bedroom. Her heavy eyes craved rest, but when she shut them, Akia's broken body and hollow eye sockets greeted her. That, and the pain in her ribs, forced her to sleep sparsely, but the broken sleep seemed to have brought forth Dea.

She sat cross-legged amongst the lush quilt and blankets built up like a nest on her bed. Her mother used to tell her: *Don't get too comfortable in this room; as soon as we get some money, we're getting away from Ron Baxter.*

That had been thirteen years ago. Now, her mother was dead, and Cassandra was locked in this mausoleum with the luxury antique furniture that would have made any other girl feel like royalty. Her bed was enchanting, with its hazy silk drapes, oak canopy, and hand-carved ivy running over the finials and through the headboard, but when she lay in it, residual death it was once shrouded in resurfaced. If she was in the right spot, she could see the gnarled old, vein-covered hand of a ghost-white woman ringing a brass servant's bell as she took her final breath, terrified and alone. Occasionally, evil revelations like that seeped from the black room and manifested as visions—the curse of the Oracle. Some events occurred years ago, but others hadn't passed yet, and it was impossible to distinguish which was which.

With each vision, a gaunt woman with the face of a china doll emerged from the black room, watching through deep, dark pits as her puckered smile rose at the corners. Her stringy black hair trickled slowly into the rippling lake that always followed her. Sometimes, at night, a soft knock would sound on Cassandra's door. The doll-faced woman, Dea's antithesis, begging hungrily for the next vision.

Cassandra flung her legs off the side of the bed and traipsed across the wooden floor, shedding her nightgown.

"Fat!" she said, regarding her curves in the tall dressing mirror and sneering at her large breasts, an affliction passed down from her mother. She hated her wide hips and thick tree-trunk legs. Her sisters had long legs and small, perky breasts, and Ron would allow them to dress for his parties while she served drinks.

Cassandra tiptoed across the room, imagining what it would be like to wear a pair of pumps and a cocktail dress to a gala. She smiled, moving with broad, sweeping steps, greeting imaginary socialites like she'd read about in *The Great Gatsby*—one of the books she'd managed to hide amongst her journals.

Her smile faded as she stumbled back onto her heels, recalling Akia's final moments and the weight behind her last whisper. "Yagi." Kissing Cassandra was the last thing Akia had done in life. She closed her eyes, inching toward the cold glass with her lips, trying to relive the moment, but all she saw were the deep black pits pumping blood onto the grass as Akia's heartbeat slowed to a stop.

*How cruel.* Cassandra's eyes fluttered open, and she pulled away from her reflection. She would never know if it was Akia or the monster inside that had kissed her. Yagi, Master Leonard. She remembered it now.

----

They had only been children, home alone, with Patricia in charge, the perfect night. Cassandra, Mary, or Nancy had never been to Ron's private quarters, but Patricia could do no wrong, so they followed her.

At the top of the stairs, a long, narrow hallway stretched forever. Mary and Nancy padded fearlessly across the pitch-black floor, but Cassandra froze at the doorway. Evil radiated like a fever from the room.

Patricia smiled like she could read the uncertainty in her face. "C'mon, it'll be fun."

Black onyx statues of dancing women lined the grand entrance on the left, and white marble versions on the right. There was a sadness in their faces, and heat bled through the stone like they were living. One appeared to be crying, but that was impossible.

"C'mon, Cassandra!" Mary yelled. The others were already standing at the other end of the hallway, so far away. She ran to catch up when a low moaning wail called out her name, not Cassandra, but a name that belonged to her in a past life. She didn't know how, but she recognized it as it drifted faintly behind her.

A strange warmth crossed her skin, like breath. Cassandra shuddered but couldn't bring herself to look. The girls were gone when she faced forward again, and the wall behind the statues fell away.

A dystopian land spread infinitely. Earthy but barren, no life could survive here. Weapons clanged as hooded figures battled snarling monsters, twelve feet tall, with blood in their jowls and death in their eyes. No two creatures were alike.

One of them eyed her, an appalling troll with long, stringy black hair, bulging eyes, and a V-shaped beak of a smile spanning from ear to ear.

"Oraculi," the creature said without moving its strained grin.

Cassandra stumbled back into comforting arms. She smelled her mother's perfume, but it was Patricia holding her. The monsters were gone, and the dimly lit hallway opened to Ron's bedroom.

"Hey, c'mon," Patricia said, worry lacing her expression. "It's all going to be okay, Cassie."

Cassandra hesitantly peered down the empty hall, where the statues stood alone. Mary and Nancy stared at exotic masks hanging above statues of Greek gods.

"Don't touch anything, you two!" Patricia said sternly. "Ron mustn't know we were here."

The walls were midnight blue, fading into black at the top with specks resembling stars. High in the rafters, large spheres revolved and rotated on rickety gears, orbiting a large glass dome in the center of the ceiling.

Underneath was the most enormous bed Cassandra had ever seen—almost the size of her entire bedroom. Carved into the headboard was a man with a goat's head holding a panicked human woman. The creature's tongue wrapped around the woman's neck, and its giant, grotesque hands fondled her breasts.

Cassandra's vision blurred. Labored breathing and the cry of something inhuman in the throes of passion bled into the still air. The bed buckled under an invisible weight.

Patricia pulled Cassandra by the arm. "What's wrong with you, Cassie? I've been calling your name."

"She's in love with that ugly old goat!" Mary said. She and Nancy bleated.

"Okay, okay, that's enough," Patricia said. Cassandra's sisters plodded toward the bathroom, but she remained. The wooden carving called to her.

"Cassandra? C'mon, we're going to play a game." Patricia placed her hand on Cassandra's shoulder, breaking her infatuation with the headboard. "It'll be fun."

The girls stood four in a row in front of a washroom mirror. Cassandra could barely see over the vanity, but the room was pitch-black, so it didn't seem to matter. Patricia lit a candle, illuminating the room in an eerie orange glow. The flame danced to match its reflection, creating lively, sweeping shadows against the wall behind them.

"Now what?" Mary asked.

"Shush Mary, or else she won't come." Patricia locked eyes with her reflection.

"Who?" Nancy asked.

"The bloody woman! Wooo!" Mary pinched Nancy's hip.

Nancy slapped her hand. "Stop that, Mary!"

"Quiet, both of you!" Patricia said. "Everyone, look into the mirror, and repeat after me."

Mary giggled.

Patricia chanted: "Bloody woman, bloody woman, bloody woman—"

Mary joined in: "Bloody woman, bloody woman, bloody woman."

Nancy watched with saucers for eyes and hesitantly joined: "Bloody woman, bloody woman, bloody woman!"

Cassandra remained silent.

"Bloody woman! Bloody woman! Bloody woman! Come!" Patricia blew out the candle. Nancy screamed and ran out of the washroom. Mary joined her, shrieking even louder, and both girls fell into a fit of giggles.

"Did you see it?" Nancy cried. "It was a woman covered in blood! Have you ever seen anything so horrible?"

Mary squealed. "I saw it!"

Patricia smiled and slunk out of the bathroom. "Pretty scary, huh, girls?"

Light poured in from the bedroom, and the mirror was again a reflective surface. Cassandra stared into her own brown eyes. Her chest tightened, and her fists clenched into clammy balls as she tried to process the actual horrors she'd seen.

Moments ago, a figure walked slowly into the reflection, wearing a mask with deep pits for eyes and a puckered little black smile. The dark oversized robe revealed no gender, and its weight forced a hunch. Each step clacked off the floor and echoed like hooves but with the gait of a human.

*Clack-clack, clack-clack, clack-clack.* It stopped behind Mary's reflection. The blade in its hand radiated the candle's light. Shadows behind it shifted, and whispers filled the room.

"Leonard."

"Mister Leonard."

"Master Leonard."

Mary's reflection grew into a young woman, beautiful and thin. She gawked at Cassandra, whispering: "It comes in the heat amidst death."

The hooded figure placed its hand behind Mary's back, and the knife exploded through her sternum. Mary fell to the floor, but her voice remained.

"It comes for the child."

It moved behind Nancy's reflection. *Clack-clack, clack-clack.* Nancy grew older, her teens, her twenties, her thirties. Her features grew gaunt, and her flesh hung from her frame before finally decaying.

The masked figure moved behind Patricia's reflection. *Clack-clack, clack-clack.* Patricia aged into a tired-looking young woman and jerked her head toward Cassandra. "It comes for you."

Cassandra shut her eyes, and the cold steel of the knife brushed against her throat. Her eyes fluttered open. The room was dark. Smoke danced off the candle, and the other girls shrieked and laughed.

"It comes through you—Oracle."

**58**

*Clack.* The bedroom door unlocked from the outside, and one of Cassandra's sisters knocked twice. It was time for chores. She opened the door and stepped into the hallway, almost tripping over Patricia, who was sitting on the floor with her back against the wall. Ron's silk robe hung off her slight frame.

Cassandra squatted beside her. "What's wrong? Are you hurt?"

"Ron and Creed are with Barbara." The whiskey-soaked words oozed from Patricia's mouth, which turned up at the corners as she forced a low belly laugh. "I guess you're the only virgin left."

Cassandra shuttered, eyeing the staircase leading to Ron's quarters. Last night, she had heard portions of Ron and Creed's conversation through the cast-iron register in her bedroom. It was the usual banter, mostly booze-soaked promises of power and money. However, Creed had brought something Ron had desperately wanted. Cassandra couldn't hear what it was, but Ron's entire cadence changed for the better once Creed presented it. Barbara must have been his reward.

Cassandra flung Patricia's limp arm over her shoulders and pulled her up. "C'mon, let's get you to bed."

Patricia mumbled inaudibly as Cassandra pushed the bedroom door open. Two immaculately made bunk beds sat on the far wall with a single trunk between them. Cassandra flopped Patricia onto one of the bottom bunks.

*This was Akia's bed.* Her heart sank, and her chest tightened, the same sensation thoughts of her mother instilled. That frigid March day when her mother died eight years ago burrowed into her conscience.

*I'm afraid it was suicide.* Ron's words were cold comfort to the eight-year-old girl, sobbing into a rag doll as the smell of death slunk down the stairs from his room.

Patricia's bloodshot eyes met Cassandra's. "Cassie, does Ron love me?"

"Ron loves us all," Cassandra responded in such an intuitive way it frightened her.

"Yes, but"—she paused—"but do you think he'll ask me to marry him?" The tears running down her tired face signified she already knew the answer.

"Get some rest, Patricia." Cassandra pushed through the bedroom door, glided down the stairs, and froze mid-step in front of the still curtains of the black room.

*We go now!* Akia's voice still lingered in the back of her mind. She clenched her fists and threw open the heavy curtains, stepping into the darkness. "You're still here," she shouted. "Still desperate—I can feel you squirming in the shadows! I want you to know I don't fear you!" The silence lingered until Cassandra felt foolish. As she turned to leave, a deep, booming voice invaded her mind. The base of her skull raddled until it almost burst, and slow words poured from the darkness.

"Veni mecum domum oraculi."

Cassandra stared into the blackness. The room was breezeless and cold, yet it still felt like hell.

She planted her feet. "I'm not scared of you!"

A deep snarl answered. "Eligere vel eligere mori vivere."

"Show yourself or begone, stop tormenting me!" Confidence faded. Cassandra edged backward.

The booming voice tore through her consciousness. "Fiat mihi te."

"I-I said show yourself!" Cassandra yelled. "Why do you hide, coward?"

"Ego nusquam et ubique." Warm, heavy breath spread across Cassandra's back and under her toga. She didn't dare turn.

"You are broken. Allow me to take you for a time. I will cure your gift of clairvoyance," it whispered against the nape of her neck. Master Leonard rose from the shadows in front of her. Its curled horns reached the ceiling, forcing a hunch, and its gaze bore a hole into Cassandra.

"W-why me?" she stammered.

The creature's hooves clacked on the ground as it approached, towering over her. "Your soul is old. It was offered to me long ago. The gods we have brought to this plane, the death merchant, the builder, the armored, and the messenger, grow weak. Those who ride upon them, Eligos, Sabnock, Marchosias, and Ronove, seek new hosts." The dialect was still foreign but familiar.

Cassandra inhaled through her nose. She was weightless in the dark. There was no sense of up or down. "Do you mean—"

"You do not ask questions of me, Oracle." The voice made the floor apparent again. "Dea remains, but now we rise, the once lesser gods, to divine power. The death merchant teeters between worlds. He is lost to me. The others will fall by their own foolhardy hands. Time grows short." The creature advanced, and its immense body heat engulfed her. She backed away slowly.

"I don't want any part of this! I don't even know what you are!" she yelled meekly.

"There is no choice, Oracle. You know me. Say my name."

"I don't know your name," she lied.

"As I have told the other one, Ronald Baxter, in many a dream, bring me the gods' spawn so I may feast. The brothers' bond has just begun to fracture. The moonchild is not yet on this plane. There is still time to control the outcome."

"Why do you speak in riddles? What are you? Where did you come from?"

"I am everyone and no one. I am life, and I am death," it whispered. "I live in the weak and timid and feast on the strong and foolish. Pay me my price, Oracle: the gods' spawn."

"Why did you kill my friend?" Cassandra pushed the creature. The heat within the wiry hair burned her hands. She reeled back.

The soulless, dead eyes dropped to Cassandra's level, and a grotesque snout slid into the daylight, beaming through the black curtains. It had a mouth wider than any mouth should be, opening slowly until the jaw dislocated with a sickening crack.

A limp human foot emerged from the gaping craw, then another, kicking wildly, and a woman's slender body covered in mucus, pus, and blood poured out. The stench was unbearable, like rotten meat. Akia's scream overlapped itself in many tones as if thousands of suffering people were screaming through her.

"Her soul is weak and unpalatable. She is my gift to you, Oracle. Pay me my price, the gods' spawn." Akia slid from the jaws to the floor with a thunk and fell deathly silent. The burning eyes vanished into the darkness, and a hush fell over the room.

Cassandra gawked at the naked woman sprawled at her feet. "Akia! Don't move!"

The daylight was like fire in her eyes as Cassandra burst through the curtains and slid her hands blindly along the console table. She brushed against the ornate base of a candlestick, and her trembling hands tore match after match against the striking strip until one ignited. She shoved her way back through the black curtains, swinging the candle against the darkness. Akia was gone. Only the horrible, putrid stench remained.

*Master Leonard.* She remembered now. The heartache and pain it thrived upon, and its true name: the Baphomet.

**59**

"Look at her, Nancy, look how fat she is!" Mary's voice carried from the kitchen.

Cassandra pushed the five-panel door open and peered in. A plump woman stuffed into an ill-fitting toga faced away. Mary and Nancy stood across the island with matching mean-spirited smiles.

*She must have been Creed's "delivery,"* Cassandra thought.

"She'll never get a private blessing from any of the followers. What an oinker!" Nancy piped in, locking eyes with Cassandra. "Just like Fat-Sandra has never had a private blessing, isn't that right, Fat-Sandra? Aren't you still a virgin?"

The plump woman turned slowly, scanning Cassandra through swollen, red eyes. She was tall and a little chubby but would only pass for fat when beside two sticks, like Mary and Nancy. A short-cropped mess of sandy-blonde hair ran partially down into her eyes. The other girls must have held her down and cut it last night.

Cassandra smiled at the new girl, ignoring her sisters as she pulled a glass out of the cabinet.

"Whatever, go suck an egg, Fat-Sandra!" Nancy said.

Mary's features softened, and she spoke in a baby-like fashion to the new girl. "Look, I feel like we got off on the wrong foot."

"Yeah, we have a long day of chores. You should have some breakfast." Nancy matched Mary's nauseating cadence and pulled the refrigerator open. "What would you like? Oh, I know!" The door closed. "Mary and I will make you an omelet!"

Nancy cranked her arm back and launched an egg at the new girl. She ducked, and the egg burst on Cassandra's sternum, running down her toga.

Nancy and Mary rushed out of the kitchen, giggling. Cassandra sighed. The new girl twisted her red face, trying unsuccessfully to hide an ugly cry. "Why are they so mean?"

Cassandra said: "I'm sorry about—"

The woman wrapped her arms around Cassandra and pressed her face into her toga, ignoring the matted yolk. "He's dead! My father is dead!"

Cassandra hesitated but ultimately wrapped her arms around the girl.

----

Deep sobs caused the girl's body to convulse. She looked almost pathetic, sitting alone on that bottom bunk. Luckily, Patricia had vacated their sisters' room. Cassandra handed her a glass of water, which the girl gulped down greedily.

"What's your name?" Cassandra asked.

"Geraldine," she said, studying Cassandra with shiny green eyes.

"Well, Geraldine, I'm Cassandra. It's a pleasure to meet you." She turned her attention to the drying egg yolk on her toga, sighed, and slipped out of it.

Geraldine slapped her palm over her eyes, and her skin flushed red. "What are you doing?"

Cassandra frowned. "I'm changing."

Geraldine stared out the window in horror. "But—you're naked! Don't you have any shame? You can't get naked in front of a stranger."

"Why not?" Cassandra furrowed her brow. "Ron encourages it."

Geraldine turned slightly toward Cassandra but couldn't seem to look directly at her. "It's—well—it's uncouth." She returned a cupped hand over her eyes.

Cassandra walked to the armoire and pulled on one of Patricia's togas. It was a little tight, but the organdy was a welcome change from the burlap she'd been wearing. She smiled and sat on the bed next to Geraldine. "Better?"

Geraldine turned her mouth into a line. "I guess." She pulled her skirt over her thighs. "Why do we have to wear these... robes anyway?"

"They're togas." Cassandra giggled. "And we wear them because—well, it's what Ron wants."

Geraldine scanned the floor and swallowed the final sip of water. "Aside from having no shame, you seem like a normal girl. How did you end up here, Cassie?" She wiped her mouth with the back of her hand.

Cassandra paused to reflect. "Well, my mother told me we lived with Ron's brother, Robert, after my father died. Then he died too, and Ron brought my mother and me here from Mexico."

Geraldine's green eyes met Cassandra's, and her tiny nose scrunched. "You mean you've basically lived in this house your whole life?"

"I think so. I don't remember much before the Sibylline Temple." Cassandra shrugged, eyeing the cracked door. She was supposed to be doing chores.

Geraldine inched closer. "And you've never left?"

*We go, now!*

"There's no need. I live here and work for Ron because no one lives for free," she echoed Ron's words automatically, like a fool.

Geraldine rose to her feet. "Cassandra, doesn't this situation feel odd to you?" She glanced at the door. "My father"—she inhaled and shut her eyes—"when he passed away yesterday, a police officer told me I had to come here. He said I didn't have a choice. Don't you find that queer? I guess Ron is my godfather or something, but I've never met him."

"Well, at least you have a home." Cassandra forced an overabundant smile. "Let me be the first to welcome you—"

"I don't know. Something feels off, Cass." Geraldine scanned the room.

Cassandra stood to meet her eye line. "Don't say that."

Geraldine glanced at the door. "This isn't how normal people live. No offense, of course. It's just—" Her breathing intensified, and a deep, face-altering cry overcame her. Cassandra guided her onto the bed and pulled her face toward her chest. Geraldine's sobbing slowed.

Cassandra placed a hand under her chin and turned her face. "Please, don't cry."

Geraldine's glazed eyes met hers, and she whimpered softly. Her eyes shut, and Cassandra felt hers do the same. She inched forward, and Geraldine's soft lips pressed against hers. Cassandra's stomach lurched into a knot. She leaned in, kissing her deeper, and something awoke, the same feeling instilled by the faceless woman: love or God, whatever people called it, family perhaps? Something Ron preached, but Ron and her sisters were a square peg in a round hole. This feeling filled the space within Cassandra perfectly.

Geraldine backed away. "I-I'm sorry, I don't know what came over me! It's the grief—"

Cassandra smiled and kissed Geraldine again. Geraldine returned the kiss and backed away slowly. Cassandra's eyes fluttered open, and both girls smiled.

"That was—"

"Ah, Geraldine, I see you've met Cassandra," a voice boomed behind them.

Cassandra spun toward the door wide-eyed. "Ron!"

Ron's bare feet padded across the floor. His skin was pink and blotchy and slick with sweat from a morning of fornication. He forced himself between the girls on the bed regarding Geraldine. "I'm Ron Baxter. Terrible news about your father. Preston Hall was a good friend, more like family, really." He sighed. "I'm so sorry, dear."

Geraldine smiled sadly. "Thank you."

"I always told Preston if the unthinkable happened, you'd have a home in the Sibylline Temple, and with your mother passing last year. Tsk, tsk, tsk."

Ron's hand found Geraldine's thigh. "Enough of this glum talk!" He shot to his feet. "You've come at a perfect time, my dear. We're having a dinner party tonight." He leaned on the top bunk, looming over the girls. "It's going to be wonderful, like Cinderella. You like Cinderella, don't you, Geraldine? Of course you do; what girl doesn't dream of being a princess? Isn't that right, Cassandra?"

"Yes, Ron."

Ron clapped his hands together. "Good, well, I'll let you get back to your chores." He sauntered to the door, stopped, and raised his index finger. "Oh, one more thing." He turned and eyed the girls, but his smile had vanished. "If I ever see that disgusting display again"—his eyes narrowed, and a bit of spittle flew from his lips—"I'll cut out both of your tongues."

"Yes, Ron," Cassandra said.

He smiled. "I'll see you tonight."

**<u>60</u>**

Cassandra leaned on the wall outside the dining room, listening to the muffled conversation on the other side of the door. She picked her cuticles nervously, following the door's inlay with her eyes, but her legs wouldn't carry her inside. She felt ridiculous with her breasts pushed up and poking out the top of the lacy, strapless evening gown, and when she tugged up, the stupid A-line flare made it seem like the world could see under her dress. She glanced into the oak-framed mirror hanging above the bar. A clown stared back, done up in too much makeup: blue eyelids, red lips, and pink cheeks. The only good thing that came of all this was Patricia cutting Cassandra's hair from a shaggy mess into a curly bob.

Patricia burst through the dining room door. "There you are!" She glanced inside and flashed an index finger before closing the door behind her. "I was beginning to worry."

Patricia's golden hair was curled and hung over her left shoulder, and her black, V-cut cocktail dress gave off an effortlessness Cassandra couldn't seem to capture in her look.

Patricia grabbed Cassandra by the arm and pushed the door open. "C'mon, silly. You're missing all the fun!"

Ron studied Cassandra from his seat at the dining room table. "You're late," he said through a phony smile. He looked dapper in his suit.

Across from him, another man sat with his back to her, his combed blonde hair shimmering in the low light. He threw an elbow over the back of the chair and smiled deviously. Cassandra swallowed her emotions and smiled, feeling more like prey than a dinner guest. *Creed.* The name forced eels to crawl through her empty stomach.

"It's no problem, Ron." Creed rose. "You can't rush this kind of beauty." His solid gray suit made his blue eyes pop, but the whole ensemble stunk of desperation. Creed pulled out the chair next to him.

Cassandra sat and smiled hollowly at him. "Hello, officer," she said in a passionless, monotone voice.

"Hello yourself." Creed's eyes danced across Cassandra's body. She shuddered to keep from squirming.

Patricia sat next to Ron and sighed happily. "Sorry, gentlemen, Cassandra was powdering her nose and lost track of time. You know how forgetful we girls can be when we're so preoccupied with looking nice for our men." Patricia wrinkled her nose at Ron. Cassandra's stomach churned at the phrase: "our men."

The chocolate-burgundy table and cream-colored walls looked gorgeous in the low candlelight, like a different house. Strange and delicious smells wafted from the kitchen behind Ron. Cassandra smiled until she noticed Geraldine staring blankly from the corner of the room.

Ron clapped his hands twice, and Mary and Barbara lugged a giant silver platter from the kitchen and placed it in the middle of the table. Mary lifted the lid, and steam rose from a crispy, red bird.

Ron eyed Geraldine. "I find this Beaujolais Nouveau pairs nicely with any kind of fowl." He smiled across the table at Creed. "I think you'll quite enjoy it."

Creed winked at Cassandra. "I think you're right," he responded.

Geraldine took the hint and filled the wine glasses with a shaky, nervous hand. Her eyes met Cassandra's, and she spilled it onto Patricia's arm.

"Watch it, you cow!" Ron spat.

Cassandra tensed and gripped the armrests of her chair.

Patricia eyed her, and a nervousness Ron could only instill danced across her eyes. "No harm, darling." She wiped her hand on a silk napkin and smiled longingly at Ron. "See? Already forgotten."

Cassandra cleared a thick lump from her throat. Ron's gaze held on Geraldine as he adjusted his lapels.

Patricia smiled at Creed. "Officer Creed, I believe you were telling us about your time in the service?"

"Please, call me Donald," he said with a slick smile. "Are all your girls so proper and rigid, Baxter?" He ran his monstrously rough hand over Cassandra's thigh under the table. "Or do they only know how to have fun when the lights go out?"

Cassandra pulled her leg away slowly to avoid offending and gulped her wine.

----

After dinner, the group retired to the parlor. Nancy and Barbara poured scotch for the men as they discussed sports, politics, and other matters over cigars. Cassandra sat quietly by the unlit fireplace, eyeing the black room's curtains through the parlor's doorway, wondering if Master Leonard was still in there.

Patricia sat down daintily on the edge of the brick. "How are you doing, Cassie?" She was all smiles, and the mascara made her green eyes pop even through all the booze she'd consumed.

Cassandra didn't want to ruin this night for Patricia, but she also found it next to impossible to lie to her. "I've been better." She looked away, studying the charred black andiron in the fireplace.

Patricia's face soured. "Cassie, sometimes you have to do things you don't necessarily like to help others." She sighed. "This is one of those times, I'm afraid."

Cassandra eyed the men, and her emotions betrayed the mask she'd been hiding behind all night. She felt her eyebrows furrow with intense sadness. "No, Patricia. Please," she pleaded quietly. "I can't. I'm not—I'm different."

Patricia rolled her eyes. "Cassandra, it's just one night. What's one—"

"Cassandra," Ron summoned. The scotch in his glass swirled slowly. "It seems Donald is an antique furniture enthusiast. Why don't you show him your room?"

Creed smiled. "I would be very interested in seeing that. I hear your bed is quite a piece to behold." Creed laughed. Ron followed suit, but it sounded hollow.

----

Cassandra could feel Creed's eyes crawling across her body as she climbed the steps ahead of him, but she dared not turn around. His shoes clicked on the marble as he closed in. She shuddered and rubbed her arms. The pain from her bruised ribs screamed, but that was nothing compared to what was to come, especially if she refused.

The walk down the hall took an eternity, but it wasn't nearly long enough. Cassandra sighed, closed her eyes, and turned the brass knob to her room. When the door clicked open, Creed was on her. He spun her around and pushed her against the armoire, forcing his lips onto hers. It was wrong; he tasted like poison and smoke, and his touch felt cold and medical. She tightened her lips. He yanked at her dress with the tenacity of a child ripping open a birthday gift. Cassandra slid away, desperately pulling her brazier over her exposed breasts.

"Please—"

Creed was on her again, kissing her shoulder with his wormish lips. She went numb but could still feel the heat of the tears on her face as he yanked her brazier off.

"I've wanted this for such a long time," he panted as he pulled off his belt and kicked his shoes off. Cassandra covered her breasts with her arms, but Creed forced them to her sides. Her ribs cried out in pain, but it paled compared to the shame and humility.

"No, no, no. I want to see all of you," Creed whispered through the stench of stale alcohol.

"Please don't." Cassandra's pleading fell on deaf ears, and he tore her underwear down.

Cassandra shuttered sharply and stared at the wall as he kissed her body. She tried to focus on the light in the corner of the room and leave her tortured body behind. The harder she stared, the more apparent it became; the light was an eye.

Creed yanked his shirt over his head and pressed his slimy skin against hers. The armoire was cold against her back. She shut her eyes, squeezing more tears out, and nodded to the watching eye.

Then it was in her.

She was powerful. She knew things, things she shouldn't have known. Cassandra gripped Creed's throat, extended her arm, and lifted him off the ground like he was a rag doll. His eyes bulged, and his face grew purple. "What are you doing?" he croaked.

"Don't trust him."

"Don't trust anyone."

"You're stupid."

"You're strong."

"Crush him."

"Mercy."

"Kill him!" A million voices echoed through her head.

"I am god," she said in a deep snarl, shaking the house and rattling the windowpanes as she, once again, surrendered herself entirely to the Baphomet.

The Empire Bulletin
Empire City, Friday, March 8, 1946
THE GODS OF EMPIRE

Last night, Salvatore DiLilo, reputed Gambino of the DiLilo family, was shot four times in his Northwell home and pronounced dead at Augusta hospital hours later. He was 73. This morning, Mayor Hall held an impromptu press conference outside City Hall in Terrytown to get ahead of rumors that he approved the execution of DiLilo himself.

In October of last year, police began cracking down on the drug trade in the Southside of Empire, causing the DiLilo family to make threats against Mayor Hall and his camp. Salvatore DiLilo told a member of Mayor Hall's team, "Stick to running this city into the ground, Preston (Hall). Bad things happen to people who step outside the bounds of their job."

 "Of course, we know who did this," Mayor Hall said after denying his involvement. "The gods of Empire. The protectors of America. Our heroes have come home from Japan, and I, for one, have never felt safer."

The mayor was referring to the League of Enforcers, who publicly announced, at the press conference, that they had ended the drug kingpin's life. Captain Wonderful, the team's leader who stood behind the mayor at his press conference, said, "Evil in Empire City knows no bounds, and any who stray from the righteous path of good or step outside the well-tread road of our justice system will face the League of Enforcers. The laws of man do not bind our justice. We operate with a purpose that police cannot, for fear of legal retribution. A downside of man's law by which we are unaffected. Beware, villains, for we are not afraid to play by your rules."

Captain Wonderful went on to speak about the victory over the DiLilo family. "(Salvatore) DiLilo was a menace. He made his fortune trafficking illegal alcohol in the '20s. Now he's flooding the Southside of our fair city with opium and all kinds of junk and smack. I won't stand for it, nor should Empire's citizens. I challenge his son, Francisco DiLilo, also known as the Fang, to leave town today or get put down like his father."

The other team members, both women, the Scarlet Sparrow and Miss Mercury, joined Captain Wonderful behind the podium; their true identities unknown. Mayor Hall seemed to fully endorse the trio and their methods with his new campaign catchphrase, "It's them or us."

"We are three against an infinite festering underbelly of evil," the Scarlet Sparrow said when asked about her leader's violent methods. "With disreputable opponents, sometimes force is the only option. Will that always be the way? I hope not, but for now, we need to adapt to survive this grisly criminal underworld. The demands of our city outweigh the lives of those who will not abide by the law."

Onlookers and Hall supporters alike seemed to be noticeably torn on the matter of the group's hasty use of violence. But whether saviors or murderers, one thing is for sure; criminals should think twice about their actions when the gods of Empire walk the streets of man.

SLOW
PACE OF
CHANGE

The shade from the awning did little to stave off the heat radiating onto the patio of Delmonico's Restaurant. Cal lifted the menu, but his eyes remained on the giant painted mural on the neighboring building that said: "Little Italy." It felt like a threat. Leering eyes from neighboring apartments and passers-by watched him fidget across from the brooding but delicate Theodora Connor. Being black in Eastwood was still out of style.

Theo twisted the charm of her necklace, glaring across Lime Street, where Club Danza loomed like a fortress. She had made up her mind. She was going to war with the mob on the word of Lily Larkin. Cal had voiced his concern at the Hall of Enforcers, but Theo was too far gone.

"I don't know, Theo; it sounds fishy." Cal followed her with his eyes as she ducked behind a partition on the far side of the Hall's war room.

She poked her freckled face over the top and met his gaze. "What's fishy about it, Bucko?"

Cal pressed a black button on the console. The tape squealed, stopped, and the cryptic message played again: "—found Bonnie—DiLilo Family has her—come quick." Theo had cleaned it up, but if anything, it sounded more contrived.

He slumped into one of the chairs positioned around the giant table in the center of the room, spinning back and forth lazily on the swivel. "Why couldn't the fastest woman on the planet rescue Bonnie from a bunch of has-been gangsters?"

"Lily is a coward," Theo sneered over the screen. "She would never engage unless the media were watching."

Cal remembered Lily as a shy young woman in Honshu, quiet as a mouse, but why would an invincible man need to speak with a field nurse anyway? He met Theo's gaze. "Didn't James kill—"

"James killed *Salvatore* DiLillo, Francisco's father." A black dress flopped over the top of the partition. "It was senseless; Big Sal was a has-been, even then. He made his fortune running booze into the city during prohibition. The only reason James insisted on killing him was because he threatened Mayor Hall. 'The stigma of his family made him too big a risk to have around,' he said. Really, James just wanted Hall's support when we had our big coming-out party.

"The DiLilos have never been a family to forget a slight, and killing the patriarch didn't do us any favors. It makes sense they would take Bonnie; I can't believe I didn't think of it sooner."

Theo emerged from behind the partition. "Well, whaddya think, Bucko? Have I still got it?"

The form-fitting red polyester was cut like a bathing suit, leaving little to the imagination. A torso-sized leather E ran over her chest, stopping between her legs. Theo spun and smirked. Her confidence offset the skimpy garb, imbuing a naturally intimidating quality, especially with the holstered Ka-Bar knife strapped to the inside of her right thigh.

"You look—" Cal cleared his throat.

Theo ran her necklace between her thumb and index finger, transforming from a statuesque goddess to a haunted young woman. Her eyes carried an innocence Cal had forgotten behind the loathsome actress and the killing machine.

"Why are you wearing that old thing?" Cal asked.

Theo chuckled. "You don't approve?"

"Well, I—"

"It's okay, Cal, I only meant that as a gag. I don't like it any more than you do." She placed her hands on her hips. "This getup is so uncomfortable; you couldn't imagine."

"Then why wear it?" Cal met her eye line, doing his best not to stare.

"This is how these people know me. These… monsters." She chuckled like she'd remembered some private joke. "Believe it or not, they fear this ridiculous uniform."

"If there's even anyone left alive who remembers," Cal said.

Theo's smile faded. "Francisco will remember."

"Why are you so sure he's still alive?"

"He's too much of a maniacal son-of-a-bitch to be dead." Theo abandoned her innocence again.

Cal crossed his arms. "Then why didn't you kill him when you had the chance? Hell, you killed everyone else."

Theo's dead brown eyes lingered on Cal's. "Well, if you must know, in the '40s, Francisco 'the Fang' DiLilo had so much pull in Empire, the Enforcers couldn't touch him. Even though Ron Baxter owned the town, DiLilo somehow held the respect of important people. Luckily, Mayor Hall was Ron's man when we killed Sal, but the DA told us we'd be charged with his murder if we so much said the name Francisco. Not in so many words, but we got the picture. After that, Francisco became a real thorn in my side. He was the one who turned his father's trickle of opium and heroin into a flood in South Valley."

Theo sauntered behind the folding screen. "But, DiLilo left town after T-Day because work dried up. I had the lowest bid to rebuild the city—one red cent." The black dress vanished from the top of the partition. "The union boys hated that, and the DiLilos' racketeering ventures took a big hit. He must have taken Bonnie to get back at me."

"Why now?" Cal sighed. "What about the person in the Shadow Butcher's uniform?" *The one who warned me about you.* "Where do they fit in? Or the thing that attacked us? Or the missing ship?"

Theo emerged, pulling the dress down over the uniform. "I don't know, Cal, but Lily said the DiLilo family has my daughter"—she adjusted the dress's bust line—"and that's the most solid lead we have." She grunted and tugged on the hemline.

Cal watched her from the oversized red chair. "What if Francisco still has pull with the right people?"

Theo looked at her reflection in the glass wall separating the war room from the rest of the Hall. "Doesn't matter." She pursed her lips and turned in the makeshift mirror. "One way or another, as soon as I have Bonnie, I'm getting out of this godforsaken city"—she regarded Cal—"you can tell people I forced you to do this if you want. Tell 'em I finally snapped—threatened Wilbur Davis or something. The DiLilos are my only surviving enemies, Cal. They have her."

"Then why haven't they made demands?" Cal shook his head. "This is a fool's errand."

Theo pulled a lipstick from her bag and eyed it sadly, losing herself in her thoughts.

"Theo?"

She snapped from her trance and glanced at him. "I'm sorry, but this is the plan. If you want to leave, no hard feelings, Bucko. It was never your fight." She spread the lipstick over her lips and pressed them together.

Cal sighed. "I'm not killing anybody."

She slipped a pair of low-top combat boots into a large purse. "Fine. Just remember, once it starts, call me the Scarlet Sparrow, and don't get in my way."

<u>62</u>

Cal set the menu down. The knot in his stomach destroyed his appetite. Theo sat silently across the table, sucking her cigarette to ash with her eyes locked on Club Danza.

"What are we waiting for?" Cal asked.

Theo sipped her wine. "I want to see if Francisco shows up."

Cal's eyes lingered on her ruby lips and her eyes that matched her dark, freckled skin. She was too perfect. A mask preventing the world from asking, *who are you, Theodora Connor? Who are you, really?*

Theo caught him staring. "What? Is my hair out of place?" She ran a palm over the top of her head.

Cal forced a smile. "No. You look great."

*But you're overcompensating. I know how broken you are.*

A shadow of a memory danced across Cal's mind. He stood in the large, empty kitchen of James Connor's old penthouse suite, peering into the parlor holding a half-empty bottle of rye. Clarity had pushed through the booze fog once people started dying.

The memory overlapped, like a folded piece of paper he could only see part of. The hot smell of iron mixing with allspice and jasmine and the chanting of the masses gathered to bear witness. Theo stood naked in the middle of it all. The gleam of wet blood coated her skin. Her shoulders heaved repeatedly. The icy grip of frost crawled along the floor, dragging the scent of ozone. Theo's breath left her in one long heave of steam like her soul had escaped the mask fastened to her face.

Her body spasmed, spun, and rose from the floor, limp and lifeless, as if something unseen had lifted her like a doll with dead black pits for eyes, staring at the onlookers.

A horse whinnied, and a shape prowled through the shadows. The creature's silhouette towered at least fifteen feet over the spectators. It was hunched and misshapen, with four legs and a wild shock of hair encircling its massive head. Sickly-looking bat wings sprouted from its twisted, arched back and folded into themselves.

"Tasa Sabnock on ca lirach," Theodora snarled in a booming voice.

The creature slunk forward. Its metallic hands threaded a black rope through the eye of something resembling a meat hook. It plunged the device into Theodora's bare arm, parting her flesh and muscle and splintering the bone. She let out a savage cry, something between agony and ecstasy, and a mad laughing fit overcame her.

The creature threaded a rope through a second hook and plunged it through her other arm. Then, two more into each leg. Whenever the steel bit Theo's flesh, she let out an elated gasp and laughed maniacally.

With a sickening crack of bone, it drove a hook through her sternum, working it into her heart. Theo's back arched, and then she fell still. The black ropes grew taught, stretching her flesh. She danced through the air like a toy and fell into a heap on the floor.

A final hook was forced into the back of Theodora's head and out her puckered black mouth. The sound of her skull fracturing made Cal's stomach churn. He tried to drown the feeling with a swig of rye but wretched anyway. He wiped his mouth with the back of his hand and peeked through the door again. Hundreds of blank white faces stared at him. Theodora stood inches away, watching with those dead black eyes. "Es Marchosais!"

Goosebumps rolled over Cal's naked skin. His breath pushed through a broad, twisted smile and hung in the cold air. Hooks threaded into his arms, legs, and chest, forcing his penis to swell and throb. The crack of his skull made Cal scream with delirious bliss, teetering on the edge of insanity. He fell limp.

Jerry, Theo, and James Connor hung suspended beside him, staring into oblivion with the same twisted grin wrapped around a protruding metal barb. They were one with their captors, gods amongst men, and damned, all at once. The numbness was in them.

----

"Have you had a chance to look over the menu?" The waiter asked. "Our ravioli is quite popular—"

"I'm far too excited to eat!" Theo became the actress again. "My fiancé promised to take me dancing at Club Danza!" She flashed her golf ball-sized wedding ring at the waiter. It shimmered in the dusk's low light, almost as if on command. "I've been dreaming of it since it was featured in *Vogue*."

"I've heard good things," the waiter said politely. "Will your fiancé be joining you here or—"

"How about you, darling?" She regarded Cal with her phony, eager eyes and matching smile. "Are you going to eat before we dance?"

The waiter looked him over like he had twelve heads. Cal traded glances between the two, and Theo raised her eyebrows, awaiting an answer.

"I'm not hungry." He smiled.

## 63

Cal watched a teal Roadster pass and darted across Lime Street with Theo's hand in his. The sun had dipped below the horizon, but sweat still pooled on his back under his pinstripe coat. When they reached the sidewalk, Cal tried to pull his hand away, but Theo yanked him closer, forcing his arm around her slender waist as they approached Club Danza.

"Pretend ya like me, Bucko. I don't bite," Theo whispered, scanning the line of people extending around the corner. "This won't do." She approached the bouncer by the front door. "Excuse me," she said in a sing-songy voice.

"Line starts down the bl—" The man scanned the length of Theo's body. "Well, hello there, doll. How can I help you?" His grin displayed his intentions plainly across his broad face.

Theo kept her distance, running her hand along the velvet rope. "We're the musical act for the evening. Is there a back entrance we can use?"

The man flicked the brim of his flatcap with his thumb and traded glances between Cal and Theo. "Ya don't say?"

Cal eyed the .38 special under the man's blazer as Theo locked her arm in his and smiled. "Ever heard of Nat King Cole? Well, this is his cousin, Alvin."

The man eyed Cal. "Alvin King Cole?" he asked with a justified smirk.

Theo smiled. "Just Alvin Cole."

"You colored folks sure can sing." He laughed boisterously and jabbed toward an alley behind him with his thumb. "Round back, tell 'em Rocco sent ya."

Kay Starr belted "Wheel of Fortune" over the speaker system as Cal pushed through droves of white people dressed in their finest suits and gowns. They laughed and drank, and conversations blended into a constant hum, drowning out the music. Cal adjusted his lapels on the suit Theo had insisted on buying and sighed. Whenever he dressed up, he felt like he was at a funeral.

Men seated at tables along the wall stared at him skeptically through curtains of cigar smoke as he made his way to a bar on the back wall. He budged into an open spot, leaning into the bar and glancing casually around the crowded room. Theo had vanished.

"What'll it be, big fella?" The bartender had slick, black hair to match his slick, black demeanor, and he chewed a toothpick as he spoke.

Cal eyed the colorful bottles lined up in a seductive row behind him. "I'm fine, thanks." He turned, taking in more of the scene and ignoring the impending ruin inches away.

The club was a middling-impressive, wide-open space with a dull purple rug, gaudy white columns, and arches someone probably thought were fancy. An empty stage was erected in the back, next to the kitchen door.

The bartender went to work on someone else's drink. "Don't get many of your type in here." Cal turned to find the man's deep-set, shifty eyes scanning him cautiously. "You ain't gonna start any trouble, are ya?"

Cal shook his head. His eyes followed the brown liquid from a cocktail shaker into a glass. He licked his lips again and glanced at the bottles on the wall.

The bartender followed his gaze. "If you don't want a drink, why the hell are you here?"

Cal looked at him. "I'm meeting someone."

"Oh yeah? Not another nigger, I hope. Get too many o' yous in here, and there's liable to be a problem."

Cal ignored him and scanned the club, desperate to find Theo before either of them did anything stupid.

"I told Frankie we can't be playing that Louis Armstrong shit. The niggers love it. Droghead and Lincoln will be emptying into our establishment before long."

Cal ground his teeth. The bartender was a twitchy mess of anxiety, probably drunk or on something. "Excuse me," Cal said, pushing himself off the bar.

"Yeah, just watch yourself, fella. You ain't so big as you think you are!"

The song ended, and the slow melody of "Changing Partners" by Patti Page began.

Theo emerged from a group of people, slipped her arm around Cal's, and pulled him away. "Dance with me, Calvin."

"Theo—" Cal slowed his pace, but she yanked him into a crowd of young lovers, too enticed by one another to notice anything else. She fell into Cal's chest, and he could smell her sweet perfume. The two swayed slowly, and the rest of the dance floor vanished.

"See anything suspicious?"

"Hm?" Cal remembered himself and looked over Theo's shoulder into the dark crowd, trying to ignore the comforting heat of her body. "How do you know the DiLilos are even here?"

"I know the family. They wouldn't miss a hoppin' Saturday night in their own—" Theo's body went rigid. "Why don't you get us a couple of drinks? I need to powder my nose. Won't be but a moment." She slithered out of his arms and vanished into the masses. Cal sighed and acquiesced, pushing through people toward the bar.

A scream erupted from across the room, then another, and the crowd shifted. Hysteria cut through the docile tones of "Changing Partners" as people rushed by Cal toward the exit in rabid droves.

"It's the Scarlet Sparrow!" someone yelled, followed by the spray of a submachine gun. Screams echoed through the room, and the phalanx moved faster, knocking Cal around. He managed to stay on his feet but was dragged backward toward the exit.

The bartender reached under the bar. A knife blade gleamed in the dim light, catching him in the eye. He stumbled backward and clutched weakly for the hilt with a half grunt as his life drained. He slumped forward and painted the bar with his blood.

Theodora sashayed across the top of the bar, kicking people's glasses away. She pulled the man up by his greasy hair, yanked the Ka-Bar knife out, and discarded him into the well.

*Rat-tat-tat-tat-tat. Click. Click.* Bullets rippled off Theo in a burst of orange thanks to her armor-harness. The man holding the empty gun fumbled a new magazine in his trembling hands. Theo squatted and grabbed a shotgun from behind the bar. She smiled.

"No, please!" The shooter dropped his gun.

*Bang!* The club walls faded in a flash. A sick, stabbing pain caught Cal in the gut, and he doubled over, wheezing. Something had ripped through his chest, but when he looked down, nothing was there.

When he looked up, the remaining people were ghostly wisps of smoke, shrieking inhumanly and pushing away from where the bar had been. Gunfire rang out. Some spirits faded to black, while others erupted in a brilliant white and vanished. Cal was watching through the eyes of his captor, he realized. Marchosias.

Theo stood alone, naked and pale. She had deep eye sockets but no eyes and a black, puckered smile. Thick ropes jutting from layers of fleshy scar tissue that had grown over the hooks dragged her forward. An unseen puppeteer forced her to pace across the bar like a rabid dog.

Cal glimpsed himself in a shattered mirror, naked, dangling by his left side like a broken marionette, spinning slowly around and back. Hooks dug into his appendages, but ropes only looped through his left arm and leg. His right arm was free and flailing.

The pain of infection from the old, rusty metal screamed through the muscle and bone of his loose appendages, head, and chest. Marchosias yanked wildly at the ropes, but Cal only bounced like a broken toy.

"Cal?" The Scarlet Sparrow stood untethered, surrounded by smoking bodies leaking blood into the purple carpet. A lone gunman fired blindly from behind an overturned table at the other end of the room.

"Make sure no one leaves through the back door," Theo said a little too stoically as she wiped her bloody knife across a tablecloth.

Cal walked begrudgingly across the blood-sodden carpet and pushed the swinging door into the kitchen if only to escape the stench of death. He turned, looking over the scattered bodies. Bonnie was never here. He threw a punch through the drywall and brick, opening a hole into a bathroom. His muscles relaxed, and he stared at the mournful face peering back from the mirror.

*I'm no better than her*, he thought. *The numbness is still inside me*. Pain shot through his arm, and he regarded the trickle of blood dripping from his knuckles, smiling. *But it's fading. Good. These gifts aren't worth my soul.* He found a towel and wrapped his hand.

The kitchen was empty. The cooks had probably left when the gunfire started, but the smell of garlic and tomatoes lingered. Cal rounded a pot rack and found a hunched old man with a bad toupee and a cigar long with ash. He paid Cal no mind and continued stirring something in a large blancher six-quart pot.

Cal watched him curiously. "Hey, old-timer. You gotta go." The man glanced up with a sour face and continued stirring.

Pots and pans clamored to the floor, and a panicked man stumbled forward, frantically scanning the shadows. "I'll fuckin' kill you!" he screamed nervously. When he saw the old man, his eyes went wide. "Nonno? Why are you still here?" He eyed Cal like a feral animal.

The old man regarded the young one with the same sour scowl he'd offered Cal and muttered in Italian.

The younger man kissed his forehead. "Nonno, your salsa don't matter. The devil is here; you have to go."

The old man removed his cigar and spat on the floor.

*Bang!* A gunshot burst through the young man's calf. He fell with a shriek and gripped his leg. "Fuck!"

Theo emerged from the shadows and grabbed the man by his slick black hair, forcing him to his feet.

"Mercy, please!"

Theo smiled. "Do you know who I am?"

The man desperately launched across the butcher's block, reaching for a cleaver. Theo pulled her Ka-Bar and drove it through his hand into the wood.

"I asked you a question." She twisted the knife, and blood poured from the wound.

He shrieked. "You're-you're—"

She twisted the knife again.

"The Scarlet Sparrow! The fucking Scarlet Sparrow!" he screamed.

Cal inched forward. "Theo—"

"Wait for me at the bar."

He placed a hand on her shoulder. "I think I'll stick around."

She shrugged him off. "You aren't going to like this."

"Get-get my grandfather out of here!" The man's pathetic eyes were on Cal as he slid to one knee, still pinned by his hand to the butcher's block. "Please—"

Theo raised the bartender's Remington shotgun and fired blindly across the room.

# The City of the Gods: Gold

*Boom!* Buckshot blasted through the old man's head, slathering the wall behind him with blood. His body dropped.

"Pay attention!" She pulled the young man up by his hair. "What is it I do to people like you?"

"Oh, noooo. You-you didn't have to do that! He was just an old man"—his face twisted with anger—"he was an old man, you fucking bitch!"

Blood collected around Cal's shoes, and the gaping hole that was the old man's skull gawked at him in his periphery. He eyed Theo with a new kind of loathing.

Theo turned the man to show him his grandfather and rested her chin on his shoulder. "Answer me," she said.

"Y-you kill people," he whimpered. "You fucking killed my Nonno!"

Cal touched Theo's shoulder. "Theo, we need to—"

"Cal, get your fucking hand off me and go to the bar."

Cal frowned and moved to the door.

"Please, don't go!" the man sobbed.

Theo nuzzled the man's shoulder. "Where is Francisco?"

"I-I don't know; he left town after T-Day. I heard he might be in Chicago."

Cal let the door swing shut behind him. There was a gunshot, and the man screamed.

"You wouldn't lie to me?"

Cal approached the bar.

"No, I swear to Christ, lady!"

*Bang!*

The man screamed again.

"Where is Miss Mercury?"

"Miss Mercury? I have no idea!"

"She told me different."

"I've never even seen Miss Mercury in my life. I swear to God! We all went straight after the Enforcers—"

"You boys were packing a lot of hardware for a crew who went straight. Where the fuck is my daughter?"

"Your—what? I don't—" A final shot echoed. There was no scream.

Cal slumped onto a barstool and wiped a drop of blood off an empty highball with his thumb. He grabbed a bottle and filled the glass. It didn't matter what with, as long as it was brown. He closed his eyes and smelled the sweet burn of alcohol, aching to slip into oblivion.

Theo took a seat on the stool next to him. The Ka-Bar was in its holster, but otherwise, she was unarmed. The Scarlet Sparrow uniform suddenly didn't seem so absurd.

They sat quietly, staring at nothing across the gore-covered bar as sirens sounded in the distance. The speakers poured the tranquil lyrics of Nat King Cole's "Too Young."

Theo's face twisted with anger. She shot from her seat and whipped a glass across the room. Cal regarded the drink he'd poured, wishing, once again, he had never met Theodora Connor, and set it on the bar.

# The City of the Gods: Gold

Theo upended a bottle of bourbon, pouring it down her gullet. When she'd had her fill, she flung that across the room, too. Cal regarded his throbbing, bandaged hand and the blood smear across the bar, reveling in the irony. Bonnie wasn't here. She was still missing, still safe from her mother's clutches.

The sirens grew louder. Cal eyed the dead bartender, waiting to meet his fate. Under the body, a few of the floorboards ran north to south rather than east to west. He crawled over the bar and found a metal ring amongst the coagulated blood. He pulled up, lifting part of the floor with a rusty creak. Theo peered over the bar curiously.

Cal sat on the floor and dipped his legs into the square hole, covering his new suit in blood. With his feet, he found a rickety metal ladder and descended into the pitch-black.

"What is it?" Theo's silhouette peered over the hole. He ignored her, and at the end of a long, dark climb, his feet touched something solid. The floor was dirt, and the air was crisp; it smelled like earth. He groped along the wall, brushing rotten timber beams. The clang of feet on rungs echoed, and Theo dropped down next to him.

"This must be the tunnel Big Sal ran booze through in the '20s." Her voice echoed through the cavernous room. "It's warmer over here."

Cal inched along the wall toward her voice and the sound of rushing water. A swollen, underground river abruptly ended the path. Light from a hole at the mouth of the river illuminated a rotten makeshift dock, too soggy and decayed to stand on, but the shore declined on either side.

Theo walked out until the water was waist-deep. "This must be Miller's River." She waded upstream, running her hand over a brick wall, and vanished around the corner.

Cal glanced back to the dark path, waiting for the police to storm the cavern. "We should leave."

No response.

Cal shook his head and carefully traversed the sloping shore into the water. The cold current tugged lightly downstream as Cal trudged toward Theo. She stood perilously on the slick, shiny rubble in front of an area where the wall looked like it had exploded outward.

"Whatever made this hole was big." Theo squinted inside. "It links up to the old subway—"

"Who's down here? Show yourself!" a stern voice echoed.

A flashlight shone on the wall across from the platform. Cal turned wide-eyed.

Theo ran a finger over the brick next to the hole. "Looks like there's something..." She pulled her Ka-Bar and screwed her face, digging into the wall.

"We need to get out of here now," Cal whispered.

"I've almost got it."

"Hey!" A circle of light darted across the room. "Who's there?"

Theo kicked Cal in the chest. He stumbled backward, tripped over debris, and splashed into the cold, rushing water. The current took him faster than expected. Cal grabbed a piece of rubble and pulled himself close as the light investigated the water around him.

"Over here!" Theo called out. The light shot across the water and stopped on Theo. Cal pressed his body against the debris pile, praying it would hold.

"Scarlet Sparrow?" the police officer called out. "What are you doing here?"

Theo dropped into the water and waded toward the cop. "The same thing as you, I imagine, looking for the creep who created the bloodbath upstairs."

The flashlight swept the water again. "Just you down here?"

"Just me and whatever tore through here." She eyed Cal. "Probably halfway to Westport by now. If you have no objections, I think I'll follow it."

"Everything alright?" a second voice called from deeper in the cave. A flashlight swept across Cal's face. "Hey! You in the water, identify yourself!"

The officer in front of Theo pulled his gun. She grabbed his arm, twisting his wrist back until it popped. His scream echoed. Theo drove the heel of her palm into his chest and dove into the water. Cal went under, swimming with the current. The gun's muzzle flash cascaded across the walls and ceiling as bullets ripped through the water around him.

The river grew deeper, and Cal spun helplessly in the current. There was no telling which way was up. He swam harder, fighting the urge to breathe.

Something snagged Cal's foot. Instinctively, he kicked and thrashed. It squeezed tighter, pulling him into the murky depths. He looked down in a panic to find Theo hugging his waist.

There was a blinding flash.

A cold metal grate pressed into Cal's back as he sucked in air. Each breath was a gift. The sound of water running through metal filled the large room until it dissipated. Next to him, Theo traded off, coughing and gasping.

Cal pushed to his elbows, scanning his surroundings. Somehow, they had made it back to the Hall of Enforcers.

"Jesus, Cal, I was only trying to save your life," Theo choked out. She was lying on her back, eyes closed, dripping into the grate. "Why'd you have to kick me?"

"What happened?" Cal asked.

Theo rolled over, pushed herself to her knees, and fell back onto her haunches. "I feel like I'm going to spew."

"What happened?" Cal repeated.

"I teleported us here, and you kicked me in the face." She adjusted her jaw.

"Teleported?"

Theo sighed. "I displaced us through space and time."

Cal's brow furrowed.

Theo laughed in a defeated manner. "In the blink of an eye, we moved almost seven miles."

"If that's true, why didn't we... teleport into that club? Why all the theatrics?"

"Well, it's exhausting. We'd have no energy to"—she paused—"for anything else." She slumped onto her back next to Cal, meeting his gaze. "Anyway, I had a good time on our little date, didn't you?"

Cal cleared his throat. "So, what made that hole in the wall?"

Theodora pulled a metal mass from a compartment in her belt and turned it between her fingers. The surface shifted in the low light of the Hall. She closed her hand into a fist. "No idea, but I found a slug in the wall with an odd metal coating. I'll have to analyze it."

Theo stood and pressed her palms against her back, stretching with a wince. "Lily went out of her way to send me on that wild-goose chase, so I wouldn't notice her taking my ship to my lab on—"

"The moon?" Cal sighed and staggered to his feet. His whole body ached, and the spinning room threatened to return him to the floor.

"The moon," Theo responded.

"Why would she kidnap Bonnie, though? It doesn't make sense," Cal said.

Theo shrugged. "Why send us to Club Danza at all? Maybe Thompson is alive, and they're working together. Nothing would surprise me at this point."

"So," Cal said. "The moon?"

"The moon."

"Great," he sneered.

SPEAK NO MORE
THAN IS SET
DOWN FOR THEM

## 64

The static hiss was deafening. Two pairs of eyes watched from the shadows fuzzed over like television sets with lousy reception—one forlorn, the other jovial but exuding insanity. The boy sat silently, his legs hugged to his chest.

Laughter exploded. The owner of the smiling eyes lunged into the light on long pencil-thin legs encumbered by a hump growing from his arched back. He towered over the boy, sputtering in black and white.

Static snow created deep creases accentuating the gaunt features on his clown face as it twisted into a grin revealing thousands of crooked teeth. He crouched slowly on creaky knees, inches from the boy, tittering, leaking noxious breath, and burst into loud, hysterical laughter. His jaw dislocated, raining spittle that smelled like burning rubber.

The clown ripped backward into the shadows.

*Crunch!*

The laughter ceased.

The boy peered into the inky black, too afraid to move. Sobbing echoed through the room. Big, cumbersome feet hobbled into the light, carrying a hunched body much like the first. Salt and pepper static crackled across the form in waves, interrupting the weeping with an eerie, technical hiss. The clown fell to his knees and slumped like he had no spine. His eyes peeked through narrow creases, and his jowls drooped almost to his shoulders, swinging like pendulums.

The boy's grip on his legs relaxed, and he rose slowly, inching forward. The clown yelped, clawing at the ground as he shot into the shadows.

*Snap!*

No more crying.

A third presence watched. Something older than the world. "Tasa Sabnock on ca lirach," it whispered. And Gordon understood.

**<u>65</u>**

Gordon's fingers dug into the firmly packed dirt. His eyes shot open. Walter stood over him, nudging his arm with a dirty shoe. "Gordie?" Walt's shirt was pulled over his nose, and his oversized hat was pushed back on his brow, leaving only his blue eyes exposed.

Gordon sat up slowly, clutching his throbbing head. "Wh—"

"Gordie? Are you alright?" Walt said. "You were sleeping for a long time, and I think— well—you peed your pants."

Gordon glanced around the dark room. "Where?" He sat up slowly, and his stomach churned, letting out a low rumble.

"The fortress, where else? Billy helped me carry you, but he left."

*Billy? We were in Sainte Marie Square—Did I help Miss Mercury?*

"Miss Merc—"

*No, that's stupid. I was there with—Billy and Walter, and—* Gordon's mind was still so foggy. He eased onto his back, closing his eyes to relieve his pulsing head. His eyes darted open. *Oh shit! Pop!*

"What time is it?"

Walter shrugged. "I don't know. It must be morning by now."

"We have to—" Gordon tried to remember, but his brain was drowning in a thick haze. *"Clowns!"* he exclaimed.

Walter jumped. "What?"

Gordon shut his eyes. *Why can't I remember?*

"What'd you say, Gordie?"

Vague shadows drifted through Gordon's mind, skewed by queer phantom-like apparitions of clowns: A cop, a pile of rubble, steel, and Pratima. "What day is it?" His chapped lips pulled tight as he spoke.

"I dunno." Walter shrugged. "Sunday night or Monday. Gordie, Pop will"—he swallowed—"we're dead meat."

Gordon wobbled onto his feet. The blood caked in his hair and on his face tightened when he blinked, and his body screamed in agony. "I need water," he croaked. Walter shrugged.

The wall bowed in and out like it was breathing, and the world upended. Gordon burst through the door, heaving Sugar Smacks into the brush.

Walter froze in the doorway. "Gross, Gordie!"

Gordon leaned against the plywood wall and shut his eyes, inhaling the damp, humid air. "How much money you got, Walt?"

Walt elephant-eared the linings of his pockets.

"Great." Gordon ran his dry tongue over his dry lips, scanning the woods. He spotted his bike leaning against a tree next to Walt's and limped across the clearing.

Walt followed closely. "Gordie, what's Pop gonna do to us?"

Something deep in the forest grinned with the soft crackle of television static dancing across its many splintered teeth. Gordon shuddered and tried to mount his bike, but pain shot through his back when he lifted his leg. "C'mon, Walter." He released the handlebars. "The bikes'll be safe here for the night."

Gordon shuffled forward, using the bone-like trees for support. The white bark glowed in the moonlight. Walt scurried beside him, clutching a stick warily. "Sure is dark out here."

*Walter focuses on the darkness when he should be grateful for the light!* The thought presented itself as a woman's voice in the back of Gordon's mind.

Walt's eyes were unblinking saucers darting every which way. "D'ya think there are monsters, Gordie?"

"There's no such thing," Gordon said. He knew it was a lie; he could feel eyes watching him.

The voice returned: *Walter has no idea! He didn't see what you saw. You know what must happen.*

Gordon's head pulsed.

*I can protect you from your father,* the voice snarled through a constant static hum. It sounded like his mother caught deep within a telephone receiver. She quoted Captain Wonderful: *There is a way to stand up for yourself and be fair and just at the same time, but it's not for the small man. It is for the righteous only!*

Walter ran ahead, swinging his stick wildly.

*Do not forget your father's schedule; that is death. Do not forget his moods; that is death.* His mother overlapped a deeper, more vile voice, knocked loose when he had been in the shadow place, where dreams and reality met, where nightmares flourished, where he'd seen those... things.

*Tasa Sabnock on ca lirach!*

Sabnock. Somehow, he knew that's what was talking to him.

*Let me in! I'll protect you.* The garbled whispers grew louder. In his mind, he could see Miss Mercury in her scantily clad uniform staring out from a television set. She pulled the zipper on the back down slowly. *Do it for me, Gordon!*

*Remember what happened last night? There's a knife on the counter,* his mother's voice said from Miss Mercury's pouty lips. Her dark hair fell playfully onto her bare shoulders as her bodice slipped off.

*Knife on the counter,* something whispered from deep in the woods.

*Through the cellar door,* a second voice joined in.

Gordon stared vacantly, trying to remember.

*Use the knife on the counter,* the voice whispered.

*Body through the cellar door,* something answered.

*Last night… Walt was watching the Uptown Clowns and—*

Every ache and pain in Gordon's body screamed suddenly.

*I fell. I fell when I was running. No, before that, my father—*

*Knife on the counter!* The reverb from the distorted scream shook his vision.

*Cellar door!* The forest blurred into glowing white fuzz.

*Last night, my father—*both voices screamed over each other like a jumbled mess of mismatched radio frequencies and fell silent—*hit me.*

"Waaahhhhoooo!" A loon's cry ripped through the night, and Gordon jumped. He placed a nervous, fidgety hand on Walt's back and picked up the pace, glancing through the ghostly white trees at the rippling black-and-white shapes darting between them.

Walt frowned. "Gordie—"

"Shh! They'll hear you!" Gordon watched the static men lumbering between the trees.

"Who?" Walt slid close.

Gordon limped on quickly over the rotten railroad ties pressed into the foliage. Something brushed the small of his back. He swung his head around, and his mother's soothing voice returned. *It's only me.*

Gordon smiled, but it was short-lived. He tried to remember how he'd gotten out of that hole in Sainte Marie Square. An eerie, nauseating feeling clung to his subconscious. Part of him thought he might have died, only for a split second, but that split second had allowed something into his soul.

*CRACK!* A jarring noise shook Gordon from his thoughts.

"Take that monster!" Walter giggled at the broken branch in his hand.

"Jesus Christ, Walt!" Gordon said. "You're going to give me a fuckin' heart attack!"

"Geeze, sorry, I only whacked a tree, Gordie." Walter tossed his broken stick into the brush and gazed at the moon. "Gordie, do you think Mom is looking at the moon?"

Gordon stared at his brother. He didn't think Walt even remembered their mother. He had only been a little over two when she left. "I-I don't know, Walt."

"It's just that she always read *Goodnight Moon* to us before bed, remember?" He scampered forward to keep pace with Gordon.

"Yeah, I remember, so what? Lotsa people read that dumb book."

"Well, it's just, she'd read it, and then we'd all go to sleep. But now I'm awake, and the moon is so big, so maybe Mom is awake looking at the moon, too. Maybe she remembers reading the book, and she's thinking about us right now."

Gordon scanned the ground to hide the tear rolling down the bridge of his nose. "That's the stupidest thing I've ever heard, Walt." He wiped it away.

"Nuh-uh, Gordie! We can ask her! We can ask her when you join the Enforcers, and she comes back to Empire on accounta you'll make it safe."

Gordon didn't respond. He didn't want his voice to shake or more tears to fall. All he wanted was to walk through the darkness in peace, to the inevitable doom waiting at the house.

**<u>66</u>**

Gordon's Poll-Parrot shoe hit the Albert Street sidewalk, and whatever had infected his mind lifted. The static clowns watched from the tree line but advanced no further. His headache dissipated, and the screaming, analog voices calmed as he recalled everything but his time in that horrible pit.

Gordon forced a sad smile. Soon, the Enforcers would summon him, and he'd have to leave Walter behind. The sting of tears pressed behind his eyes. He placed a hand on Walt's back. "You-you're a good Junior Enforcer, ya know?"

"Yeah, I know it, Gordie." Walt swung his stick wildly in front of him. "I'm second-best on the team!"

"Third best," Gordon teased.

"Nu-uh! I'm way better than that whiny baby, Billy. Ukrit talks funny, and Pratima is a girl. I'm second best!"

"Okay, okay. You're second best." Gordon laughed and scanned the sidewalk to gather the right words. "I probably won't be around much longer—I mean, now that I finished the fort, it's only a matter of time before the League recruits me."

Walter dropped his stick. "Can't I go with you, Gordie? I won't get in the way—honest Injun, I won't!" He grabbed Gordon's arm.

Gordon smiled sadly. "Walt, I need someone here to run the Junior Enforcers, and since you're second best, it has to be you."

Walt met his gaze with a puzzled expression. "But Gordie, I—"

"It's not a request, Private! It's an order!"

"Okay, Gordie," Walt squeaked.

"I'll come back and visit. Every chance I get," Gordon said. "And when I marry Miss Mercury, I'll be the leader. Then, I'll recruit you myself—should only be a couple of years."

"Oh!" Walter's face brightened. "That's why you want to marry a girl, so you can be in charge of the Enforcers." He sniffled and wiped his nose on the back of his hand.

Gordon smiled and slapped the brim of Walt's hat over his eyes. "Betcha can't catch me!" he yelled, running down the Signal Ridge hill.

----

The old Victorian eclipsed the moon. Gordon sighed, trudging past his father's beat-up Chevrolet, sitting in the driveway at an angle that suggested he was not sober. No matter how brave Gordon had told himself he was, his body refused to take him up to the door.

Walt moved close behind him. "Do you think you can ask Captain Wonderful to talk to Pop, Gordie? Ya know, after you're the leader of the Enforcers. Maybe he can tell him to stop hittin' us?"

*You can protect Walter. Forever.* That familiar, distant voice returned. *There's a knife on the counter and a root cellar where no one goes.*

Gordon scanned the paint-chipped railings, the missing shutters, the ugly blue porch.

*The knife.*

"I don't think Pop would listen to Captain Wonderful, Walt. Some foes refuse to be reasoned with. That's when the Enforcers take action." He quoted the radio show again as he climbed the stairs with a new sense of fortitude.

*The cellar door.*

The door behind the screen was wide open, which meant his father had been too drunk to close it. Gordon ripped the screen door open and stepped inside. "Go to bed, Walt."

Walter scampered up the stairs quietly. Gordon stopped in the living room, eyeing the empty sofa. He peered into the kitchen, half expecting his father to be passed out on the floor with the refrigerator open again, but the house was silent.

The gleam of the water faucet caught his attention. He stumbled across the kitchen floor, bracing himself on the counter, and pulled up the handle. The cold liquid washed over his tongue and down his parched throat, spilling across his blood-soaked shirt. He gulped until his body refused water and shut the faucet off. Sick but satisfied, he couldn't help but smile.

Metal glinted on the counter. Gordon pushed aside a few old newspapers and overdue bills to reveal a dirty butcher knife.

*The knife.*

He saw himself standing over his father with blood running across the knife's blade. In his final death throes, Sam Ross stared wide-eyed at the child he had neglected to raise peacefully.

*The cellar door.*

His father's final words were muffled by the blood ejecting from his throat as his soul faded from his wide eyes. Gordon dragged the lifeless body down the four steps to the other staircase leading into the forgotten root cellar. A smile crawled across Gordon's lips. He shook his head and gasped, lifting the knife between his index finger and thumb like a dead rat and dropping it into the garbage can by the back door.

Light from the backyard flickered through the window. Gordon hovered over the sink, craning his neck. It looked like it was coming from Mister Storier's tool shed, but the unfinished picket fence on the property line blocked his view.

"Old man Storier is as useless as tits on a nun," his father had said the last time he'd discovered the oil lantern left burning in the shed. "*He* could have burned down the whole fucking neighborhood." A few drinks later, Sam had marched over in the dead of night to berate the old man.

Gordon stared at the light bleeding through the fence. Even if Mister Storier had left it on, it was nearly two-thirty. Someone should have noticed it by now. He opened the back door slowly. "Hello?" He inched across the shared stone patio.

Behind the oil lamp, a dark figure hunched over a workbench. Gordon crept around the beat-up wrought iron furniture, keeping his eyes locked on the shed door.

"Mister Storier? It's Gordon—Gordon Ross—I live next door. I saw the light on—" Gordon glanced down at the patio to ensure he didn't lose his footing and followed droplets of blood to the shed with his eyes.

Inside, the outline of a man shifted in the light, throwing a long shadow across the back wall. He was working diligently.

Gordon gripped the door frame, and words caught in his throat. It was his father, hunched over a workbench, muttering to himself humorlessly over the screech of the radio.

"Bore times bore times stroke three point eight seven five times three point four. Four times three point eight five times point seven eight five four times six equals two forty-three point four."

*He must be drunk,* Gordon thought, but something was horrifically precise about Pop's movements. His voice didn't sound slurred or erratic, but he favored his left arm, which was odd because Pop was right-handed.

"*Pop?*" Gordon whispered.

His father spun quickly, peering over Gordon, eyes like a wild animal. He turned back to the workbench and continued muttering. "Vessel—control—uranium two thirty-three ninety-two."

Gordon inched inside. "Pop, are you alright?" he asked. On the workbench, a mangled eyeball stared from a puddle of red pus. Gordon gasped, stumbling backward into the lawnmower, knocking it onto the ground. The clamor interrupted the radio, and his father turned his head like he'd just noticed Gordon was in the room.

"P-Pop?"

In the lantern's glow, he could see his father's face. Blood ran from a deep gash where his left eye should have been, collecting in his black and gray beard. The socket to his cheekbone was swollen, blue, and puffy like he'd been digging inside.

Gordon stared in horror, and when he could finally find it in himself to move, he turned and tripped over the lawnmower. "What did you do? *What did you do?*" he screamed from the shed floor.

There was a glimmer of humanity in his father's face and a hint of terror as his shaky hand raised slowly and touched the bloody eye socket. Gordon pulled himself to his feet. His father's face twisted, ready to cry.

Gordon lunged forward, wrapping his arms around his father. "I'm sorry, Pop!" Flashes of the blood-covered knife shot through his mind. "I was going to—I wanted to—I'm sorry." His father's body shook. He sobbed so intensely that the sound reverberated off the shed's walls.

A deafening, mechanical shriek ended the bawling. Gordon's father pushed him to the ground. He hummed a low guttural vibration, increasing the tone until it matched the high-pitched radio waves.

"End function," he said as he reached for a hacksaw pinned to the wall.

"No!" Gordon sprang to his feet and grabbed the saw from the opposite end, holding the bar running in a C-shape over the blade. "Pop, what are you doing?" He tried to wrestle the saw away, but his father shoved him to the floor.

Pop pressed the hacksaw to his bicep. Gordon pulled himself to his feet and stumbled toward his dad, but he pushed Gordon back to the ground.

Sam Ross stared longingly at his son, and Gordon watched whatever remained of his father fade as the dull metal blade parted his flesh and muscle. The sound grew louder as the teeth scraped across bone like he was cutting wood.

"Please… stop." Gordon stared up from the dusty wooden floor in a daze, watching blood run down his father's arm and onto the ground. Pop shuttered, and a sick smile crossed his lips as the saw ran clean through the other side.

*Thump!* His arm landed next to Gordon. Pop never screamed.

"Build, conquer, two-hundred thousand"—he lit the drip pan on a kerosene blowtorch—"from the water." When the flame in the flash pan died, he turned the valve and lit the front nozzle.

Gordon crawled backward across the floor, anxious about what his father might do with the torch.

"Revenge from the water—ex equals el one cosign zero one el two cosign—zero one plus zero two." He brought the tip of the flame to the bloody stump, running the fire evenly over it. "Cosign zero one plus zero two plus zero three." His face reddened, and sweat droplets formed on his forehead. "Received. Final Solution realized." The screaming radio silenced.

The smell of seared flesh filled the shed as the wound bubbled and closed. Sam lifted a thin metal rod from the table, forcing it into the scar tissue. He welded the metal to flesh and bone with the torch.

"*Help*," Gordon whispered as he pressed himself against the far wall, staring at his father.

"Error, non-linear equations. Effector coordinates and joint coordinates—reevaluating." His father lifted his thin, stained undershirt, holding it between his teeth, and pressed the hacksaw to his torso. As the workbench and tools disintegrated slowly, the metal rod expanded and grew into a bulky, malformed mass resembling a crop duster.

"Help! Somebody help!" Gordon yelled. His father stared at him, working the hacksaw back and forth across his abdomen, spilling blood onto the floor.

"No!" Gordon pulled himself to his feet and grabbed the hacksaw again, but the object seared onto Sam's bloody stump raised and gripped Gordon's throat like a mechanical hand. Gordon kicked wildly, but the ice-cold grip tightened. His kicks became weaker and weaker as his final breath stuck in his lungs.

"What in God's name is going on out here?" Mister Storier stood in the doorway, brandishing a shaky butcher's knife.

*Thump!* Sam dropped Gordon.

"Sam? Jesus Christ! Y'almost gave me a heart attack. I thought you were a Negro come over from Droghead again." His eyes shot open. "Holy shit, what happened t' yer—get away from him, boy!" The old man stepped inside the shed and yanked Gordon up by his shirt. Sam advanced slowly with a blank look on his face.

"Now, don't do anything crazy, Sam. I called the cops, and they'll be here any second!" Mister Storier pushed Gordon behind him, holding the trembling knife high.

Gordon's father gripped Mister Storier's throat with his metal arm, lifting him off his feet. Mister Storier stabbed wildly with the knife, but the attack grew weaker as the air left the old man's lungs in a squeaky whimper.

Gordon jumped on his father's metal arm. "Stop it, Pop! Stop it!"

Pop grabbed Gordon's shirt with his human hand and launched him out of the shed. He rolled across the grass and into the trunk of a tree. Something in his back popped, and stars burst when his head smacked against the root. There was a sickening, wet, tearing noise from the shed. Mister Storier fell to the ground, expelling dust. He lay still briefly before shaking and gurgling. Then, all at once, it stopped.

Gordon stared at Mister Storier, lying at his father's feet. *Get up. Please get up!*

Gordon's father lifted the hacksaw and let out a jovial grunt as he lined it up against his torso.

*Do it! You don't deserve to live!* The thought ran through Gordon's mind in his mother's voice.

The sound of sirens bled through the night, and red lights beat against the back of the shed, trading off with darkness.

"They're over here!" a man yelled. Sam dropped the hacksaw and lifted the knife. Gordon watched from the foot of the tree. A smile crossed his lips, and somewhere in the distance, the howl of a loon brought him peace.

"Drop the knife! Now!" another man yelled. Although they were standing next to him, Gordon could only make out their shapes. The red lights were relentless, so bright and beautiful, illuminating what he couldn't see before.

Behind the shed, purple eyes watched from deep within the outline of a face with long, pointed ears and savage, untamed hair. It was fourteen feet tall, sitting atop a horse in glistening armor, the clown killer, Sabnock. Its face was illuminated with a loud bang and a bright flash, the gunshot that killed his father. Gordon smiled, and the world vanished.

**<u>67</u>**

Red lights beat against the clouds that had rolled over the moon. Gordon sat on his front porch in a hospital gown, wrapped in an itchy gray blanket, with no recollection of how he got there. His wounds had been dressed.

Walt was huddled under another blanket to his right, his eyelids heavy. Gordon tried to speak but found he was still a little foggy. "Where—what—"

"Gordie!" Walt called out excitedly when he heard his brother's voice. "Are you okay? You've been staring at that police car for a long time."

"Yeah, I think so. What happened?" Gordon watched the circus of cops, medics, and men in black suits parade against a backdrop of spinning red lights. Two black Chrysler

Imperial sedans were parked diagonally across the driveway behind his father's car. Three police cruisers, a maroon Ford station wagon marked "Miller's County Coroner," an ambulance, and an unmarked black Dodge van lined the street.

Two men emerged from the side of the house, wheeling a gurney. On top sat a black bag with the unmistakable outline of a human body against the broadcloth. They managed across the street and worked the gurney into a vehicle marked: "Miller's County Coroner." Two men in black suits followed, pushing another gurney with another black bag. Behind them, a third man in a black suit carried a bag marked evidence containing something resembling a giant crop duster.

*Pop*, Gordon thought. "Hey, Walt." Gordon maneuvered between his brother and the carnage. "Do you remember what you said about Mom and the moon?"

"Sure, I do. Why?"

A man in a black fedora watched the men in black load the black bag into the black van across the street. "Allied Science, sub-two." The man slammed the door and slapped the back of the car twice, sending it off into the night.

"Well, I think you're right," Gordon said, smiling weakly.

"Gee," Walt said. "Ya really think so?" He craned his neck to gaze at the moon.

Down the street, Missus Storier sat on the back bumper of an ambulance and stared catatonically at the street.

"Hey, there he is! Back in the world of the living?" A uniformed officer approached the boys, holding two steaming Styrofoam cups.

*Officer Kane,* the golden tag pinned to his breast pocket, gleamed proudly. He handed a cup to Gordon and one to Walter. Whatever was inside smelled like chocolate. Gordon set the cup on the porch, watching Missus Storier stare into oblivion. *I wonder if she sees clowns too.*

Walter slurped his beverage and sighed happily. "Gee, thanks, mister!" He grinned at the cop with a chocolate mustache.

The officer plopped his hat on Walter's head and smiled. "You're welcome, young man." He had the same slick hair and chiseled features as the other cops, but his eyes smiled. He took a seat on the steps next to Walt. "So, what grade are you in, young fella?"

Gordon watched Missus Storier intently. "What happened to her?" He knew the answer, but he needed confirmation. He needed to know what he had seen was real.

"You mean you don't remember, son?" The officer turned his mouth into a line.

"Mmmmm no, not really—" Flashes of his father's crazed, smiling face, staring at the hacksaw with one excited, dead eye stuck with him.

"Well, I'll be sure to have someone come check in with you. I'm more of a—well, I'm here to get you boys anything you need."

"Can I have a butterscotch sundae?" Walter asked excitedly.

Gordon shook his head. "Walter."

The officer chuckled. "I'll see what I can do. In the meantime—"

"What happened here?" A man in a fedora asked as he stomped across the yard. He had loose jowls and a no-nonsense stare that cut through the discomfort of the situation. He wore no police uniform, but he was obviously someone important.

The officer shot to his feet. "Hey, c'mon now. These boys have been through enough. Lay off, huh?" He stepped between the man and the porch steps.

The man in the fedora eyed the officer, then looked around him at Gordon. "Were you attacked? Or did you initiate contact with the—your father?"

"My father?" The sound of metal sawing through bone took Gordon into the scar tissue of repressed memory. He recalled the sick thunk as Pop's arm hit the wooden floor of the shed.

The officer placed a hand on the man's shoulder. "He's just a kid. He didn't see anything."

"Officer," the old man interrupted, "this is a federal investigation."

The cop put his hands on his hips. "Oh yeah? Boy, I'd like to—"

"It's true. I didn't see anything. I wasn't wearing my glasses," Gordon lied. "I had just gotten up for a glass of water when—"

"What about your bloody shirt? Or the—*urine*—in your pants?"

"Well, I guess when I hit my noggin, I lost control." Gordon shrugged.

The man eyed him carefully. "Fine." He turned in a huff.

"Fuckin' G-men," the cop muttered. He turned back to the boys and smiled. "Is your mother home? We didn't see her inside."

Walter eyed Gordon. "She's—"

"She's at work. She works nights at Schiller Hospital over on Wilmore. She should be back in a few hours," Gordon lied again. If the police found out the truth, they'd take Walt and him away and maybe separate them.

The officer eyed the ambulance. "Hm. She should have been contacted—"

"Oh, wait a minute"—Gordon slapped his forehead—"I guess my mind is still kinda fuzzy. She's up in Northwell, visiting Auntie Lauren. She'll be back tomorrow."

The officer put one leg on the stoop and leaned in on his knee. "Well, we'll get an officer out there—"

"She's camping. I forgot all about it." He tried to maneuver the lie, so the officer had no recourse.

"Camping, huh? Is she out there looking for Bigfoot, too?" Officer Kane smirked.

"No, she's out there on Whitetail trail," Walter piped in unexpectedly, "honest! She told me last week."

Gordon eyed his brother and smiled.

"Well, alright, then. I'll stay with you boys until she gets home. How'd that be?" The cop was smiling, but his eyes said he didn't believe anything they'd said.

Gordon scanned the lawn, looking for a way out. "We don't really—"

"Officer, we need to round up the others," the man in the black fedora yelled from the sidewalk.

Officer Kane sighed. "What am I supposed to do with these boys?" he called back.

"We have bigger problems. I'm getting reports of more of these"—he eyed the boys—"just come with me. We need all hands. Social Services will handle them."

"I'm staying until I talk to Social Services myself," he said.

The man scowled and moved toward the street, grumbling. The Enforcers had to come now; it was Gordon's only option.

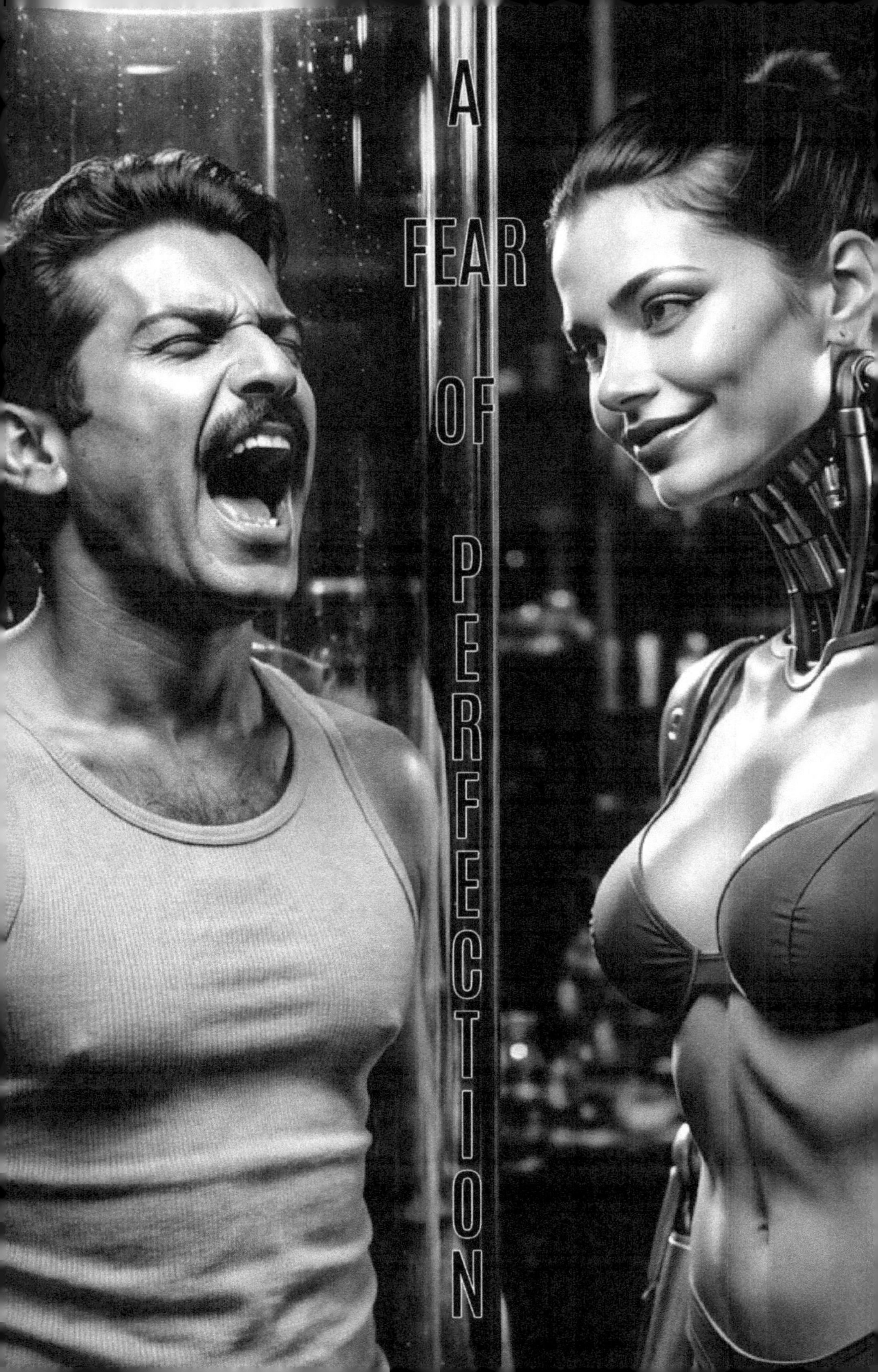

A
FEAR
OF
PERFECTION

"And Gordon replied, 'I'll find out how we can help and report back. Until then, at ease, Junior Enforcers.' And then he told the policeman the Junior Enforcers had arrived!" Ukrit said, looking over the family with wide, excited eyes.

Nadir sipped his coffee, scanning the *Bulletin* for news of his blunder at Allied Science. When the print blurred, he pinched the bridge of his nose, shut his eyes, and set the paper beside his plate.

"Are you alright, darling?" Anila whispered.

"I must be tired," Nadir responded.

"And the police said you can't go, but Gordon went anyway!"

"Police? These boys sound quite dangerous, Ukrit." Anila said.

"It's only a game, Mother," Pratima interjected. "They pretend to be heroes, and I pretend to be their science officer. There aren't really any police." She eyed her brother.

"There, you see, Anila? Just good, clean fun." Nadir said, helping himself to more poha. "I think it's wonderful Pratima and Ukrit have found a way to fit in."

"So long as no one gets hurt." Anila scowled and took a dainty bite of poha. "The Junior Enforcers," she muttered, shaking her head.

Nadir winked at Ukrit and smirked at Anila. "It wasn't long ago you were just a girl, my dear, alone and scared in the strange new world of England. Wouldn't you have liked to have had a friend? Even one who called herself a Junior Enforcer?"

Anila grimaced. "I had no time for friends."

Nadir chuckled. "That's true. Knowing your father, I'm sure he would rather you play with the schoolmarm."

"Was Grandfather strict, Mother?" Pratima asked.

A soft, rapid knock ended the conversation, and the Singhs regarded the front door. The knock came again, still timid, but Nadir's breath caught in his chest as he got up. "Y-your grandfather was the strictest man I'd ever known." He strolled to the door, feigning a smile. "There were porcupines less prickly."

"Are we expecting anyone?" Anila asked.

Nadir shrugged, turned the knob, and peered out. "Frank? What on earth are you doing here?"

Frank eyed Nadir with a look that said: *we have a problem.*

Nadir scanned the empty hallway behind him, trying to mask his concern.

"Mornin' Singh. We need to talk," Frank replied quietly.

Nadir watched him hesitantly. "Alright. Would you like to come in?"

Frank's eyes shrunk to slits, and his cheeks rose, twisting his face into a disgustingly phony smile as he waved to Anila and the children. "I think this is an outside conversation," he muttered.

Nadir regarded his family, held up his index finger, and joined Frank in the hallway, closing the door behind him.

Frank sighed. "I'm not going to jerk you around, Singh. Last night, Sam Ross, one of the firemen from the lab—" He paused and glanced up the stairway. "Somethin' happened to him, somethin' bad."

Nadir furrowed his eyebrows. "What?"

"Classified," Frank said sheepishly.

Nadir sighed, raised his arms, and rolled his eyes.

"I know, I know. Bottom line is, the higher-ups are requesting we come in for some tests."

Nadir crossed his arms. "I don't work for Allied Science anymore—"

"They're requesting hard," Frank said. "I talked them into letting me collect you rather than embarrassing you with an armed guard. Your family doesn't deserve that."

The door creaked open behind Nadir. He shut his eyes and bit his lip.

"Hello, Missus Singh. I'm Frank Rivoli. I had the pleasure of speaking with you on the telephone a few nights ago." Frank offered his weathered hand and another off-putting smile.

Anila shook his hand. "Is everything okay?" Her gaze fell on Nadir.

"Just fine," Frank replied. "I know the two of you just started your long-awaited vacation, but you know how it is with these eggheads. Us normal folks don't know which way is up without them. We'll only need a few hours of your husband's time, and then he's all yours. Big brain 'n all."

Anila eyed Nadir skeptically. "Alright, would you like some breakfast, Frank? I've made poha."

"No, thank you, sweetheart. It smells wonderful, but exotic cuisine doesn't usually agree with me." Frank's smile faded. "We'll just be a few hours."

Nadir turned to Anila. "I-I'll be right back, my dear." He tried to keep his voice from trembling.

"Okay." Anila scanned the hallway and stepped back across the threshold into the apartment. "We're still going to Currie Park this afternoon, right? When the children are out of school?" She shot Nadir a doe-eyed glance.

"Try and stop me!" Nadir kissed her. "Tell the children—I'll see them this afternoon." Tears welled in his eyes. He turned before his wife could see. "Shall we, Frank? After all, science waits for no man." Frank waved to Anila, and Nadir heard the door click shut.

----

As the mismatched pair walked in silence through the busy streets, Nadir watched Frank for any warning of what was to come, but the man was as stone-faced as ever. He turned scenarios over in his head, inspecting them from every angle. *We all signed waivers. There's no way a lawsuit would hold up in any court, so they aren't bringing us in for legal reasons. They had every chance to shoot us last night and would have if they wanted to keep this whole affair quiet.*

Frank placed a hand on Nadir's shoulder as if he could read his mind. "Hey, don't worry, Singh, it's all routine." His smile seemed sincere, but Nadir was still a skeptic where the government was concerned.

They turned the all too familiar left onto Sunrise Drive. Allied Science sat at the end of the joyless square, an empty husk of what it once stood for. They trudged across the sapling-lined cobblestone. The Powersphere spun with its usual soft hum, and Athena watched from atop her stone perch until she faded from view.

Nadir pulled the heavy door open, eying the vacant guard stations. "A little light on security—"

"Allied Science is closed," Frank responded coolly.

Nadir nodded, and nerves crept up again. Tunnel vision made the room spin out. He leaned on Zeus' wall, and his fingers brushed the raised lettering: "Onward."

"You okay?" Frank asked a little too casually.

Nadir glanced at him and noticed he was eyeing his watch. "Never better, old boy. Can you say the same?"

Frank called the elevator with his key and glanced around the lobby. "It's going to be fine." He wiped his brow with the back of his arm and met Nadir's troubled gaze. "What?"

Nadir stared wide-eyed. "You're scared, Frank."

Frank eyed his watch again and grumbled.

"Frank, this is no time to be stubborn." Nadir gripped his shoulders. "We need to leave, now!"

"It's not that simple," he whispered, glancing around.

"I know you have no love for me, but think of my wife, my children!" Nadir pleaded.

"We'll be fine!" Frank's eyes drifted over Nadir's shoulder. Nadir turned and found a newly mounted protrusion in the far corner.

*Surveillance.*

There was a ding, and the elevator doors slid open. "You-you're sentencing me to death."

"We're going to be fine!" Frank growled.

Nadir's breath came heavy and fast through his nose, but he had no more words. Frank guided him into the elevator. The doors shut. Frank turned a second key and pressed the button for subbasement one.

"Sub-one?" Nadir said. Frank faced forward as the elevator lurched down. "Disease control?" Nadir fought to catch his breath. The elevator stopped with a jarring bang. "Frank, it's not too late—"

"Stop it, Singh!"

"Turn the key, and go back up! Give me a chance, please!" Nadir barely uttered the final word before his voice betrayed him with a series of sobs.

The doors slid open. Frank motioned for Nadir to exit and offered his hand. "It's been a pleasure, Doctor Singh."

"Wait! What will happen to me, Frank? You owe me that!"

"Singh, I—"

He grabbed his longtime handler by the lapels. "Tell me, you bloody bastard!"

"I don't know!"

Nadir's arms fell limp to his side as he stared into Frank's now mournful eyes. Frank tightened his lips over his teeth and placed a hand on Nadir's shoulder. "Good luck, Nadir. I'll be sure to"—he cleared his throat—"I promise you'll make it out of here."

Nadir watched Frank slip into the darkness. "You promise? *You promise?*" Nadir's voice cracked. "You piece of shit, Frank! You bloody puppet!" Flashes of Thompson's red face danced across his mind. *The world will burn!* He felt the words on his lips, but they never came.

**<u>69</u>**

The bright white room smelled too clean, like death had been scrubbed away recently, and the fluorescent lights hummed like an interrogation lamp. Nadir squinted and stumbled

380

through the sterile room until his hand pressed flat on a glass wall. A man in a black hazmat suit watched him from behind a plate glass window to his left, scribbling on a clipboard.

Nadir eyed the man, awaiting instruction, staring at his reflection in that lifeless mask. Other men in similar suits stood single file in the next room, armed with identical service rifles. Across from them were Doctors Brown and Wendell, Nicholas, and the other two guards who had been present when they opened the vessel.

When the man was satisfied with his notes, he pressed a button, and his muffled voice filled the room. "Move to the door," he said with a mix of authority and boredom. Nadir obeyed, and the glass door hissed open. The same phony, clean scent wafted from the new room.

All the men turned and watched Nadir from their semi-circle of folding chairs. Doctor Brown was crying. Even Wendell, who rarely showed emotion, had a hint of gloom in his eyes. Nadir stepped into the room hesitantly.

"Stop!"

Nadir froze, and a sheet of air blasted over his body, the source of the sterile scent.

"Move into the room," the voice said.

Nadir sighed and took the open seat between Brown and Wendell, slapping Brown's back. "Buck up, old boy, everything will be alright."

The man who'd invited Nadir into the room walked from behind the glass panel. His movements seemed military, but his aggressive notetaking said otherwise. "You're all here because something... troubling occurred last night. This situation is highly confidential, so we will conduct individual interviews, and if we like your answers, you'll be released. Cooperation is all we ask."

A former guard leaped to his feet. "He's lying! The firemen and the contractors, they're all dead!"

"Sit down!" an armed guard in a hazmat suit yelled in a garbled voice.

The man glared like a wild dog. "I won't die here!"

The man with the clipboard sighed, turning his attention to a device on the wall matching the protrusion Nadir had seen in the lobby.

"Calm down!" The hazmat guard lifted his rifle.

Nadir took the opportunity to whisper to Brown, who was white as the room itself. "Are you chaps alright?" He felt a light tap on his shoulder and turned to meet Wendell's gaze.

"Where's Frank?" Wendell eyed the man in charge and whispered: "I need to get my notes from home—I think I know what's happening, but I need my notes. We need to contact Jacob Landry in Windwood Prison."

Nadir squinted. "Windwood? What's—"

The captive man lunged for the door. The hazmat guard jammed the stock of his gun into the man's nose, demolishing his face. He staggered, cupping a pool of blood with a shaky hand. The guard raised his rifle. "I won't warn you again!"

"I ain't going out like this!" the man mumbled through broken teeth as he stormed the door.

*Brap!* His head exploded, painting the glass wall in blood and fragments of bone and brain.

"You killed him!" Brown shot up. "He-he was telling the truth!"

The guard trained his gun on Brown, trying to steady it on his trembling shoulder. "And you'll get the same!"

"No!" Nadir pushed between them. "Please, that's enough. We're going to cooperate, right, gentlemen?"

The hostages looked each other over, nodding cautiously, aside from Wendell, who stared forward, lost in thought.

"Thank you." Nadir helped Brown back to his seat, eyeing Wendell. He was never known to be a liar; he wasn't even an exaggerator, and the information in his notes was most likely substantial.

"That's all we ask." The man with the clipboard regarded the dead man sprawled on the floor. "This was as unnecessary as it was unfortunate." He sighed. "I need to know if anyone else was in the vicinity of storage item number 100334A or, as you have coined it, 'the ship' or 'the craft.'"

Nadir watched his nervous reflection in the man's facemask. Then his gaze fell desperately on Nicholas, the only one who knew Pratima had seen the ship. Sweat trickled down his face as each man said no. Nicholas glanced at Nadir with sad eyes, waiting for his turn.

Nadir shook his head slightly at Nicholas, hoping the man in the respirator wouldn't notice. He licked his dry lips.

"Something you want to tell us, Doctor Singh?" the man with the clipboard asked, standing directly over him.

"N-no." Nadir fought the lump in his throat.

"Why don't I believe you?"

A tear spilled down his face. "I'm telling the truth."

One of the guards lowered his gun to Nadir's head.

"I promise." Nadir stared past the barrel of the rifle into the lifeless facemask. Another tear followed the trail from his eye to his chin. "There was no one else," he said firmly, shutting his eyes.

The man's pencil froze over the clipboard. "We're going to find out, anyhow. Go easy on yourself. Tell us, Doctor Singh."

Nadir shuddered, waiting to be thrust into eternity.

"Wait," Nicholas said.

Nadir jerked to his feet. "No!"

The man with the gun shoved him back into the chair. "Sit down!"

"Please—" Nadir closed his eyes and saw Pratima smiling at him with those big brown doe-eyes. *My little duckling.*

"Lieutenant Frank Rivoli and Lieutenant Joseph Falso were in sub-three when we opened the ship." Nicholas found the floor with his eyes.

Nadir tried to look angry at the man who had saved his daughter's life as air filled his lungs again.

The man with the clipboard eyed the device on the wall behind him, then regarded the group. "We know about Rivoli and Falso. They're being questioned in a location more fitting of men of their ranks." The man turned back to Nadir. "Is that it?"

Nadir nodded silently, letting the tears fall where they may. They lied better than he ever could.

The man with the clipboard reviewed his notes and looked up. "You will all be escorted to individual quarters and questioned further."

**<u>70</u>**

Nadir sat on the edge of a hospital bed in another blinding white room, stinking of sterility. After his adrenaline fell, his headache became unbearable. Countless men had come and gone, berating him with questions about his past from behind masks as they scribbled fastidiously on clipboards—his ties with Robert Oppenheimer, Henry Thompson, Theodora Connor, and the League of Enforcers. They asked if he was or had ever been a member of the Communist Party, why he was in the country, and what his plans were for the future. He answered truthfully, with as much enthusiasm as he could. Nadir's optimism returned when they told him he'd be on his way home after a physical.

A mechanism on the far wall clicked, and the door slid open as the lights cut.

"Hello?" Nadir waited in silence. "Doctor?" He crept slowly toward the door. The hallway was dark, aside from the dim emergency track lighting running along the wall a foot from the floor.

"I-I believe the door malfunctioned." Nadir poked his head around the corner. "Hel—"

*Bang!* A thunderclap of gunfire echoed down the hall. Nadir ducked his head into the room, staring at the open door. Silence returned with a faint sulfur smell overcoming the clean, sanitary scent.

Frank exploded through the doorway. "Singh! We need to leave!"

Nadir studied each speck of blood on Frank's shirt behind the M1 Garand he was white-knuckling. "Frank, but—"

"Now!" Frank glanced in the direction the shot had come from.

Nadir scowled. "What have you done? I was on my way home—"

"No, you weren't. They played us for fools." Frank crept into the hallway, looking strangely in his element, clutching the rifle.

"What about Brown and Wendell," Nadir said, "and poor Nicholas?"

"Dead," Frank replied bluntly. "Everyone, except us. C'mon, before they send more guards." Frank pressed against the wall, moving in the opposite direction the gunshot had come from; his fingers jumped and fidgeted nervously around the rifle's stock.

Nadir followed. "What happened—"

"Quiet." Frank peered around the wall into a dark corridor.

"My family—" Nadir whispered.

Frank edged forward and spoke without turning. "Forget 'em. It's best for everyone."

Nadir glanced back down the dark hallway behind them and followed closely. Frank was right, but if he died here, they wouldn't know why he'd abandoned them. *All because I had to see what was inside that craft*, he thought, *all because of my damnable curiosity*.

The marching footsteps of soldiers echoed off the high walls. Frank picked up the pace. Nadir matched his speed. Beams of light shot down the hallway. Frank gripped Nadir's shirt, slowing when the hall split into three. He pulled Nadir to the right, down a hallway with far sparser lighting, and froze.

"Shit! Wrong way!"

"What do you mean *wrong way*?" Nadir said.

Frank motioned with the gun in the dim light across the corridor. "Exit's on that side. Fuck."

Nadir squinted into the darkness. "We need to make a run for it." Yellow beams scoured the perpendicular hallway.

"They'll gun us down," Frank said.

"Well, why don't you just… shoot back? You are holding a gun, Frank," Nadir snapped.

"I'm outgunned and rusty. These boys will massacre me."

"Doctor Nadir Singh! Lieutenant Frank Rivoli! Throw down your weapons and step out with your hands over your head!" a voice called from down the hall. "We can work something out. You're both well-respected men."

Nadir gripped Frank's shoulder. "What now?"

Frank pressed the stock of the gun to his shoulder. "Make a run for it. I'll cover you."

Nadir watched the lights chase each other around the hallway. "No, I have a better idea."

"Last chance, gentlemen!" the voice called through the darkness. Light danced across the wall on their side.

Nadir extended his hand. "Give me the gun," he whispered.

"Why the hell would I do that?"

"Trust me!"

Frank sighed and shoved the heavy M1 Garand into Nadir's hands. "Be careful."

Nadir cleared his throat. "I've apprehended Frank Rivoli!"

"What the hell are you doing, Singh?" Frank whispered vehemently.

"I'm willing to trade him for my freedom! He has killed men down here. I have not!"

"Come out, and we'll talk about it," the befuddled voice answered.

"They're going to kill you, too," Frank spat.

"When we step out, run across the corridor toward the exit," Nadir whispered.

Frank nodded.

"I'm coming out, don't shoot!" Nadir yelled. The two men stepped into the open, and flashlights jumped from the floor to their faces. Nadir froze. Frank grabbed his arm and bolted across the hallway. Thunderous gunshots echoed in all directions, strobing like flashbulbs. Nadir fumbled the rifle from his sweaty grip. "Bloody hell! Stupid bloody klutz!"

Ricocheted bullets sparked against steel, revealing smeared blood on the floor. If it was Nadir's, adrenaline hadn't allowed him to feel any pain. The gunfire ceased, and the negotiator barked out orders. Footsteps rumbled down the hall.

Nadir scrambled toward Frank, who was leaning on the wall, inches from a giant metal door, groaning, favoring his left leg. Blood soaked through his trousers.

"Forget me, get out of here!" Frank drooled as he forced the words.

Nadir slid under Frank's arm and edged toward the door to freedom as the sound of hundreds of feet on steel beat behind them. The negotiator called out something inaudible from down the hall, and the footsteps ceased. Flashlights beamed.

Nadir leaned into a metal wheel bolted to the center of the door. Frank steadied himself on his good leg, peering nervously at the bullet-riddled wall. The wheel budged, and the door lurched open. Natural light blinded Nadir as a fishy odor overtook the stale, sanitized air. Gulls cried in the distance.

A distorted voice called forth another deafening bullet storm. Nadir helped Frank outside, following closely. When they were clear, Frank put all his weight behind the heavy door, slamming it in place, spinning the spoked wheel, and forcing three rusty deadbolts. He hobbled away from the structure. "C'mon! They'll be right behind us!"

The wheel spun the opposite way with an ominous creak, but there was a satisfying clang as the door hit the deadbolts. Nadir pushed his way up under Frank's arm again, and they limped across the concrete.

Daylight flooded over a hundred-foot wall with a single weathered ladder running up the center.

"Where are we, Frank?" Nadir sputtered.

Frank tore one of his sleeves from his shirt with two forceful tugs and eyed the door. "That won't hold them long." He tied his sleeve tightly around his thigh, then hobbled toward the ladder bolted perilously to the wall. The door was eerily silent.

"Can you swim?" Frank asked.

Nadir gripped the side of the ladder, testing its stability. "I haven't since I was a child."

Frank ascended the ladder slowly, wincing and grunting. "Well, are you bulletproof? Those are your choices."

Nadir scampered after him, pausing intermittently to allow Frank to suffer up a few more rungs. His legs burned, but the sound of a buzzsaw screaming behind them caused him to forget the discomfort.

Frank moved a bit quicker as the blade audibly caught the steel door. "Won't be long now," he yelled.

Nadir's arms weakened with his resolve as he climbed hand over exhausted hand. Frank vanished over the top, and Nadir made the mistake of looking down.

Sparks poured from the door, dissipating amongst the concrete. Nadir panicked, missing a rung with his sweaty hand, and his shoe slipped. The ladder groaned at the sudden weight shift.

Frank grabbed his wrist and pulled him up. "C'mon, Singh! You're going to survive a hail of gunfire only to let a ladder finish the job?"

Nadir struggled to grip the slick surface, covered in milky-white bird droppings, and eyed Frank. "Thank you."

*Clang!* The door fell to the concrete, expelling a storm of dust. Soldiers in black respirators spilled like cockroaches from the hole, scattering across the white floor. The same men tasked with protecting folks like Nadir and Frank for nearly eight years aimed their guns as others rushed to the ladder.

"It's now or never," Frank said, eerily calm. Nadir watched him fall one hundred feet into the Basalt River. He looked at the soldiers, closed his eyes, and leaped into the bright afternoon sky. Bullets audibly riddled the concrete, scattering birds.

The salty air rose, and Nadir tightened his limbs flush against his body. The wind tugged at his clothes. The water's surface was concrete, engulfing him with an abusive sting and submerging him into its refreshing blue-green depths.

He kicked and pulled his way to the surface, hacking and gasping for air. A few blinks revealed the current had carried him far enough away from Allied Science to render guns useless.

Frank drifted nearby. Nadir swam to him in a panic and grabbed his shoulder. "Frank!"

"I'm just resting my eyes," he responded weakly.

Nadir forced a nervous smile. "If I don't get to rest, you certainly don't."

Frank coughed. "I've had the worst goddamn headache all day, and th' way th' sun is hittin' the water—it's painful as hell."

Nadir sighed and went limp, becoming one with the current. "Where will we go?"

Frank's eyes fluttered open. "They'll be looking for us. No way in hell they jump in the water with all that gear on, but it won't be long until they deploy the frogmen." His eyes slid shut again. "My cousin has a fishing boat docked at Shelly's Marina. We'll take it to my place in Northwell, where we can lay low and figure out our next move."

**<u>71</u>**

Nadir navigated the maze of docks through the fishy stink toward the sign reading "office," offering folks a smile or nod to let them know he was just another boat enthusiast. After pulling himself ashore a half-mile downriver, his clothes and hair were still damp enough to draw the attention of anyone who cared to look closely. His eyelids were heavy, and his limbs sluggish. Swimming had been more taxing than he had anticipated, and all that kept him moving now was the fear of death.

He took a deep, reassuring breath and pushed through the office door into a small room with photos and fishing paraphernalia vomited on the walls. A phony, forced grin stretched his face to queer proportions as he rang the bell on the desk amongst bobbers, hooks, and tourism pamphlets.

"Yes?" the man sitting in front of the counter on a barely functional stool asked. The word seemed to ooze from his droopy face he couldn't bother to lift from a newspaper.

Nadir regarded the lumpy man. "Oh, do you work here?"

The man didn't look up from the newspaper. "No, I just enjoy sitting in the office."

Nadir cleared his throat. "Yes, well, I am here to retrieve Henry Rivoli's Barrett 22 Cabin Cruiser… boat. We're going fishing!"

"Congratulations." The man pushed himself up from the counter, eyeing Nadir through a pair of glasses far too thick for anyone who regularly operated a boat.

"What was the name?" The man's thick gray eyebrows met in the center of his forehead.

"Henry Rivoli," Nadir repeated. "Barrett 22 Cabin Cruiser. 'The North Runner,' I believe it's called."

The man looked Nadir over and meandered casually behind the counter. "Uh-huh, uh-huh. I know the boat."

Nadir maintained his worthless smirk, eyeing the clock behind the man. "Look, Henry is waiting for me, and he's no doubt loaded the fishing... sticks, beer, and sandwiches he's promised."

The man approached the desk. "Right."

Nadir paused, recalling what Frank told him. "We're fishing for Marlin, Atlantic Marlin. Off Sharktooth Cove, on Broadshall."

The man froze, staring at Nadir until a wide grin invaded his morose face. "I just come back from Sharktooth yesterday! They're biting out there this year, boy!" He turned and unlocked a box fastened to the wall behind him. "If you find yourself heading ashore, make sure you go to Jimmy's Bait n' Tackle! Tell 'em ol' Pete sent ya." He pulled out a set of keys. "Good luck out there, fella! Not that you'll need it."

Nadir took the keys, hiding his bewilderment behind the same phony smile he'd been sporting since he crossed the threshold to the office until he was safely outside.

----

Fresh salt air licked Nadir's face and whipped through his hair as the boat glided across the water. The sun shimmered, and the soft hum of the motor forced a smile. They passed under the Bunche Bridge, brushing the edge of Brookfield. The cityscape gave way to suburban homes and serene wooded areas where bare branches climbed toward the sun with false hope of Spring.

Frank said he still had friends from the war who owed him favors, and as soon as things cooled off, he could get a message to Nadir's family and retrieve poor Wendell's notes.

*Jacob Landry.* The name still haunted him; the name sounded familiar, but the fact that he was associated with Windwood gave Nadir pause. *What would a con know about the work we do at Allied Science?*

Frank also told Nadir that the dam they jumped off was a safety protocol installed by the Scarlet Sparrow. If the Powersphere ever malfunctioned, the embankment would be blown to flood Allied Science. The glowing orb on top was just something for the tourists. The actual nuclear reactor was in sub-ten.

Frank pulled the boat parallel to a dock beside a large maple tree and an American flag snapping in the wind. He killed the engine, leaped off with a wince, and gripped the starboard edge to steady it. "C'mon, Singh." He looked over the hull. "It's a shame I have to let this boat go, but we can't leave any trace. A lot of people saw us pulling away from Shelly's"—he looked at Nadir—"and you aren't exactly inconspicuous."

"I don't blend in at the boating club? How offensive." Nadir smirked.

Frank laughed. "C'mon, let's get inside."

Nadir climbed carefully off the boat, shaking the hull under his weight. Frank said something apologetic and shoved 'the North Runner' into the Basalt River. "I'll reach out to my cousin in time"—he watched the craft drift with his hands perched on his hips—"he'll understand."

"I appreciate this, Frank," Nadir said.

"Thank me later, Singh. This is just the beginning." Frank limped slowly across a sprawling lawn peppered with maple and oak trees. Leaves danced at their feet. Those that didn't crunched underfoot.

A modest, rustic log cabin sat behind a row of giant evergreens, far enough from the river not to be spotted by any boaters. A shallow porch jutted from the front with a hand-carved rocking chair as its only piece of furniture.

Frank glanced at Nadir over his shoulder. "This was the retirement plan, Singh, whaddya think?"

"It's lovely, Frank," Nadir said. "Thank you for your hospitality."

Frank nodded uncomfortably, slid an obviously out-of-place rock aside, and removed a key, which he wrestled into the lock. "Hungry?" He threw the door open.

"Surprisingly, I'm not," Nadir responded.

"Yeah, me neither. Probably nerves," Frank replied.

Dust floated amongst the few remaining sunbeams shining through the curtainless windows. There was still enough daylight where turning on a lamp seemed silly, but not enough to where the artificial light wouldn't be a welcome addition. Nadir waited patiently for his eyes to adjust as the scent of mothballs and freshly cut wood combined into something else altogether.

The interior was decorated exclusively with heads of various dead animals and fish, all mounted on plaques with gold inscriptions. It was a rustic house built for a man by a man, and it was the second time Nadir had felt out of his element today. The idea of living in this primitive little dwelling wasn't as bad as being shot, but close. A single lonely door sat in the back of the cabin, which Nadir assumed to be the bedroom. The lack of any other entrance shot down his hope of indoor plumbing.

Frank grunted and fell back on the old, dusty recliner. "Make yourself at home."

Nadir blinked through the expelled dust, rubbing his left eye. "Shall we get that bullet out of your leg?" he asked.

Frank snickered. "Ya know, I forgot all about that. Must be my adrenaline."

Nadir found himself drawn to the lush curves and knobs of an old RCA Victor radio cabinet in the corner. "Do you mind if I turn on the radio?" He pressed his thumb into his itchy eye, and warm pus dribbled down his cheek.

"By all means." Frank pushed himself off the recliner. "I'll be right back."

Nadir ran his hand over the radio's smooth wood finish and clicked it on. The speaker hissed and screamed like the reception was nonexistent. He smiled. The message became more evident.

Frank reemerged through the bedroom door, handed a hacksaw to Nadir, and propped his leg on the arm of the easy chair. Nadir pressed the saw into Frank's thigh and slid it noisily back and forth, blending with the radio's screech. Blood spilled over the chair into the cracks of the hardwood floor. Nadir muscled through the bone until Frank's leg dropped with a thunk. He looked up blankly, and Nadir could see his brother emerge within Frank's features until his face blurred.

Nadir dropped the saw and dug a thumb into his left eye socket, displacing his eyeball. Warm, soothing blood flowed down his cheek. He yanked his eyeball free of the optic nerve with a swift jerk and tossed it away, then he ran his hands over the speaker. The message was clear; they were to construct their initial forms. Frank smiled.

Inside his own body, Nadir screamed. As his mind faded, he forgot how it was and what could have been.

I, David T Wendell, was murdered by Allied Science to cover the link between Theodora Connor and Henry Thompson. Whoever should find this, the answer is in the metal. Find Jacob Landry.

PASSING
THROUGH
NATURE
TO
ETERNITY

*We go now.*

Akia's voice echoed through Cassandra's dream, where Creed still smiled perversely. His sodden lips sucked her neck, and his greedy hands groped her as he forced his sweaty body against hers.

*We go now!*

Cassandra shuddered awake. Creed was gone, but his stench still hung in the stale morning air: cigarettes, booze, and hair tonic. It was enough to turn her stomach. She peered out from under the blankets at her assailant's clothes, strewn across the floor, and remembered the medics who removed his broken body.

"I hope he's dead," she said. The words sounded like a beautiful melody. Cassandra threw the blanket off and smiled. "I hope he's dead!"

Since she'd allowed Master Leonard in, her thoughts were an open book. She could feel it sifting through her mind's catalog, repelling the faceless woman from her dreams. However, it was partly a two-way street. Selective memories flooded back, and she recalled Master Leonard's last visit—

—when she was still called Rosalita.

Her mother dragged her along Wexford Street through the mounting snow, blanketing the eerily empty city. "We're late!" she said with none of her usual accent. "I hope you're happy!"

*I remember the blizzard of '44, but my mother was never so stern.*

The wind sighed between Hemsford's tall buildings, biting through seven-year-old Rosalita's jacket. She followed the smattering of lights along the face of the elaborate

Ironleaf building, arching her back to discover the top vanished into the clouds like a magical castle. Her mother argued with the doorman: "What do you mean, service elevator? Do you know who you're speaking to?"

"Sorry, Mister Connor's orders."

Rosalita's mother scoffed, yanked her through the service door, and pushed her into the waiting elevator. The doors shut, and the elevator lurched upward.

A bell dinged, and the metal doors parted. The inviting warmth and the enticing smell of savory food flooded the hallway. Rosalita's mother helped her out of her jacket with the tact and grace of an angry bear as she nervously scanned the dimly lit hallway. "We are so late!"

*This is wrong. Ron brought me to the penthouse; Mother had already been there.*

The memory cut, like a missing scene on a film reel. Only her mother's voice remained, with the heavy Mexican accent Cassandra remembered. "Ron must not receive a gift. If you ever want to be free. Never Ron."

Rosalita's warm breath filled the ceramic mask clinging to her face. She followed her mother through elegant French doors into a makeshift ballroom, moving amongst the sea of strangers with broad smiles and small, puckered doll faces. The garbled mess of their conversations made everyone inaudible. Deeper in the room, sweaty people convulsed against each other like animals with no shame.

"Ah, the guest of honor has arrived." Ron's voice boomed as he sauntered over, swirling a glass of brandy. Sweat bled through his white silk robe. Another man walked next to him, dressed in a more reserved black tuxedo. He had slick brown hair, kind eyes, and a matching smile. He crouched. "Hello, sweetheart. I'm glad you could make it."

The handsome man winked at her mother, and she blushed as if he'd willed it out of her. Rosalita ducked behind her mother's leg, peering out timidly.

"Don't be rude, Rosalita!" Her mother pushed her forward. "Mister Conner was nice enough to host your party."

"It's alright." James stood and winked. "I'm accustomed to a woman's rejection."

"I doubt that." Rosalita's mother offered a wicked smile. James chuckled politely as a woman slipped her arm through his. She was wearing a beautiful black off-the-shoulder ball gown, and a white gardenia clung to her auburn hair. Her ensemble was muted, however, by the glimmering diamond ring adorning her left hand.

James slipped an arm around her waist. "Carmella, I'd like you to meet Theodora Byrne, soon-to-be Connor."

Rosalita's mother's fist clenched. "Charmed." She placed a hand on Rosalita's shoulder. "This is my Rosalita, the reason we're all here."

Theodora smiled with her whole face, and orange light danced across her eyes. "A pleasure to meet you." She regarded the doorway nervously. "This is some party, huh? Not necessarily my cup of tea, but to each his own, I guess."

A gong sounded, and a hush fell over the room. White masks peered out from hooded robes, leering at Rosalita.

"Are you ready?" Ron asked.

"These people are all here for you," James said.

"Isn't it divine?" Theodora smiled.

Cassandra's eyes widened. *No, Theodora was bitter and angry when I met her. James had to force her to stay at the party. She can't be——*

She saw Theodora standing alone in a dark room through Master Leonard's eyes, whispering: "I offer unto you the pure soul of my firstborn——"

There was a soft rap on the door. Cassandra pulled the heavy comforter over her head and tried to will whoever it was away. The door clicked open, and footsteps padded across the floor. The mattress creaked and sagged in the middle. "Can you ever forgive me?" It was Ron's voice.

Cassandra ripped the comforter off and faced him with wild, angry eyes. She pictured his eyes bulging, like Creed's had, and felt a slight smile creep across her lips.

"I was never supposed to let anything happen to you, Rosalita." He watched the door, refusing to face her. A sudden moment of clarity forced her to reel away and press her back against the headboard as her breath left her in a gasp. Ron stood. She balked.

"Creed will survive. I thought you should know," Ron said.

Cassandra followed the folds in his toga to his clenched fist, waiting for her punishment. It would be more fitting than whatever this pathetic display was. Still, something deep within her enjoyed seeing this sniveling dog suffer.

Ron turned but didn't quite look at her. "The ceremony is tonight. Creed's actions released the Baphomet into you. I saw it in a dream." He sighed deeply. "I love you, Rosalita, and I'm sorry."

Cassandra's newfound bravery abandoned her, and she hugged a pillow to her chest to stop it from heaving. Acceptance of the creature inside her was sobering, and it seemed to enjoy her anguish as much as it did Ron's.

"I'll send a girl up with your clothes." Ron padded to the door and met her gaze. He looked surprisingly human. "If tonight goes well, I'll tell you about your father." He finished with a desperate smile and left quietly, shutting the door behind him.

*How could he know about my father?* she thought. *He died before Ron met me.*

Cassandra threw the pillow and inched to the edge of the bed. The floor seemed so far away. It would be much easier to lie back down and forget the world, but she sighed and strutted to the mirror, stopping inches from the glass. She followed the curves of her body with her eyes, smiling, running her tongue over her teeth, losing herself in her cool gaze.

There was another knock. Before Cassandra could say go away, the door creaked open. "Cass?" Geraldine stepped cautiously into the room, holding a garment bag. She pulled the door shut behind her.

Cassandra watched her stagnantly. "What do you want?"

"Ron wanted me to bring this gown—"

"Leave it."

Geraldine lumbered to the bed, keeping her eyes forward, and set the garment bag down. "I hope you feel better," she said.

"Geraldine?" Cassandra watched her in the reflection curiously. "I didn't hear you come in."

Geraldine met Cassandra's eyes in the mirror. Her eyebrows fell. "But—"

Cassandra stumbled across the room and wrapped her arms around Geraldine, blaring deep sobs and breathing the comforting smell of her skin. "I'm so scared."

Geraldine ran her hand through Cassandra's hair. "There, there, Cassie. Creed can't hurt you anymore."

Her words were cold comfort. Cassandra peered over Geraldine's shoulder into the mirror, the real source of her terror. *Maybe Akia was right.* She eyed the open window. *Maybe death is the only way to escape it.*

**<u>73</u>**

Geraldine sat on the edge of the bed, bobbing her knee. The rapid, repetitive movement was an eyesore in Cassandra's periphery as she ran her hands over the folds of her dress in the mirror. "Stop it!"

Geraldine froze and scanned the floor. "Sorry, I guess I'm anxious."

"Don't pout." Cassandra smiled maliciously.

Geraldine looked up and scowled. "You've changed, Cass. I don't like it."

*She's jealous.* Cassandra pushed her breasts up in the red bodice. *Just like Mother was.* The cascading silk was uninhibiting, like she was wearing nothing at all.

*Are you ready?*

*These people are all here for you.*

*Isn't it divine?*

Cassandra met her reflection with wide eyes, pulling the silk garment up. "Geraldine, I can't wear this." She turned, and her reflection revealed the gown was backless. "I feel ridiculous."

Geraldine's face softened. "You look beautiful. What is this party tonight?" Geraldine asked. "It's not"—she paused—"it won't be like last night, will it?"

In her mind, Cassandra saw flashes of Donald Creed pleading from the ground through a hushed, damaged voice, and a smile crept across her lips. "We'll see."

Cassandra scowled at her queer response and turned, taking Geraldine's hands in hers. "You need to get away from here. Tonight, Ron will be so distracted you'll be able to slip out. Don't go to the police. Get out of Empire. Do you have any family?"

Geraldine's eyes met hers. "We could both run."

Cassandra turned away and shook her head.

"Why not?" Geraldine rose, grabbing Cassandra's hand again.

"I can't." Cassandra pulled away and returned to the mirror.

"You can't, or you won't?"

"I don't know."

Geraldine placed a hand on her shoulder. "Cassandra, maybe this is fate, our meeting like this."

Cassandra broke her gaze and frowned at her reflection. "You're in danger here."

Geraldine wrapped her arms around her neck. Outside, nature was dying, but the scent of summer was still hanging onto this angel. She watched Geraldine's face in the mirror, then glanced at the door and pushed her away. "If Ron saw us—"

Geraldine sighed and released her, shutting her eyes. The silence was intoxicating. Cassandra wished she could live in it for the rest of her life, but the sun was setting. It was almost time.

She gripped Geraldine's shoulders. "Promise me you'll run when the sun goes down."

Geraldine scanned the floor.

"Geraldine, please." Cassandra saw the last ceremony in her mind. Naked men and women deep in the throes of passion amongst the blood running from those deemed the misfits of society as appetizers to the new gods they would create in death.

*Never Ron.* Her mother's words echoed.

She took Geraldine's hand. "Please."

Geraldine pulled her close. "Why won't you come with me?"

Cassandra closed her eyes. Master Leonard allowed a few memories of her mother's death to seep into her conscious mind like a faucet turned to a slow drip. "Your father"—she sighed, and a single tear ran down her face—"was it a suicide?"

Geraldine's eyes widened. "How did you know? I mean, that's what the policeman said, but I never saw—"

*Damnatio memoriae.* Cassandra shut her eyes, but it did nothing to save her from the horrors etched in her mind, like thumbing through a horrid photo album.

"Ron killed your father like he did my mother, so we'd be his. Soon, all records of our father's life will vanish." She inhaled slowly through her nose, and her lip curled. "The only remains of my mother is what little memory I have left of her. If Ron kills me, her memory dies too. That's why I can't go with you."

"Then let's kill Ron!" Geraldine shot to her feet, and her wild eyes searched Cassandra's for something she couldn't give her. Cassandra shook her head.

Geraldine moved grimly toward the door and stopped. "Cassandra," she said in a hushed tone. "If Ron killed my father, then I'll murder that rotten bastard myself."

Cassandra regarded the mirror as the door clicked shut and smoothed the wrinkles from her bodice. *She's right. Ron needs to die.*

Master Leonard agreed.

**74**

A series of candles lit Cassandra's way as she moved like a ghost into Hell, descending the marble stairs into madness. She pulled her mask down, but it didn't matter. They'd all know her. This was her party.

Her sisters served cocktails on silver platters, clad only in doll masks. Whatever beasts Master Leonard brought to this plane walked unseen amongst the lechery as guests of honor. Cassandra could sense them observing from the shadows as she weaved through the orgy. Master Leonard writhed in ecstasy inside her.

She parted the black curtains and stepped into the ceremonial black room. It no longer frightened her; it was only brick and plaster, like the rest of the house. Her sisters had drawn circles and symbols in chalk on the floor. Along the sides, six-foot candelabras were set apart in four-foot increments. Hundreds of small flames danced.

"Are you ready?" Ron emerged from the shadows as a mass of darkness in his hooded, black, floor-length robe. The light of the candles made his gray eyes dance behind a golden mask, ornate with black symbols matching those scrawled on the floor.

Before she could answer, two men in matching blue collared shirts, pleated trousers, and pistols on their hips pushed through the curtain.

"It's done," The older man said. Ron took him aside. The younger one studied Cassandra, but his gaze was too serious to be lewd.

*Your sister Barbara is no more,* Master Leonard whispered.

----

A gong sounded, and the noise in the foyer ceased. Cassandra took her place on the platform behind the elaborate podium, running her fingers over the raised glyphs around the edges.

Memories came like a spring river, too fast to distinguish one from the last. The religion was new. Believers and skeptics alike gathered in the Ironleaf's penthouse to witness Rosalita host the Baphomet. Men offered it wealth and power, but Theodora provided the most valued prize in the end, and four gained the power of gods. This time, the Baphomet wanted something Ron didn't have. Tonight, would not go well.

The congregation filed into the room, a sea of dead-eyed masks tucked into hooded black robes, china dolls with sad, little, puckered smiles, and round faces with big, sinister grins staring forward.

A hush swept the crowd as Ron stepped onto a lower platform beside Cassandra. To his left, someone lit incense. Lavender and jasmine shouldered the stench of shameless perversion into the ether.

"My brothers and sisters!" Ron's voice thundered through the room.

The congregation looked on. In the back, a woman stood alone in the doorway, watching through a bone-white mask, missing its painted puckered lips. Something about her energy was familiar and alluring.

"Tonight, whoever so the Baphomet chooses will be blessed with gifts! The League of Enforcers were but an inkling of its power."

Cassandra scanned the congregation. When she looked back to the door, the woman was gone.

*Isn't it divine?*

She smiled. *Dea.* The name whispered through her mind. Master Leonard lashed out inside her like a spoiled child.

Another gong sounded. Congregants shoved two naked men with sacks over their heads to Ron's feet. He nodded, and the flickering candles cascaded down his golden mask, giving it the illusion of life. Men in the robes yanked the sacks from the prisoner's heads.

"Where am I?" a black man murmured after a few disoriented blinks. He was older, tall, and lanky with a slight paunch for a belly, and his long salt-and-pepper hair stood up straight. He scanned the onlookers with wide, terrified eyes. "What in the world? I'm s'posed t' be on my way home. I served my time. I need t' see my son."

The white prisoner glowered from his knees. The top of his sweaty, pink head was bald, but long, stringy hair ran from the sides down past his shoulders. His thick brow threw a complete shadow over his eyes, and his saggy face made him look like a happy thought had never crossed his mind.

Ron stepped off the platform and approached the black man. "You are here to offer something greater than your pathetic existence. Tonight, you will fight to the death for the Oracle's amusement."

Cassandra quivered, and the corners of her lips curled into a smile.

The black man's eyebrows furrowed. He scanned the emotionless parishioners behind him. "My son's expecting me!" His gaze fell on Cassandra. "I served my time! Did a little opium down in Hell's Gate, sure, but I'm clean!"

The second man pushed himself up and jammed a finger in Ron's face. "This nigger ain't worth the energy, an' neither are any o' you." He spat a gob of phlegm on the floor and eyed Cassandra. "An' that goes double for you bitch, I see th' way you're lookin' at me." He smiled a toothless smile. "But you're a little too old, sweetheart!" He yanked up twice on his crotch and rasped out a laugh. "You think you can intimidate me by strippin' me down? You obviously never did time in Windwood." He shoved Ron.

The men in the blue collared shirts lurched forward, but Ron raised his hand. His gaze held on the prisoner as he pulled a bone-white blade from his robe and buried it in the man's shoulder.

The convict screamed and stumbled backward. Ron pushed the knife's hilt, forcing the white man to his knees.

"Now, you're at a disadvantage." Blood oozed onto the floor.

"Oh, god," the black man gasped.

"God is dead," Ron yelled. "We are god."

"Deus est mortuus, non sumus Deus," the congregation muttered in unison.

The black man scanned the onlookers until his gaze locked on Cassandra, lingered, and fell back to the injured white man. "I-I'm sorry about this, for what it's worth." He ripped the knife from the white man's shoulder.

The con threw his head back and shrieked. Insatiable bloodlust awoke something primal inside Cassandra. She licked her lips, and her breathing quickened as she ran her hands over her silk dress.

"Please, mercy!" The white man drooled. The black man gripped the bloody hilt of the knife and stared at Cassandra with wide eyes as if begging for another way. She answered with a nod.

"No, wait!" the white man screamed his final words as the knife found his throat. He fell to the floor, gargling. Cassandra shuddered in ecstasy, stepping off her platform into the warm puddle of blood.

The black man fell to his knees. "I need t' see my son, you understand, don't ya?" He sobbed silently. "You understand."

"Homo sacer! Homo sacer!" the onlookers chanted. The man gripped the corpse's shoulders, staring blankly into the void. "I'm not a violent man. I just need to see my son, is all."

Ron pulled the knife from the dead man's throat and grabbed a handful of the other man's hair, dragging him into the middle of a five-pointed star scrawled on the floor in chalk. Cassandra watched in horror, a prisoner in her own body, as Master Leonard took her form, shrugging out of her silk dress.

The gong sounded, and one of her sisters stepped forward, holding a silver bell. In unison, the congregation dropped their robes, embracing the darkness with their exposed bodies.

The man on his knees rubbernecked around the room in horror. "Mercy, please."

Cassandra collected the blade from Ron. He retreated into the shadows behind her and dropped his robe.

"Please," the con pleaded. She grabbed a handful of his hair and raked the blade across his throat. The hot iron scent overcame the incense, and the spatter soothed her exposed skin as he sprayed a final, gory cough.

Cassandra shuddered, bit her lip, and closed her eyes. The warmth of the blood swaddled her, and she convulsed as she pressed the man's head against her stomach. The final death throes forced more blood to pulse from the open wound down her thighs.

Ron placed a large book on the pedestal. "Now, we may begin."

Something within the recesses of Cassandra's soul wailed as Ron split open the supple leather pages of the great tome. A lock of hair sewn into the spine marked the ceremonial words. She closed her eyes and ran her left hand over the slick blood coating her body as she held the dead man close to her with her right.

Cassandra's sisters placed scrying mirrors as Ron's voice carried through the room. "About me, flames the star of the Baphomet!"

Cassandra dropped the dead man to the ground. His blood ran around him unnaturally in a perfect circle, then across the floor along the chalk outline of the five-pointed star.

"Within me burns the black flame of eternal fire!" Ron boomed.

The star burst into flames under Cassandra's feet, enveloping the corpse in a fury of blinding heat. Cassandra remained in the blaze, threw her head back, and licked her lips with pure elation.

The fire settled, simmering across the five-pointed star. The believers' chests heaved in unison as if becoming one, a single being larger than themselves.

A woman stepped forward from the sea of people, holding a black goblet. She dropped to one knee and raised the chalice slowly over her head. Ron lifted it from her grasp, presenting it to the gathering. He circled the flaming star, yelling his prayer. The flames faded and reignited, onyx black, sipping all color from the room. The bell rang, echoing around the chamber and continuing into some deep, unseen crevice.

Cassandra's back arched and spasmed, and her knees buckled. Unbridled pleasure rushed through her body until she cried out in a queer, high-pitched squeal, tensing every muscle.

Ron continued the prayer. Cassandra's head snapped forward, and her chest heaved. A naked woman with red-stained skin glared at her from the mirror, but her reflection no longer obeyed her.

Her body was massive and powerful, like each step, echoing through the black room, might crack the marble floor. She kissed Ron's mask and took the black goblet from his hands, drinking the thick elixir. The sting of the poison made her choke, but still, she drank.

"I am the true manifestation of superiority. I am god!" Ron yelled triumphantly.

"We are god!" The processions repeated.

Cassandra spat into the flames. The fire erupted, engulfing the ceiling.

"I proclaim the old God is dead!" Ron yelled over the roar of the flames.

"God is dead!" The crowd responded.

"I reject all false knowledge! I am god!"

"We are god!"

"Bring forth the offering!" Ron yelled. Men, clad in robes, escorted a train of listless naked women into the light of the, once again, normal fire. Their eyes were empty, lobotomized. Drool trailed from their gaping jaws. They smelled foul, like rotten meat; offering these souls was an insult.

"No." Her deep, rumbling voice shook the room. "I was promised the spawn of the gods."

Ron eyed the legions of white masks behind him. "We didn't—we couldn't—"

"Then, I will take something you love," she said.

Ron gripped the podium. "I just need time. I can get anything you want." His groveling disgusted her almost as much as the appalling offering.

"Bring forth your concubines." Cassandra stepped forward. *Clack-clack.*

Terror and doubt danced across Ron's eyes through his eloquent mask. She stared at him, waiting for him to disobey so she could rid the world of this sniveling rodent. Ron dropped his head and nodded slowly.

A gong sounded, and the girls lined up beside the simmering flames. Soft murmurs trickled through the mass of spectators, but they fell silent when Cassandra stomped across the room. *Clack-clack, clack-clack, clack-clack.*

"Remove your masks," she boomed.

Ron nodded again. The girls slowly revealed their faces. Mary, Nancy, Patricia, and Geraldine.

Cassandra watched, frozen inside her own body, as Master Leonard lifted the knife next to the cursed men's charred remains.

Mary watched through wide eyes as Cassandra pressed the knife to her throat. "I will take two souls and, in return, offer you one gift and four premonitions."

Mary quivered and looked to Ron for help. Ron slammed his fist on the podium. "I implore you, take the sacrifices, leave my girls!"

"Nine years ago, four gods were born on this plane. One was vanquished. One was replaced. Four of the five were lovers and offered their future spawn for power.

"On this day, I was promised a second spawn. You have failed me. For this inconvenience, the Oracle will take what's yours. When I return, twelve years hence, you will bring me the second spawn, or I will take everything."

With one quick pull, the knife glided through Mary's neck. Ron dropped his head. Cassandra flailed desperately inside the recesses of her mind.

Mary fell to her knees, gripping her throat. She stared at Ron helplessly and released her neck to touch him before she collapsed and gurgled a last breath.

Blood ran from Mary's throat, creating two identical children's faces staring profile on either side of her body. "Find the brothers Ross, stolen from death's door. One is crippled, and one is strong. One is light, the other is night. One brings salvation, the other doom."

Cassandra stomped her foot, and the faces ignited. Gasps filled the room, and the congregation pushed forward.

Blood seeped under Mary's body, forming a baby surrounded by a circle. "The child of the moon is as unnatural as its creators. It will bring death to all things." The image of the baby ignited, and the circle around it burst outward, spreading the flame. Gasps rode the crowd. "Salvation."

When the room fell silent again, Nancy's stifled whimpers echoed through the hall. Cassandra inched toward her. *Clack-clack. Clack-clack.* She pressed the blade to her throat. Nancy stiffened, and the chords in her neck popped. Her bottom lip quivered.

"Do you fear me, child?" Cassandra asked. Nancy forced a nod through tremors of fear.

"Good." Cassandra smiled wickedly at Ron and pressed the blade through Patricia's throat instead. She stumbled forward with panic in her wide eyes, clutching at her neck as she dropped to her knees. Ron turned away. Blood flowed slowly in a perfect circle around Cassandra's feet. "In nineteen-hundred and eighty-four, the moon will fall from the sky."

Patricia released a sickening choke as she pulled her limp body toward Ron. Desperation fought the fear in her eyes as she struggled to find validation from the man she loved, but he refused to look.

"And in two-thousand and two, the earth will burn. Apocalypse. Cessation of life."

Patricia dragged streaky blood through the premonition, and her body ignited. There was a noiseless scream and the passing image of raw terror on her face as she expired. Cassandra screeched into the cold emptiness of oblivion that was her mind for her fallen sister.

Ron stared blankly at the floor as Patricia's body burned. He lurched forward and grabbed Cassandra by the arm. "Enough of this! Where is my gift?"

Cassandra only stared. "I have allowed you to keep your life. That is your gift." The congregation began to file out of the room.

Ron traded glances between his dwindling throng and the crackling ash that was once his lover. "No! I paid the price for the power of a god! I demand it!"

Cassandra turned calmly. Her bare feet clacked slowly across the onyx marble. *Clack-clack. Clack-clack. Clack-clack.* "You do not command me. Bring me the spawn of the gods, and you'll have your gift." The ground spun out from under Cassandra, and the floor rushed at her as the world faded to black.

**<u>75</u>**

"Cassandra?" Geraldine's voice cut through the darkness. "Oh, thank god. How do you feel?" She smiled. Behind her, Nancy glared from the doorway through puffy eyes and tear-stained cheeks. The afternoon sun cascaded softly through the window.

"Where am I?" Cassandra asked weakly.

Geraldine eyed Nancy. "We moved you into the guestroom. Ron insisted."

"What happened?"

Geraldine watched Nancy leave and turned back to Cassandra curiously. "You mean—you don't remember?" she whispered. "You killed people, two of the girls who lived here."

Cassandra shook her head. "No, I—"

"They were horrible, horrible girls, but they didn't deserve that." Geraldine glanced at the door. "Ron's been crying all night."

Cassandra eyed the door. "Why didn't you leave?"

"I won't go without you!" Geraldine pulled her chair forward with a shrill squeak. "We can still—"

Ron exploded through the eastern door, naked, eyes wild. "You finally decided to wake up, you bitch?" He stomped toward the bed, grabbing Cassandra by the throat. His breath smelled like poison.

"Stop it!" Geraldine leaped on his back. He staggered to one knee and elbowed her in the face. Her nose exploded like a tomato. She sat on her haunches, between dazed and shocked, watching blood collect on her toga.

Ron pulled himself to his feet and picked up a lamp from the nightstand, throwing it at the far wall. "I didn't even receive my gift!" He ripped Cassandra from the bed by the arm. She heard her shoulder dislocate, but the pain didn't bite until she was rolling across the floor.

"What did you mean by '*find the brothers Ross?*'" He towered over her. "The brothers, Ross. The brothers, the brothers. Where have I heard that before?"

A book launched through the air and missed Ron wide left. "Get off of her!" Geraldine yelled.

Ron stomped across the room and grabbed a letter opener from the desk.

Ron Baxter's Journal

December 20, 1944

My worst fear has come to pass. My love, Carmella, is dead at her own daughter's hand. The same way Robert died all those years ago. I would kill the girl myself if not for the fact she is Robert's daughter.

James, Theodora, and those caterers all received gifts, and I remain with the burden of being Rosalita's keeper. What did they offer that I didn't?




Ron Baxter's Journal

December 21, 1944

Rosalita now insists on being called Cassandra, as is the Oracle's designation, and comes to my bedroom each night, speaking about past lives, staring through me as she shakes my room with her inhuman voice. I lock her in her bedroom, and still, every night, she finds a way to stand over me, haunting me, torturing me. However, I can sense Master Leonard's grip weakening.

In the waking hours, I must keep her under my thumb, humiliate her, and make her believe I am still in control. I fear her, but I have a greater fear of what will happen if I ignore her warnings. I may be a slave to Master Leonard but not to Cassandra.

For my religion, I must focus on the premonitions Master Leonard spoke of, but they become hazy as time passes. Brothers, children, the name Ross. What does it mean?

During the ceremony, I caught glimpses of the girl inside the monster, fighting against Master Leonard. Something she saw forced her true self forward. What did she see that night? What did Cassandra see to weaken Master Leonard?

WAKE NOT
A SLEEPING LION

*I should go home.*

Gibson swallowed whiskey to drown the irritating voice of reason screaming over the jukebox's rendition of "Please, Mr. Sun." He tapped the rim of the glass. Eddie poured another two fingers of Old Fitzgerald, offered a half-smile, and moved back to the end of the bar.

Next to him, Slim drank, exhaled, dried his mouth with his sleeve, and repeated. "Fuck!"

"You said it, partner." Gibson turned Baxter's journal in his hands. "Maybe we missed something—"

"We been over it an' over it. Back an' forth, up an' down. There ain't nothin' in there, Skipper, but the ramblings of a lunatic. An' I ain't your partner."

The booze-soaked hours spent at Eddie's had bled together as a collection of false hope and headaches, but the old dive seemed to be hallowed ground for Harper. If he'd left another clue, it would be here. Plus, getting Slim to work without a drink had been like pulling teeth since Murphy sent him packing. So, they sat in the barren watering hole amongst the drunks with money left over from the weekend, working a case that was no longer theirs.

"Maybe you're right," Gibson said.

Slim scowled. "Maybe I'm right? What are ya, quittin' on me?"

"Then maybe whatever you found at the Connor estate would shed some light."

"It don't pertain t' this. Drop it."

Eddie sat at the end of the bar, lazily scanning the *Bulletin* with a lit cigarette dangling from his lips. "You fellas okay down there?" he yelled.

"Just ducky, Eddie," Gibson responded, lazily flipping through the pages of the journal.

Slim pounded the bar. "'Nother round."

Eddie casually dropped the paper, stretched, and slunk at a snail's pace to where Gibson and Slim sat. "Ya know, I don't make it my business to pry, especially into the lives of two of my best customers, but it's eleven in the AM, and you fellas are in here the second day in a row drinking like the Zephyrs got swept in the World Series. What gives? It's Monday morning, for Christ's sake." He grabbed the bottle of Old Fitzgerald from the shelf.

Slim smirked. "Best customers, ha! Yer gonna make me blush."

Eddie forced one of his half-smiles and poured two more fingers into each of their glasses.

Slim downed it. "Leave th' bottle."

Eddie loyally poured him another and returned the bottle to the shelf. "Seriously, fellas, everything alright?"

Gibson placed a Lucky between his lips. "Rough couple days at the office, is all." He struck a match and lit the cigarette.

Eddie slid an ashtray in front of Gibson with an attentive half-smile. He seemed to have a half-smile for every occasion. "This one's on me, boys."

Gibson nodded. "Much obliged."

Slim downed the whiskey as Eddie trudged back to his paper. Gibson took a long drag of his cigarette. Everything was tasteless ash in his mouth since he'd started this case; even whiskey was an unenjoyable means to an end. He swallowed the drink anyway.

Slim removed a cigarette from his breast pocket and placed it between his lips. He flipped open his lighter and fell into a coughing fit, launching the unlit cigarette onto the bar.

"You alright, old man?" Gibson tried to be nonchalant, but Slim's sunken eyes made him look like he already had one foot in the grave.

Slim waved him off. "I'm fine. Just worked up, is all." A few lingering coughs escaped, then he lit the cigarette, sucking on it like he needed it to survive. He lifted his empty glass. "Although I'm liable to die of thirst!"

"Maybe you should take it easy, Slim," Gibson said.

"Ha! Didn't realize my ex-wife was here. You done bein' a cop, Skipper? Now that yer suspended, you resigned to bein' a tired old shrew?" Slim forced a smile. "Besides, I'm retired. I can do whatever th' fuck I want."

"Alright, alright, settle down," Gibson responded.

Eddie was already inching along the bar. He poured Slim another drink and hovered the bottle over Gibson's glass.

Gibson waved him off. "Had my fill, thanks, Eddie."

Slim swirled his drink, staring nonchalantly at a Pabst Blue Ribbon ad behind the bar. "Ya know, Skipper, I'm just talking here, but maybe th' answer isn't in a book or a letter. Maybe we should drive up to Baxter's house an' check up on him." His hooded eyes met Gibson's. "After all, the poor guy's dear sex slave, or servant girl, or whoever the fuck died a few days ago. The poor fella is probably all broken up. We'd be doin' him a service. Me, a concerned party"—he poked Gibson's chest—"an' you, a cop."

Gibson ran his fingers over the edge of Baxter's journal mindlessly. "I don't know, Slim—I could lose my badge, or—"

"Yeah? Well, little Bonnie Connor stands to lose more!"

Eddie dipped the corner of the paper and glanced across the bar. Gibson waved him off, and Eddie vanished behind the black-and-white print.

Gibson slid another cigarette out of the pack, ran a palm over the stubble on his face, and stared at the Pabst ad with a snarky college boy in tennis garb beaming, pouring a beer. "It's blended...it's splendid," it said. He placed the cigarette in his mouth, struck a match, and nodded.

**<u>77</u>**

The ride up north was quiet, aside from Slim's cough. Gibson made a right off the Bunche Bridge onto North Avenue, past the Connor estate. The gate was still open, waiting impatiently for Bonnie's return, and the grandfather clock was probably still inside, counting the time they had wasted. No matter how much cheap whiskey Gibson drank, he remembered Theodora's words exactly.

*What if the laws of man don't apply anymore? What if there's so much more of the universe that you don't understand?*

The drawings and Latin phrases scribbled by a madman in the book in Ron's study were still so visceral.

*It's not your fault; you couldn't possibly understand. You see, I've seen things, detective—*

Gibson turned onto Pleasant. *I've seen things too*, he thought, *but I don't necessarily want to believe them.*

*How do you, as a man of the law, a man who I can only assume has a moral compass, behave when the world you know and love comes crashing down around you, and there's no right or wrong, just survival, just preservation of life?*

Breath came in shallow gulps. *I go against my better judgment and risk it all to save one little girl.*

*I have faith in you, detective, but I'm afraid you don't quite understand what faith is.*

Gibson wheeled the Plymouth onto the grass outside Baxter's gate and cut the engine, eyeing the mansion, trying to remember why he'd agreed to this. There was no plan, no way to tell what they were walking into, and no backup if it went south. A crow's screech drew his attention to the finials on the iron gate. Death never strayed far from this house.

Slim slapped his dented flask into Gibson's chest. He took a swig. It burned like hell, but he got it down and pushed the car door open.

Slim gripped his shoulder, forcing him into the seat. "We only get one shot at this, Skipper. Don't hesitate; blow Baxter out of his boots if you have to. We're so far off the book now, it don't matter."

The old man was clearly drunk, but that might have been the most reasonable thing he'd ever said. Still, Gibson had his reservations. "I'm not killing anyone, Slim."

"It might come down to him or us." Slim drew a Colt Commander from his belt. "And I'm not dyin' here."

Gibson followed Slim up the driveway, gravel crunching beneath his shoes. He scanned the three rows of windows on the mansion's flawless face. There were a lot of eyes in the house; all it would take was one set to unravel this whole caper.

The weight of the pistol in Gibson's shoulder holster gave him the courage to follow Slim onto the porch. The old man leaned slowly into the creaky door, peering inside. He smirked and whispered: "Folks in Brookfield never lock their doors."

The two-story Zeus and Athena statues watched them inch across the foyer with solemn faces. A thick, nauseating stench spiked the stale air, like booze in the punch at a debutante ball. Slim crept toward the staircase to the left of the statues and glanced back with a scrunched look on his face that said he smelled it, too. The air grew thicker around the newel post—rotten and sweet, like old food.

Slim pressed a finger against his lips. Gibson froze and listened; the staircase was buzzing frantically, like a hornet's nest. Slim pulled his gun, aimed it at the doorway, and motioned toward the black curtain. Gibson exhaled and yanked it away.

The stench rushed out. Gibson tasted it, gagging and retching until his eyes teared. Charred skeletal remains were everywhere, like spilled firewood. Dried blood spread across the floor, creating elaborate designs flowing from dead women slumped against the wall with twisted visages recounting their final moments in life. The walls rippled as thick swarms of gluttonous black flies crawled in droves. The buzz was deafening.

Gibson stumbled backward and leaned against a white console table. "Jesus," he managed through the warm bile inching up the back of his throat.

Slim moved behind him and whispered in a gruff whiskey-soaked voice: "Keep it together, Skipper. Focus on the task at hand. We came in with no probable cause, no warrant. Nothin' we saw would hold up in court."

Stay here, an' keep watch. I need to check something." Slim pressed a handkerchief from his pocket over his face and vanished behind the curtain. Gibson took a few deep breaths to subdue the taste of death, cleared his sinuses, and spat on the floor.

Slim slipped back into the foyer with a contorted lip, like someone offered food he didn't particularly care for. "Ya never get used t' that," he whispered. "Th' good news is, all of these people appear to be adults. No sign o' Bonnie Connor." He shoved his handkerchief back into his breast pocket and placed a hand on Gibson's shoulder. "You okay, Skipper? My old partner used t' say, if you can handle a homicide scene, you can handle anything this job throws at ya.

"You think this is bad? I remember ol' Harper and  me—"

*Thump! Thump! Thump!* Angry footsteps traveled above them. Slim drew his gun, eyed Gibson, and crept slowly up the staircase. Gibson made sure to stay at least three steps behind and pulled the Colt snub nose revolver from its holster, trying to keep it steady in his shaking hand.

Slim halted, stopping Gibson with a balled fist and peering over the cusp of the staircase. They stood in a silent purgatory until Slim inched forward again.

Gibson's eyes slowly adjusted to the dreary, second-floor hallway, stretching into complete darkness. The thumping returned on the other side of the banister, behind Zeus's head.

Slim tried to suppress a coughing fit, but it was still loud enough to give them away. He doubled over, hacking stringy, bloody phlegm into his handkerchief, shaking with each cough.

*Bang!* A door slammed into a wall.

"You finally decided to wake up, you bitch?" a man yelled. Three more thumps and the voice grew quieter.

Gibson crouched by Slim. "Are you okay?"

Ropes of blood drooled onto Slim's shirt. "Forget me, Skipper," he wheezed, "get up there."

Gibson watched the blood dribble from Slim's lips and cursed under his breath as he tiptoed hesitantly up the rest of the marble staircase.

"Stop it!" a woman screamed.

Gibson slunk down the hallway toward the far room. The snub-nose had a good enough weight to steady his pounding heart. Something crashed against the other side of the wall.

"I didn't even receive my gift!" the man screamed.

Gibson peered through the open door at a silhouette dancing against the bright window.

"What did you mean '*find the brothers Ross?*'" The voice sounded like Baxter's.

Gibson slipped into the room and ducked behind an armoire.

"The brothers, Ross. The brothers, the brothers. Where have I heard that before?"

Cassandra was sprawled on the floor, trembling. Another woman with a broken nose, too old to be Bonnie Connor, threw a book at Baxter but missed by a mile. "Get off of her!"

Baxter moved to the desk, lifting a gleaming blade. "Who are the Ross brothers?"

Gibson stood and raised his gun. "Freeze, Baxter!" The Colt shook harder than his voice.

Baxter spun. He was naked. His glazed eyes had too broad a range of emotions to be sane, and his broken smile was out of place. "This doesn't concern you," he whispered, staring through Gibson.

"Back away from the girls, Baxter!" Gibson said, moving along the floor counterclockwise, keeping distance.

Baxter white-knuckled the letter opener. "There's more going on here than you can possibly comprehend."

The gun steadied as Gibson found a stitch of courage in the wide eyes of the terrified girls. "Baxter!" he growled, "I'm going to count to three, and I want your hands on your head!"

Baxter spat on the floor. "Look at you, a scared child!" He smiled deviously and inched forward. "Why do you tremble, little man? Are you afraid to take a life, or because you face God?" The veins bulged in his neck, and his eyes grew wide with something akin to glee.

"One." Gibson's finger found the trigger. Over Baxter's shoulder, the girls huddled together on the floor. "I mean it, Baxter, hands on your head! Two!" Sweat snaked down Gibson's face. He thought about the charred remains in the black room, scattered around the corpses left to bleed out. They all used to be people with lives and families. "Three!" Still, his finger wouldn't squeeze.

"Now what?" Baxter edged forward, forcing Gibson backward.

A Colt Commander jammed into Baxter's temple from the open door. "Now, I blow that sick fucking brain of yours onto the wall," Slim said, forcing Baxter to the center of the room with the barrel of his gun.

Baxter smiled nervously. "You would never—"

*Bang!* Everyone jumped. Gibson's ears screamed. Slim had fired inches from Baxter's head and blown out a window across the room. Baxter dropped the letter opener and cringed like a beaten dog.

"Oh yes, I would, gladly. You see, I have what they call a terminal affliction. So, I gotta get my affairs in order an' make peace with folks, etcetera, etcetera.

"Seein' as my ex-wife skipped town, you're th' only one who I still have outstanding matters with. You wronged me more'n anyone, Baxter, an' I can't wait to paint this room with that sick shit you keep between your ears." Slim's finger caressed the trigger. "But first, where's little Bonnie Connor?"

Gibson slid his pistol back into its holster and took a deep breath.

"I don't know!" Baxter shrunk away from Slim's gun.

Slim shook his head and pulled the trigger again. *Bang!* The gun exploded inches from Baxter's head. A bullet stuck in the wall. One of the girls let out a terrified squeal. Another c-note screamed in Gibson's ear.

"Try again," Slim said casually.

Baxter stammered: "I had nothing to do—"

"Bullshit! You don't walk away from this. If you're God, then I'm the fucking Devil, and I've come to end you! Where is she?"

Baxter fell to his knees. The stench of piss engulfed the room as a puddle grew on the floor between his legs. "I—"

Slim chuckled, which turned into a wheezing laugh. He pulled the hammer back. Baxter tried to look up but couldn't make eye contact with the Colt Commander pressed against his forehead.

"You're a dead man," Baxter growled. "This city is mine—the politicians, the lawyers, even the police force. I am the puppet master, and any who stand in my way are fodder to burn through. Your disease is a paradise compared to what the Sibylline religion will do to both of you." He drooled on himself as he exhaled sharply in and out through gritted teeth, ready to meet his maker.

"Maybe, but you'll go b'fore me." Slim steadied his hand. "An' as far as your reach goes—I know a secret, Baxter, your old pal Jim Connor ain't in yer pocket. Hell, he don't even respect you. An' Missus Connor hates your sick, twisted guts. Smith brothers despise you, always have. Hell, probably Miss Mercury, too. The *real* gods your cult created abandoned you."

"Shut up!" Baxter sneered.

Slim pressed his gun into Baxter's face again. "I seen th' love letters you been sendin' Jimmy Connor on the desk in his study, an' I thought, why would Baxter be so cordial when the Enforcers turned their back on him? Then, I realized you needed to get back in his good graces t' get a hold o' Bonnie. But why Bonnie Connor? She's just a little girl. Even too young for a pervert like you. Well, seein' that room o' horrors you left downstairs, I had all my questions answered and wrapped up with a little bow.

"I saw one or two o' your girls amongst the dead. Flies got to 'em pretty good, but I recognized 'em. Been a detective for a while, so I got a thing about rememberin' faces, even mangled ones. I imagine it don't look good for the followers of your religion to see their own flock die. Far as I can see, you needed Bonnie for whatever sick ritual you performed in that fucking room. Th' spawn of th' gods or somethin', that shit's beyond me." Slim chuckled. "But you were too stupid t' find her, so your girls had t' stand in her place—"

"Fuck you, you fat coward!" Baxter pressed his forehead against the gun. "Strike me down, and the power of the Sibylline Religion will tear you asunder. I am God!"

"It's funny; the harder I press this here handgun into your face, the closer you come to soiling yourself. *Again*. Some god." Slim's smile faded. "This is for Bill Harper. For those two terrified girls over there in the corner. For the poor souls whose bodies you desecrated downstairs. Hell, for the puppy you probably tortured when you were a kid."

Gibson locked eyes with Cassandra. "Slim, wait!"

"Why should I?" Slim kept his eyes on Baxter, not bothering to hide the tears. His lips pressed up into a sour sneer, and his hand shook.

"Kill him now, and he'll become a martyr," Gibson whispered. "This religion will take off out of the gate with nothing to slow it down. That's how it works. They erase anything from the past that doesn't agree with them and celebrate what does. You kill him, and he *will* become a god in his followers' eyes."

"What are you waiting for? Kill him!" the fat girl screamed from the corner.

Slim's face twisted, and the gun rang out again. Baxter doubled over, holding his leg, screaming and rolling across the blood-spattered floorboards.

"You're lucky my partner's a softie, Baxter." Slim holstered his gun. "If I had my way, I'd be scrapin' your godly brain off my size-thirteens right now. Think of yer knee as something to remember me by."

"It's a new dawn, detective!" Baxter yelled. "Don't you see? How do you behave when the world, as you know it, falls apart around you? There's no right and wrong!"

*Just survival,* Gibson thought.

"Shut yer mouth." Slim nodded toward the two girls huddled together. "Those girls in the corner there, an' anyone else you're hidin' in this house, are coming with us. You say boo about it, an' I'll blow another, more permanent, hole right through you. I don't care what Skipper says."

Baxter twisted his body to make eye contact with Cassandra, laughing like a seething lunatic from where he lay. An unsettling noise full of pain and shame in place of glee. "Cassandra, do you want to go with the detective?"

Cassandra blinked her swollen eyes at the sound of her name, and life returned to her face. She shuddered out quick, sobbing breaths as she watched Baxter squirm on the ground. "I want to stay with Ron," she whispered.

"What?" the fat girl yelled. She grasped Cassandra's shoulders. "Cassie? The detectives—"

"I want to stay with Ron!"

Baxter wheezed from the floor. Blood pumped in rivers from his injured leg. "The matter is settled."

Gibson eyed Slim, who watched Baxter like a vulture, waiting for him to bleed out. "Rot in Hell." Slim took his leave through the same door he'd heroically entered moments ago.

"Nancy!" Baxter yelled.

Gibson followed Slim into the dim hallway and glanced down the long corridor opposite the stairs. A tall, thin girl stared out from a doorway.

"Nancy!"

She snapped out of her daze and vanished into the room.

"Good luck," Gibson whispered, remembering Betty Burton's lifeless stare and the deer his uncle killed all those years ago.

**<u>78</u>**

*Bang!* Slim let the front door crash shut. The crunching gravel remained the only sound as the two men walked to the car. It was fitting and almost poetic; their last blaze of glory as a team was a dud, just as the entire partnership had been.

Gibson pulled open the car door and looked at the house that seemed to feed upon women. The weight of Bonnie Connor had been lifted off his shoulders and dropped squarely onto his soul. "What do we do now, Slim?"

Slim pushed his fedora back and ran his forearm over his brow. "Nothin', you go on, an' I fade away."

"But I'll be walking around with a target on my back," Gibson said, surprised at his selfishness.

Slim shrugged. "Shoulda let me kill him." He rubbed his chin. "Remember when I asked if you have a wife or kids? I was makin' sure you didn't have anyone for Baxter t' go after."

Gibson scowled. "So, this whole thing was your private crusade to kill Baxter? Bonnie's still out there—"

"So are a million other lost people. Like I said before, Baxter's real power is influence, like the DiLilo family before him. You made me realize if we weed him out, someone else will sprout up. There's no ending this pattern. Better a clown like Baxter than some unknown puppet master."

"Well, if Baxter kills us, who will stand up to him?"

Slim chuckled. "Goddamn, first week on th' job, and you're already lettin' your head grow to such monumental proportions? You're a rookie detective, Skipper, not an Enforcer, which is why he might not go after you at all. An' if he does—well, maybe it's time you said goodbye to this godawful city."

"This is my home, Slim."

"Shoulda let me kill him, then." He smiled and turned away from the house. "Sky doesn't look so good. Maybe we're finally due for some rain."

"So what now? We ride into the sunset like Bill Elliot? That felt like a loss in there."

"This ain't a movie, Skipper. That felt like a loss because it was a loss. Baxter beat us. Whoever took Bonnie Connor beat us." He smiled a sad smile. "The world is changing, partner. It's more corrupt and vile than ever, an' there ain't no room in it for hard-boiled old-timers like me. Had too many losses to count in my lifetime. Hell, I can't even keep track of 'em anymore." He glanced across the car at Gibson. "So what now? We go home and lick our wounds. Tomorrow's another day"—he planted a cigarette in his mouth—"or it's not."

"Tell me what you found at the Connor estate," Gibson said.

Slim sighed. "Theodora's love letter to Jerry Smith. I didn't want ya gettin' all gung-ho and lettin' it distract you or doin' somethin' stupid with it. You're still just a rookie, an' ya think like one."

"Love letter? But why—"

"See? Rookie thinking. The why don't matter; it don't concern this case anyway, as I said."

Gibson looked back to the house. "Well, we need to do something."

Slim lit his cigarette and coughed. "All we could do was kill that bastard—but you were right—it would just make him a martyr. A guy like Baxter can walk away from a pile of bodies as high as his house. He can turn ol' Bill Harper into something he ain't, a dirty cop, which turned him into a drunk, which ended up killin' him in the end—not in a conventional way, mind you, but because the booze fed him the courage to seek the truth.

"In death, Baxter'd be an idea, a goal for other sickos to strive for. Eh, maybe I'm wrong. Maybe there is something we can do, but that notion is beyond me. I'm jus' a tired old man who's had enough of this shit. Like Baxter said, ain't no right and wrong anymore in this city. Now, there's all these gray areas.

"Enforcers killed people. Shit, they had more bodies on their hands than most folks I knew in th' war. An' we were supposed t' believe they were righteous?" Slim took a long drag. "Then, on th' other hand, Baxter kills a bunch o' people, and he's evil? Then you and I kill a bunch of people, an' we're patriots fighting for our country? Gray areas." He tossed his cigarette stub into the driveway. "Makes a man pine for simpler times."

"But, we're supposed to be the good guys," Gibson said, "the only non-grey area in this whole equation."

"Bein' the white knight is exhausting, an' a fool's errand. Baxter thinks he's God. Maybe he is. Maybe God is just a spoiled child with unlimited reach." Slim chuckled and spat into the gravel. "This city's gone t' shit. If I were you, I'd leave, find some young girl, marry her, knock her up an' live happily ever after. Yer young yet, Skipper, go be young. Don't ruin your life like I did. You'll never win against the likes o' Baxter, or DiLilo, or whoever comes next. Leave that shit for other people like the Enforcers who operate in gray areas with the rest o' th' chicken-shit creeps." He chuckled. "Took me a whole lifetime t' figure that out. Don't be a MacIntire, like I was."

Gibson looked his former partner over. "No, Slim. This is my city, not Baxter's. I know people who live here are inherently good. Like you said, guys like Baxter are a dime a dozen, but people who'll stand up to them, people like you and me, now that's a rare breed."

Slim smiled. "You really have gone soft, kid, or maybe you were born like that. I only known you a couplea days. That's not a bad thing, mind you. Maybe that's what Empire needs: someone soft, understanding, trustworthy. I'm set in my ways, an' th' sun is setting on the world I once knew. Th' League killed off all the colorful villains like Torment and th' Dark Plunderer. Folks who let you know they were the bad guys. But evil isn't gone from Empire because of the Enforcers. It just changed—blended into everyday life. "If you insist on stayin' here, maybe you can change how the folks in Empire think and act. Influence over people trumps abilities like superspeed any day o' the week. That goes for Baxter, but it goes double fer you. We lost this one. Bonnie Connor is probably dead. That doesn't mean there won't be more Bonnie Connors in the future." Slim slapped the roof of the car. "Right now, I got a stool with my name on it down at Eddie's. Care to join me?"

Gibson shook his head. "I'll join you once Bonnie Connor is safely back with her mother."

Slim wheezed out a laugh.

"Something funny?" Gibson asked.

"I get it now." He shook his head somberly. "God is dead. We are god. Ya know, th' thing Baxter said? Truth and justice went out the window, everything good people used to stand for. Now, the gods of Empire rule, not the Enforcers, the rich and powerful. Drop me at Eddie's on your way home. The only alter I care t' bow to."

GREAT
AND
PRECIOUS
THINGS

## 79

"Oh, good, you're awake," Theo said.

Cal sauntered across the Hall's hangar, flexing his bandaged hand and rubbing the sleep from his eyes, still unable to get used to the form-fitting impact suit he'd changed into after his suit had been ruined. "What time is it?"

Theo eyed her watch. "Quarter past five."

"PM?"

"Monday morning."

Cal pinched the bridge of his nose. "Jesus."

"I ran tests on that slug we found beneath Club Danza and found a material resembling corundum or aluminum oxide coating it. The same stuff was on my clothes after our fight with that thing in the penthouse."

Cal nodded. "So, it was down there?"

"It most likely made the hole in the wall, then someone shot it." Theo flashed a shallow, tired smile. "I've finished the alterations. The Bluebird's rarin' to go into space." She took a long drag off her cigarette. "You should head home. I appreciate all you've done, but frankly, something is missing inside you."

"No, I'm coming with you."

Her gaze lingered, and in her dead brown eyes, what Cal assumed had been a dream of her insanity gained validation. "Suit yourself. Just remember, I tried to save your life." She was unhinged but right. The numbness inside Cal was fading. Still, his nagging aches made him feel more himself than he had in ten years. When the brain fog lifted, he knew he couldn't abandon Bonnie to this creature.

Cal glanced away, unable to look at the haggard face of this thing that was once Theodora Connor, regarding the ship instead. The thin frame looked like a Lockheed P-80 with hinged wings and a blue Enforcer logo on each side. The sleek silver body with blue trim reminded him of a Jaguar racecar.

Theo ashed her cigarette and shuffled to a control panel flush against a miniature city of spinning gears. "Hold still." She pulled a lever and pressed a few buttons, opening a portion of the ceiling. "If you insist on coming, you'll need a spacesuit."

Robotic arms dropped and stamped white rubber armor over Cal's impact suit in a symphony of whirring and clicking. Pieces scalloped around a box fastened to his chest while a second machine bolted the plates to each other. A small cylindrical device pulled metallic fabric over his arms and legs and seamlessly adhered it to gloves and boots with a welding beam. As the machine finished sealing him in, he smiled to hide the churning of nerves in his stomach.

Theo clamped the cigarette between her lips and looked him up and down, slapping another button. As she walked toward the ship, a second machine composed of drills, lasers, and robotic arms followed her along a run of steel girders, fastening components over her impact suit. A painted, scarlet "E," faded and scratched, stood prominently on her chest to the left of a box with a glowing green line across its face.

She ousted her cigarette on a console and stopped at an old industrial metal shelf where she removed a fishbowl helmet with an antenna. Cal took the hint and grabbed an identical one.

Theo pressed a red button on a device that looked like a parking meter linked to the Bluebird by a thick, black wire. A hatch door hissed and dropped slowly on a hydraulic mechanism, spewing steam and creating a ramp. Lights inside flickered. Theo removed the cable from an outlet on the hull and walked up the ramp. Cal followed, maneuvering down the narrow aisle between the four seats.

Theo propped her helmet on the yoke. A panel arched under the domed glass roof, covered with buttons, levers, gauges, and screens marked with old, yellowed masking tape and hastily written words that seemed important.

"Allow me." She grabbed his helmet, twisted it into place over his head, and slapped the back with a playful smile. Cal could hear the air flowing. It sounded like the conch shell he'd found on Eastview Beach as a boy. He remembered what his mother had told him that day: *The place you're from never truly leaves you, like the ocean inside this shell. Empire City is inside you and me, Calvin, no matter where we go.*

Theo popped her helmet on. "Can ya hear me, Bucko?" she asked through mounting static. Her voice sounded like the old Theo, hopeful and lighthearted. Another mask?

Cal nodded and lowered himself onto the front seat, staring out the two inches of glass that would separate them from the vacuum of space.

"You need to buckle in," she said.

Cal carefully pulled the nylon over his helmet and clipped the metal buckle between his legs. Theo nudged him and pulled a second belt across her lap, which he emulated. The snap of the clip invoked the same sense of dread as that old, rickety roller coaster in Steel Harbor—that slow cranking sound as the cars climbed before the drop.

"Ready?" Theo's garbled voice sputtered in his helmet.

"As I'll ever be."

She went to work on the console, and the whooshing of engines brought the Bluebird to life. She flipped up a transparent cover and punched a red button. The engines coughed mechanically as the ship spun a choppy one hundred eighty degrees and stopped. A blank, gray wall stood about fifty feet away.

Cal eyed her hesitantly.

"We'll be fine," Theo said, like she was a mind reader.

She fiddled with a few knobs. A giant gun above the ship spun to face the wall. "Attention," an automated voice said, "please clear the area. There will be an atmospheric pressure drop in t-minus ten seconds."

The countdown invoked the same apprehension as parachuting out of the C-47 Skytrain over Kyushu, excitement painted over with a coat of fear. At "three," a green ray shot from the gun above the ship, transforming the wall from a gray surface to an endless star-smattered universe. The moon was so close the entirety wasn't visible through the gateway—a desert of deep craters and jutting mountains. Theo's cigarette stub rolled and shot into the darkness of space. The other ships in the hangar whined. Theo gripped the throttle. Cal held his breath.

"One," the automated voice said. "Have a nice day."

Theo yanked the throttle. The engines thundered, and the ship shot forward. Cal slammed against the seat as the universe expanded, leaving his stomach back on Earth.

Theo squealed like a schoolgirl. Cal eyed her in his peripheral, afraid to look away from the windshield. The landing gear retracted audibly, vibrating the floor.

"Boy, oh boy, what a rush! You look three shades greener, Calvin." She laughed. "We jumped about two hundred thirty-nine thousand miles through an Einstein-Rosen Bridge, but we're still around three hundred miles from the moon." Theo pushed the throttle forward, and the speed dropped. "We'll be there in about an hour."

Cal felt her gaze lingering. "I see the way you look at me, Calvin. It's the same way I look at James."

Cal stared into the void of space, searching for a response but finding only tranquility. Up here, his issues with Theodora Connor seemed insignificant. "Theo—"

"James is a maniac," she said in a low, dejected tone. "I've been walking on eggshells for so long, afraid of what he might do to Bonnie or me.

"Ironically, the Enforcers used to put maniacs down, like dogs, and after the kill, James would smile. Sure, taking lives came easier with time, but it was never fun, and James' disgusting smile became harder to look at each time."

"Easier doesn't mean right," Cal said.

"Maybe, maybe not. Do you remember the Anti-Angel? She thought she was doing society a favor, eradicating sick people. 'I'm sending them to God,' she would write on the hospital walls. I caught up to her in Hemsford, connecting hoses to the HVAC system of a children's hospital, about to pump sarin through the ducts."

Theo lifted her glazed eyes. "I shot her right in the head without a word." A tear slipped down her cheek. "Painted her baby-blue van with her demented brain, and… I smiled.

"The *Bulletin* dubbing everyone with funny names allowed me to disassociate. The Anti-Angel was less than human, and the Scarlet Sparrow smiled when she killed her. Theodora Connor didn't; she was innocent." A tear ran down her cheek. "Thanks to the radio show, most people think the Ivory Icicle is an old man plotting ice-related crimes, complete with puns and a dog sled. Really, he was a Japanese sniper who went on a spree in December '45. I put him down with a Springfield aught-three, but I didn't smile back then.

"When Thompson attacked the city, I was pregnant. I knew he targeted Empire to get to me because I was the one who proposed the shutdown of the Manhattan Project. James killed him or said he did, and I hated him for it. I wanted the kill. I knew taking his life would make Theodora smile, not just the Scarlet Sparrow, and that feeling scared me.

"After that, nothing was the same. Rebuilding the city—surrendering to all that power—nearly drove me mad. So I retired before I completely became a monster." She laughed, which turned into a tear-filled mix of joy and pain on her face. "When Bonnie vanished, something awoke in me. I lost myself. I smiled when I murdered those men in Club Danza. I loved every second of it."

"I know," Cal responded.

"Cal, if you see it again…don't let it take me." She placed a Martian-looking modified Colt Government pistol onto the console. "And watch over Bonnie if it comes to that."

Cal sighed. "Theo—"

"This gun is designed to put me down, remove my life essence—a god killer. If you see me slip again, take the shot. I can't be a monster anymore."

The sincerity in her voice terrified Cal more than any vision he'd had. Cal looked from the gun to Theo. His problem was solved, but he wished it wasn't.

**80**

"We're coming up on the moon," Theo said redundantly. The desert-like rock spanned the entire windshield. In the distance, an emerging series of man-made domes peppered the surface. Sunlight glinted off the glass and metal, which seemed alien in the eternal night of space. Theo twisted knobs and pulled levers. The ship responded with hisses and whines as it slowed.

"Seatbelt," she said without looking up. Cal clicked both into place. There was a final loud hiss, and they were still. She smiled. "I appreciate how great you've been through all this, Calvin."

Cal nodded. After Theo's crisis, something didn't sit right. He still couldn't tell who the real Theodora Connor was: The tired, over-exasperated mother at the end of her rope, the pitiful self-loathing killer, or this pleasant old friend. Cal eyed the gun on the console—the god killer—and thought better of it. Perhaps she was still in that messy head somewhere.

"Ready, Bucko?" She unbelted and stood. "Careful. The gravity is much different here than it is on Earth." She pressed a button by the door, air expelled, and the ramp dropped slowly.

Cal followed between the seats, glancing back to the front of the ship. The cosmos unfolded through the windshield, but all he could see was that damn gun on the console.

"You okay, Cal?" Theo asked.

Cal's eyes lingered on the weapon. "Just nerves, I guess."

Theo smiled up from the moon's surface. "They'll pass."

Cal struggled down the stairs. Theo pressed a button on the Bluebird, and the gun disappeared behind the closing ramp.

"C'mon." She turned to make sure he was following. "We don't have a lot of oxygen."

The Earth's deep blues, loamy browns, and swirling whites popped against the black backdrop. Cal glanced past it to the sparkling expanse. He wasn't religious, but the magnificence made him believe anything could exist out there, even his mother.

*What can be big or small? Anywhere in the world, near or far, can stay the same or change over time? It's different for everyone, but everyone has one.*

Even Jerry.

Theo hopped away from the ship, towing a long, black cable, and plugged it into another parking meter. The lights inside the Bluebird flickered in appreciation, and the craft powered down. Theo's mouth moved, but only static sounded in Cal's helmet. She leaped into the air, landing about eight feet away. Then again, until she vanished into a dust cloud. Static sputtered.

Cal exhaled and bound after her. Launching himself eight feet in the air made him smile; he couldn't help himself. A few more hops and they stood outside the structure he had seen on arrival. Thirty-foot walls of seamless metal and towering glass domes stretched for miles in each direction. There were no screws or evidence of metal bunching at the seams from welding. It was uncannily perfect. He approached a fifteen-foot steepled glass entrance.

Theo occupied herself with a small control panel. The door slid open. She nodded to Cal, and they entered a small chamber about the size of the kitchen at Wilbur's. The door shut, and an oversized digital clock on the wall counted down from sixty.

A loud buzz filled the room, the interior door opened, and lights powered on in succession down a long corridor. Theo removed her helmet and shook out her auburn locks. Cal removed his.

"Radios must be on the fritz; sorry about that, Cal. I was saying we entered through the mess hall because Lily wouldn't be caught dead here. I've never seen that woman eat." Theo smirked. Cal didn't. She cleared her throat. "With any luck, I can track her activity without her spotting us. If she knows we're here, she'll be in the wind." There was hatred in her tone, sparking a sense of urgency, and suddenly, Cal felt like he was talking to James.

The gravity had returned to normal, and each step sent a severe shock through Cal's muscles. Theo led him down the newly lit corridor into a large cafeteria. Four long banquet tables with bench seating stood in the middle. Dusty, alien-looking machines laid dormant around the exterior, including two giant metal cases with waist-high slots carved into each. One said "food," the other "drink."

Theo set her helmet down. "Actually, Lily might expect us to scan the base from the control room." She stared vacantly, pressing her index finger against her bottom lip. "We should start in the hangar, track her the old-fashioned way." She scampered to a blank wall in the rear of the cafeteria. A hidden panel flipped down, and Theo pressed a few buttons. A hatch in the wall opened, revealing an elevator. She held the door with her forearm. "C'mon."

Cal set his helmet on the table and shuffled in next to her. Deep in thought, Theo swiped her index finger repeatedly across a giant screen. "Ah-ha! Sorry, Cal, I haven't been up here in a while."

"Hangar," an automated woman's voice said. The elevator shifted sideways abruptly. Theo squealed as she fell into Cal's arms, forcing him against the wall. Their eyes locked. Theo smiled and pressed her soft lips to his.

Cal froze. A vision of a little girl flashed in his mind, not Bonnie, but close to her age. *The end of all things,* something whispered. He recoiled, but before he could speak, the door opened. Cal cleared his throat and released Theo.

"Peachy!" She pressed herself off Cal's chest and stepped out of the elevator into the gasoline-scented room. "The Redbird is here, I knew it would be." Lights hummed overhead as Theo traversed the massive space toward the ship.

Cal watched her lithe frame, and a crude and animalistic sensation stirred, demanding something on the razor's edge between violence and sex. He flexed his injured hand painlessly and followed. The door sealed behind him.

The hangar seemed to be the heart of the structure. Doorways similar in size and shape lined the curved walls, branching off and honeycombing into other domes. The ship, identical to the one they had arrived in, except with red trim, was the only thing in the room.

"Now, all we need to do is follow the lights that Lily's left on." Theo motioned to a hallway, but her eyes lingered on Cal's.

Cal exhaled through clenched teeth, unable to look away. Desire rippled under his skin. She turned and stalked toward the hallway. Cal watched her, wary that a similar sentiment lurked behind her lascivious glance.

Her silhouette waited in the doorway. Cal approached slowly, eyeing the pistol in her hand; the sight of it sobered him. It was familiar; the odd, rounded barrel and fin on top looked like a fish, and the tip had small rings running along a center antenna that grew smaller toward the front. Similar to the gun on the Bluebird's console, the god killer. Theo spun on her heel. "C'mon, we haven't got all day."

Cal hesitantly followed through the maze of hallways, corridors, and open spaces. Each area looked vaguely similar: arching glass domes linked together with long, joyless hallways that ended abruptly.

"This is it, Bucko, end of the line." Theo pressed her hand flat on the wall, and a small panel flipped out of the metal. She tapped on the exposed screen, and Cal eyed the pistol hanging off her hip.

An alarm screamed through the corridor, and a red light flashed. Theo punched the panel and cursed. She tried again with the same result. "So much for the surprise entrance. Janice, report."

"Afternoon, Missus Connor," the same monotonic voice from the elevator replied. "You are unauthorized to enter this room."

Theo eyed the ceiling. "On whose authority."

"I'm afraid that's classified," the voice responded. "Please vacate the area. Thank you, and have a nice day."

Cal turned. The silhouette of a little girl watched from the end of the hallway. *The end of everything,* a woman's voice whispered.

*Clang!* Theo dropped the panel she'd pulled off the wall and plunged her hands into the square hole. "Oh, that Lily Larkin!"

Cal shook his head, trying to remember what he'd just seen.

*Woosh!* The door slid open.

"Access granted."

"That's what I thought," Theo responded.

"Who's Janice?" Cal asked, glancing up at the rafters.

"This whole base is Janice, Cal. Artificial intelligence I built to run the joint while I'm on Earth." Theo's irritation slathered each word. "Janice, you're to do as I say, no one else, understand?" She stomped down another empty hallway, then stopped. "Janice?"

"Error," the voice called out. "This interferes with my current program."

Theo made a noise between a grunt and a sigh. "Override code: Bravo, Oscar, November, November, India, Echo."

There was a pause. "Accepted, but all programming will revert to current settings in twenty-four hours."

"Janice, on whose authority?"

"Classified."

"Janice, override code: Oscar Mike Echo Golf Alfa."

"Accepted."

"Now, I'm asking again—on whose authority did you override me as primary caretaker?"

"Classified."

"Janice, why is this information classified to the primary caretaker?" Theo yelled.

"The information is classified because the information is unknown."

Theo took off in a mad dash down the hallway. Cal ran after her as best he could in the clunky spacesuit, gritting his teeth through the pain each step yielded.

"What is—"

*Woosh!* The opening door interrupted Cal, and Theo's concerned glance stopped his question. He followed her into the largest room since the hangar. A hive of transparent staircases and platforms ascended the glass to the highest point of the dome. Each floor was unique, all containing dangerous-looking, unfamiliar equipment.

"There!" Theo said. The clang of her boots on the metal grate grew fainter as she ran over the suspended bridge and ascended a ladder. When Cal caught up, she was already twenty feet in the air, climbing fast. He watched her disappear over the edge.

Cal climbed quicker than expected, painlessly pulling himself rung over rung with a tenacity he thought had long abandoned him. As he neared the top of the ladder, an unfamiliar woman's voice said: "Theodora? Thank goodness you're here."

<u>81</u>

# The City of the Gods: Gold

Lily Larkin stood at the far end of the room in front of a curved console smattered with buttons, knobs, and screens. She regarded Cal with a go-to-hell look as he climbed through the open hatch. Her heavy eyelids and pouty lips exuded unfounded self-importance, framed by her dark hair, pushed back with oversized goggles, and falling in curls past her bare shoulders, almost reaching her blue bathing suit, masquerading as a uniform.

Theo stared daggers. In the flawless Lily Larkin's presence, her recent deterioration became much more apparent.

"Lily! This is low, even for you." Theo pulled the gun from her belt. "Where's my daughter?"

Lily raised an eyebrow. "I have no idea where Bonnie is. I only told you the DiLilos had her to keep you from following me to your little lab. That was a mistake. I really do need your help, dear."

"Bullshit!" Theo took a step forward. "Where is she?"

Lily sighed, vanished, and appeared next to Theo. "Always the lady, eh? What are you going to do, shoot me?" she asked lazily.

Theo pressed a button, and the pistol hummed as a red bar built on the side.

"Theodora, you can't possibly think I'd have anything to do with kidnapping your little Bonnie. Think about it, dear. It's a good thing you're pretty because you certainly don't have a head on your shoulders. I needed to use your equipment, and I thought it would be easier if you weren't in my way."

Theo lowered her weapon. "Why do you need my equipment?"

"I'd be better off showing you." Lily carried herself with confidence and poise, no longer the quiet, bookish woman she had been in Japan before inheriting Jerry's speed. Cal blinked, and she was across the room, standing by a glass staircase along the dome's wall. "Come, come."

As the three scaled the winding stairs, Theo placed a hand on Cal's chest and watched Lily ascend a few more steps before she whispered: "I don't like this, Cal. Lily has the upper hand if this goes south."

Cal watched the dying light in Theo's eyes. "What choice do we have?"

"Just stay on your toes."

The serpentine staircase opened into a large room at the top of the dome. Even this high up, the ceiling stood about twenty feet over their heads. Cal's stomach lurched as he stepped onto the transparent floor and glanced nearly three hundred feet down to the moon's surface.

A collection of consoles with blinking lights and monitors quartered the room into sections. One machine fastened to a steel support beam flashed in the corner.

The stench of rot hit. Theo scrunched her nose and shot Cal a concerned look. Lily grabbed two vinyl vests from what looked like a coat rack and threw one to each, then slid into one of her own.

Theo begrudgingly put on the harness. "Lily, have you been monkeying with the gravity-pump?"

Lily rolled her eyes. "It was the only way I could move him." She opened a small hatch in the blinking machine, yanked out two stubborn stainless-steel cables, and handed them to Cal and Theo. "Clip these to your vests."

Theo snatched the carabiner clip and shot Lily a stern look. Still, she obliged. Cal followed suit.

"Move who?" Theo asked.

Lily sped across the room, unraveled an identical cable from another support beam, and hooked it to her vest. "Why, James, of course."

Theo's eyes grew wide. She stomped across the room toward Lily, but the cable snapped tight.

Lily watched her with that terrible smirk on her face. "Trust me; you won't be so excitable when you see him." She darted from console to console, flipping switches and pressing buttons until a large metal table rose slowly into view with an ominous, mechanical whirring. Theo gasped.

Shackled to the table, no more than ten feet away, was the creature that had brought down the building in Hemsford. A hodgepodge of exposed bone and metal appendages pulled frantically against the restraints. Wires had been clipped and plugs inserted along the metal part of its body. Its rotten skin had been cut and peeled back where the neck met the shoulder, exposing a sickening combination of muscle fiber, bone, and metal. Screens with bouncing lines and graphs spiked and fell as the creature struggled. James Connor—the once-proud hero—reduced to a crooked, malformed monster locked on a metal slab in space.

Theo's glazed eyes followed Lily, snapping back to the creature whenever it jerked against its bonds. Her mouth moved silently until one word emerged: "James?"

Lily maneuvered around the table, watching the monster writhe with a beaming smile. "We found some sort of UFO wreckage a few nights ago. On the fifteenth, I think. The big lug insisted on opening it," she recalled the event as if it were a picnic in Miller's Run.

"The fifteenth? Was Bonnie with you?" Theo whispered.

"Of course not! This isn't the radio show, dear Theodora; there are no Junior Enforcers with decoder rings following our every move. You really must get your head out of the clouds." Lily regarded James. "Anyway, I wanted nothing to do with it, so I left. James returned to the Hall a while later, upset because someone had reported the vessel to

Allied Science after he'd opened it, and the FBI had pulled rank on him. When I heard the FBI was involved, I returned to Brookfield to ensure the UFO reached its destination. We wouldn't want something like this to fall into the wrong hands. I'm still a team player, Theodora, even though there isn't much of a team anymore. When I returned to the Hall, James looked like this." She chuckled. "I'd be lying if I told you the nurse in me isn't a bit intrigued."

Cal scanned the creature. It was a horrific, malformed shadow of a human body: twisted appendages and wide red eyes the size of silver dollars, with no eyelids, but he could almost see James' features amongst the chaos.

Lily said: "Naturally, I was horrified until I saw a bit of his personality come through, a smile here, a nod there..."

The creature flailed against its shackles. Theo approached the table slowly. It seemed to calm down when it saw her.

Cal regarded Lily. "How did you get him here?"

Lily sighed. "He escaped me for a time and managed to build a weapon he launched it into Sainte Marie Square. Luckily, I made quick work of it, no thanks to the two of you."

"That's why he stole my blueprints," Theo whispered. "Why would he want to destroy—"

"How did you get him *here*?" Cal asked. "We put him through a building. It didn't even slow him down."

"Because I'm better than you, dear, it's that simple. I followed the weapon's trajectory and tracked him to the old subway tunnel. He had broken through the wall to where Miller's River flows under Club Danza and was using it to travel under the city. I returned with the Redbird, and a few non-lethal shots pacified him enough for relocation.

"I knew you'd never let me bring him here, so I created a distraction. I'm sorry about involving Bonnie, but I knew it was the only way to get you out of my hair for a few hours."

Theo's stagnant gaze remained on James.

"That still doesn't explain how you got it here. It must weigh five tons," Cal said.

"*He* isn't as heavy as you might think," she corrected. "I calmed him down, and then he wanted to come here so I could cure him." She smiled.

Theo's shock melted away. "Lily, you closet case!" She lurched forward and snapped the cable taut. "I know what's inside him. He doesn't want you, and he certainly doesn't want a cure. He wants my technology! Unhook him quickly before it's too late! You're feeding him information through the computer, my blueprints, my weapons, everything!" Theo bound to the edge of the table, grabbing a wire from the thing's bicep.

Lily grabbed Theo's arm in a blur of speed. "You really must think this through!"

Theo's mournful eyes scanned the remains of her husband. She released the wire and yanked her arm from Lily's grasp. "Why are you so obsessed with curing my husband anyway, Lily Larkin?"

Lily sighed. "I suppose being blunt is best. Theodora—dear, sweet Theodora—James and I are in love."

Theo stared at her husband until Lily touched her shoulder, and she shrunk away.

"Can't we be adults about this?" Lily said. "You can still do the right thing and help me get him out of this state. Bonnie needs her father."

Theo stared through glossy eyes at the monster. Cal placed a hand on her shoulder, and she flinched. Tears in stasis spilled over.

"It's better he's on the moon," Cal said, "rather than running wild through Empire."

Theo shut her eyes. "Turn the gravity off."

Lily pursed her lips to speak but thought better of it and sped over to the console with the flashing warning light. She pressed a large red button and glanced at Theo. Cal sighed as his feet lifted slowly from the floor. He took in slack from his stainless-steel lifeline.

A tear rose over Theo's head as she closed her eyes. Her eyebrows narrowed, and she ground her teeth. "I'll help you if you help me find Bonnie. You can have James. You two deserve each other."

"Of course, darling, I am a hero after all. James and I would be thrilled to help."

Theo floated next to the table, scanning the creature. This time, when it saw her, it lashed out.

"Is that really you in there, James?" she asked.

The creature ripped its enormous, crooked arm away from the table, shattering the restraint. Theo trained her gun on its head, but Lily slapped it away in a blur of speed.

"No! Don't hurt him!" Lily screamed. "Don't you dare!" The creature backhanded Theo, sending her flying until the cable jerked. She grunted, suspended limply in the air. The monster ripped its other arm free and sat up. Cal pulled himself along the steel cable toward Theo. "Are you alright?"

"I have you, my dear," Lily said, wrapping her arms around James' pulsing, rotten neck from behind.

Theo snatched Cal's hand, and his feet touched the ground. "This is going to be bad," she said, watching Lily and James. "We need to leave." The rest of the open room still seemed unaffected by gravity. The gadget on Theo's chest displayed a full green bar, beeping wildly. "Lily, we need to go!"

# The City of the Gods: Gold

Lily scampered around on James's back, narrowly avoiding his long reach. "I'm not leaving him!" The creature grabbed her arm and threw her like a rag doll. She slammed into a table and hung in stasis as blood floated from her head.

James ripped the shackles from his feet and leaped to the edge of the glass dome.

"Shit!" Theo dragged Cal toward the stairs.

Cal craned his neck around. "What about Lily?"

"She'll be right behind us. She's fast, remember? Now, stop fighting."

A thunderous noise reverberated, and Theo's pace quickened. Cal turned his head to find the origin, but it was out of sight. The ear-shattering bang repeated until it was unbearable.

"Lily, come on!" Cal yelled over the echoing insanity. A large crack traveled up the side of the dome. Cal's eyes followed the abrasion to the creature pounding on the glass.

Lily hung lifeless as blood continued to trickle up from her head.

"Theo, wait! We need to go back for her!" Cal yelled.

Theo sprinted toward the stairs with Cal in tow, dragging him like a child. He couldn't break her grip.

A booming crash gave way to the vacuum of space. The hands of death pulled, but Cal's feet never left the ground. Theo pressed on, yanking him along step by labored step as her hair whipped around her determined face.

"Whatever you do, do not let go of my hand!" she screamed. As they inched forward, the meter on her chest dropped from full green to a quarter, blinking yellow bar as they inched forward. Debris shot past them on either side. Some of the smaller consoles jostled and launched into space.

Theo ripped the cable from her vest halfway down the stairs, and Cal did the same. Both steel cords shot back up through the ceiling, pointing at the open gash.

"Janice"—Theo's chest piece blinked a sliver of red—"quarantine section niner four seven dash Alfa!"

"Authorization?" the all too calm voice answered.

Theo shook the hair from her face. "Bravo, Oscar, November, November, India, Echo!" An orange light spun on top of the console marked "caution" in the room above, and the ceiling closed slowly.

When the atmosphere returned to a standstill, Theo ejected a charred mass from the box on her chest. "Whew, who knew the gravity-stabilizer would work against the vacuum of space?"

Cal stared through the ceiling at Lily Larkin's floating corpse, tethered to the structure's new roof. Her long black hair flowed around her frozen, terrified face like a winding river, and her blood-red eyes glared at nothing from their sockets.

"We need to get back in there."

Theo shook her head. "Cal—"

"We need to get back in there!"

Theo tumbled to a seated position, fell onto her back, and stretched out on the transparent step. Her chest heaved under the spacesuit. She closed her eyes and laughed. "There's no oxygen in that room, Cal. Hell, it isn't even a room anymore. If you went out there, you'd end up like Lily. I'm sorry, Bucko, she's gone."

Cal saw Jerry's bloody smile, like a horrific Cheshire cat in his mind.

"We have to try!" he said.

Theo ignored him. "Of course, that thing is James," she said through a chuckle as she wiped a stray tear away. "I don't know why I didn't make the connection earlier. I knew he'd open that vessel if he ever found it. He was always looking for more power, more women, more everything. That man was never satisfied."

"You knew about the vessel?" Cal asked.

Theo sighed, "Well, I guess there's no use keeping secrets when the people you're supposed to be keeping them from are dead—or as good as dead." She closed her eyes and exhaled. "Years ago, when Thompson and Oppenheimer were developing the uranium and plutonium cores that would eventually lead to the atom bomb. I was busy developing my nano-mites. Atom-sized robots that could build where the bomb would destroy, but I didn't stop there."

Theo traced the stars with her eyes. "After the Anti-Angel attacked all those hospitals, I had the idea of adding an organic component. One that would help people afflicted with disease heal themselves. A miracle cure for anything. They were just so expensive and time-consuming to make."

Cal's eyes widened. "That's what you put inside me on top of that building in Hemsford, isn't it?"

Theo's eyes jumped back and forth between his pupils.

"*Isn't it?*"

"Yes, but Cal, you need to understand. You would have died if I didn't. You were in no condition to even stand, let alone put up a fight."

Cal glowered. "So, I'm going to turn into… whatever James is?"

"No. I was successful. My nano-mites bought my mother a few more years of life, even with her terminal pulmonary fibrosis diagnosis. But my designs were stolen in '45, along with the designs for my disbursement unit. And from the sound of things, that was what James and Lily found"—she paused thoughtfully—"I came across one of the phony disbursement units back in '47, in the Basalt River. Luckily, it was rusted shut, and James never saw it. Since their conception, he was constantly pestering me to test my new nano-mites on him. He thought it would make us more powerful.

"I always told him no and managed to hide the poor counterfeit at Allied Science before he even knew it existed." Theo sat up and scanned the surface of the moon. "The thing is, I still have no idea who stole my designs, but I always assumed it was Thompson."

Cal watched the Earth float innocently above them. Whatever James had become was still out there. He couldn't save Lily, but he could still protect his city.

Theo forced an exaggerated smile. "Did you see the state of him? Low-grade science." She chuckled. "Maybe he's working with Thompson after all. Maybe when James threatened to kill him, Thompson offered to turn him into that."

Cal watched the Bluebird lift off in the distance. "Theo, we need to get back to Empire—"

"I feel like it's all connected, Thompson, Bonnie, James becoming a kitchen appliance." She laughed. "It's too much of a coincidence not to be."

"Then let's go." Cal scampered down the stairs to the ladder. "The Redbird is still in the hanger."

He stopped and glanced up at Lily Larkin's corpse. There was nothing more they could do for her, but he hesitated anyway.

He saw Jerry smile, his bloody smile. *What a ride. Huh, Cal?*

He sighed and gripped the rung of the ladder. *I'll be back for you, I swear.*

Cassle Cola
QUENCH YOUR THIRST IN A HURRY!
Cassle

THOSE
WITH GREATNESS
THRUST UPON THEM

## 82

"Home at last." Nadir shut the door gently. It must have been close to midnight, and he felt every hour of the day in his aching back. The apartment was darker than usual, darker than ever, actually, like being submerged in ink. Streetlights were absent, and the usually chaotic city was silent. He groped the wall but couldn't find the light switch. The coat rack was missing too.

*Perhaps I've stumbled into the wrong apartment,* he thought, inching carefully toward the kitchen. At once, the apartment illuminated, and the street lit up, clamoring like someone jump-started a carnival.

Nadir flinched and scanned the red Formica table and three chairs. Bare counters stretched around the kitchen's edge, and a pink Admiral refrigerator hummed. A cream-colored velvet tufted sofa sat across from a radio in the living quarters and a lonely ornate mirror against the wall next to the door.

Something was off. Nadir adjusted the edge of the mirror a quarter inch. "There we are." He regarded the radio in the reflection. Something was still off. He glanced between the white Admiral refrigerator and the green tufted sofa when a yawn caught him off guard. *I better get to bed. I need to do... something tomorrow, a favor for a friend*—he froze thoughtfully.

*Nadir, old boy, it seems you've finally lost your marbles.* He ambled down the hallway, past the children's closed bedroom doors, on his right. *That's not where those go.* When he eyed them again, both doors were in their proper location on the opposite wall. "Perfect." He turned and marched toward his bedroom, trying to remember his plans, but a deafening grinding sound flooded the hallway when he tried to focus on anything that happened earlier than his arrival home. Luckily, his family remained undisturbed.

"I think I know what's going on," a voice intruded. "Where's Frank?"

Nadir turned abruptly. "Who's there?"

"I need to get my notes from home." The voice crawled the length of his shoulders. "I think I know what's happening, but I need my notes. We need to contact Jacob Landry."

Nadir's panicked gaze jumped around the empty hallway.

"Where's Frank?" the voice thundered down the hall. "I need to get my notes from home. I think I know what's happening, but I need my notes. We need to contact Jacob Landry."

*Bang!* The door at the end of the hallway slammed shut. The sound of a locking mechanism rotated and clicked. Nadir ran toward it, but with each step, it pushed away, stretching the hall to an inconceivable length. He slowed to catch his breath. The children's rooms were still beside him. He twisted the brass knob on the lefthand door. It wouldn't budge. He knocked quietly. Silence. The tiresome phrase regarding "notes" repeated until it was ambient background noise.

Nadir turned the knob to the other room, and the door flung inward. He squinted and lifted his hand to shield his eyes from the glare. "Anyone in there?" He entered. The light was so luminous it made the room virtually featureless, far more lacking than even the darkest black could render it. There were no walls, just blank, white space expanding infinitely in each direction.

*What used to be here?* He forced himself to think, which shifted something in his stomach, and warm bile climbed the back of his throat. His chest muscles tensed. He whirled around, stumbled back to the hallway, and slammed the door.

*I've lost my mind.* Nadir stared helplessly at the blue and brown floral wallpaper. *Am I in the wrong apartment?* He scanned the churning teal and orange leaf design on the wall. The photos of his family were gone, as was the oriental runner.

"Where's Frank?"

# The City of the Gods: Gold

He trudged toward the kitchen, running his hand over the black and gold wallpaper to stop the world from spinning. A soothing voice sang in high soprano. He exhaled and smiled.

"I need to get my notes from home. I think I know what's happening, but—" The voice cut.

A woman, a girl, and a boy sat silently around the blue Formica table, facing away, existing as three heads of black hair atop beige fabric. Aside from the table, the only furniture was a purple tufted sofa and a radio.

"I'm terribly sorry for the intrusion," Nadir said, "but can you tell me what apartment number this is?"

They were so motionless that they didn't even seem to be breathing.

"Please." Nadir reached forward. The people and the orange Formica table they occupied lurched just out of his grasp. "I think something is wrong with me." Nadir swallowed panic and moved around to confront the mysterious people. Each time he'd try to catch a glimpse of their faces, their heads would turn away.

The high-pitched singing demanded his attention. He snapped to order, approaching the mirror and bringing his face slowly into the frame. An Indian man with a Roman nose and a thin mustache stared back. He had two eyes, a weak chin, and a fat, soggy eggplant body that could never perform the task required of it. The mirror dropped, exploding into a million pieces.

*The world will burn.*

He tried to understand the message reverberating through the song as he slumped onto the sofa. The people vanished with the table, the chairs, and the mirror shards.

He spun the volume knob on the radio, and the dulcet, treble-heavy hiss shook plaster from the ceiling. It was calling him home. This had been the wrong apartment, after all.

*The world will burn.*

He understood now.

## 83

He was born on an unforgiving wooden floor in a small cabin in Northwell. Thrust into this world with only the information The Elder Brother instilled upon him through the frequencies.

Bright light piercing the window seared his sensitive new eyes, and the sudden growth of appendages replacing the bloody stumps from the old body left him in constant, seething agony. However, pain was all he knew, so he loved it like a son would love a mother. He understood basic ideas like this, but this form would never utilize the full capabilities of the mind growing inside him.

Material composed of metal, wood, rock, and bone were broken down to their molecular levels and transformed into raw materials on the atomic level via exoenzymes. They replaced extracted appendages and rebuilt the body. The waste was left where it fell.

His dry mouth moved, but the habit of speech had been broken with the extraction of his vocal cords. Soon, other flaws would fade, food and oxygen cravings, thirst, longing for socialization, and love.

Unnecessary organs—lungs, heart, liver, intestines, bladder, and kidneys—had been removed in preparation for the life that would grow inside him. Nutrients— polysaccharides, lipids, and proteins—were absorbed through the same exoenzymes that created his body. The same compound that metastasized in the blood of the tumor called *Nadir Singh.*

# The City of the Gods: Gold

A feeling of loss for the organism's loved ones lingered, but The Elder Brother insisted these thoughts would fade as the new life within him absorbed the tumor. Still, the mental anguish rivaled the physical torture of living.

He and His Twin Brother had been born simultaneously through the same spores. Although the two looked different, they would comprise similar genetic makeup as The Elder once this phase was complete.

His Twin still had traces of the organism Frank Rivoli in his facial features, but the muscles had failed due to a ruptured blood vessel in the brain. So, his features hung as a drooping mass of flesh.

The radio emitted a constant symphony of commands and information from The Elder:

*The creation of our primary objective was meant to be a distraction. It was easily dismembered by the organism: Lily Larkin—deceased—in Sainte Marie Square. That primary objective was to leave the city broken but not yet decimated. Status: success.*

*The secondary objective remains under construction in Steel Harbor. Status: compromised. We must move production west, through Miller's River.*

Coordinates followed.

*This Elder Brother has confiscated technology from Earth's moon, salvaged at significant risk from the organism Theodora Connor. Your task is to relocate and complete the secondary objective, achieving our purpose for these forms.*

This One staggered to his feet. His Twin watched silently. It was of the utmost importance that This One learn how to exist independently for the safety of the life that would grow within him.

*You must ensure your body is strong enough.* His Twin's words drifted over the frequency. *There will be many hardships before the Final Solution is reached, and this is but the first form.*

This One stumbled. His movements were sluggish from the new unwieldy appendages and the tumor Nadir Singh's internal struggle.

His Twin watched, unencumbered by his host's persistent meddling. When the brain died, the tumor Frank Rivoli was purged. Now, His Twin could focus on rebuilding.

Beasts watched from the wall, dead flesh stuffed with fat and wood shavings, and furniture lay in ruin across the floor. Little remained to extract after His Twin absorbed the robust material, and the host Nadir Singh was not chosen for its powerful body. It was not chosen at all, merely happened upon.

The log cabin shrunk, and the door didn't fit the wall. No, This One was growing. Exoenzymes absorbed what they could from the couch, but the parasite still thought about things like the room's size as it resisted. It was solid of mind, a formidable opponent.

*Anila.* The word was a strong tether, keeping the tumor from pacifying. It burned in This One's body where life should have been growing.

*Don't let it win,* His Twin hissed over the frequency. *Be more assertive. Use the parasite's weapon against itself.*

**84**

Darkness pushed in like a rising tide around the green velvet tufted sofa. Nadir was nowhere. The radio floated in pitch-black, illuminated from the inside, a distraction as his body slowly withered away like a piece of human fruit, fallen too far from the tree.

He tried to recall his life and what kind of man he'd been, but he couldn't even remember his name. He tried to think of familiar things: his parents' faces, the address of his childhood home, where he had worked, his family, his wife, but only the soft hiss of the radio filled the vacuum.

"Nadir." A woman's voice broke through the static.

"Anila," he said, but the word was meaningless.

"Stop fighting, my love, let go." The voice sounded like a spring rain pattering against a tin roof on a country house in England. He remembered an old stone chimney, the back farmhouse window looking over the sprawling countryside, and clean, crisp air. Each day, the love between the shamed man and wife grew stronger as life took hold inside the woman. It was to be a girl called Pratima, after her grandmother.

"Anila." He remembered her almond-shaped eyes, her cascading hair like a silk waterfall. The laugh that sometimes made her snort. He smiled, recalling the smell of her soft skin as they made love on the cotton sheets. Two kids with no responsibility but to each other. "Anila." His face twisted, and hope melted with his heart. That life was gone.

"If I let go, how will I find you again?" he asked.

"Forget me, my dear. That is how it must be—"

"The world will burn!" A second voice cut through the static, and Nadir remembered—not everything, but enough. He gritted his teeth, dug his fingers into the couch, and pushed up with all his strength. He summoned all the energy remaining in his withered old body and shoved the radio to the floor.

## <u>85</u>

The storm calmed inside This One's head, and he staggered to his feet.

*You've purged the parasite,* His Twin said through the frequency.

*Yes,* This One replied. *I feel—*

Something spiked internally, sending him into the wall and expelling dust. *Bang! Bang! Bang! Bang!* He violently threw his head against the wood. A sharp ringing brought the frequency to an abrupt halt as a crack formed in the skull, reminding him of the moment he was born. Pain—his nurturing mother—felt natural.

*Don't give in to the satisfaction,* His Twin hissed. *That is the tumor's pleasure, not yours.*

This One's jaw dropped, and an inhuman howl rode air left in the chest cavity up through the dry, gaping mouth, "Annnaaaiiiiaaaa!" His legs buckled.

*The parasite Nadir Singh is trying to destroy the body!* This One cried desperately through the frequency to The Elder Brother. He scanned the room, focusing on the large mirror hanging over the fireplace.

**86**

Nadir turned away from the broken radio, and the world reemerged. His favorite song, "Someday I'll Find You," dribbled through the walls. He tasted poha, smelled fresh-cut grass, and felt silk brush his skin. Everything returned in one overwhelming sensation until he couldn't separate smell from taste or touch from sound. Sensory overload propelled him from the hypnotic trance, returning his strength. The audio spewing from the radio's remains seemed like volatile static and clatter not of this world.

The apartment returned to its original state, and the city was alive through the window. Nadir's family called to him from the hallway across the kitchen. He rose from the couch and leaped over the back, toppling it over.

"My duckling! My family! Oh, god!" Tears welled in his eyes. "I didn't give up. I wouldn't!" He staggered past the door, the walnut coat rack, the shoe rack, and the mirror and leaned on the smooth finish of one of the *four* red Formica chairs to steady his shaking body.

He froze, eyeing the mirror. Something watched from the other side. Nadir could sense it crawling inside his skin, leeching off his body.

"Darling?" Anila's voice drew him back to his family, but that bloody mirror still demanded his attention.

"You need to look," Anila said.

He regarded the love of his life. "I'm not ready to go."

Anila smiled through tears. "We will be alright, my love."

"It's okay, Father," Ukrit said.

"My brave boy." Nadir smiled. "You take good care of your sister."

Pratima cupped her hands on her face, and her slight shoulders bounced silently.

"My little duckling," he whispered. There was much more to say, but somehow, he knew these were only apparitions of people he had loved in life. "Anila, I'm so sorry."

*Look in the mirror*—Nadir's voice called through the scramble of the radio frequency—*end this.*

He regarded his reflection with a terrible sinking pain in his heart. A horrific mix of metal, exposed bone, and dehydrated flesh watched him with a hopelessly artificial stare through one exposed, bulging human eye and one cybernetic.

Nadir Singh's body was no more. The hands that shaped his career, the legs that brought him to this country, the knee he proposed to Anila upon, and the heart that beat for his family were all discarded. Now, some terrible, writhing monster grew inside this shell, feeding off everything he ever loved.

Plaster cracked, and the ceiling crumbled. Furniture danced across the floor, crashing onto the hardwood as the apartment shook. Nadir stood motionless, watching his family's mournful faces. The hall light cut out. He kept his eyes on his family's stagnant form until the kitchen light dimmed, and they vanished into the void.

"Goodbye."

Behind him, the docile tone on the now pristine radio became crystal clear. The song was sweet and sad, happy and triumphant like his life had been. However, it was not infinite. It would eventually come to an end, as all things did.

**<u>87</u>**

The mirror told the truth. Shadows that had clouded This One's mind dissipated as the parasite Nadir Singh heaved its final death throes and dissolved. Pain was no longer his caretaker. It was the enemy, and the agony of life was a farce the tumor had instilled upon him.

This One's head throbbed, his body ached, but development flourished. His mind was his own. This was no longer a log cabin in Northwell. This was material, nourishment, and protection for the life growing inside him—a step toward the Final Solution.

He regarded His Twin and staggered onto his wobbly legs with the help of the cabin wall. *It's done.* The splintered bone jutting from his left shoulder craved material. As the phantom limb flexed, he scanned the room, envisioning what could be. *The material here is substandard.*

The Elder's voice traveled over the frequency: *Make do. Your form will be reinforced later. We must prepare for what comes next.*

Wooden timber dissolved, broken down into its base elements and redistributed over the exposed portions of This One's body.

His Twin approached. *The frequency tells me we are hunted by those pursuing the parasites Nadir Singh and Frank Rivoli. We must change locations.*

Atoms crawled over This One's slight frame, creating a rudimentary arm and developing his physique into a considerable bulk of mediocrity. His intense appetite tore the wall asunder. *First, I must feed.*

His Twin nodded. *Not too much. If you assemble entirely, it will render you immobile and complete this form's life cycle. There is still much to be done before this phase concludes.*

All traces of the parasite Frank Rivoli had been adequately purged from His Twin's face. His impressively colossal body now towered eleven feet four inches tall and weighed six hundred and twenty-three pounds and four ounces—a worthy protector of the creation growing inside.

Life stirred in the genetic bath within This One's chest cavity, awakening, requesting nourishment. This One would be weak while it fed on the tumor, Nadir Singh. He regarded the mirror and recognized the face, slowly reemerging over the neoplasm. Metallic chrome fused to flesh. One eye, replaced by cybernetics designed by the organism Theodora Connor, retrieved by The Elder and distributed over the frequency. The remaining meat was half of a face above the nose, a partially exposed brain, and a lower jaw. The inorganic portion of his body continually shifted as unstable molecules rippled.

The radio exuded a beautiful hum, and This One knew The Elder had succeeded. Information and technology required to complete this life cycle had been obtained from Theodora Connor. The Elder would bestow it upon phase two.

*The world will burn.* It echoed in This One's head as a war cry. A final gift from the parasite Nadir Singh.

Outside, rubber rolled over gravel and skidded to a stop. A vehicle had arrived, followed by another, then a third. This One stopped absorbing questionable nutrients and said to His Twin: *There will be raw material in the vehicles. However, I am far too weak to take it from the organisms as the life feeds inside me.*

His Twin turned toward the window. *I shall take it for you.*

Outside, twigs snapped, and leaves rustled. This One could perceive every movement the organisms made, sensing the steel that made up their guns and the fear buried underneath the adrenaline. There was no more taste, smell, sight, sound, or touch. Instead, all five senses were experienced at once.

His Twin regarded the door facing the river. The vehicles were behind him, but the organisms were everywhere. This One cycled through his functions and expelled sufficient energy into his defenses. The life inside him stopped feeding and grew irritable.

The radio hissed and squealed instructions. This One turned toward the thinning wall as His Twin opened the door and stepped onto the porch.

"Hey, stop right there!" one of the organisms yelled.

"Holy shit! What is that thing?"

The guns exploded, and bullets rattled off His Twin. Strays pierced the cabin's walls. This One waited next to the mounted head of an animal, sensing the molecules leaping off the vehicles. They were close, but there were still too many organisms to fortify his body safely.

His Twin advanced from the porch onto the lawn. More gunfire and more steel riddled the walls.

"Everybody, get over here, now!"

This One could sense perspiration and fear, then blood, as His Twin ripped heads from bodies and stripped flesh from bones. The organisms were frail, but their weapons were too dangerous a risk to the life inside him. It jolted and convulsed against his abdomen, and he nearly doubled over.

This One couldn't wait any longer. He punched the wall, forcing the wood to jump. Pain ran down the length of his arm. He punched again. The logs bent and splintered, and he pressed his hands through the wall, pulling the wood apart.

The cars sat unguarded on the gravel road behind the cabin. This One stumbled through the broken timber and collapsed on a police vehicle's hood. The shocks buckled, and the tires blew simultaneously as the metal crumpled under his body. He absorbed the steel into his form and slowly rose from the heap of rapidly decaying material.

*Not too much*, the frequency hissed from a police radio. *We have not yet completed this stage of the Final Solution.*

The gunfire ceased. This One abandoned the nearly consumed car and joined His Twin on the other side of the cabin. Together, the brothers moved through the row of towering evergreens toward the water.

More vehicles barreled across the lawn, filled with the same vulnerable human organisms. A black Plymouth plowed into His Twin. He buried his hands into the engine block before it overtook him and flipped the car, launching it into the air. It landed on a second car twelve feet away with exact precision. The vehicles caught fire.

The wind changed, rocking the dock back and forth. The river was a means to end this unplanned phase of unwarranted destruction and act as salvation for a time. The brothers didn't require oxygen, but those chasing them did. They marched across the lawn as flames caught the gas tank of the overturned car. Both vehicles erupted into a towering inferno. Black smoke writhed and swirled into the air.

Sirens announced the next wave of vehicles, two this time. The click of a door and the cocking mechanism of a gun alerted This One to their next would-be aggressor.

"Freeze, that's far enough!" the organism said. This One turned. The organism was different, with no palpable fear intertwined with its rage. It thought it was safe behind the car.

His Twin bolted toward the organism and dove through the passenger-side door, tackling it onto the grass. It emptied its clip ineffectively as His Twin rose, towering over it.

The organism spoke fearlessly: "See you in—"

His Twin interrupted by repeatedly burying his fist into its head until nothing, but pulp remained. His Twin continued slowly toward the water until another organism discharged its weapon from the second car.

This One gripped the organism's head in his large metal palm. It fought, kicked, and screamed something muffled and inaudible. He squeezed. Its head burst, and its body dropped as a listless bag of meat, blood, and bone.

That was the last organism that opposed them. The others lingered on the opposite side of the house. More pulled up in boats and demanded surrender through megaphones. The two brothers walked into the water under a hail of gunfire and vanished under the current. The next stage of the Final Solution was safe inside of them.

They moved steel and other raw materials under Empire City through Miller's River until the frequency told them to stop. This One and His Twin ceased primary functions, allowing the life inside them to feed.

A craft splashed into the water. The Elder emerged from the hatch in an expulsion of air bubbles, and This One could sense the potent life inside him without the frequency. It was almost the end of this phase.

The Elder also had something more: the necessary data to complete their weapon.

*The world will burn.*

The other two of his kind agreed.

From: Commanding Officer, Special Services Division.

To: Chief of Detectives

Subject: Unknown Hostiles

Date: 10-19-53

Location: Northwell

1.	Police Lieutenant Richard Hill, Shield #274, assigned to this matter under the supervision of the undersigned reports as follows.

2.	On October 19th, 3:12 PM, eyewitnesses reported seeing fugitives Dr. Nadir Singh, M/36, and Lt. Frank Rivoli, M/63, on the southeastern shoreline of Northwell. All available units were dispatched, arriving at 4 Southshore Lane, the domicile of Lt. Frank Rivoli, at 3:52. Officers came upon resistance in what can only be described as two half-mechanical creatures. Overall, there were 13 casualties, all declared dead by the Northwell County coroner. The bodies of Dr. Singh and Lt. Rivoli were not recovered.

3.	The suspects are two unknown entities. They are still at large and considered extremely dangerous. Dr. Nadir Singh and Lt. Frank Rivoli are also missing and considered dangerous.

4.	The FBI took command of this case after a rendezvous with local law enforcement where they obtained clearance from the commanding officer. Agent Danvers of the FBI has requested all available units remain on high alert.

5.	There were 13 incidents in connection with this attack, 13 resulting in death.

6.         This matter will receive continued attention until such time as all entities are captured or terminated.

Howard Norman

Captain

NEEDS AND
WANTS

It had been a few hours since they'd carted Pop's body off, and the skewed world in front of Gordon's pillow didn't yet seem real. When he closed his eyes, he was forced to watch the hacksaw tear through his old man's exposed arm bone. Pop had the same haunted look in his eyes, dismembering himself as he did after hitting his son—longing for a peaceful past life just out of reach.

Walt stirred in his bed and exhaled, falling back to sleep. Gordon peeled his face off the pillow and slouched on the edge of his mattress, leering out the window, humming his mother's tune. Across the street, next to the police cruiser, Officer Kane spoke with a man who looked like a corpse stuffed into a suit as a chickadee sang its "see-saw" melody.

Gordon rose, stumbling against the torn wallpaper as a sudden bout of dizziness overcame him. His head throbbed, and with each pounding beat, the world fuzzed with static. In his mind, he saw Miss Mercury dancing across a pixelated screen, swaying to his mother's song. He shut his eyes, and she climbed from the television, sputtering with static and white noise. He could smell her sweet perfume amongst the electricity, Coty L'Origan, like Mom used to wear. She placed a hand on his shoulder and shook her dark hair out of her eyes. "I can't wait to marry you, Gordon."

Something in his belly jumped like he was on the roller coaster in Steel Harbor.

"Get the knife, Gordon," she said in a low, distorted voice, "wait for the police officer, and—"

Gordon's eyes shot open. He was standing in the kitchen over the garbage can, staring past unpaid bills, dented beer cans, and TV dinner boxes at the knife he'd thrown away last night. He gasped and ran up the stairs back to his bedroom, slamming the door and putting his weight against it.

"Gordie?" Walt sat up in bed, rubbing his eyes. "Where's Pop? I had the strangest dream..."

Gordon cracked the door and peered out into the empty hallway. "He's sick, Walt. Remember, the ambulance took him?"

"Oh yeah! Heck, I thought he'd be better by now! Silly ol' Pop was probably three sleet to the wind again!"

"Three *sheets* to the wind, Walt," Gordon said in an unavoidably sad tone. "But, you're right. I bet he was."

"Pop is such a nut!" Walt's eyes glazed over, and a tear rolled down his cheek.

Gordon ignored it. "Hungry?"

"Nah." Walt looked up hopefully. "Where's Officer Kane? He told me we could go for a ride in his cruiser today instada going to school."

Gordon sighed. "About that, Walt. I looked into it"—he kicked around the clothes on the floor, looking for the least dirty pair of pants—"Officer Kane works for the Dark Plunderer."

"No foolin'?" Walter's eyes went wide. "Geez! Too bad the radio doesn't work. We could see if the Enforcers were on. Ya know? To see if they talk about him."

Gordon glanced out the window, watching the cop and the ghoul in the suit through a dizzy haze. He remembered the static hiss of the radio reverberating around the shed as Pop mumbled math equations and something else—revenge from the water.

"Gordie?" Walter was standing, pulling on his sleeve. "Are you okay?"

Outside, Officer Kane shook the man in the suit's hand and started across the street.

# The City of the Gods: Gold

"Shit!" Gordon ducked and scampered across the floor, keeping his head under the window. He dumped school supplies out of Walt's rucksack.

Walt stared wide-eyed at the door. "Is that mean ol' Officer Kane coming, Gordie?"

"Shh!" Gordon nodded and loaded his decoder ring, Walt's BB gun, and whatever clothes fit into the sack. Downstairs, the screen door squealed.

"Boys? Are you awake?" Officer Kane called.

Gordon could see his father's bedroom through the crack in the door. Inside was a duffle bag he'd planned to fill with more clothes and whatever food was in the kitchen.

"Gordon? Walt?" The voice was distant.

Gordon scrambled across the room. "Quick, out the window. I'll meet you at the fortress."

The insides of Walt's eyebrows raised like they always did right before he was about to cry.

"I need you to be brave, Walt, like a real Enforcer."

Walt swallowed and nodded earnestly.

"Boys? How'd you like to take a ride in my cruiser?" Officer Kane called again. The stairs creaked.

Gordon quietly slid the window open and slipped an old *Velveteen Rabbit* book between the frame and the chipped sill. He tossed the rucksack through and listened for a thump on the grass.

*The knife!*

He eyed Walt. "Now you—"

"Boys? Walter? Gordon? You aren't in any trouble, fellas. That man I was talking to was a friend." Empty cans and bottles clinked as he moved past Pop's room.

*The cellar door!*

Walt eased himself through the window and onto the grass a few feet below.

"Remember, the fortress," Gordon said. The bedroom door creaked open slowly. "Go!"

Walt broke his wide-eyed gaze, grabbed the rucksack, and ran like a scared rabbit.

"Oh, Gordon, there you are. Didn't you hear me calling you?"

Gordon turned to meet Officer Kane's smiling face.

"How'd you boys like to take a ride in my black and white?" He placed his hands on his hips, barring the doorway. "Say, where's your brother?"

*Don't trust him. The man he was talking to will separate you and Walter. You'll never join the League of Enforcers,* the woman's distorted voice boomed through his head.

"He—he went to school." Gordon slumped onto the edge of the bed.

"I see," Officer Kane said, removing his hat. "Funny, I didn't see him leave, and I've been outside all morning."

Gordon shrugged and looked past the cop at the static fuzz dancing along the hallway wall.

Officer Kane took a seat on the bed. He smelled like Lifebuoy soap, like Pop used to. Gordon scooted away and eyed the baseball bat leaning against the wall in the back of the closet.

"Look, Gordon. I'm trying to help you, but all these stories about Walt going to school and your mother camping in Northwell." He chuckled and shook his head. "I was young once, too, you know? And boy, did I tell my share of whoppers."

*The knife!*

Gordon watched the cop's mouth move, but the voice reverberating around his skull drowned the words.

*The cellar door! Do it!*

Miss Mercury's static, black-and-white visage rose from the floorboards, pulling a robe over her slim frame. A tear drew a trail of mascara down her cheek as she moved silently to the door. *I thought you wanted to marry me, Gordon.* She strode into the hall, where her cries echoed.

"I do!" Gordon said.

"What?" Officer Kane replied.

*Then do as I say!*

Static danced around the room with laughs and sobs resounding. The sounds were like scraping a shard of glass over an open wound.

*ThE kNiFe!*

"Gordon?" The officer placed his hand on Gordon's shoulder.

*tHe CelLaR dOoR!*

"I know where Walt is." Gordon shut his eyes. "I'll take you to him."

"Great! Don't worry, I'm here to help you, boys, I promise." Officer Kane smiled with his whole face, even his eyes, just like Walt did. The same way Pop used to.

Gordon slid off the bed. "Let me grab my rucksack." He kicked dirty clothes aside on his way to the closet.

*Do it, Gordon!*

Gordon gripped the handle of the baseball bat. The bed squeaked as the cop stood.

*Do it!*

"Boy, we sure could use some rain." Officer Kane flopped his hat onto his head and flipped the brim back, gazing out the window. "I think a storm is just the thing to break this heatwa—"

The bat cracked and vibrated. Officer Kane's body dropped like a broken marionette. Blood spread across the wooden planks, soaking the rug under the bed.

"I-I'm sorry! I never meant—"

Officer Kane gurgled and twitched, staring through Gordon until the light faded from his eyes. Gordon dropped the bat and ran into the hallway. The door slammed, and he stopped to suck in air in short, audible gulps.

"I-I'm sorry—I'm so sorry!"

Through his watery eyes, Gordon saw Miss Mercury backlit in the living room.

*I can solve all your problems if you listen!*

Gordon straightened his back and stood a little taller.

She raised her finger to the sky. *Sabnock is waiting.*

**<u>89</u>**

"Why do you got such a big bag, Gordie?" Walt whispered vehemently through the broken balusters at the end of the porch.

Gordon hoisted Pop's old duffel bag onto his shoulder and locked the front door. "Because I'm never coming back here, Walt." He thumped down the rotten steps onto the sidewalk and dropped the key into the sewer grate.

"Whadja do that for?" Walt scampered ahead to try for some eye contact. "What'll happen to me?" He turned his attention to the empty police cruiser across the street. "Didja give that mean ol' cop the slip?"

Gordon picked up the pace. "You'll live at the fortress until you're old enough to join the Enforcers."

Walt kicked a rock into the street. "I never get to do anything!"

The boys trudged up Signal Ridge. "Walt, you're a good Junior Enforcer. You're just too little right now." Gordon looked over Steel Harbor one last time. Soon, summer would break, and childhood would vanish with it. Gordon turned away from the beach, from his hometown, his past. He turned away from games of hide-and-seek and kick-the-can. Gordon Ross, the man, couldn't be bothered with such things.

They moved through the stark white birch trees, hopping across the old railroad trusses scattered incrementally along the path until colorful leaves overtook them. The wind kept the bare branches alive.

Gordon spotted his bike leaning against a tree outside the fort. He pushed the door open and sank into one of the hunting chairs.

"The bikes are still outside," Walt announced proudly from the doorway.

"Good job, Walt," Gordon said with his back to the door as he rifled through the duffle bag.

Walter moved in front of Gordon, grinning. "Does that mean I get to come with you and the Enforcers? I'm a good guard, remember?"

Gordon sighed. "I don't want you getting hurt."

Walt's eyebrows turned up in the corners. "I won't get hurt, Gordie! I'm a good Junior Enforcer! Just like you said!"

Gordon burst from the chair, rushing past Walt, through the door, and into the pale white woods. The little fort was too claustrophobic; he couldn't breathe in there.

Walt exploded through the door behind him. "Please, Gordon! You can't leave me with Pop!"

Gordon closed his eyes. The final zip of the black bag containing his father's corpse echoed through the woods. He could see the emotionless G-men carting his body to the black van. The police were probably in the backyard now, looking for any reason a man would do what his father did. Maybe they'd find Officer Kane inside.

"Walt." He turned to his brother. "Pop's not going to hurt you anymore."

"How do you know?" Walter yelled.

"Because—" Gordon saw his father's gleeful face as he cranked the hacksaw through his arm. "I just know." He placed a hand on his brother's arm. "I'll check on you when I can, but you need to stay here!"

Walter pouted. "Okay, Gordon, whatever you say."

When the sun went down, the sound of the Coastal Highway lulled Walt to sleep, but when Gordon closed his eyes, he could only see Officer Kane sprawled across his bedroom in his final death throes.

*Boy, we sure could use some rain. I think a storm is just the thing to break this heatwa—*

**<u>90</u>**

After a breakfast of Cheez-Whiz and Oreo cookies from the duffel bag, Gordon made sure the fortress walls were sturdy and piled fresh leaves around the edges for insolation. He eyed the tree line protecting him from the prying eyes of Baggata Elementary, wondering where the Junior Enforcers had been. Even Billy hadn't come out yesterday.

Walter chased a squirrel around a tree until it vanished into a bush. "Fuck!"

Gordon chuckled. "Don't say that, Walt."

"How come? Pop says it."

Gordon tousled his brother's hair. "Remember what the Enforcers say? The words you use are the same as the face you present to the world."

"I know, Gordon. Please don't tell them I swore!"

"Well, alright," he teased, "but don't do it again."

Shadows vanished as the sun disappeared behind black, sluggish clouds. Crisp air whipped leaves around Gordon's feet. He closed his eyes and inhaled, but all he could see was the friendly smile of Officer Kane. *Boy, we sure could use some rain. I think a storm is just the thing to break this heatwa—*

"Where the fuck have you been?" Billy said, crawling through the brush. "The cops came to Baggata yesterday, lookin' for you."

Gordon turned to greet his friend, who stared at him through big saucer-like eyes.

"I-I wasn't feeling well—"

"Nuts to that. What about the cops? They asked if I seen you, but I didn't tell 'em nothin'."

487

"Thanks, pal," Gordon said.

Billy gawked at him like he had two heads. "What the hell did the coppers want with a guy like you? Your old man's gonna—"

"Pop went to the hospital," Walter chimed in from a tree he was climbing.

Billy hadn't blinked since he'd arrived. "The hospital?"

The bushes rustled, and Ukrit emerged, followed by a reserved Pratima. Billy scoffed, and Gordon adjusted the fortress's door, ignoring them. He watched Pratima approach from the corner of his eye and cleared a nervous tinge from his throat. "I didn't expect—"

Pratima fell into his arms, and Gordon's animosity faded. He pulled her close, inhaling the scent of her shampoo. She sobbed against his shoulder as the wind shifted through the branches and the clouds opened up, dumping rain.

"I'm sorry I left you at Sainte Marie Square, Gordon." She pushed back to meet his gaze. "I meant to apologize yesterday, but—my father is—well, he's missing!"

Gordon pulled her into his chest. Hugging her invited a dizzy flutter, and suddenly, the rain was as inconsequential as the horrors he'd experienced the past few days. "There, there. The Junior Enforcers will—"

Pratima pushed away. Her teeth and fists clenched. "Enough with your bloody Junior Enforcers! This is serious!"

"The Junior Enforcers are serious!" Gordon yelled, stepping forward. His shoulders heaved. "You're just like my mother! She—"

Pratima yelped and recoiled. Gordon noticed all eyes were on him as he clutched a large stick he never remembered picking up. He dropped it like it was on fire.

# The City of the Gods: Gold

*The knife.*

"Stay away from me!" Gordon screamed. "I have work to do!" He turned back to the fortress.

*The cellar door.*

Billy, Ukrit, and Walter all displayed various levels of worry but remained silent. Pratima stomped forward and pursed her lips to speak when the low hum of an air-raid siren interrupted everything.

Lightning flashed against the black sky, followed by the low rumble of thunder. Everyone shifted their attention toward the school as the siren's scream grew louder. Gordon smiled. That sound would bring the Enforcers.

"Oh shit, Gordon," Billy said. "I bet it's the Commies. Joey Taylor said they have a bomb that'll destroy a whole city." He stood halfway in the fortress, peering out hesitantly at the sky.

Gordon pushed past him into the fortress and upended the rucksack. He slid his decoder ring onto his finger and loaded the BB gun as the Junior Enforcers filed in behind him.

"What's the plan, Gordon? Ukrit here looks like he might shit his pants." Billy smirked and tossed his wet hair to the side.

"Shut up!" Ukrit said.

Gordon loaded the BB gun and the ammo back into the rucksack, leaving clothes in a heap on the ground. "Bill and I will scout ahead. You guys wait here."

Pratima snatched Ukrit's arm. "We're leaving! We just lost Father, and I'll not have you staying here to die in this godforsaken place."

Ukrit's jaw dropped. "But—"

"No buts, I'm your big sister!" She yanked him toward the door. "Can't you hear those horrible air-raid sirens? We need to seek shelter in a safe place."

Billy placed his hands on his hips and puffed out his chest. "This fortress is the safest place around, toots! See Gordon? I told you the Junior Enforcers was no place for girls!"

"Ready, Private Billy?" Gordon bit his lip to hide a smile.

Pratima pressed her hand on Gordon's chest. "This is real, don't you understand? If you go out there, you could *die!*"

Billy laughed. "I knew this broad was daffy. We're the Junior *Enforcers!*"

Walter glanced timidly out into the rain-soaked world as thunder rocked the fort. "I don't know, Gordie. Maybe she's right."

Gordon pushed through the group. "Walter, I need you to watch over the fort. Whoever is attacking the city might try to double back and attack us where we live."

"I want to go!" Ukrit yelled.

"No, Ukrit!" Pratima stepped in front of Gordon. "Please don't do this."

Billy ran out into the pouring rain. "Ha! Stay here with the skirt, you sissies."

"I'm not a sissy, you fatass!" Walt called after him. He pouted. "I'm not a sissy, Gordon!"

Gordon crouched to meet his brother's eye line, ignoring Pratima's pleas. "I know, Walt, but you're in charge while I'm gone. Can you handle that?"

Walter wiped a tear away and crossed his arms over his chest. "I can handle it, Gordon!"

"Good, I feel bad for any villains who come here lookin' for trouble!" Gordon gave Walt a playful shot to the arm, and the all too familiar sting returned behind his eyes. "I guess...I'll see you in a couple of years. You know, when the Enforcers and I come to get you. There's food and clothes in the duffle bag."

Gordon looked away and cleared his throat. Walt wrapped his arms around his brother's neck and squeezed.

"It'll be here before you know it. Take care of the Junior Enforcers while I'm gone, alright? Don't let 'em walk all over you." Gordon managed.

"I love you, Gordie," Walt said.

"I love you too, Walt." Gordon snatched the rucksack and pushed through the door into the rain before Pratima could see he was crying.

**<u>91</u>**

The air-raid siren shrieked. Gordon cranked his bike pedals, climbing Lovers Lane with Billy in tow. He skidded to a stop at the abandoned make out overlook and scanned the towering skyscrapers through the sheets of rain.

"Jesus Christ," Billy wheezed, stopping behind him breathlessly.

"Do you think the Sears on Broadway still has that Viking console set on display in the front window?"

"It's worth a—there!" Billy yelled. Gordon followed his outstretched finger to a small swarm buzzing near the western shore.

"It looks like it's in Calway or Westport, maybe," Gordon said.

Billy squinted. "Who do you think it is? The… Bee?"

Gordon rolled his eyes. "That's not even a real bad guy." He shrugged. "Could be the Dark Plunderer's minions."

Billy stared wide-eyed. "They can't fly, can they?"

A helicopter burst from behind the tree line, dusting the boys and shooting like a dart into the city. Gordon stared in awe.

Billy recoiled. "Jesus!"

The helicopter grew smaller, and the swarm darted angrily at the thumping blades until the fuselage spun out and careened into a building.

"Holy shit! Did you see that? Those things ripped that fucking helicopter to smithereens!" Billy cried.

"Let's get down there!" Gordon said.

"But I—aren't we supposed to—don't we need backup?" Billy worked to form a coherent sentence.

"C'mon, don't you want to be a hero?" Gordon stood on his pedals and let the bike carry him down the hill. Lightning lit up the city, followed by a loud thunderclap.

"Junior Enforcers, away!" Water shot out under the tires as Gordon blasted like a rocket down the hill, speeding onto Jasper Street. "The bigger they are, the harder they fall! Bud-um bud-uh! Here come the Junior Enforcers!"

Gordon hopped onto the curb to dodge debris and ride around stalled cars. Billy rode more conservatively, watching the sky. They took a left on Sunrise Drive and a right down Wolf Street. Screams echoed between the tall buildings, followed by a low mechanical hum and the same distant buzz of a broken radio Gordon had heard in the shed.

Fallen stonework and glass forced them west along Grant Road. They rode against panicked groups, fleeing for their lives. Filthy people covered in dust, mud, and torn clothing stared out from alleyways, shouting warnings. Billy stopped next to a station wagon, nervously staring into the distance.

Gordon continued toward the mechanical whirring until a barricade of overturned cars blocked Lincoln. He hopped off and walked his bike around, stopping to yell: "C'mon, you sissy! Where's your sense of—"

A woman's scream reverberated down the street, and hordes of shrieking people exploded around the corner from Wilmore Drive.

The earth quaked, and some smaller debris leaped off the concrete rhythmically. Shards of glass and pieces of ornamental arches and stone pillars fell from the skyscrapers, shattering on the sidewalk.

Gordon squinted through the rain to the west. A few blocks down, something enormous and metallic trudged between the buildings on four legs. Above the fifteen-story thing, human-sized insects carried people, vanishing on top of the four-legged monster.

Billy's brakes squealed next to him. He gawked down the street. "Gordon, what the hell is that thing?"

Another crowd bolted by, screaming and sprinting around and over cars, debris, and other people. Gordon ditched his bike and inched along the edges of abandoned vehicles, moving against the masses. He pressed into a doorway, clutching the rucksack. When the crowd dwindled, Gordon stepped into the street, pulled out his BB gun, and raised it to eye level. The metallic creature lurched forward, forcing cars to bounce on their shocks and sending rubble falling from the buildings with each deafening step. It tore through the suspended train tracks over Scorpio Drive.

Gordon aimed. "Alright, ugly, you messed with the wrong city."

Billy skidded to a stop behind him. "Holy shit, Gordon! Maybe we should hold back for a second—let the Enforcers—ya know—catch up."

The walker's gears and pistons hissed and churned. Gordon dropped the barrel of the gun and squinted through the rain. Something was on top, fighting the swarm.

Gordon pointed excitedly. "Look up there, Bill! I bet that's Captain Wonderful!"

Shots rang out, and a blast of light split the gray sky. A woman leaped from a building onto the back of the walking thing. "Look, Billy! It's the Scarlet Sparrow! They're here; they're all finally here!"

People around them scanned the sky, frantically calling out to their loved ones. While others dragged injured and bloodied bodies out of the fray.

"Gordon, we gotta get outta here," Billy said.

Gordon dug in the rucksack for a box of BBs and reloaded. "I'll cover you, Scarlet Sparrow!" He pulled the cocking lever and aimed.

"You're on your own, Gordon!" He heard Billy's tires rolling over the wet concrete until they vanished.

Gordon turned to yell after him when a voice in his head whispered, *you don't need him. You don't need anyone but me.*

"Junior Enforcers, away!" Gordon advanced toward the hulking creature, pumping the cocking lever and firing with each step, walking past structures that looked like they had been gutted, spilling debris from their bowels onto the street. Part of a train jutted from an office building with the wheels still sparking. Lifeless people hung out the windows in a mess of blood and flesh. *Those dumb cops can't stop me. Pop can't stop me. I'll show 'em all! I'm an Enforcer!*

# The City of the Gods: Gold

The robot was three blocks away. The world jumped and crumbled. Gordon aimed the shaking barrel at the thing's leg, waiting for a clear shot. As much as he reveled in the idea of being a hero, part of him couldn't wait until this was over. He'd get a victory kiss from Miss Mercury, talk strategy with Captain Wonderful, and try out the Scarlet Sparrow's latest invention. One good shot was all he needed.

"Gordie?" Behind him, Walter straddled his bike in the middle of the street. Rain trailed from his soaking wet hair into his squinting eyes. "Gordie, we have to go home. Pop'll be mad."

The shrill, scraping metal grew louder. Gordon turned back to face the beast and steadied his gun. The monster's foot crushed a Studebaker like a soda can. He fingered the trigger. "Not now, Walter!"

"But the sun's probably down, Gordie. And Pop won't like that we're all wet."

Gordon shook his head and aimed the gun. "Walter, go back to the fortress." He pushed the words out through the lump choking his throat.

The ground repeatedly detonated under enormous metal feet. Puddles rippled, and cracks in the street crawled outward.

Gordon heard Walt's bike drop, and his brother's hand was on his shoulder. "I can't go back without you, Gordie, please!"

Gordon shut his burning eyes. The slam of the metallic foot echoed through the buildings.

"Gordie, please, let's just go home," Walter said. Gordon could hear his voice shaking, but he couldn't bring himself to tell his brother there was no more home to go back to. Pop was dead, Mom was gone, and he had killed a man to protect what little family he had left.

"I can't," Gordon said weakly and steadied the gun. "Not till I prove I'm worth something!"

Concrete shook, and a crack in the ground climbed a building. Gordon looked up as a mass of stone fell. He shoved Walt aside as an ornamental gargoyle pinned him to the street. Pain shot through his legs and faded.

"Gordie!" Walter ran to his brother's side.

Gordon watched the black sky and took a deep, shuddering breath. The gargoyle grinned. Flashes of static covered its features and faded. It should have been heavy across his lap, but it felt weightless. In the distance, a loon howled over the laughter of a clown.

Walt held him close, sobbing into his wet clothes.

"Walt," Gordon croaked, "run." The robot's metallic hoof gleamed as it rose.

*Boom!* The streetlights flickered on; it was time to go.

*Boom!* A crack parted the sidewalk they were pinned to.

*Boom!* Gordon hugged his brother, and the earth shook itself apart underneath them.

FATE
INTERCEPTS
DESTINY

Gibson set the Colt Commander back onto the table and reached for the cigarette perched on the ashtray next to the Corby's bottle. He took a shaky drag and clicked on the radio for a reprieve from the carnival that was his mind. The speaker sputtered and buzzed. He turned it off; he was sick of that song.

*Bang!* The neighbor's door slammed shut. Gibson spun and eyed his front door, still bolted and chain locked. He wiped his brow.

*Maybe Slim's right. Maybe I should get the hell outta Empire, find a girl, have a normal life.* He pictured Ann standing on the boardwalk, smiling as the sea air whipped through her blonde curls. He could call her, win her back, go someplace where it was warm year-round, and people had never heard of Ron Baxter.

No. Escaping with Ann was a nice dream, but it wasn't in the cards while he had a target on his back. Instead, Gibson crammed himself into the breakfast nook with the pistol and a half bottle of whiskey to keep him company. He lifted the *Bulletin*, but his racing mind blurred the black and white, so he folded the paper and gazed out the window at the sleek buildings cutting into the gray sky. Bonnie was out there somewhere; she had to be.

Something Slim had mentioned refused to relent—something involving human sacrifices and the Enforcers, and how Bonnie could be wrapped up in it. Baxter wanted her, but maybe someone else did, too. The cold, dead stare of the woman with the deer antlers nailed to her head watched Gibson from his thoughts.

He abandoned the breakfast nook and wandered to the windowsill with his pack of Luckys, lighting another cigarette. A middle-aged man in a suit too expensive for this neighborhood loitered by the Plymouth. Gibson picked up the Colt again. The weapon's weight calmed his quick breathing.

# The City of the Gods: Gold

The man split time between checking his watch and glancing down the street. Gibson double-checked the gun was loaded. It was. A young woman approached, and the man smiled with a false sense of confidence. Gibson followed them with his eyes until they turned on Scorpio and vanished.

He exhaled and returned to the horizon, fixating on the unfinished building Slim had pointed out at Wilbur's. It stood out like a sore thumb, but he'd never noticed it until it was spilled in his lap by a half-drunk old man. Maybe Gibson was a shitty detective after all. Still, his thoughts refused to leave Bonnie, even when his own life was in danger, and that obsession had to count for something.

Gibson thought about the gray areas Slim had mentioned. The place outside law and decency. He glanced at the *Eddie Wilbur* file, sitting amongst old beer cans on his coffee table, and considered the dirty, rotten cops who made up the ECPD. He thought about Baxter and that mountain of bodies in his house. He thought about the bodies the Enforcers were hypothetically sitting on—all people operating in gray areas with no retribution. Gibson leaned on the window frame, watching the black clouds churn. The asphalt smelled like rain.

*Was Murphy lying? Had this been our case before we got too close?*

*Did Creed try to get me on Baxter's payroll so I'd stop asking questions?*

*How do James and Theodora Connor fit in? Are they victims, or is there something more nefarious under the surface?*

*Was Slim lying? Is he involved?*

Gibson's head was swimming, so he clung to what Theodora had said: *How do you behave when the world you know and love comes crashing down around you, and there is no right or wrong anymore, just survival? Just preservation of life?*

He took a long, thoughtful drag from his cigarette. *How would I—as Theodora Connor—behave when there's no right and wrong anymore? How do I survive when the rest of the world is full of people operating outside the law?*

Gibson's eyes widened; he mashed the cigarette into an ashtray and shot to his feet. *I'd kidnap my own daughter to keep her safe!*

**<u>93</u>**

The shocks wheezed as the Concord sped off the Bunche Bridge into suburbia. Gibson took a hard right onto North Avenue and slowed to a crawl through the Connors' open gate. He couldn't shake the nagging feeling he was missing something. It would have been nice to talk it through with Slim, but there was no time.

Gibson killed the engine, fired up a Lucky, and leaned on the hood of his car, scanning the glass domes and the metal walls of the Connor estate.

*Well, here I am. What now? I can't just knock on the door and ask if they've kidnapped their daughter.*

Thunderheads rumbled, and the patter of rain landing amongst the dead leaves made Gibson pine for his bed. The heat broke, as promised, and the sweeping drizzle picked up. Lightning ripped above the house, and another ominous rumble of thunder.

Gibson sucked on his cigarette. The front door creaked open, and Theodora stepped onto the porch. Her white, flowing dress whipped and cracked in the wind. She threw her long hair back and yelled into the storm: "Beautiful day, isn't it?"

Gibson lifted himself off the hood and deposited the cigarette stub into the overgrown lawn, feeling every ounce of the Colt hanging from the shoulder holster. "Sure."

Theodora laughed. "Are you going to stand in the rain all day?"

Gibson sheepishly slid his hands into his pockets and kicked his way through piles of heavy, wet leaves to the porch. He forced a smile.

Theodora smiled back. It seemed genuine until Gibson remembered what she had said last time he was here. *Lucky for me, my mother was an actress. She taught me all the tricks.*

"You're all wet, detective," she said. "Come in, won't you?"

Gibson took his hat in his hands. "Just checking in. I wouldn't want to drip all over your floor."

"Nonsense." Theodora motioned for Gibson to follow. "Come, we'll chat in the parlor."

Gibson's socks squished in his shoes, and his heavy, wet clothes stuck to his body like plaster, dripping all over the oriental rug. "I don't mean to impose; I was in the neighborhood, and I thought—" Gibson didn't know what he'd been thinking.

Theodora's bare feet padded along the floor ahead of him. "Would you like some dry clothes? I'm sure James has something that would fit you."

"No, I won't be staying long."

"Are you sure?"

"Yeah, I have an appointment with the Chief of Detectives in an hour," he lied. "Thanks anyway."

"Suit yourself." She turned, entering the parlor.

Gibson followed cautiously. "Is your husband home?"

Theodora stopped suddenly and turned. "You look like you could use a drink." Behind her, a fire crackled in the fireplace, but Empire had been an oven until a few minutes ago.

"I'm fine, thank you."

The rain beat relentlessly against the windows. Fingers of lightning threw unrecognizable shadows against the far wall.

"Well, don't mind if I do. It's been quite a day." She moved to the bar cart and played with the bottles. "Please have a seat by the fire. Maybe you can dry off before your appointment."

Ice cubes clinked into a glass, followed by a smooth pouring sound. Gibson eased onto the edge of the velvet couch next to the fireplace. "Are you sure you wouldn't like me to sit somewhere... less expensive?"

Theodora took a swallow and sauntered to the matching chair opposite him. "It's just a sofa. Are you sure I can't get you anything, detective?"

"No, thank you, ma'am." The formality was another piece moved in the mental chess match they'd been involved in since he'd arrived.

"Ma'am?" she asked.

*Check.*

"I thought we were better acquainted, Skipper." She pouted playfully. "Aw, you really are going to make me drink alone, aren't you?"

*Check.*

Gibson eyed the doorway and cleared his throat. "Fine. Whiskey, neat."

Theodora smiled. "That's the spirit." She strolled across the room to the bar cart. "As I recall, you prefer Corby's?"

"That's just something my partner teases me about."

Lightning turned the lawn from gray to gold. In the distance, an air-raid siren hummed faintly.

"It sounds like Empire's in trouble," Gibson said.

"Sounds like it," Theodora responded.

"I read somewhere the Russians have some kind of world-ending bomb." Gibson moved to the window, but nothing looked out of sorts except the weather.

"Don't worry, it's not that."

*Check.*

Gibson eyed her curiously. "How do you know?" he asked, returning to his wet spot on the sofa.

"We'll get to that." She floated daintily across the room and handed Gibson his drink.

*Checkmate.*

Gibson had lost when he pulled through the gate that had been purposefully left open and entered this absurd house where Theodora Connor had been waiting for him. She watched him with the light from the out-of-place crackling fire dancing in her eyes. The air-raid siren sang. Gibson sipped his whiskey. Perhaps it would be his last drink.

She regarded the window. "Boy, some storm out there. We needed it, I suppose. That heat was—"

"What have you done with Bonnie?" Gibson set his drink down.

She sank into the armchair and smiled. "Where's your partner today?"

"He has the day off."

Theodora studied him with her eager eyes. "Just you and me all alone in this big house?" She brushed her hair over her shoulder. "What will the neighbors think?"

"I believe I asked you a question."

"We'll get to that." She smiled earnestly and ran a finger over her clavicle. "I'd like to enjoy my drink first."

Gibson watched her raise the glass to her lips. There was still no ring on her finger, and the sheer dress clinging to her body left little to the imagination.

"Where is your husband?"

Theodora burst into laughter so suddenly it made him jump. "Aren't you tenacious?"

"Well?" Gibson eyed the window. "Last time I saw you, you were covered in dirt."

"He isn't buried in the backyard if that's what you're implying. The last time you were here, I had just finished planting marigolds. They're Bonnie's favorite." The smile wouldn't leave her face. "I've been waiting for you for a long time, detective. Longer than you've been alive." She sipped her drink, but her eyes never left his.

"What does that mean? I'm in no mood for riddles."

Theodora placed a hand over her lips to stifle a giggle. "Let's start with a question; why do you think you're here? To what do I owe the pleasure of your company this afternoon, Detective Gibson?"

He eyed the door. "You knew I was coming."

Theodora leaned back in her chair as a lightning bolt lit up the sky. "I did." She smiled, and thunder cracked like a tree splitting in half. "I knew you'd come back, just like you knew I had Bonnie since we met. Isn't that right, Skip?"

# The City of the Gods: Gold

Gibson fingered his gun.

"There's no need for that," Theodora said, eyeing the Colt. "We're just talking. Believe it or not, we're on the same side."

"Then, why kidnap Bonnie?" He watched Theodora's face for any tell, but her features were stone.

"Well"—she traced the floor with her eyes—"the short answer is, to protect the city, you can hear the air-raid siren from here." She smiled. "You mentioned that. You see, Bonnie needs to be missing for the ultimate sacrifice to take place." Her face grew somber and unsettled. "I also missed her; she's my daughter—"

"Exactly!" Gibson interrupted. "She's your daughter. Why put everyone through this?"

"For the greater good," she said. "I can't tell you everything, but you must trust me." A rumble of thunder shook the house, and the lights flickered. Theodora didn't flinch. "Unfortunately, you will find everything out in time, Skip, and I can't tell you how sorry I am for that."

"Are you protecting her from Ron?" Gibson pressed her.

"No. Ron is playing with things he doesn't understand. Like many other faiths we've misinterpreted, the Sibylline Religion is just one man's desires broadcast as the word of something greater. Ron's in love with his cult because he's in love with power. He's using people, which is terrible, but none of his actions inspire loyalty." She glanced out the window thoughtfully. "No, Skip, it's not Ron we need to worry about. I kidnapped Bonnie to protect her from myself."

"That makes no sense!"

"The Theodora Connor you know from the papers is unhinged and dangerous. I should know; I used to be her."

Gibson shot to his feet. "So, you're what? From the future? A Martian shapeshifter? A spirit? Tell me when I'm getting close."

Theodora laughed. "You watch too many movies, Skip, and that's coming from someone who adores the silver screen."

Gibson could only stare, more insulted than bewildered. This was a pitiful lie, even for someone as off her rocker as Theodora.

"I know how absurd this sounds," she said, "but you need to trust me." She rose and took his hands; he was a child again, unencumbered by the weight of the world. He smiled, and his eyes welled up as reservations abandoned him. For one beautiful moment, he was one with the universe, falling in love with the idea of something infinite he couldn't name because there was no word for it. He saw the creation of galaxies. Entire lives of people he cared about, beginning and ending. Tears streamed down his face.

Gibson yanked his hands away, refusing to believe what he'd seen. It was a flash of lightning, a trick of the eye, a drug in his drink—anything but that. He blinked away a few stray tears.

Theodora drifted to the window. "I used to be like you, running into situations without thinking them through. Like you did in Sainte Marie Square and Ron's house. And like you did here today. It's not a bad quality, but luck has to be on your side." She glanced back at Gibson. He felt two inches tall.

"I caused a lot of problems by not thinking things through. So here I am, atoning for my past. It's my penance, self-appointed, but a penance, nonetheless. Helping you is just a small part of it. And really, it's self-serving in the end, but isn't anything we do for the greater good always self-serving?"

"Unless you're a hero," Gibson answered. "Or a martyr."

"And which one are you? I know you risked your life to find my daughter."

Gibson shook his head. "I'm just doing my job."

"And who do you work for? Ron Baxter's police department?"

"I'm still a cop." He tried to stop his hand from shaking as he reached for the cuffs hanging from his belt.

Theodora laughed. "Don't do that."

Gibson released the cuffs and sighed.

Theodora turned to the window, watching the rain patter against the glass. "Skip, didn't you learn anything through all this?" She walked back across the room to where he was standing.

Gibson studied her golden-brown eyes with flecks of the divine still lingering in the unnatural color.

"I'm sorry to drag you through this mess, but I couldn't reveal I had Bonnie until I knew for certain you were the man I was waiting for."

"I'm a rookie detective, that's all," he said firmly.

She placed her soft hand on his face, and he saw her clearly again: magnificent, flawless. The universe expanded across her skin, and her freckles became burning stars, forming galaxies. She was a creator, a destroyer, the Alpha, and the Omega. He fell in love with her and hated her. She was life, she was death, and all the experiences in between. She was all around him, and her voice boomed through his mind.

"I'm not who you think I am, Skip. Not really, anyway. I look like Theodora Connor, sure, and once upon a time, I was her, but—it's all so complex."

"Who are you then?" he asked through a broad, uncontrollable smile as tears streamed down his face. He knew the answer, but he needed to hear it.

"I've been called many things in my many lives, but the answer you're looking for is Dea."

"Dea." The word tumbled from his mouth.

Theodora released her grip. The room's four walls became very apparent, the furniture was back, and she was flesh and blood again. She sighed. "You aren't ready."

Gibson watched her, unsure who or what he was speaking with. He remembered her touching his face, but not the exact details. "So, where is Bonnie now?" he stammered.

Theodora smiled. "I'm glad you came here today. You didn't know what you'd find, but you came anyway. It gives me hope. You aren't ready yet, but you will be. I have faith in you, Skipper."

He cocked an eyebrow. "What do you mean I'll be ready? Ready for what?"

"The end," she said with a tight smirk. "You'll see in time, but I've already said too much." She stifled a laugh. "It's like watching a movie you've seen a thousand times with someone who's never seen it! You'd never forgive me if I spoiled the ending."

The grandfather clock chimed. Her face grew somber and troubled. "I'm afraid I need to leave. You'll find Bonnie down the hall, sleeping peacefully." A fearful look washed over her face as she chose her words. "This disturbance in Empire will be the most horrific thing the city has seen since T-Day." She took a deep breath. "Bring Bonnie into the heart of it. Theodora Connor needs to know her sacrifice wasn't in vain once Sabnock leaves her. Her mind is so clouded right now. Bonnie will bring clarity." She glanced away. "You'll find her in a place she and I love dearly. She won't know you because she's never met you, but when you see her, help her. She may look strong, but it's all an act to save face. She's weak, and she's scared. Please let her know you're there for her. And be there for Bonnie. Especially for Bonnie. Can you do that? Can you finish what I started?"

# The City of the Gods: Gold

There was a tangible shift in the universe, and Gibson remembered what he'd experienced moments ago. This woman, whoever or whatever she was, didn't have a secret agenda or a diabolical plan. She wasn't trying to hurt him or anyone. She was surviving in a world full of gray areas, just like he was. He nodded.

She approached slowly, gazing into his eyes with an unspirited look. The spark had faded, and only embers of her soul shone through. "I hope you find your way soon, for Empire's sake, for the world's sake, and especially, for your sake. For now, please find Theodora. I—she needs to say goodbye."

She pulled him close and held him tight. The world dropped away again, but he closed his eyes. He'd seen enough of that. Her skin was soft, and she smelled like a woman, like summer at the beach. Salt and earth, like Ann once had. He thought her name again: *Dea*.

"Skip, I think this is the beginning of a beautiful friendship," she said.

Gibson peeled himself away, gazed into her eyes, and smiled genuinely for the first time in a long time. "Casablanca."

She nodded.

"How do I know I can trust you?" he asked.

"You don't," she said with an impish smile, "but please have some faith. Just like I have faith in you, I'm trusting you with Bonnie, the most important person to me, the most important person in all of this."

The room fell away behind her, and Gibson squinted at the image of a little white cottage sitting alone beside a shimmering body of water. He blinked, and it was gone.

She smiled. "If all else fails, and it will—find the Oracle. She's the constant." As she faded into the light, her fiery eyes watched him, and her smile told Gibson this was how it had to be.

"Wait, what does that mean?"

The light faded. The room returned to normal; the material possessions of a woman who may or may not have existed anymore lingered to gather dust. The oddly shaped house built into the side of a hill, made of metal, wood, rock, and glass, now felt like a mausoleum.

Gibson watched the puddles gathered on the patio through the window. Drops trickled across the still water and came to a complete and sudden stop. Reality caught him, and he shook his head. The kidnapper had escaped on faith, terms she had decided. He chose to ignore what he'd seen if only to keep a shred of his sanity. Still, the name stuck in his head. *Dea.*

Gibson shuffled through the hallway, lined with framed news clippings of the League of Enforcers' adventures. The heroics of Empire City's saviors, frozen in time, they seemed meaningless now. He paid them no mind as he moved down the hall and pushed open a cracked door. Bonnie was sleeping soundly, her auburn curls spread across the pillow under her small, peaceful face. *Maybe faith is what I've been missing. I've gone by the book, and it's gotten me nowhere. I've thrown the book out the window, and it's gotten me nowhere. So far, faith got Bonnie back*—he smiled—*and at the end of the day, she's what matters.*

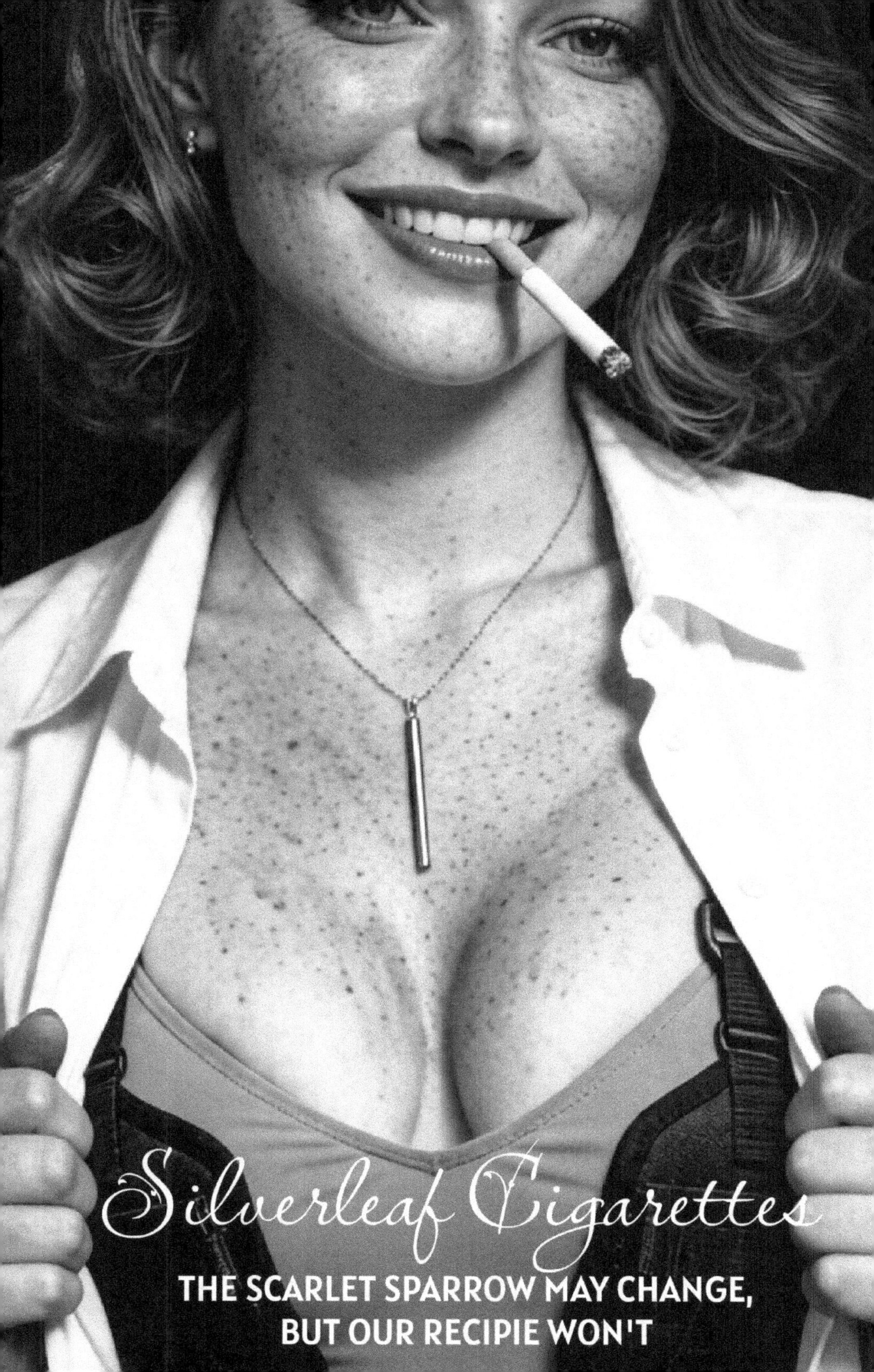
Silverleaf Cigarettes
THE SCARLET SPARROW MAY CHANGE,
BUT OUR RECIPIE WON'T

A
GOOD
DEED
IN A
WEARY
WORLD

## 94

Cal ground his teeth as the Redbird careened into Earth's atmosphere, jolting the fuselage and nearly rocking him unconscious.

Theo maintained her death grip on the shuttering yoke. "It looks like our ugly friend ditched my ship in the river near Calway," she yelled over the engine. "If I hadn't had to fix the Einstein-Rosen Bridge Generator, we would have intercepted it."

The Redbird steadied. Theo grabbed the radio handset. "Washington International approach, this is Redbird Delta Eco November four miles south of your location, at twelve thousand feet, heading two sixty, requesting to transition into your airspace to the south."

Static answered. Theo pulled back on the throttle, slowing the ship. "Approach, come back. Redbird Delta Eco November, requesting squawk code and local altimeter." Static crackled again.

"I guess we aren't landing in Terrytown," she grumbled, thrusting the ship forward through the pea-soup clouds, giving way to the sprawling terrain. Water droplets ran over the windshield. "Looks like it might finally rain."

From this height, Empire was a slab of concrete, but as the Redbird soared closer, the city became a complex machine, with moving parts pumping life into the pavement. Cal smiled. He was almost home.

Theo glanced between her equipment on the console and a black screen with jumping green lines. "What the hell is that in the water?" She pressed a button below the screen, cycling through graphs and charts. "I can't get a reading. Hang on." She spun the yoke, and the right side of the Redbird dipped, spreading the city out under Cal again. "See anything?"

Cal leaned forward and looked downstream. A mass stirred beneath the surface, like a school of fish the size of a city block. "It's a—"

A swarm exploded from the water in a fury of flashing metal. Cal lost visual as the ship righted itself. "Wait!"

"I saw it." Theo flipped a few levers and yanked back on the yoke. The ship quaked as it climbed. Cal's stomach dropped.

"Woah!" Theo rolled the Redbird left as something whizzed by the nose cone into the clouds. More silvery shapes rushed past on each side. Cal's head snapped back as the Redbird shot forward like a bullet.

"So much for staying out of commercial airspace." The Redbird spun left and right, narrowly avoiding the swarm shooting upward from the city. One careened off the ship's protective shield in an orange flash of light. It looked human, only larger, and covered in armor.

"This hunk of junk," Theo said through gritted teeth. "These shields are already almost spent. Another couple hits, and we're toast." She flipped up two clear covers and pressed red buttons on either end of the yoke.

*Thunk! Thunk! Thunk! Thunk! Thunk!* Heavy rounds exploded from mounted guns, shaking the floor as the chambers emptied. Bullets ripped a hole in the swarm. The ship spun back and forth and upside down, each move narrowly avoiding the dangerous new air traffic. A Douglas DC-6 commercial aircraft dropped below the clouds ahead.

"Theo!" Cal yelled.

"I see it," Theo muttered, pressing a button under her monitor, cycling through the charts and graphs. "Damnit. Hang on!" The swarm came up fast.

*Thunk! Thunk! Thunk! Thunk! Thunk!* The machine gun blew through it, sending chunks of metal plummeting to Earth. Theo navigated through the debris and surviving members of the horde.

"These things'll tear that DC-6 to shreds." She grabbed the radio handpiece. "Mayday! Mayday! Commercial aircraft, divert course. This is Scarlet Sparrow of the League of Enforcers, hailing from Redbird Delta Eco November. I repeat, divert course immediately!"

The radio hissed. Theo slammed the handpiece. "We need to help them."

Cal eyed the flyers' reinforcements, veering toward the DC-6. "Help them how?"

Theo throttled up, and the Redbird shot directly at the front of the aircraft.

Cal clutched the armrests. "Theo?"

The sound of the DC-6's engines was deafening. Something on the console screamed a warning to match a flashing red light. Cal met the stunned gaze of the aircraft's pilot just before Theo dipped the nose cone, falling directly beneath the plane.

Cal's frame turned to jelly as the DC-6's engines roared overhead. Theo yanked back on the yoke, and the Redbird shot straight up behind the plane, hovering upside down over the fuselage.

Machine-gun fire split the incoming horde. Some exploded, others tumbled to the Earth, bullet-riddled and limp, but a larger mass waited ahead. Lightning cut through the sky, followed by a low rumble of thunder. Theo accelerated in front of the commercial aircraft and righted the ship.

In the distance, an air-raid siren shrieked. The throng obscured the sky. Theo pumped a small black button in the middle of the console. The fuel gauges dropped at once, and alarms cried a warning on deaf ears. "I diverted all power to the shields."

The swarm was on them, but the orange barrier plowed through. Alarms continued their needless song as the ship dropped, collecting the creatures. The Douglas DC-6 roared overhead. The Redbird died with a coughing sputter, and her gadgets became inert.

Theo slammed a red button, and the hatch in the back opened. "I'm sorry," she yelled, springing to her feet. "I made a promise, and I intend to keep it."

"What?" Cal pressed against the seat, but the seatbelt held him in place.

"Please forgive me." She snatched both parachutes off the wall and sprinted toward the open door, leaping into the dark, overcast sky.

"Theo, wait!"

Metal bent and whined as gnashing claws tore at the hull, turning it into a sieve. Cal ripped his seatbelt off and moved to the ship's rear, searching unsuccessfully for another parachute. The horde sunk their claws in and lifted what remained of the Redbird straight up into the dark sky.

One of the wings ripped off and spun away in a frenzy of fire and smoke. The plane whirled in the opposite direction, forcing Cal toward the door. His back hit the metal frame, and a gust of wind pulled him into the cool air. He spun helplessly like a ragdoll, trading the view of a gray overcast sky with Empire City until it became one indecipherable blur. The air-raid siren sang in the distance. Above him, creatures ripped through the Redbird's carcass until an explosion lit up the sky and scattered the horde. Fire and debris rained over the city, and smoke remained suspended like a painting over the cloud coverage.

He didn't bother to scream as the city shot toward him. There was a quick thump, then nothing.

**95**

Cal awoke in a featureless room, waiting for pain that never arrived. His breath left in a thick huff of steam, and the overpowering aroma of jasmine and sandalwood made him want to wretch.

# The City of the Gods: Gold

Smoke trailed from the darkness at infinite points, meeting in the east, where it created a thin visage of a wolf's head, staring through piercing red eyes.

*Rat-tat-tat-tat!* Cal jumped at the sudden chatter from a Japanese M1 carbine. He held Jerry close, watching him cough blood onto his uniform. "Cal, go get Theo. Tell her to tell Baxter I'm ready. It's time for Plan B." He smiled, and his head dropped. Cal sat in the bunker, holding his dead brother for hours, days, or centuries. Time was meaningless here.

"Find the brothers, Ross," something whispered over his shoulder. He spun but only found darkness. When he faced forward again, his brother was gone, and a young girl watched him through black, soulless eyes. She had long dark hair and too solemn a face for a child.

Jerry stood behind her, smirking. "What is broken if it's not kept?"

Giant red eyes opened, hundreds of feet in the air, and a roar with a stuttering click reminded Cal of what Jerry had bought with his soul to win in Japan. Plan B. Dzoavits.

"Goodbye, Calvin."

"Wait!" Cal staggered to his feet. "Was the sacrifice worth it?"

Jerry's smile faded. "Preservation of life is always worth it, no matter how small the contribution."

Cold rain pattered against Cal's face. His eyes fluttered open to find skyscrapers towering over him, like old friends, welcoming him back to the world of the living. Lightning flashed, and a crack of thunder returned his memory.

*Empire.*

Throbbing, dull aches informed Cal he'd survived the fall. The numbness was there, but it was fading. Finally, he was almost free of Marchosias. Rain trickled down his dry throat, and he smiled.

The wailing started or resumed; he couldn't be sure. Screams weaved into the roar of the air-raid siren as legions of people scrambled around him.

The concrete under his back quaked in a pattern matching footsteps. Puddles rippled, and panes of glass rattled in the buildings.

Cal pulled himself up and twisted his body to glance at the street signs. Milnor Avenue and Grant Road. He'd landed in Calway.

Further down the street, lightning illuminated a giant crawling horror lumbering toward him. It was mechanical, with four legs, at least fifteen stories high, but Cal couldn't make out much more through the pouring rain. He staggered to his feet and limped against the screaming masses toward the thing they were fleeing. That's where he'd find Theo and, hopefully, answers.

The crowd dwindled as Cal got closer. The entire world convulsed with each sluggish step. Its body and legs were a hodgepodge of girders, metal sheets, and tools held together by a metallic substance, running like a river amongst the clutter. Other appendages jutted from the front, sweeping over streets and buildings like feelers on a bug. Below them, a giant orb surveyed in short, rapid bursts. Above it, the flyers swarmed but never intersected, like an oversized beehive blotting out the sky. On top of the lumbering behemoth, colorful light beams tore through the giant's flying spawn.

"Theo."

*Thud!* A flier landed—ten feet of soldered junk and flowing liquid metal. Wings folded into its back as the small orb on top snapped around like a giant bird. Radio static crackled. It lunged, trying to grab him. Cal caught a metal finger in each hand. His eyes widened as the thing's strength forced his feet into the cracking pavement, and his spine bowed under its strength.

# The City of the Gods: Gold

Behind it, the walker's hoof pancaked a Triumph Roadster and sent a crack rippling up the side of a building. The ground heaved, uprooting trees and lampposts. The scent of gasoline threatened to turn the street into a tinderbox.

The flier faltered, and Cal pushed back. A quick right hook sent the monster stumbling into a phone booth.

The robot surged forward and yanked Cal up by his arm. It ripped a right hook with the force of a truck across his face. He dangled helplessly as blood and broken teeth ran down his chin. His left eye was swollen and throbbing with his heartbeat.

Metallic, bat-like wings jutted from the flier's back and thumped as it hoisted Cal into the sky. He hung like a ragdoll, swinging in the cold, whipping breeze. Other fliers circled amongst the tops of the buildings, emitting high-pitched frequencies. Cal punched and grabbed the closed fist wrapped around his sleeping arm, twisting and pulling frantically, but its grip was ironclad.

The flier landed on the giant walker, dragging Cal toward an open chute near the rear. He beat his knuckles bloody against the metal body as it forced him to his knees. The smell of warm rot burst from the chute. Cal gripped the frame, but the surface was slick, and his power was waning. He elbowed the creature's forearm to no avail. A second flier landed, grabbing his legs and forcing his face into the hole.

Grinding gears churned over pulp with fingers and other human parts floating amongst the paste. Cal yelled and kicked the flier holding his feet, sending it careening backward. He swung at the other one, catching it flush in its little pea head, busting it open like an overripe cantaloupe. The analog screams they emitted were like music, but he felt every bump and bruise. The numbness was gone.

More fliers were on him. Too many to count. They turned him upside down and fed his body into the death pit.

Cal jolted defiantly. "Come on, you sons-of-bitches! Is that all you got?"

More gripped his body where they could. The metal frame whined and bent under the last of his strength, and his face inched into the hole. Gears churned gurgling slop. Bloody spray licked his face. He was laughing, he realized. He was finally free. His arms gave out, and his fingers slipped.

One of the creatures ripped backward, then another. Gunshots muffled Theo's voice. Cal instinctively pushed his hand forward to catch himself.

The pain was indescribable, but the sound was worse as flesh and bone mangled in the gears. Cal thought he heard himself scream, but he couldn't be sure. Darkness took him.

----

Consciousness was a narrow, dream-like beacon, but Cal's mangled stump leaking blood onto the steel back of the walker seemed real enough.

"Oh, Calvin," Theo said, standing over him, holding a pistol. "I couldn't let you suffer at the hands of these creatures." She sighed. "I wish you had died in the Redbird."

The swarm of fliers circled, throwing themselves at an orange, domed barrier encasing Cal and Theo.

Cal tried to climb to his feet but stumbled and sat in a slump as his body betrayed him. "Why?" he choked through his split lip and broken teeth.

Theo sighed. "Jerry was my soulmate, and I promised to share his fate."

Cal shook his head. "You're insane."

"No, I just lost my way. After Jerry died, I leaked some of my blueprints, including my nano-mites, to associates of Thompson's. I knew he'd attack the city to get revenge, but when T-Day happened, I was pregnant with Bonnie. I couldn't sacrifice myself. She deserved to live. Years later, I found one of Thompson's nano-mite disbursement units floating in the Basalt River. Bonnie needed her family, so I hid it at Allied Science, where James or I couldn't get to it.

"Then, a few nights ago, I came across another one while searching for Bonnie. It was open. The counterfeit nano-mites were out. It was destiny. I called Allied Science to get rid of the evidence and left the safe in my apartment open for whatever came out of that vessel, the blueprints for another T-Day."

"You're sick, Theo. You need help," Cal said.

"I reached out to you in a moment of weakness, but I never expected you to help me. You gave me hope for Bonnie for a time, but after Club Danza—" She shook her head. "I tried to spare you, but when you insisted on coming to the moon, even with your powers waning, I knew you were just like your brother. You wouldn't hesitate to give your life for Empire." She raised the gun. "I can't send you to that hell. I can't let your soul surfer. I'm sorry. I wish you had died in the Redbird."

Cal spat. "What about Bonnie?"

A tear slipped down Theo's cheek. "The-the city needs me."

"This city never needed you. You, James, and Lily created the need for you in Empire." Cal chuckled and smiled his bloody smile. "The Enforcers were always the problem, and it's time for Plan B." He closed his eyes, calling out to his creator.

The last sound he heard was a gun discharge. There was no pain.

**<u>96</u>**

"I know you're here. Answer me!" Cal called into a shrouded black room. He stood naked, but the hooks and ropes binding him to Marchosias had vanished.

The faint smell of cinnamon and allspice clung to the still air. "I need to make a deal!"

521

Red-slitted eyes suspended twelve feet in the air opened slowly. A snarl revealed the inhuman snout, dripping liquid fire across thick black fur.

"Et Nunc absolvo vos." In the glow of the dripping orange flame, feathered wings spread behind the lupine-like head, and a scaly tail flicked. "Educ me ad alterum."

"I can't understand you," Cal said. The creature watched him for a moment longer, then retreated silently into the shadows.

"Wait—"

*In your darkest hour, I saved you from yourself.* An eerie voice whispered faintly. *Now, I must serve another.*

"Why have you come here?" a second, unseen voice boomed over the clack of hooves as a young girl in a black robe slowly stepped forward. Her glowing red eyes lifted and met his. "Answer me!" The deep register didn't match her young, delicate features. Something shifted in the shadows behind her.

Cal stepped forward. "I'm here to make a deal, like Jerry did, my soul for Empire's safety."

The girl's face was stone as her glowing eyes studied him. "Your soul is worthless. You are broken. You are dead. There is nothing to offer me, Calvin Smith."

"Please, I'll do whatever it takes."

Shadows shifted behind her, and faint, scattered whispers chattered around them.

"Salvation will come." The girl lifted her arm slowly and extended a finger. "The builder has offered itself in exchange for Dzoavits."

Cal slowly followed her finger with his eyes to Theo's limp body, hanging from ropes and hooks. "No. Please, take me."

"It is done," the voice rang out as the girl returned to the shadows. "Its soul is forfeit. Sabnock has abandoned it. Now, Sabnock serves another."

"No, wait!" Cal's eyes fluttered open to the whine of metal as the walker inched through Empire. He touched the hole in his chest that had killed him, but he felt no pain as Marchosias and Sabnock drove his lifeless body forward. The fliers circled like vultures but didn't attack—a grim reminder he was already dead.

Cal slumped on top of the walker's head, searching for the reason he was allowed to exist. A cool breeze whipped through the buildings, and he smiled. *I guess summer is over.*

Two children screamed in the middle of the road, one pinned under a stone gargoyle, the other trying desperately to pull him to safety. Cal saw himself and Jerry pinned in a foxhole. The creatures riding his mortal coil stirred. *Find the brothers, Ross.*

Cal gritted his teeth and tumbled off the front of the walker. He limped toward the boys, grunting, but the dead couldn't speak. In the distance, the sky tore open in a blinding burst of energy. Empire's salvation fell from the laceration into the river. Dzoavits.

*No.* Cal stopped short. He could feel Marchosias and Sabnock forcing his dead body forward. *I can't give them what they want.*

The boys stared wide-eyed over Cal's shoulder as the walker thumped forward. *But I won't let them die.* Cal hugged the gargoyle, desperately trying to move it, but he had no more strength for such feats.

The Earth trembled, and the statue's hold tightened. Cal shoved the smaller boy to the sidewalk and gathered the pinned one in his arms.

*I'm sorry, Wilbur. Take solace in the fact that I tried to do the right thing.*

His vision went.

*Part of me is still in the kitchen in the back of the diner, trading witty jabs with you, old man. Happy and free. Part of me will always be there.*

*Mom—*

Gears whined, and pistons screamed.

"Gordie!" The smaller child slid next to Cal. He held both boys tight.

*—I'm on my way.*

Jerry,

This is the most difficult letter I've ever had to write, and harder still knowing no one will ever read it.

I wish I had told you when I had the chance. Just before that night in December that changed us, I found out I was pregnant with your child. Before James could force me to get an abortion, I made a pact with whatever was inside Rosalita. We would receive gifts and a chance at a life together, but our unborn child would never draw breath. I realize now what a mistake I'd made.

I'm tired. Each day, I feel my soul dim as Sabnock's grip closes. When I lost you, I realized it would be easier to face the unknown embrace of death than the numbness. I gave my enemy the upper hand in hopes of sacrificing myself as you did and reaching the same eternity. Perhaps our daughter is there too. Perhaps our family can be together again.

Today, I discovered I was expecting another baby with James. A girl. I can't sacrifice myself, knowing it would end another child's life. I hope you understand.

I know I'll see you again one day. If I bide my time, another opportunity will present itself. When that day comes, I will not make the mistake of letting either of you go again. For now, memories of the risks we took to be together, and a photograph, are all I have.

Love Always,

Theodora

A MEASURE OF
WORTH

The putrid scent of death pushed through the handkerchief wrapped around Cassandra's face. She grasped Mary's cold wrists, scanning the ceiling to avoid her vacant stare as she dragged her corpse to the chute on the far wall. The weight of Mary's body pulled back. Coagulated blood snagged her hair, twisting her head, and air escaped as a moan like Mary was fighting for a second chance at life.

Cassandra dropped her dead sister's limp wrists, blinking away tears and repeating Ron's words: "This is your penance. You brought death to this house." Ron had said more, but Cassandra was too distracted by the tears streaming down his face to hear him.

Last night, Cassandra had a lucid dream for the first time since the Baphomet left her. Two moons, vying for control of the sky. One full, the other eclipsed. The faceless woman stood on the edge of a cliff, gazing across the water. Cassandra ran to her, but she fell into the raging surf as the eclipsed moon tore across the sky and consumed the full one. Below, Mary and Patricia danced naked on a shore of bones as waves lapped their feet and tears streamed down their doll-like faces.

*These were people I loved,* Cassandra thought, scanning the pile of remains near the chute. Bile clawed up her throat. It wasn't the smell that made the black room unbearable. It was other details. Bloated bellies, yellow root-like appendages, and unidentifiable bone mashed into the floor. Flies and other insects that walk hand-in-hand with death, swarming in incessant buzzing masses. Across the room, Geraldine scrubbed the floor, remaining uncharacteristically silent.

"Geraldine," Cassandra squeaked. "Are you still angry?"

The wish-wash scrubbing sound ceased. Geraldine threw her brush against the wall, scattering a group of flies, and stood, swatting something in front of her grimacing face. "What do you think, Cassandra? We had a chance to get away from this!" She motioned to the pile of corpses.

Cassandra couldn't bear to look. "I—you don't understand. I can't just leave."

"You can't, or you won't? An hour ago, I didn't think I could move a dead body, but guess what? I threw three into a pile *and* cleaned the rest of them off the floor!" She stomped across the room and pushed through the black curtain.

Cassandra followed hesitantly. As her eyes adjusted to the intense white of the marble foyer, Athena and Zeus stared down in judgment from their pedestals, not for what she'd done in the black room but for her cowardice—staying here, in the safety of routine.

Cassandra glanced up the marble staircase. "We should finish cleaning."

Geraldine ripped the handkerchief off her face and threw it onto the floor, glaring at her through swollen black and blue eyes. A little white bandage rode the bridge of her nose. "Cassie, don't you see? That cop shot Ron to give us a head start! There is no way he could catch up to us, and I think Nancy is frightened of you after—well—"

The pause was a knife in Cassandra's heart. She scanned the floor. "The police would hunt us and kill us, or worse, bring us back. I wish I could explain—Ron would never let me go."

Geraldine lifted Cassandra's chin. "We could kill him!" The words looked like they tasted like candy. "We could kill Ron Baxter!"

Cassandra guided her away from the open staircase. "Shh. What if he hears you?"

"He won't." She grinned spitefully. "He's up there with that hussy Nancy, doing Heaven knows what."

"We aren't murderers."

"Says the girl who just—" Geraldine paused.

Cassandra eyed the curtain over the black room as rain pattered against the windowpane. Lightning lit the house like a flashbulb. Thunder rolled. The crisp air whipping and snapping the drapes finally felt like October.

"You're right," Cassandra said, "I'm a murderer."

Geraldine placed her hand on Cassandra's shoulder. "I didn't mean—"

"You need to get away from me! I'm poison!" Cassandra choked out something Ron had told her and ran across the room, through the swinging door into the kitchen. She fell to her knees, sobbing with her entire body.

A bone-white object propped on a shelf in the pantry caught her eye. Her tongue was acidic and sour, and the lingering dread tied to the premonitions of the doll-faced woman she had suffered in the past reemerged—the tortured thoughts of a troubled girl.

Still, she inched forward. A white face stared out blankly. Cassandra's bare feet padded across the cold linoleum, and she tried to call out, but her throat was dry.

*Isn't it divine?*

She stopped at the threshold. A mask painted in a brilliant, sparkling pale color—not quite silver, but not quite white—was propped on one of the shelves. Cassandra lifted the mask with a shaky hand, turning the featureless object and watching it glow in the low light. It was lightweight with a smooth finish but no material she'd ever felt. *Dea,* she thought as she clutched it to her chest and raced through the back door.

Cassandra looked to the sky and shut her eyes as the storm washed over her. Chilly autumn air tugged at her toga. She ran into the yard, kicking leaves with the elation of a child, and spun in the downpour, laughing. Thunder roared overhead. She yelled along with it, finally free, if only for a moment.

She dropped back into a pile of wet leaves and stared at the rolling thunderheads, reminding her of an old dream where the moon exploded, and Empire burned.

She smiled and fingered the smooth mask. *I survived.* In her mind, she watched the faceless woman tumble off the cliff. *When the sky fell, and the world burned, I was spared to bear witness. I survived.*

Cassandra sat up and took a blade of grass between her fingers. Ron's mansion didn't look so big or threatening from here. There was a vast world outside those walls, and the Sibylline Religion couldn't control all of it. Akia, Barbara, Patricia, and Mary had escaped Ron the only way they could. The same way Cassandra was told she would one day. Death was inevitable, but how she lived until that day was still undecided.

*Maybe Geraldine's right.*

Her name sent butterflies fluttering through Cassandra's insides. She smiled, but it faded when she remembered the genuine fear pressed in Geraldine's eyes after the ceremony.

*Could she love me unconditionally after I killed so ruthlessly?*

Cassandra suddenly recalled the end of her latest dream. After the faceless woman fell, Empire was ashes, buildings sat in ruins beneath a moonless sky, and the streets were choked with the dead. The lucky ones had been burnt to nothing. However, some still moved through the desolate city with their skin hanging from their bones. In her dream, she knew the faceless woman was dead.

The rain soaking her skin was cold now. In the distance, the faint whine of an air-raid siren competed with the thunder. Cassandra shut her eyes. When they fluttered open, she stood alone in an empty black room. The rain had ceased. She was dry and naked. Boorish sniffing discharged moist air on her neck, forcing her hair to stand on end.

"I hear you summoning me, Oracle." The familiar, booming voice erupted from all around. "Have you brought me the godspawn?"

It was another of her dreams, precisely as she had dreamt it. She could smell the decaying flesh of the dead gods and taste the sulfur amid the putrid humidity.

She exhaled. "A man comes to you—"

"Yes, Calvin Smith," the voice reverberated. "What concern is it of yours, Oracle?"

"He means to trade his soul for Dzoavits." She turned. The Baphomet's eyes bled through the black emptiness.

"Calvin Smith's life is meaningless, forfeit. He teeters on edge as a nonbeliever and a dead man."

Cassandra shut her eyes and shuddered. "Take my soul," she whispered. This was not her dream anymore. The vision she had seen could still be changed. The faceless woman never had to exist and, therefore, could never die.

"I demand the soul of a god. You are no god."

"I will stand in the god's place!" She clenched her fists to steady her quaking voice. "Take me, or I refuse to be your oracle!".

The voice growled. "You do not refuse me. I create gods, and I extinguish gods. The death merchant and the messenger are trapped between worlds. The armored passes to another. The builder is all that remains."

Cassandra stepped forward. "No, please." She knew the builder was somehow the faceless woman's inception. "I can give you—"

"The deal is made of her own volition. The god is damned. The champion emerges. Behold, Dzoavits."

Cassandra stood alone in the backyard, soaked, holding the mask. Cold rain dumped like pellets. Everything was as it had been before.

"Wait!"

Lightning lit the sky.

"Take me!" she screamed.

Soft arms wrapped around her, and a familiar scent emerged through the rain, floral and comforting. "It's okay, Cassie, I'm here," Geraldine whispered.

In the distance, the sky ripped open. Cassandra's dream had been fulfilled. This event would create the faceless woman who would live only to suffer. A being burst from the cosmos into Empire City, a horrific creature, not of this world or even this plane of reality, but perhaps the city's last hope for survival.

Cassandra stared into the black, stellar laceration gouged into reality and remembered Japan. As a little girl, she had brokered this same deal. Jerry Smith's soul, for Dzoavits to intervene in a war of men, only to be forgotten.

Geraldine guided Cassandra toward the house. "Let's get you inside."

Water pooled underneath the girls as their togas dripped onto the kitchen floor. Cassandra shivered.

"Can you believe this rain?" Geraldine asked. "Finally, everything is going to cool—"

"We need to go now," Cassandra said.

**<u>98</u>**

The overcast sky accelerated dusk into night. Cassandra inched across her dead sisters' bedroom, dragging a sheet from the bunk bed to the armoire. She laid all the clothes Ron had bought Patricia on the sheet as Geraldine stood guard by the door.

"Hurry up!" she whispered. "I think I heard something!"

Cassandra quickly changed into one of Patricia's least formal dresses, which bunched above her hips and fell below her calf, but it would have to do. She wrapped the mask in a silk blouse and hissed to get Geraldine's attention.

The women switched places, doing their best to not disturb the creaky wooden floor. Cassandra leaned on the doorframe and stared into the black hallway toward Ron's private staircase, listening intently for footsteps.

"How do I look?" Geraldine whispered.

"Fine," Cassandra responded, focusing on the hall.

"You didn't even look!" Geraldine folded the blanket into a sack, flinging it over her shoulder, and crept back to the door. "I feel like a sausage."

Cassandra eyed the room one last time. It looked strange, like she hadn't known the people who lived there, even though the wounds of loss were still fresh. She took Geraldine by the hand and stepped into the hallway. Soon, they would be gone, and this would be another bad dream in her mounting repertoire.

A door creaked somewhere behind them. Cassandra gasped, pulling Geraldine down the hallway and carefully paddling down the stairs. There was no time to collect her journals.

A burst of lightning lit the foyer, and the curtain to the black room shifted. The door to the kitchen swung quietly back and forth as something stepped through. Cassandra stopped short, staring wide-eyed into the darkness.

"Did you see that?" Geraldine whispered.

Cassandra remembered the inhuman moan Mary emitted as she dragged her corpse. She pulled Geraldine by the hand toward the kitchen anyway, swallowing her words, afraid her voice would quiver if she tried to speak.

"We're not going back there, are we?" Geraldine hissed, pulling Cassandra away. "What if that was Ron?"

The form had been feminine, and the gate slight; it was a woman. Cassandra's pulse quickened. "The front door will make too much noise. Besides, Ron can't walk."

Lightning illuminated the house again, and Cassandra squinted into the kitchen through the porthole. Clumped shadows shuffled against the back wall. Cassandra pushed through the door.

The overhead light clicked on. "Where do you think you're going?" Nancy said. She stood in front of the exit wearing one of Ron's silk robes, with her brown hair up in curlers. "I knew you'd try something like this."

Geraldine burst forward, grabbing a steak knife off the island. "We're so close! We have to kill her!"

"No!" Cassandra grabbed her arm.

"Tell her to put down the knife!" Nancy hissed. Her terrified eyes locked on Geraldine.

"Cassie, we have to!" Geraldine held the knife out straight.

"I mean it, Cassandra!" Tears welled in Nancy's eyes. "I'll scream! I'll wake Ron up, and then there will be hell to pay!"

"There's been too much killing. Even if it means our freedom, I can't allow my only remaining sister to be murdered."

Geraldine lowered the weapon. "But—"

"Nancy," Cassandra said, "come with us. There's nothing for you here." She inched toward the frightened girl.

Nancy's blue eyes floated back and forth between Cassandra's. She waited for an insult, some snide remark about her weight, or for her to call out to Ron, but Nancy just stood still until her face scrunched to cry.

Cassandra took another step forward and touched Nancy's slender shoulder. "Please—"

"There's nothing out there." Nancy shrugged out of Cassandra's embrace. "I've lived out there, on the streets of Hell's Gate. Trust me, this is the best life someone like you or me can hope to have."

"But, we'll be free."

"No, you'll die." Nancy shook her head. "We've lost too many. Cassandra, I know it was Master Leonard who killed our sisters. Ron told me." She smiled, but tears still fell. "Go back to your room. This can be our little secret."

Cassandra tried to find the spiteful little stooge she had known Nancy to be in her words, but the sincerity in her eyes was genuine. "Nancy, we're leaving," she said.

Nancy sighed. "Fine, but I warned you." She opened a cupboard behind her, removed a box of Soilax that Cassandra had never seen before, and hugged it to her chest.

"What's that?" Geraldine asked.

"Before the ceremony, when the police found Barbara at the end of Pleasant Street. She was carrying this box, among other, more valuable things." Nancy licked her lips and peered inside the box. "The police returned the valuables to Ron but gave this dumb box to me to put away." She laughed. "Those dopey cops thought she had taken it to poison Ron. They didn't even bother to look inside."

Nancy placed the box on the island and met Cassandra's gaze. "God, Cassandra, they—" Her face screwed slowly, and she burst into tears, slumping over the island and gripping her head. "Oh, god!"

Cassandra placed her hand on Nancy's back. "I know, Nancy. I know what they did."

"No, you don't! How could you?" she scowled. "You were the chosen one! You had your own room! You had everything, Cassandra!" Nancy pushed away and backed against the wall. "Those rotten police officers brought poor Barbara to the basement and lined all of us girls up next to her. Mary, Patricia, and me." She bit her lip, and her chest heaved. "We watched—we knew what was going to happen—but we watched anyway. We had to, Cassandra! We had to!" She sniffled, wiping her eyes.

"Nancy, you don't have to talk about it—"

"Yes, I do! Barbara deserves to be remembered! She was our sister!" Nancy shuttered a breath out. "Those cops picked up Barbara—she was flailing wildly, flailing for her life! All of us girls knew what was going to happen. Patricia tried to step in, but one of the cops anticipated it and pulled his gun. 'Ron's orders,' he said.

"They threw her into the incinerator, and"—Nancy shut her eyes—"they turned it on."

Geraldine dropped the knife and gripped her mouth with both hands. "Oh, god."

"We could all hear her screaming. She was screaming for so long." Nancy snapped out of her trance and glared at Cassandra. "It was to be a lesson for the rest of us girls, but not for you, Cassandra, not Ron's perfect oracle. You were never to know!"

"Nancy, I—"

"Save it!" Nancy sneered. She upended the box of Soilax onto the island, and rolls of rubber-banded money tumbled across the linoleum. "If you're going to go, take this with you. Patricia had been sneaking it from Ron little by little. She was trying to help Barbara get out, trying to make sure she never had to go back to Hell's Gate again." She locked eyes with Cassandra. "A fresh start."

Cassandra took Nancy's hand. "There's plenty here. We could all start fresh."

Nancy stared past the money at the table. "You don't get it, Cassandra. You were always Patricia's favorite, and she was always Ron's favorite—"

"Nancy—"

"After you, of course." Nancy's eyes glazed over. "Patricia would want you to have this now that Barbara's gone, and when you're gone"—she smiled—"I'll be Ron's favorite."

Cassandra shook her head. "Nancy, Ron doesn't love anyone but himself."

"Get out of here, Cassandra!" Nancy shoved her. "Never come back! Ron is mine, do you hear me? Mine! At least let me have this! You've taken everything else!"

Cassandra nodded slowly. She had lost another sister.

"C'mon!" Geraldine eyed Nancy with an untrusting glance and dumped the money into her makeshift sack. "This is our chance!" She took Cassandra by the hand. Nancy grabbed her other wrist, and Cassandra's eyes shot to meet hers.

"Don't come back, Cassandra, don't you *ever* come back!"

Cassandra nodded, and Nancy released her.

She watched the remnants of the only family she'd ever known standing alone in her childhood home and turned away before grief consumed her.

Geraldine pulled on a pair of rubber galoshes, and Cassandra stepped into her fur-lined winter boots. Nancy remained a statue with a furious, tear-stained face.

"I won't forget this, Nancy," Cassandra said. "If you ever change your mind, find me. You'll always be my sister."

Nancy's face grew slightly apprehensive, but she remained still.

Cassandra glanced through the kitchen door's porthole, past the black room, and into the foyer where the Greek gods stood sentinel.

*C'mon, Cassie, it'll be fun!* Patricia called from the shadow of a memory. *We have nothing to worry about!*

They were both finally free.

Ron Baxter's Journal

January 1, 1947

Cassandra is once again a little girl, and all traces of Master Leonard are gone. She seems to remember very little of what's transpired. I count that as a blessing, and for now, I am at peace. However, before it departed, Master Leonard told me it would return with the unnatural heat and crave the godspawn. That will be my chance to gain the power of a god and rid humanity of this creature. Until then, I must maintain control of Cassandra and never let her out of sight.

WHEN THE
SWORD OF
DAMOCLES
FALLS

**<u>99</u>**

*Empire is burning.*

Gibson watched plumes of smoke dissipate amongst the dark clouds as the Concord took a hard left onto the Bunche Bridge. Bonnie slid across the bench seat, giggling. Gibson wiped his brow and pressed his Oxford on the pedal, still unsure where he was going, only knowing he needed to get there fast.

The Concord growled as it accelerated, the bridge hummed under them, and the autumn wind whipped through the open windows, carrying the stench of death. Traffic choked the opposite side of the bridge. Horns blasted, and people on foot weaved through discarded vehicles to a backdrop of smoke and fire. The memory of T-Day rode the ashes of the dying city, and the survivors' facial expressions all told the same story: *Don't go into Empire.*

Above the city's skyline, a cluster swarmed like wasps. *Helicopters?* Gibson thought, but on approach, they seemed to be flying men. Still, it wasn't the craziest thing he'd seen today.

The gas pedal was almost through the floorboard as the Concord tore through the toll lane. There was no one inside the booth to take money or comment on today's weather. The air-raid siren continued humming its familiar tune: annihilation incarnate, an old favorite in Empire.

In Eastport, something had dragged itself onto the shore. The boats in Shelly's Marina were on fire and sinking, with their bows pointing up like tombstones. Gibson followed tumbling swells of smoke up with wide eyes and discovered stars glittering through a gash in the sky. He blinked and squinted. Whatever strange happenings he'd experienced at the Connor estate had followed him into the city.

542

A choir of horns turned his attention back to the street. He slammed on the brakes and shot a concerned arm across Bonnie's chest. Cars were at a dead stop, scattered across Bunche Avenue, pointed north toward the bridge to salvation.

"Hang on." Gibson jerked the wheel. The Plymouth hopped the curb onto the sidewalk, and Bonnie giggled, jostling back and forth. The car weaved between buildings and the abandoned vehicles with puttering engines jamming the street.

Gibson positioned his hand over the horn, freezing when a primal cry flooded the city, stuttering at the end like a powerful engine turning over. Panicked masses abandoned their vehicles and hurried away on foot.

"What was that noise?" Bonnie asked.

Gibson met her curious gaze, wrestling with the same question. "It's nothing."

"But I heard a noise," Bonnie said.

Gibson swallowed, examining the sky for the sound's origin as the Concord inched forward. "I'm sure it's far away from here."

Bonnie stared silently out the window as they passed exposed offices and apartments. Further down the street, a sparking train track blocked the road, one side propped up by a crushed Studebaker, the other jutting from the front of a department store. Gibson dropped the Plymouth off the curb, turning on Windham and weaving around broken furniture and brick. Silhouettes of looters slithered out of windows and shifted in alleys.

Bonnie watched what she could see over the dashboard. "Where are we going?" Her innocent eyes locked on Gibson. "Mommy told me you were bringing me to see her."

"I'm afraid it's not that simple—" Gibson slammed on the brakes as a scruffy man with dirty clothes and a radio under his arm slapped the Concord's hood. Bonnie screamed, but the man's eyes remained locked on the sky as he hurried into the shadows.

Gibson exhaled. "You okay?"

Bonnie nodded.

Gibson eyed his own radio curiously and turned the knob.

"—code two. I repeat, some sort of giant mechanical creature and a—it looks like a damn horror picture down here! Is anyone out there? Please respond. Code two, New Hastings, code—" The radio cut.

"New Hastings," Gibson whispered as he took a left onto Jasper Street.

Garbage barrels burned, and shadows moved through the umbrae. Sirens wailed in the distance, and another roar reverberated through the buildings with the same ominous, stuttered grumble at the end.

Bonnie gasped. "Where's Mommy?"

"We'll see her soon."

Gibson took a right onto Broadway, left on Union, and right on Mosley, remembering Slim's words. *Being the white knight is exhausting and a fool's errand.*

He lifted the radio's handset. "Gibson for Shanahan, come in, Shanahan." He flipped desperately through the channels, but only static answered. The Plymouth crawled past Wilbur's. "Closed for repairs," a sign read.

Gibson pulled over and eyed Bonnie, drumming his restless fingers on the steering wheel. He gripped the handset again. "Slim, if you're out there, I need you, partner. Please, come back, it's Skipper." Hope died amongst the static. He slammed the handset back onto the receiver and gazed out the window.

"Gibson? Is that you?" the radio answered. The taste of bile in the back of his throat placed the voice. "This is Creed for Gibson. Come back, Gibson. If you're out there, I need to talk to you."

He clicked the radio off.

Bonnie tugged on his shirt sleeve. "Mister? Where's my mommy?"

Gibson shut his eyes and exhaled. "I told you; we'll see her soon." He shifted into drive and wheeled into a U-turn as Slim's voice invaded his mind again.

*I told you not t' get involved. Big thing like that requires a big response, bigger n' we can handle.*

Bonnie pulled herself up onto the armrest and peered out the window. "I want my mommy!"

Gibson placed a hand on her shoulder and eased her back into the passenger seat before the sight of death and destruction ruined her. "I need you to be brave right now, sweetheart, I'm going to take you to your mommy, but there might be some... monsters along the way."

She sniffled. "My daddy said there's no such thing as monsters anymore."

"I sure hope your daddy's right." Gibson slowed the Plymouth to a crawl and glanced anxiously down Wilmore Drive at a downed telephone pole. "Shit." He ran his shirt sleeve over his brow and flashed Bonnie a fake, shallow smile as they made a left on Baggata and a right onto Scorpio.

*Screeeeeee.* The sound of metal scraping across concrete carried down the street, echoing off the buildings. Gibson eased on the brakes. A silhouette emerged through the dust, dragging a parade of sparks. A man, no, it was too big, standing at least eight feet tall. Hunched but still imposing. It limped forward, revealing a face gruesome enough to disprove Bonnie's father. Monsters did still exist.

Two more creatures emerged behind the first, emitting the same eerie, potent scrape. They looked like they'd fallen into a trash compactor and survived to tell the tale.

The one in front had metal fastened to part of its face and a single red eye staring relentlessly through Gibson. What was left of its skin looked like a burn victim's. The rest of the body was a mess of man and machine, grotesque arms cobbled together with scrap metal riveted into exposed meat and bone. Its tube-like torso bubbled endlessly. Inside, a mass floated, resembling a carnival sideshow. Gibson could feel it watching him, reaching out, grasping at his mind like a low radio frequency. The others shuffled into view, each grislier than the last—horrors resembling Boris Karloff as Frankenstein's monster.

The one in front stopped. Gibson threw the car in park and popped the door open. Tears welled in his eyes as an unnerving but familiar tune floated through the air, with notes as gentle as the breeze. He smiled. The song's title escaped him. It was childhood incarnate: A game of stickball, the corner store, penny candy, his first kiss.

"What are those?" Bonnie's voice broke Gibson's trance. She stood on the seat with her hands on the dash, peering through curious eyes at the grotesques.

Gibson regarded her. "Th—" A sudden jolt of pain fired into his head. He cringed, and tears poured down his cheeks. Everything ceased.

**<u>100</u>**

"Hey, you okay, Gibson?" a familiar voice called over the hum of a Curtiss C-46 Commando as it took to the air. In the distance, a mountain range brushed the cloudless sky, and the spray of salty air fought for dominance over humidity. Gibson was back in Korea.

"You okay, pal?" Creed watched him with his usual amused gaze and jammed a spade into the ground. "Boy, you looked like you were gonna pass out." He was shirtless, and his bronze skin glistened with sweat.

# The City of the Gods: Gold

*No, I met Creed after Korea.*

The world flickered, and the man's face became a fleshy, featureless mass. The sun dropped like a stone, and Creed's features returned. He wiped smeared dirt from his brow and plunged his shovel into the ground, leaning on the handle. Gibson looked over his callused hands, remembering the trenches they'd been digging. He licked his dry lips and sat, collecting his canteen from the grass.

Creed offered Gibson a Lucky from a pack in his pocket. "Good idea, pal. I could use a break myself."

The cigarette burned fine, but it tasted synthetic. Gibson regarded it curiously, dangling his feet into the trench that suddenly had no bottom. "How long have we been digging?"

"Well, Shanahan would say not long enough. Boy, what a slave driver, huh?" Creed scanned the sunset, which threw a red filter over his face. "I'll say one thing, it sure is pretty here." Smoke snaked from his smirk. "You have anyone special back home?"

"Back home? You mean Empire?" Gibson reached for the cigarette between his lips, but it had vanished.

"No, I mean France. Of course, Empire, you knucklehead."

Gibson stared over Creed's shoulder at an old Dutch Colonial that hadn't been there before. It was white, with green shutters, across the street from the beach. He knew the house.

The sun dipped below the horizon, cicadas sang their summer song, and Gibson was walking. A cool breeze carried the familiar scent of the ocean as it crashed against the shore. Buildings rose, and houses dotted the landscape in the distance.

*This isn't Korea, this is Steel Isle, and that's Ann's house.*

"Ann! Ann's my girl back home." Gibson turned to find Creed, but he was alone, outfitted in his Army dress uniform, holding a fresh bouquet of lilies.

Something in his pocket was bogging him down as he jogged across Sunrise Drive and bounced onto the old rickety porch with the salt-worn paint. He fished around and pulled out an engagement ring. It wasn't much, but under the full moon, it looked like he'd plucked a star from the sky. He smiled and opened the swinging screen door. "Ann?"

No answer. Gibson inched into the foyer and peered up the stairway. "Ann, are you home?"

"C'mon up, Skipper. Might as well get this over with," Slim said, his voice echoing.

Gibson climbed the stairs and faced an old five-panel door with peeling paint. Slim leaned against the torn wallpaper and lit a cigarette, illuminating the deep creases in his face. "On second thought, I wouldn't go in there if I were you." He shook out the match and vanished into the shadows. Gibson pushed through the door.

The room was pitch-black save for a single light hanging over the bed. Ann's skin was slick with blood, her blonde curls splayed over her pillow. She was cold, pale, dead.

The lilies dropped from Gibson's hand. "No."

*You have anyone back home?* He could hear Creed's voice in his head. *You can never be too careful in Empire, now that the heroes are gone.*

"Ann?" He fell to his knees and caressed her cold cheek. Her soulless, doll eyes stared through him.

"You fucked up, Skipper." Slim stepped out of the shadows with a grim expression carved into his gray features. "You messed with Baxter, pulled the lion's tail. Now we're dead, and you're next."

"No, this isn't real!" Through the window, Gibson heard the waves crash against the shore methodically, but something was off. There were no other sounds. He scanned her frozen body. "Ann? C'mon." His clothes were soaked through with blood. Sirens sounded in the distance.

The overhead light cut off, and indistinguishable whispers cascaded through the darkness until one booming voice silenced them. "I can save you from this."

A man in a lab coat extended his hand. He had a white combover and a thin, serious face, radiating kindness. Gibson reached out, and their fingers brushed. But something more potent demanded attention.

"Mister?" Bonnie's voice ripped Gibson from his personal hell.

He inhaled dusty city air, gripped the Concord's leather seat, and remembered. "Bonnie?"

Bonnie gawked past Gibson. The lumbering hodgepodge of metal flesh and bone slunk forward, moving its gaping mouth wordlessly.

*I can help you*—It was a whisper like the rustle of leaves with no origin—*I can reunite you with Ann.*

The giant half-man, half-machine lunged forward with an analog screech. Gibson stumbled into the driver's seat, and the radio filled the car with the same ominous whine.

He jammed the pedal to the floor. The Plymouth shot backward down Scorpio and whipped around the curb onto Spring. Bonnie's scream meshed with the radio's. Gibson slammed on the brakes and shifted into drive as the thing closed in.

Tires squealed on the wet cement, and the Concord bottomed out when the creature's fist dented the trunk. He floored it down Spring, weaving between detritus and abandoned cars. In the rearview, the thing grew smaller, watching them through its fading red eye.

Gibson hooked a left on Maurice Avenue, scanning the dark windows of the groaning buildings with exposed, twisted girders. He turned slowly onto Wolf Street.

*Thump!*

The concrete quaked, sending rubble crashing to the ground. Gibson threw the car in park, breathing in nervous gulps.

*Thump!*

Bonnie stood on the seat. "What's—"

"Shh!" Gibson scanned the horizon and fingered the gear shift.

Bonnie's face scrunched. "Where's my mommy?"

*Boom!*

A row of buildings exploded. Neighboring structures went up like a tinderbox, raining brick and glass. Another building collapsed, kicking up a dust storm. A massive silhouette rose through the haze.

The Concord shot in reverse down Wolf, overtaken by a maelstrom of dust. Bonnie screamed over a choir of mechanical whirring and snarls. Something rolled in front of the car, and the concrete heaved. The Plymouth veered, but Gibson spun the wheel hard and darted backward down Lincoln Drive.

As they rolled to a stop, Gibson's eyes darted around the still darkness. The air stunk like sulfur. Bonnie stared dumbfounded, inhaling through deep sobs.

*Thoom!* A hoof twice as large as a tank slammed into the road, churning the concrete and rocking the Plymouth like a boat. Something massive fell through a building, expelling more dust into the thick air. Pieces of the city scattered onto the ground. A crack spiderwebbed across the windshield. Bonnie screamed, but it was eclipsed by an ear-shattering shriek with an unsettling, familiar sputter at the end.

A massive outline rose from the rubble, the details obscured with dust. Gibson flipped the Concord in reverse and jammed his foot onto the pedal as the cloven hoof of something not of this world stepped over the car, lumbering toward the first being. Bonnie screamed. Walls fell in thunderous succession. Bricks careened off the Concord's roof, windshield, and hood. Gibson kept the wheel steady as he tried to press his foot through the gas pedal. Dust consumed them. He was blind.

Gibson eased off the gas, but the car had a mind of its own. The driver's side scraped against a brick building, shooting sparks. He jerked the wheel and bounced over debris. Tears streamed down Bonnie's horrified face. The car skidded sideways.

"Shit!" Gibson wrapped his arms around Bonnie. The Concord hopped onto two wheels and turned end-over-end into a violent, whirling box of screams and pain.

The car uprighted and skidded to a stop. Gibson sucked in oxygen. "Are you alright?"

Bonnie nodded, her face frozen in fear.

The world was eerily silent. Dust fell like snow. Gibson inched his hand toward the door handle. "We need—"

*Thunk!* Something hit the roof. Then again. *Thunk, thunk, thunk, thunk.* It sounded like hail, only heavier. A brick crashed through the windshield. The building next to them whined. A violent, ear-shattering crash dropped the ceiling a few inches, shattering the windows. Bonnie screamed. Gibson pushed against the driver's side door, but it was stuck. The stench of asphalt choked the air. He pulled Bonnie onto his lap and slid across the seat, pushing against the passenger door; it wouldn't budge. Panic intervened. He turned the key. "C'mon, ol' girl."

The engine sputtered and stalled. "Fuck!" He leaned back in the seat and kicked at the windshield until it cracked and peeled away. More dust filtered in. He shut his burning eyes, scooped Bonnie up, and scrambled over the hood. Part of the wall fell, and a sudden jolt of pain rushed up Gibson's arm. He winced and yanked his hand away. Bonnie screamed into his ear. He ran east as buildings buried the Plymouth.

Gibson leaned on the Maple Lane street sign. His burning chest heaved as he sucked in the freshest air Empire had to offer between abrupt hacks. The sputtering growl faded further into the city. He stumbled into a building, sliding his back down the rough brick. Bonnie fell into him and whimpered into his dusty, stained shirt. Heavy eyelids fell, and his body was weightless.

A car door slammed, and Gibson's eyes opened to a figure hurrying down the block with something under its arm. Muffled purples and reds bled through the falling dust as the sun set. Gibson placed a hand on his stiff neck and glanced at Bonnie, sleeping peacefully on his chest. He brushed chalky ash from her face.

Bonnie's eyes fluttered, then shot open. "I want my mommy!"

"I know." Gibson stood slowly, nursing his throbbing hand. "C'mon. We can't stay here." He led Bonnie across Robincroft, turned the corner, and ran headfirst into a uniformed police officer.

"Woah, hold on there, fella." The officer placed a hand on Gibson's shoulder. He was short and stocky, the type of guy you couldn't move an inch if your life depended on it. The cop pulled his belt up under his gut and looked the two over. Gibson couldn't make him; the floodlights pointing into a crater further down the street drowned his features. "You folks are going the wrong way."

Gibson rubbed his chin to hide his identity, in case he was one of Baxter's. "We're just out for a walk." He placed a hand flat on Bonnie's back, turning her.

The officer tilted his hat back and screwed his face. "Out for a walk? Pal, you gotta evacuate."

Gibson turned. "I'd just like to get my daughter home."

The cop grabbed his shoulder. "You serious? Look around. It's another goddamn T-Day. You folks need to get across the Bunche Bridge—"

"That's where we came from," Bonnie said. "My mommy's house, across the bridge."

The cop eyed Gibson with a look that would curdle milk, then regarded Bonnie with a smile. "Darlin', is this your father?"

"This one's alive!" a voice called out from the illuminated hole behind the cop. "Hey! These boys are breathing! Farley, get over here!"

"What about the colored fella?" The officer shuffled toward the hole.

Gibson pulled Bonnie back across Wolf Street. His head was pounding, and his grit was waning. A few gawkers stood peppered throughout the street, staring blankly at the chaos. Further north, the crowd thickened, and theories of what was happening traveled with the ash on the breeze.

Gibson ignored the chatter and pressed through the crowd, tightening his grip on Bonnie's hand as she stopped to listen to each argument. "C'mon. You don't need to hear this."

Bonnie pulled back. "We need to find my mommy now!" Tears welled in her big green eyes.

Gibson ground his teeth. "I don't know where your mom is! I'm sorry!"

"C'mon!" Bonnie smacked him. "My mommy always says we have to finish everything we start! We can't give up!"

Gibson's eyes widened as he gazed at the unfinished building on the horizon.

**<u>101</u>**

People watched Gibson and Bonnie from alleys like feral cats as they moved down a barren Fernwood Street. Gibson patted his chest. The gun and holster were gone, and the city had only a few fleeting minutes of daylight.

Behind them, screams echoed through the buildings. Gibson grabbed Bonnie's hand as a stampede of people thundered down the street. Something shot into the sky, like a giant mechanical bat, with a young boy locked in its talons. His terrified screams carried above the others before they vanished in the lingering dust amongst the rooftops.

Another metallic bat creature dove into the crowd and snatched a woman. Gibson lifted Bonnie by her arm and hugged her to his chest, pumping his aching legs down Fernwood. More cries reverberated through the buildings. Gibson pushed himself to stay ahead of the hysterical pack.

Mechanical whines and white noise screeched, and cold steel brushed against his shoulder. He ducked into an alley near Wilmore as the woman next to him lifted off the ground. Bonnie squirmed from his grip and took his hand. Gibson pushed through the fearful people lining the brick walls and darted out of the other side of the alley onto Huntly Street, sidestepping abandoned cars and burning rubble. He slammed against a brick wall on Smith Drive. The structure whined. Gibson eyed Bonnie and held a finger to his lips. She nodded. Above them, the gleam of a metal monster faded with the screams of its latest victim.

Gibson sprinted across Clark Street. Bonnie's hand slipped. She was frozen, watching another robotic creature land a few feet away. It shrieked. Gibson pulled Bonnie behind a car and covered her mouth before a scream escaped. Crackling static obscured all other sounds in the city. Metal scraped across the car's hood in a taunting, high-pitched squeal.

Gibson lifted Bonnie like a sack and sprinted across the street. The whine of the radio followed, and metal claws ripped at his shirt. He closed his eyes, lunged through a rotting board in the construction hoarding, and skidded across the mud, sending Bonnie careening into the unfinished building. The creature exploded through the fence, unphased.

Gibson staggered to his feet, gripping a piece of rebar. "Stay back!"

Metal claws lunged. Gibson swung. Vibrating agony shot through his arms, and the rebar fell. The creature reeled and screeched, stumbling into the fence.

Two solid kicks dented the metal door to the building, and one more blew it open. The robot surged forward as Gibson yanked Bonnie inside and slammed the door, throwing the deadbolt across the frame. They sat in the stillness, bathed in dim light. Gibson's burning chest heaved, but the door remained motionless.

He pulled his tattered shirt off, wiped the mud from his face, and inspected Bonnie for injuries. "You okay?" She wrapped her arms around him and burst into tears. His undershirt was soaked and had a red tinge, but neither of them seemed to have any open wounds.

Ornate chandeliers hung two stories overhead, bathing the room in a calming, dim light. "We'll Meet Again," by Vera Lynn, played on a nearby record player.

Gibson stood, guided Bonnie behind him, and inched along an oriental runner spread across the marble floor. "Hello?"

They edged through a mishmash of handcrafted furniture and towering marble statues brought to life by dancing shadows. Each was different: a mother and a daughter, a husband and a wife. There was an unfinished piece in the corner with a striking similarity to Bonnie.

"Hello?" A sickening twist surged in the pit of Gibson's stomach. *What if I'm delivering Bonnie to the enemy?* He reached for his gun and tightened his lips when he remembered it was lost.

A lonely glass of wine with a faint, red lip print on the rim sat on a half-finished, hand-carved end table. The record player cut and crackled until "We'll Meet Again" started over. Gibson locked eyes with an onyx statue of a creature with a lion's head in medieval armor sitting atop a pale marble horse.

"Who are you?" a detached voice asked from across the room. Theodora faced away, spreading paint across a canvas. Her eyes met his in an ornate mirror from deep within the sockets of a haggard face. She wore an oversized button-down shirt splattered with color, and her hair was pulled back into a tight ponytail. If she was surprised to see him or even cautious of his presence, she didn't show it.

Gibson clenched his fists. "You're painting? The city is—"

"Mommy!" Bonnie scampered around Gibson.

Theodora spun, and her eyes grew wide. She discarded her palette and dropped to her knees, collecting her daughter in her arms. "Oh my god! My baby!" Her eyes shot up. The fire that had burned so erratically within them had been smothered. "I'll ask again, who are you? And what are you doing with my daughter?"

"Detective Gibson. Skipper, to my friends." He flashed his badge. "I found her—well—" He couldn't find the words, not ones she deserved anyway.

Theodora ignored him and pulled Bonnie close. "Where have you been?"

Bonnie pulled back and furrowed her brow. "I was with you, Mommy."

Theodora looked at Gibson; her face hardened, and her eyebrows dropped.

"You wouldn't believe me if I told you."

"Well, you had better say something."

Gibson did his best to explain, but it sounded like the fever dream of an over-imaginative child.

Theodora regarded Bonnie. "What happened to you, Munchkin?"

Gibson cleared his throat. "I don't mean to break up the reunion, but are you aware of what's happening in Empire?"

Her fingers ran over the charm of her necklace. "The part of me that's needed is out there." She offered an obligatory smile. "I'm sure you can find your way out."

Gibson crossed his arms. "What does that mean—"

"Look, Detective Gibson, I appreciate what you've done. Truly, I do, but the only reason I've accepted your story as the truth is that mine is even stranger. Just know, I'm fighting for Empire with everything I have."

Gibson shook his head. "You don't remember meeting me, do you?"

She sighed. "No. Goodbye."

"I can't leave until I know why you're not out there."

She scowled. "Detective—"

Gibson stepped forward. "Look, I went through hell to bring your daughter to you"—he eyed Bonnie—"and I'd do it again, for her, but I think the least you can do is explain to me how hiding in this building, painting, is going to save the city!"

Theodora sighed. "You're right." She glided across the floor to her wine glass, moving with manufactured elegance, not at all the person he'd met in Brookfield. She gulped the glass of red. "But please, you mustn't tell Bonnie. Do I have your word?"

Gibson nodded.

Theodora closed her eyes. "My life is void. My soul is forfeit. I gave up both to save this city. I don't know what that entails, but it's a debt I must pay." A sad smile crossed her lips. "A good friend of mine suffered the same fate. Jerry. He was the bravest man I knew. Someone I aspired to be like." She chuckled. "I guess now, I will be." Her words softened as they suffered her emotions. "I'm sorry I'll never get to see my daughter become a woman, but in the end, I'm this city's defender. I didn't ask to be, but I am, and I've come to terms with that."

Gibson glared. "That doesn't explain why you're in here, painting away while my city burns."

Theodora shook her head. "Our city. Out there, that monster with the stuttering growl, that's me. It's my soul or something even more profound. I don't quite understand it, but it's out there fighting for Empire. In here, I'm a dead woman, a shell of my former self. It's only a matter of time before this is over. That's why I'm in here, painting. There isn't much else to do."

She chuckled. "The things in this building are all I have in this damn city. I wanted to leave as much behind as possible before it was too late."

"What do you mean this is all you have? I've been to your mansion in Brookfield, and everyone knows you have a penthouse in the Ironleaf building. Hell, you built this whole damn city," Gibson responded.

"I built the nano-mites that built this city. It almost killed me, but when it was finished, I still felt empty."

"Nano-mites?" Gibson asked.

Theodora sighed. "The day I saw the detonation of the nuclear device in New Mexico, I knew what we had created was wrong. So, I invented atom-sized robots that created, where the atomic bomb destroyed. Two sides of the same coin: good and evil, life and death, God and the Devil, whatever you want to call it. It's a balance, and one shouldn't exist without the other."

In his mind, Gibson saw the decaying bodies spread across the black room in Baxter's house, the woman with antlers nailed to her head. "Is that what this is about, playing God after playing the Devil? You'll have to forgive me, but after the things I've seen, I guess I don't put much stock in your definition of God, especially when it's twisted to fit the needs of the few at the expense of many.

"You may have the best intentions, but the gray areas you're willing to exist in to do good is the most despicable thing about you."

"Feeling that way is your prerogative," Theodora responded. "The Enforcers were divisive, but we got results. America avoided nuclear war. I stopped a lot of innocent people from dying."

"People are dying now! And you're painting!" Gibson scowled.

Theodora nodded. "I'm compelled to build and create, just as I'm compelled to destroy and kill. As everyone is to a point." Her dead eyes found his. "You see, Detective Gibson, we're all a two-sided coin. We're each our own devil, and faith that our consciousness will overcome our primal desires is what keeps us from giving in to that devil."

"Well, it seems you killed God and became the Devil full-time." Gibson clenched his fist.

"Maybe, or maybe God was never what we thought, and killing it was necessary." Theodora looked to Bonnie, busy spreading paint over the marble. "Forget the platitudes. Forget me. She's all that matters. She's the future."

"At least we can agree on that."

Tears welled in Theodora's eyes. "Now, do you mind if I have a moment with my daughter?"

"Fine." Gibson turned toward the exit and looked over his shoulder. "Why not have your nano-mites finish this building now that you're—?"

"Same reason I never fixed the Southside," Theodora said. "I hope others will finish what I started. I fought monsters for so many years that I became one. I've outstayed my welcome, and this unfinished building represents a future without the Enforcers or me. My hope is that someone will be better than we were." Theodora smiled. "Thank you for finding my daughter."

"I'd do it all again in a second."

She nodded. "I know."

**<u>102</u>**

Gibson lit a cigarette to combat the stench of ash and rot in the wind as he peered out through the window in the construction hoarding. Robots lay in broken heaps and hung limp off cars, awnings, and telephone wires. People roamed the dust-covered streets again.

An inhuman howl shook Empire but faded before the sputter. Gibson knew Theodora's work was finished.

This was the first victory in a long time for Skip Gibson. He shut his eyes and smiled regardless of the pounding headache, throbbing hand, and nagging voice in the back of his mind, screaming this would never be over.

Theodora emerged from the building, hand in hand with Bonnie. Gibson tossed the cigarette stub to the ground, watching them approach.

Theodora squatted to face Bonnie. "If I only had a brain," she sang sadly.

"A heart," Bonnie answered.

"A home." A tear rolled down Theodora's haggard face.

"Da noive!" Bonnie yelled out excitedly.

Theodora laughed and released her necklace's clasp, balling it in her fist and placing it in Bonnie's palm. "I'll miss you most of all, Scarecrow." She hugged her daughter tight. "I want you to turn around, Munchkin, and listen to the sound of my voice." She pulled away and bit her quivering lip.

"Like a game?" Bonnie asked.

"Like a game." Theodora knuckled away a tear. "Look at Detective Gibson."

Gibson took the hint and crouched in front of Bonnie, taking her shoulders in his hands and forcing a smile.

The ground split and yawned. Theodora closed her eyes as white-hot flame licked the air, spewing black ash. Gaunt, faceless men erupted from the crevice. Bonnie squirmed, but Gibson held her close.

"Mommy?" She pushed against him frantically. "Mommy!"

Gibson locked his arms around her.

"Listen to my voice!" Theodora yelled as the creatures wrestled her into the bubbling molten earth. "Bonnie, I love you so, so much. Always remember that!" Her face was tight with pain, but each word sounded natural. "I'll come back to you, baby girl, I promise! Nothing can keep me away!"

Bonnie thrashed against Gibson. She tried to turn her head, but he held tight.

"Mommy!" she screamed.

Gibson shut his eyes and forced a tear down his cheek.

"It's going to be alright, Munchkin, I promise!" Theodora's chin dipped beneath the ground. "Be better than I was, Bonnie! I love y—"

The earth cooled, and the gravel sat undisturbed. All that remained of Theodora Connor was a paint-splattered button-down shirt.

Bonnie pushed from Gibson's grasp and scanned the construction site with Theodora's necklace clenched tight in her hand. "Mommy? Mommy, come back!"

Gibson glanced up at the unfinished building. There was work to do.

The Empire Bulletin
News
Empire City, Wednesday, October 21, 1953
18, 1953
NORTHSIDE BECOMES A WAR ZONE
IN THE BATTLE FOR EMPIRE

Yesterday, Empire City was attacked by unknown entities, both mechanical and organic, devastating the city and killing tens of thousands. The cause and person or persons responsible are still unknown.

The first warnings of danger came at 4:25 PM, when a large mechanical creature rose from the West River, causing mass panic along the shoreline in Westport as citizens commuted home. Witnesses on Sandy Lane reported "a four-legged creature" crawling from the river with swarms of "man-sized" robots circling it. The "swarm" of creatures carried people to a still undisclosed location as the giant moved unopposed through Calway and into Cork. Although eyewitnesses said the Enforcers were on the scene, it's still unclear if the team of heroes was present. Contradictory reports of the battle lead to speculation.

Around 5:00, another object fell from the sky, landing in the Basalt River on the city's east side. The (sky tear) above New Hastings is still visible as speculation circles amongst witnesses as to what the beast was.

The organic creature moved across New Hastings, causing little to no damage until it found its robotic counterpart in Cork. The two beings then battled across Cork, New Hastings, and into Baggataway, killing thousands and causing structural damage.

Though the cause of the disturbance is still unknown, many speculate it was warring alien races, each trying to assert its dominance over the world. Others insist it was something created in a lab at Allied Science. The recent closing of the building could validate their claim. The Mayor's Office has stated that this is "an ongoing investigation," and Allied Science declined to comment.

"Usually, at this point, someone comes forward to claim responsibility," Chief of Detectives Brendan Murphy said. "We've had a few crazies call in, but nothing solid yet. It's still unclear if this is over or not." Murphy refused to comment when asked about the Enforcers' role, saying, "We appreciate what they did, and if they're out there now, we could sure use their help."

In a statement issued today, Mayor Stanz pleaded, "We hope that the Scarlet Sparrow will come forward now in our hour of need. The city has suffered so much. We could use assistance rebuilding."

As of press time, none of the Enforcers have come forward. President Eisenhower rallied the Salvation Army to aid the relief efforts and erected temporary housing in the Bullet's Stadium as responders continue searching the rubble for survivors.

## BAXTER ADOPTS MIRACLE ORPHAN

Local philanthropist and self-appointed leader of the Sibylline Temple, Doctor Ronald Baxter, began the paperwork to adopt one of the "miracle children" found on Grant Road yesterday.

Authorities discovered Gordon Ross, paralyzed from the neck down, alongside Walter Ross, his brother, and an unidentified deceased man.

Although doctors at Schiller Hospital remain skeptical about Ross's survival, Baxter hopes he can help the boy through the power of prayer.

Samuel Ross, the boy's father, was a fireman and first responder in the Battle of Empire. He is currently missing and thought to be deceased.

At Press time, Gordon Ross is still unresponsive to medicine and external stimuli.

THE
CHIMES
AT
MIDNIGHT

## 103

Pratima sat quietly on the windowsill. Her body wanted to move, but this would probably be the last time she'd ever see the city in the daylight. They were to fly out of Washington International at nine o'clock. Bleak, gray buildings reached into an overcast skyline, slowly fading to black as the sun dipped in the west. Pratima saw them as tombstones. She wanted to cry again, but the exhaustion was too much, and there were no more tears left for this city. Although she despised Empire, she couldn't convince herself she actually wanted to leave.

Giant snowflakes fluttered past the window and turned transparent as they melted against the glass. It would be Christmas soon, her favorite time of year, but joy was such a rare commodity in the Singh household. Since Pratima's mother announced they'd return to England, unwieldy battles had been the only lines of communication left open. Still, Pratima convinced herself that holding onto hope was necessary, even if it caused a rift between her and her mother. Anila had no response to her daughter's swear-riddled tirade about "bloody" this and "fucking" that, except, *what would your father say if he saw you?* She knew how to twist the knife, but so did Pratima.

*How will we ever find Papa when we're hiding from our problems in the countryside? If you loved him, you'd stay.*

Still, nothing could have been crueler than Anila's final response:

*He's dead!*

The words still haunted her, the end of faith, the demise of optimism.

Her mother did search for a time. The night after Father disappeared, Anila frantically called Allied Science. When there was no response, she called the police, but the Battle of Empire had thinned their ranks considerably. The officers who finally did take Anila's statement were ornery and cruel and too tired to care about a missing foreign man. They said they would "do what they could," but when they left, Anila was inconsolable.

That was the day something inside her died. Her healthy glow faded, and her need to see this through with it. Nadir Singh, her husband, was dead to her.

Allied Science finally returned her mother's telephone call, explaining Nadir had been terminated after an incredibly costly mistake destroyed one of their labs a few days before he had been reported missing.

Pratima took it upon herself to phone the vile man who had shown up on their doorstep the day her father had vanished, Frank, but the line had been disconnected. Although she had never met him, blaming him quelled the pain for a time. Still, the truth festered in the back of her mind. Her father found a way to open that craft buried deep within the recesses of the Allied Science building, and something inside that cursed vessel had destroyed him.

Outside, the city refused to fall silent. Life moved on. Pratima took a final longing glimpse out the window and wandered through what used to be the dining area into the kitchen. She placed her hands flat on the countertop beside the decommissioned phone jack, the very spot where her mother spent tireless nights on the telephone. Pratima closed her eyes and tried to imagine what it was like to be Anila Singh. A single tear escaped.

*She's lost everything, and I was so mean.*

Pratima's eyebrows furrowed. *No, she gave up too quickly!* She steadied her shaking fist and inhaled, desperately trying to forgive the woman who raised her. Losing both parents to Empire City was not something she could abide by. Still, she found it hard to love her mother, the person who tore their family apart by abandoning all hope.

*It's time to move on.* Pratima's mother insisted after their latest screaming match had come to a fruitless conclusion. *We'll return to England and pick up where we left off.*

Even through her blinding rage, Pratima could see the sorrow and uncertainty eating away at her mother. She carried it in her gaunt, tired face, and the more Anila tried to keep up the facade of optimism for her children, the harder she seemed to cry herself to sleep at night. Pratima would listen through the wall as reality ate away at her mother and annulled faith throughout the whole apartment. Sometimes, Pratima would wake up early to find her mother sleeping on the couch. She focused on that to humanize her, but something was blocking any remorse she might have felt. When Pratima's eyes fluttered open, the natural light faded from the room, and there wasn't a shred of sympathy left in her body for Anila Singh.

"Goddamn it, Father! Why did you do this to us?" she screamed, slapping the countertop.

Wisps of memories returned as Pratima meandered through her childhood home. Each room told a story, but the spirit had been sucked out and left to die. Now, the apartment existed only as plaster, wood, and brick, waiting to be filled with some stranger's life and consume their new memories. That was the way of life in the city, always moving, constantly changing. Existence was rented, and if you couldn't conform to the flow of the metropolis, it moved on without you. The only constant was the buildings themselves. An entirely different group of people would be inhabiting this city in one hundred years, but these buildings would still be here. This apartment would always be where it stood now, drinking the new memories while the old ones were left to rot under fresh plaster and paint.

The Singhs had moved before, but never without Nadir, the glue that had held the family together. Without him, they existed as a shattered collection of bitter, angry people leaving behind their souls for what seemed to be greener pastures—the coward's way into a life hardly worth living.

The hallway looked much too narrow without family photos cluttering the walls. Pratima stopped on the cusp of Ukrit's room and scrunched her nose as she peered in. The stench of old sweat socks still lingered, and the big juice stain on the far wall seemed to be winking, as it always had.

# The City of the Gods: Gold

Pratima chuckled at the memory of finding her fashion doll stuffed inside Ukrit's toybox, stripped of its clothes. Ukrit had begged her not to tell Mother or Father. She teased him mercilessly but never told, and they had never been closer.

Pratima frowned at the pieces of glass from a broken lamp in the corner. "Oh, Ukrit." There was no reasoning with him after he found out about Walter and Gordon.

Walter had changed schools, but the three of them met at the fortress one final time before he left. The poor, disturbed boy spun some fantastic story about a man who had tried to save him and his brother from a gargoyle and died. Somehow, in this far-fetched tale, he and Gordon survived being crushed by the thing that destroyed the city, and Gordon was captive in Brookfield. Walter and Ukrit agreed it was the Junior Enforcers' job to rescue him, but Pratima knew the truth. Gordon was dead.

She twisted her face to keep the tears at bay. Pratima had experienced a summer love a few months too late, and now he was gone, just as her father was. She shuffled down the dark hallway, leaned into her room, and slid her hand along the cold, smooth wall until the light switch flipped.

The wave of finality sent a lump into her throat. Her childhood had been stripped bare and left for some other little girl or boy to inhabit.

Pratima scanned the wire hangers peeking out from the closet through a veil of tears. She had grown up too fast in the city that eats its young and regurgitates them as soulless shells. In only a month, she had discovered her love for science and found a boy she liked, ushering in the best times of her life if only she had realized it. Now, her father was missing, that boy was dead, and her room was empty.

"I told you, Gordon," she whispered. "I knew it would end like this."

Pratima walked hesitantly to the end of the hall and glanced into her parents' room, stopping short.

*It's empty. It's just a stupid empty room!*

She burst across the threshold. Her warm breath spread out, and she shivered, but the chill in this room felt natural. She scanned the empty walls until she found a tear in the wallpaper next to where the armoire would have been and lost herself in the odd shape, remembering a simpler time when she was a small child.

A jewel had fallen off of her toy tiara. When her father found her crying, he took her onto his lap and said: *take pride in imperfect things, Duckling. The tiara is still stunning, but flawed, just like you and me. Imperfections add character and make us who we are.*

The anguish was crippling. Pratima fell to her knees in the middle of the empty room. "It's your fault, Father! It's all your fault! You've ruined everything!" Her cries echoed and bounced off the bare walls.

The thought of him never returning had been lying dormant outside her consciousness until she saw that stupid tear in the wallpaper. "You were obsessed, and now you're *dead*!" The word was a dagger in her heart. She tumbled into a heap.

Pratima's face pressed against the wooden floor, and when it felt like she had no more tears to be shed, she turned away from the tear in the wallpaper, allowing warm, shuttered breaths to escape.

Something peeked out from the crack in the closet door. It was small and almost invisible in the shadows, but it was there.

Pratima stood and brushed her dress off. She smoothed out the wrinkles like her mother had taught her a lady should and released a long, calming breath. When she felt composed, she moved to the closet and opened the door.

A small, unassuming envelope lay upside down on the floor. Pratima stared at it silently and ran her eyes along the crease where the flap ended. Something in her head told her to leave it. Whatever was in there was none of her business. This was her parent's room, after all.

However, something with more pull in her mind told her to open it or at least look for an address. She crouched, lifted it from the floor with a shaky hand, and turned it over. Pratima gasped and dropped the envelope.

*To my duckling, on her graduation day,* it said.

**104**

Pratima sat on the floor and stared vacantly at the tear in the wallpaper, turning the envelope in her hands, catching the edge of the smooth white paper on her fingertips. She held it up to the light but couldn't make out the jumbled letters folded over on top of each other. Finally, she sighed and tore it open.

*Dear Pratima,*

*As you venture out into the wonderful, awe-inspiring, frightening world, you must never forget: There is an exciting opportunity ahead. Perhaps the most incredible opportunity of all. Life: A long road of never-ending possibilities.*

*Be wary and steadfast in your travels, however. This road is full of wonders and pitfalls alike. Do not be afraid to take detours, but do not stray far.*

*Question and explore everything. If you are curious enough and willing to work, the world will always reveal its secrets.*

*Follow your passions, but never lose sight of what's truly important. People. If you focus too hard on one thing, such as a career, the rest of the world blurs around you into nothing, and that's what you're left with. Nothing. You're left alone.*

*You'll meet many people in the vast, wonderful world if you are open to it. Extraordinary people who will change everything for you, for better or worse. Friends, lovers, enemies, all kinds of unique, remarkable, complicated people. Experience all they have to offer, but never forget your family or, more importantly, yourself. After all, that is your foundation.*

*As difficult as things may seem, you must always have faith. Life is beautiful if you give it time to bloom, and people are inherently good. Be open to relationships. I have a hard time doing this, and I feel, as my daughter, you will, too. I'm afraid this is why I was never much of a father to you or Ukrit, and for that, I am more sorry than you can ever know. You and your brother are my life, my greatest legacy, and I regret only learning this in my thirties. However, it's never too late, and I strive to course-correct each day.*

*No matter where this incredible journey of life takes you, never forget your past or where you came from. When your mother and I are gone, you will be stronger for having known us, as we are stronger now for having you in our lives.*

*I don't know how to end this letter. In the same way, you don't know where your journey will take you. Just know I love you, and I will always be here for you. If you ever need advice, I'm only a phone call away.*

*I'm so proud of you, Pratima, and no matter how much you grow, you will always be my little duckling.*

*Love Always,*

*Papa*

Pratima slid the letter back into the envelope and sat in silence. She was a little girl again until the harshness of reality took hold. This house felt like an empty shell she had outgrown. The family would never be the same. Her mother was becoming cold and distant, and Ukrit acted out in violence as Pratima sank deeper into herself.

*This is not what Papa would want for us.*

She smiled sadly and left the room for the final time. This chapter of her life was closed, and no amount of wanting or hoping would bring her innocence back. She couldn't be Daddy's little girl with no father, but she could still be the great woman he intended her to become.

Pratima stepped into what used to be the dining area and slumped against the wall, sliding down the smooth plaster to the floor. Her eyes followed the wood grain in the light of the moon as she sat in silence and clutched the letter in both hands.

The door creaked open. Light flooded the dark, callous room. Pratima glanced up to call her father's name, but something inside her knew it wasn't him, and that was alright.

Her mother stood in the doorway, backlit, like an angel, and Ukrit beside her. Her family. Her rock.

"It's time to go, my dear."

Pratima smiled. "I know, Mother."

Nadir Singh was gone, but he'd live on through his daughter. She'd flourish with the guidance he'd instilled. Now, she was the glue that would keep this fractured family from shattering completely, and her new purpose gave her the strength to carry on.

THE GHOSTS OF
MISJUDGMENT
TIP THE
SCALES AWAY

## 105

Gibson turned left out of Wilbur's Diner and cranked the window down. A warm, damp breeze rolled in, wet concrete glistened, and surplus runoff poured into the storm drains. Lingering snow had been pushed off the streets into piles that were finally dwindling as a semblance of spring emerged.

The sun dipped, counting the seconds until nightfall. Gibson eyed his watch, weaved around a Pontiac Streamliner, and accelerated. The new Ford Crestline handled well enough, but he missed the ol' Plymouth Concord. This V8 engine was "too much car," as Slim would say. Gibson smiled. He examined the palette of warm yellows and oranges snuffing out the blue sky, and his smile faded.

Driving to Brookfield had been a chore since the Battle of Empire, but promises were made, and Gibson wasn't about to dishonor the dead by breaking them.

The city was rife with theories on what had transpired that late October day: murderous aliens, religious wars, Torment's return. Gibson knew better, but whether he believed what he saw was another matter. In his wildest nightmares, nothing was as horrific as watching those pale hands pull Theodora Connor into the molten earth.

The mayor's office told the *Bulletin* the battle was still an ongoing investigation, but it wasn't Gibson's. A few months back, he'd left the force and opened his own Private Investigator outfit. Business was slow, but tailing cheating husbands was far less dangerous than being the white knight.

In Droghead, the excitement of spring clung to the scent of blooming honeysuckle. The Crestline rolled to a stop at Union Avenue, where a carefree group of kids crossed at the light. Gibson smiled. *In a city that suffers through disaster after disaster, the people always bounce back. Maybe we'll be okay without them.*

As of October, all that remained of the Enforcers was a fading golden statue in Armory Square. Although they'd carried themselves as gods, they were only flesh and blood—people with needs, desires, and expiration dates. Empire had forgotten about its guardians as soon as they left the public eye. *Onward and Upward.*

The light turned green, and Gibson made a left onto Lock Alley, dipping into Hell's Gate. The walking dead still roamed the streets, riding the end of an old high or starting a new one. Gibson eyed a young, thin officer nervously walking his beat amidst the quiet chaos.

*Don't be a McIntyre,* Gibson thought as the cop vanished in the rearview.

It had been four months since Slim's funeral. They'd put him in the ground before the city froze, and no one shed a tear. If his wife was still alive, she didn't bother to show. The only attendees had been a handful of cops who felt duty-bound to the old man. Gibson remembered scanning the crowd and thinking ol' Slim would have hated all their dirty guts. It seemed Baxter had forgotten all about Leonard "Slim" Shanahan, an old, broken man who had burned every bridge he'd ever crossed. That was how he'd always be remembered, but at least he'd be remembered.

There was only enough money in Slim's life insurance policy to pay for a moderate tombstone. Gibson threw in a few bucks out of respect, but when the engraver asked what he or the family wanted it to say, he didn't know. So, in the end, it simply read:

"Leonard "Slim" Shanahan

# The City of the Gods: Gold

June 4th, 1897 - October 19th, 1953

Live every day as if it was your last."

Gibson called in a few favors to read the official autopsy, toxicology, medical, and police reports. Slim had died of adenocarcinoma. Lung cancer. No murder, no suicide, and no foul play. Still, there was always a whisper of uncertainty in the back of Gibson's mind, and he'd catch himself acting overcautious more often than not.

Now and then, he'd visit Morningside Cemetery to make sure Baxter didn't have the stone removed, or so he told himself. There was no more room in the Eddie Wilbur file for the likes of Slim Shanahan. He'd sit amongst the slate gray tombstones and sip Corby's with the old man. He'd tell him how things were changing, and nothing worked out the way he thought it would, but he might be better for it. He'd blame Slim for shining light on the corruption in the ECPD, which helped him resign. He'd blame him for allowing Gibson to grow accustomed to the name Skipper and making him self-conscious whenever he drank Corby's Whiskey. He'd bare his soul and laugh at the irony; the loudmouth, raucous old-timer was the best listener he knew.

Gibson eyed the setting sun in the rearview and accelerated through a yellow light. Temple's Coffee Shop shot past and vanished. The Crestline merged onto the Coastal highway and groaned like an old man. Fresh, salty air rode a frosty ocean breeze through the window, winter's death rattle. He glanced at Broadshall Island, imagining bringing Eleanor on that first trip to Schooners for a banana split as soon as the snow melted.

Gibson had met his new flame at Otto's Tiki Bar at a "Winter in Hawaii Party." Eleanor was one of the hula girls. One look at her graceful figure swaying to the songs of Hal Aloma and his Orchestra made Gibson forget all his troubles. She placed a lei around his neck and kissed his cheek. It wasn't until later he found out it was customary, but it gave him the courage to spark a conversation with the prettiest girl in the room.

Heavy traffic slowed the crawling vehicles until they broke into a wave of inaction. Gibson groaned. In the rearview, an endless sea of cars stretched until the end couldn't be determined. Monotonous honking filled the air.

A train whizzed by as a steel blur with a jarring whine. Gibson eyed his watch and jabbed the horn.

Traffic converged into one lane, and vehicles alternated between inching forward and grinding to a halt. Jackhammers and cement mixers pounded, beeped, and clunked. Sunburned men in hardhats yelled over the commotion as the highway slowly returned to its former glory.

To the west, a scar ravaged the pretty face of Empire, but skeletal frames of buildings littered the horizon, erected slowly and steadily, as the Scarlet Sparrow intended.

Gibson often found himself thinking of Theodora Connor. Before he'd met her, he imagined her as an amalgamation of her radio personality and various *Bulletin* articles. The city's spirit embodied in the quixotic woman, but she wasn't flesh and blood. When he'd finally met her, she was perfect until she wasn't. Behind the facade was a scared, broken woman with faults and problems.

*We're each our own devil.*

The difference was she recognized her shortcomings and faced them for the benefit of her city.

*How do you behave when the world you know and love comes crashing down around you, and there is no right or wrong anymore, just survival? Just preservation of life?*

Gibson would never forget her words or the answer she finally found. *You sacrifice yourself for the greater good.*

The certainty of her fate was Gibson's burden alone, for fear of anarchy overtaking the city. Knowing the citizens were left unguarded was a loaded gun held to the head of Empire, and if the wrong person found out, they wouldn't hesitate to pull the trigger.

A horn blasted, and Gibson inched forward with an apologetic wave. He twisted the radio on to kill the silence. "We'll Meet Again" was halfway through its first verse.

Gibson glanced in the side mirror at Theodora's unfinished building. He closed his eyes and traveled through the hidden lobby. The marble statues, the paintings, the handcrafted furniture all appeared as Vera Lynn serenaded him. When Gibson opened his eyes, the red girders had blended into the rusty red sky. He checked his watch and pulled through the toll booth.

The Crestline bounced off the bridge and onto North Avenue. The setting sun cascaded down the Connors' house, giving the metal shutters an appropriate, scarlet glow as it passed. Behind it, the city sat peacefully, reflective of a job well done, but still injured and recovering. *Rest in peace, Theodora. We'll take it from here.*

Gibson turned onto Pleasant, where haunted memories of bodies crawling with flies and maggots and the girl with blood pulsing from her eye sockets watched him from the nightmare they inhabited. He pulled off the road onto a patch of grass and put the car in park.

Behind a row of unkempt evergreen bushes, the Crestline was invisible. Ron Baxter's house loomed like a watchtower through a disconcerting black iron gate on the other side of the hedges.

Gibson scanned the mansion, remembering Dea's words.

*I'm trusting you with Bonnie, after all, the most important person to me. The most important person in all of this.*

In early November, Gibson had almost gone bankrupt trying to fight for custody of Bonnie. Not only did Baxter have a team of lawyers and the judge on his side, but through the public lens, it looked like Gibson was after the Connors' estate through their daughter.

He scanned the row of dark second-story windows, searching for the right one. A promise was a promise, even if it meant sitting on the outskirts of Hell and staring into the abyss. Slowly, he counted to one hundred and back again to keep insanity at bay as he waited, watched, and hoped little Bonnie Connor remembered the system.

Darkness stole over the suburban neighborhood. Gibson studied what he could see of the house between the overgrown hedges and the silhouettes of blooming trees. Any minute, he'd know if Bonnie was still alive.

Gibson fired up a cigarette and bounced it anxiously between his index and middle fingers. He scanned the dark windows as the crickets' song faded into ambient noise, and the Browning twelve-gauge shotgun called to him from the trunk.

*There's still time to go inside and get her.* Gibson sucked a long drag from his cigarette. *Unless she's already dead.* He watched the inky darkness and the pile of bodies in his mind stacked one higher. Hordes of flies and maggots crawled across Bonnie's gray skin from her dead eyes into her gaping mouth. He shut his eyes.

The heat of the ember burned across his fingers, and he disregarded the stub into Baxter's shrubbery.

A light in a window flickered on for five seconds, off for ten, on, off, on, off, on in quick succession. Bonnie had been a little late tonight but hadn't missed a beat. Gibson exhaled and leaned his head back on the seat, going limp. It felt good to smile.

"Until tomorrow, Bonnie. Goodnight." He gripped the stick shift, when a small bicycle sitting ominously at the end of the driveway caught his attention.

*Clang! Clang! Clang!* The padlock and chain slammed into the wrought iron gate further up the driveway. Gibson killed the engine, stepped onto the sodden grass, and squinted into the darkness. Bathed dimly in Baxter's porchlight, a small child yanked at the chain.

"Pst! Hey, kid. What are you doing?" Gibson whispered, eyeing the house, waiting for more lights to turn on.

A small, scrawny boy with an oversized flatcap sneered at him and regarded the padlocked chain again.

Gibson scooted closer. "Do you live here?"

The lock whined and snapped, and the heavy chain uncoiled.

"No!" the boy scoffed.

"Jesus! Did you—" Gibson approached the boy slowly and eyed the broken lock on the pavement. "What are you doing here, son?" He traded glances between the boy and the house. The kid gripped the iron bars and pulled them apart like pipe cleaners.

"Holy shit!" Gibson whispered. "Stop that!" He placed a hand on the boy's shoulder.

The kid's eyes glinted in the low light under his cap, full of desperation and rage. "My brother's in there!" he yelled.

Gibson reeled back. "It's okay, pal. I'm on your side"—he eyed the mansion—"a friend of mine is in there too."

The boy turned back to the fence and gripped the bars again, bending them further with a creaky whine.

"Hey!" Gibson gripped the boy's arm. "You can't go breaking into people's houses."

"Why not?" The boy pulled away and swung, denting the iron bar. "This old man took my brother, and I want him back!" He wiped his nose across his dirty sleeve and sniffled. "He's supposed to join the League of Enforcers; he said so himself! He's not supposed to be in this dumb old man's house!"

Gibson inched forward hesitantly. "Hey now, no more tears, pal. My name's Skipper, what's yours?" The gravel shifted under his feet, and he glanced at the house uneasily.

"Why do you care?" The kid crossed his arms in a huff.

Gibson shrugged. "I only want to be friends." He smiled to mask his nerves.

"Walter," he said. "Walter Ross."

"Where are your folks, Walter?"

"Pop's dead, and my mom left us!" he yelled and turned into a hard right hook, knocking the gate off its hinges. It landed in the yard with a loud thud. In the distance, birds took flight, and a dog barked down the street.

The house lit up. Gibson scampered behind the shrubs, scanning the porch from the shadows. "Say, how would you like some ice cream?" He tried to hide the desperation in his voice. "And maybe you and I can talk about getting your brother out of there?"

The boy broke his sulk and eyed Gibson cautiously. "Chocolate?"

The front door opened.

"Sure." Gibson nodded.

"Hello? Who's out there?" a young woman's voice called. Gibson shuffled Walter along the wet grass and into the passenger seat of his car.

"Oh my god! Who's out there? Who did that to the gate? Ron! Ron, the gate! Donald, the gate is in the yard!" The woman's voice grew fainter as she retreated into the house. Gibson rolled over the car's hood and leaped in the driver's seat. He peeled out into a U-turn across the wet patch of grass.

Gibson watched a silhouette emerge from the hedges and vanish in the rearview as the Crestline sped down Pleasant. He turned the corner onto North Avenue but kept his eyes on the rearview. "Listen, kid, we left your bike behind—"

"That was my brother's bike," Walter said. "I was bringin' it to him so he could escape." The boy's angry eyes never left the windshield.

Gibson smiled. "Of course you were."

Silence spread through the car, and "We'll Meet Again" continued to run on repeat through Gibson's head. He eyed the radio but thought better of it.

"So, where do you live?" Gibson glanced in the rearview and flipped the headlights on.

"Eastwood, in Monticello Group Home."

Gibson whistled. "That's a long way away from Brookfield. I'll bet you left pretty early, huh? Do the people at Monticello know you're gone?"

"No, I ran away!"

Gibson nodded slowly. "Well, I live in Eastwood too, Walter, and I come up north quite a bit." He paused thoughtfully. "As I said, I have a friend in that house, like your brother. Maybe we can work something out with the folks at Monticello, and we could come up here together every once in a while. We could stop for ice cream, too, if you want?"

Walter watched the world pass out the window.

"Walter, listen—"

"Why would Captain Wonderful let that dumb old man take my brother?" he yelled. "Gordie was s'posed to join the League of Enforcers and marry Miss Mercury. He said so himself!"

Gibson smiled. "Marry Miss Mercury? That's quite ambitious—"

"He was supposed to. He said so! Gordon isn't a liar!" Walter screamed until his face grew red.

Gibson eyed the rearview and pulled the car to the side of the road. Walter crossed his arms and glared into the tree line.

"Look, Walter—" Gibson considered telling the boy about Theodora Connor's gruesome fate, or Miss Mercury, saving his life in Sainte Marie Square. He wanted to tell him some bull-shit, feel-good story with a moral or a parable to give him hope.

*The heroes are gone, and now, ordinary people like you and I need to finish what they'd started.* But he didn't know if he believed that. The Enforcers had never necessarily been good for this city, and this kid obviously had something inside him like they did—something that needed curbing.

Gibson smiled and placed a hand on Walter's shoulder. "Let me tell you something my old partner used to tell me. Live every day as if it was your last— don't worry about the future—and don't worry about things you can't control, like the Enforcers. You can't rely on that. You do what you can for your brother today, like bringing his bike to him. The rest will work itself out in time."

Walter's eyes remained fixed on the hedges on the side of the road. "You really think so?"

"I know it, and I'd like to help you, Walter, if you'd let me."

Walter eyed him thoughtfully from under his oversized flatcap and smiled with his whole face.

Gibson didn't know where the power inside this small boy had come from. However, there were usually only two paths someone like him could inevitably take: right or wrong, good or evil.

*We're each our own devil.*

Gibson saw a third path, a gray area where Walter could live a normal life without heroics or villainy. No one needed to know about the boy who could bend metal. He'd never grace the cover of the *Bulletin* or any other rag. He could be an average kid with an average life, and the world would be none the wiser.

Gibson pulled the gear shift into drive and pulled onto North Avenue. The Crestline wheeled past the oversized mausoleum that had once been The Connors' residence. The crickets still sang, the moonlight still dripped off the branches of trees, and life went on. Skip Gibson had lost his battle, and helping Walter was his penance. Self-appointed, but a penance, nonetheless.

The heroes were gone, and the world wasn't perfect, but it wasn't expected to be. Life moved on after the League of Enforcers.

*This wasn't some radio show,* Skip thought. *Heroes fall, along with their cities, but people are inherently strong and resilient. Empire will rebuild, and her people will endure. Even in death, Theodora Connor didn't see fit to give up on Empire City, and neither would its citizens. Time passes, and there is too much to rebuild to celebrate. But hope remains. Faith remains. And I finally know what that means.*

**Acknowledgments**

I want to thank everyone who has contributed to the creation of this book.

First and foremost, I'd like to thank my wife, Alex, who put up with my long nights and weekends working and providing encouragement through the highs and lows of the writing process.

I am indebted to Tracy Wood, Danny Decillis, Paige Lawson, and Carol Roy, whose invaluable feedback and constructive criticism helped shape this manuscript into its final form.

I want to thank Frank, Bev, Jim, and Florence, whose stories and anecdotes helped me shape the world of 1950s Empire City and all its characters.

I am grateful to my family and friends for their support.

Last but not least, I want to thank the readers who will embark on this journey with me. Your enthusiasm and support mean the world to me.

Thank you from the bottom of my heart.

See you in the next book.

Zach Erwin

May 23, 2024

Pompton Lakes, NJ

www.ingramcontent.com/pod-product-compliance
Lightning Source LLC
Chambersburg PA
CBHW060558300726
48975CB00005B/1369